Praise for the novels of Scott Mackay

The Meek

"Scott Mackay toasts the optimistic inevitablility of the human spirit with a culturally shocking and disturbing, but quite enjoyable, novel."
—*The Midwest Book Review*

"In this fast-paced read with plenty of action and suspense, Mr. Mackay embroiders *The Meek* with emotional depth and hard scientific details."
—*Romantic Times*

"Poses some intriguing ethical problems within a satisfyingly complex plot." —*Science Fiction Chronicle*

Outpost

"Mackay avoids the grandiosity that is an occupational hazard of science fiction writers who dabble in cosmic themes. . . . Provocative."
—*The New York Times Book Review*

"A fast-paced action adventure."
—*The Washington Post*

continued . . .

ORBIS

SCOTT MACKAY

A ROC BOOK

ROC
Published by New American Library, a division of
Penguin Putnam Inc., 375 Hudson Street,
New York, New York 10014, U.S.A.
Penguin Books Ltd, 80 Strand,
London WC2R 0RL, England
Penguin Books Australia Ltd, Ringwood,
Victoria, Australia
Penguin Books Canada Ltd, 10 Alcorn Avenue,
Toronto, Ontario, Canada M4V 3B2
Penguin Books (N.Z.) Ltd, 182–190 Wairau Road,
Auckland 10, New Zealand

Penguin Books Ltd, Registered Offices:
Harmondsworth, Middlesex, England

First published by Roc, an imprint of New American Library,
a division of Penguin Putnam Inc.

First Printing, April 2002
10   9   8   7   6   5   4   3   2   1

ROC REGISTERED TRADEMARK—MARCA REGISTRADA

Printed in the United States of America

PUBLISHER'S NOTE
This is a work of fiction. Names, characters, places, and incidents either
are the product of the author's imagination or are used fictitiously,
and any resemblance to actual persons, living or dead, business
establishments, events, or locales is entirely coincidental.

To my brother, Grant

ACKNOWLEDGMENTS

I would like to thank John Jackson for helping me with the Latin in this book. *Factum optime,* John.

I would also like to thank my wife, Joanie; my mother, Claire; and my son, Colin, for their various contributions.

PART 1

FRIENDS

CHAPTER 1

"I could have walked," said June.

"I don't mind drivin' you," said Mickey. "I consider it an honor, June."

Mickey was giving June a lift to the train station to meet her brother Henry. The Odd Fellows meeting was over, and dusk was settling over the town of St. Lucius. Through her open window June smelled the Mississippi.

"I still could have walked the four blocks," she said.

"I won't let a lady walk four blocks if she don't have to," said Mickey.

June felt she had to make things clear to Mickey again. "Neil is getting out of the Seminary in two weeks," she said.

He took a deep breath and pressed his lips together. "I know," he said. "You already told me a hundred times."

"Then why doesn't it sink in?"

"Because you haven't seen him in two years," he said.

"So?"

"So . . . a pretty girl like you needs company every now and again, that's all."

"I just want you to understand."

"I understand," he said. He changed the subject. "I can't believe the Benefactors are made of . . . what did you say again? Hydrogen?"

"A special kind of hydrogen," she said.

"And the Prussians actually caught one?"

"We went over this at the meeting, Mickey."

"I know . . . but I—"

"You just want to talk about the Benefactors as an excuse to give me a lift. So you can be near me."

"That's not true," said Mickey.

"Then why are you driving so slow? We could have been there by now."

"They caught it in a big magnet?" he asked.

"Something like that."

"And he's just hydrogen?"

"A special kind of hydrogen."

"So the Benefactors ain't Angels after all?"

"Nope."

"So ever since they came here, they just bin foolin' us, tellin' us they're the Lord's own Heavenly Host, tellin' us they're from Heaven and whatnot when they're not from Heaven at all?" He whistled in amazement, then gave her a sideways glance and smiled. "You sure look pretty tonight, June. I was going to bring you some flowers."

"It still hasn't sunk in, has it?"

He looked away, made a quick retreat to the subject of the Benefactors again. "So they ain't from Heaven?" he asked, grinning weakly.

"Nope."

"So if they ain't from Heaven, where are they from?"

"We're not sure," she said. "We're talking about that. We've come up with some theories."

"Like . . . maybe from Mars?" he asked.

"Why do you always harp on Mars?"

His face stiffened. "Because of all them canals on Mars," he said. "Someone had to build 'em. Why not the Benefactors?"

"Well . . ." she said, "not Mars. They're made out of gas, Mickey. We're thinking maybe one of the gas giants, like Jupiter or Saturn."

Mickey shook his head. "And they've fooled us for two thousand years?"

"Actually, there's new evidence that says they came to Australia as far back as five thousand years ago. The Odd Fellows have discovered some Aborigine rock paintings. So, you see, there's a lot we still don't know. But rest assured, they aren't Angels. They're just so much hot air, Mickey. I've always suspected as much."

"Can I wait in the train station with you?" he asked.

"Do you think that would be a good idea?" she asked.

He looked away. "No," he said. "I reckon it wouldn't."

"You can drop me off," she said sternly. "And I won't see you again until the next meeting. Is that clear?"

He sighed. "Yes, ma'am."

June sat in the train station diner sipping coffee while she waited for her brother. What was she going to do about Mickey? A police officer, a stout man wearing a black skullcap and a cross-and-orbis badge, sat at the counter five stools away. Mickey was hopelessly in love with her, despite the fact that she was engaged to Neil. The police officer was making her nervous. Maybe he knew about Henry's arrival. She put the problem of Mickey from her mind for the time being and concentrated on the officer.

"Nice evening," she said, wanting to sound him out.

He turned to her. "Too hot for May, if you ask me," he said. "And too many flies."

She didn't detect anything suspicious in his voice.

"We could use some rain to keep this dust down," she said.

"That's a fact," he said, then studied the menu above the soda fountain.

She glanced at the menu as well. Her stomach growled. She was hungry, but she didn't have much money. All she could afford was coffee. She was shocked by the prices the train station diner charged. A hamburger cost twenty-five cents. A Western sandwich with fries was forty cents. And a soda was ten cents. She was starving, and all the food up there looked so good. She'd lost so much weight, eating all that clay-bred food. Her pleated skirt hung over her bony legs like a sheet over a clothesline. What she needed was a plate of real ham and eggs, not clay-bred stuff.

"Are you waiting for the *Silver Bullet*?" asked the officer.

"Yes," she said.

"They're saying it's going to be late."

"Maybe I'll wait out on the platform," said June.

The officer glanced at his newspaper. "You see the Ministry of War thinks the Prussians have developed a superbomb?"

"Yes," she said.

"I sure hope they don't use it on St. Lucius," he said, grinning amiably. "I think a superbomb might ruin my day."

She grinned back. "I think a superbomb might ruin my day too." She took out her change purse and scrounged through her meager collection of coins until she found a dime. She pulled it out, examined the head of Pope Gregorio V, turned it over, looked at the cross and orbis, and slid it grudgingly across the counter. "Nice talking to you," she said.

"Likewise," said the police officer.

Henry alighted from the *Silver Bullet* twenty minutes later. He looked as dapper as ever in a new gabardine suit, a silk necktie, and a handsome fedora. He gave the platform a good once-over, looking for police and Benefactors, then walked toward her, carrying a small suitcase in one hand and a package wrapped in green-and-silver gift paper in the other.

"There she is," he said. "How are you, sis?"

He gave her a hug.

"Missing you and George as always," she said. "Is he all right?" She was always so worried about her oldest brother. "Europe's just so darn dangerous these days."

"For the most capable man in the world," said Henry, "I'd say he's fine."

They walked down the platform together. As they

passed the diner, she glanced in the window and saw that the police officer was still there. She took Henry by the elbow and directed him away from the depot.

"Let's go around here," she said, "through the parking lot."

"You have a car now?"

"Are you kidding?" she said. "There's a bull in the coffee shop."

Henry nodded. They made their way to the parking lot. A few Fords, Chryslers, and Daimlers lay scattered about, covered in the dust that clung to everything in St. Lucius in the summer. Beyond the parking lot she saw the Citadel up on the hill. All the other buildings around it were fifty or sixty years old, the neo-Romanesque edifices of a growing prairie town, red brick, with lancet arch windows. But the Citadel had to be at least five hundred years old. She saw Henry looking at it.

"I hate those places," he said. "I wish the Benefactors had never built them. I hate to think of all those Benefactors sleeping inside. That's all they ever do these days. It gives me the creeps."

A short while later they came to a tavern and went inside.

It was smiles all around from the people sitting at the tables and at the bar when they saw Henry Upshaw. Henry talked to his old friends for a bit while June made her way to a table at the back to wait for him.

She was full of anticipation, wanting to see what was inside the gift-wrapped box George had sent from Europe. Everything George sent was always a revelation. Oh, to reach back through the stagnant years of

the Dark Ages, to unearth and understand all those
archaeological sites the Benefactors had put off-limits,
to finally *know* what had happened. Especially to
know the Romans, that wondrous race of ancients who
had been chased away and crushed two thousand
years ago by the Benefactors because they had dared
to put up a fight. She wished some day someone would
invent a time machine so she could go back and see
for herself all the things she had missed, meet all the
great Romans who had lived and died back then, been
a part of those magnificent events—the War of the
Gens, the Great Theft, the Exodus—all those things
that were never fully explained in any of the text-
books, other than to say each was a great victory for
the Benefactors.

Henry finally came to her table ten minutes later.
Big Danny walked over and put a mickey of whiskey
and two shot glasses on the table. Henry gave him a
fifty-cent piece, then poured a hefty shot in each glass.

"Drink that before I show you what I brought,"
he said.

She drank, then waited patiently while he pulled the
silver ribbon away. A folder lay inside. He opened the
folder . . . and there they were. Photographs. Not from
a standard Kodak box camera, but old Roman photographs, ones that used an imaging technique the covert
chemists of the Odd Fellows still hadn't figured out.
Photographs of buildings. Ancient ones. This one reminded her of the Basilica Aemilia in Rome, this one
of the Temple of Hercules in Agrigento, and this one
of the amphitheater in Arles.

"These are buildings," she said, trying to hide her
disappointment. "I've seen buildings before."

"Keep going," he said, enjoying himself.

The next photograph perplexed her. What she saw was a conglomeration of buildings—the lofty, heroic, arch-and-column forms prevalent in Roman architecture—a city made out of a curious gray-brown stone the likes of which she had never seen before. What she found perplexing was the large glass bubble over the city. It rose into a starry black sky and sat on a dusty gray plain. Nothing, not a single shrub or stalk of grass, grew on the plain. A blue-and-white half-disk hovered above the city. When she stared at it she saw brownish-green shapes on it. Continents. She recognized the Horn of Africa. The boot of Italy. The subcontinent of Hindustan. She looked at her brother.

"Yes," he said, nodding like a crazy man. "It's true," he said. "The Romans made it to the moon. The Romans built there."

CHAPTER 2

Once she had assimilated the shock of this new discovery, June spoke of Hesperus, the primary Benefactor in St. Lucius.

"He's still following me around," she said. "He's been following me for a year."

"Has he ever hurt you?" asked Henry.

"No," she said. "But I don't think you should stay with me in my apartment. He parks outside at night. I wouldn't want to put you at any risk."

"I'll stay in a hotel." Henry looked worried. "But why has he taken such an interest in you?"

"I don't know," she said.

"Does he suspect you're a member of the Odd Fellows?"

"I don't think so," she said. "But he seems weak, and confused."

"Does your head . . . you know . . . do you feel dizzy, or do you get a headache whenever he's around?"

"No . . . I don't think he can . . . he can't get inside anymore."

Henry nodded. "They're growing weak."

"I think he . . . maybe he's lonely," she said.

"Don't kid yourself, June," he replied. "They have no feelings. They're like fish. They don't have any feelings at all."

But she had to wonder if this was true. "Everyone's worried about him, Henry."

"Is he still fat? He's not playing masquerade these days, is he? No dragons or griffins, or other such nonsense."

"No, just that fat old rector."

"I wouldn't feel sorry for him, June. That's the worst thing you can do."

"I don't feel sorry for him. It's just that . . . I don't know . . . I guess it's the war. I guess the war's got him all upset."

"Good. That's what we want."

But as she walked home by herself later on, she couldn't help wondering. From Mars, Jupiter, or Heaven, it made no difference. She sensed something sad and vulnerable in Hesperus now. Just because half the world waged war against the Benefactors didn't mean the Benefactors weren't capable of at least a little human feeling.

She turned left on Rainey Street. Not too many people had cars in this part of town. The only car parked on the street was . . . yes . . . Hesperus's black 1925 Ford Model T Coupe. She had known he would be parked somewhere along her street. He always was. Especially at this time of night. She stopped. The air was heavy with that smell he had, like the electrical smell from George's old toy train set. She approached, acutely conscious of the old Roman photographs she carried in the folder under her arm. They were enough to get her hanged.

Hesperus opened the car door and got out. Always the same suit day after day, year after year. And always the same broad-brimmed rector's hat. His waist hung over his belt in an unsightly roll, straining at the buttons of his black clergyman's shirt. His thighs were monstrous, of such gargantuan proportions they hardly looked human. He had a pug nose, small mean eyes, and pocked greasy skin. What was the rationale behind such a hideous form? To inspire revulsion?

He walked around to the front of the car. She knelt, bowed, averted her eyes. He extended his hand. She forced herself to kiss it.

"Why do you follow me, Canon?" she asked.

"Kiss my hand again, child," said Hesperus.

June did as she was told. Hesperus shuddered. As if he actually enjoyed the kiss. She stood up.

He looked at her in mild surprise. His head was as big as a ten-gallon pail. "Can you call me by my name, child?" he asked. "Must you always call me Canon?"

Her lips felt cold. She wanted to tell him that George was in Prussia fighting against the Benefactors, and that it was largely through his efforts as an agent of the Prussian Abwehr that the Benefactors and the soldiers of the Holy League were finally being turned out of Paris. It was all she could do to stop from spitting on the man's shoes. Yet in his tiny dark eyes she saw something that momentarily distressed her, a chronic sadness, an element of forlorn compassion and regret.

"Answer me, my child," he prodded.

"I call you Canon because I don't want to be disrespectful," she said.

A light went on in the house across the street, and an old woman pulled the drapes aside. The woman looked at them, then quickly let the drapes slide back into place.

"Do people still like us, June?" asked Hesperus.

The question surprised her. "I don't know how to answer that, Canon," she said.

"Do *you* still like us, June?"

She felt scared. She saw before her an aging, corpulent clergyman who never bothered to bathe and who now carried around in his eyes a pathetic helplessness he couldn't seem to hide. Ostensibly he was someone she should pity. But she knew he was great and horrible, as the Bible often described him, and not to be trusted at all. He was huge. He blotted out the light of the moon. She sensed her own fragility and stepped back.

"Canon, I don't know why you've taken an interest in me," she said. "I'm just a high school teacher. I don't know the answers to your questions. I like you. I like you fine."

He made a face, as if annoyed with her. The smell of raw energy came from him like heat from a coal furnace. "Learn to trust me, my child," he said. "That's all I ask."

"I trust you, Canon," she replied. "I've always trusted you. Ever since I was a little girl. You've brought us peace and prosperity. You've taught us to live in harmony. You look after us. Everything that is good in the world is good because of you."

She parroted the words of the Sunday School song.

They tasted like bile in her mouth. Hesperus simply shook his head and looked more disappointed than ever. Without another word he turned from her and got back in his car. She moved out of the way. The front wheels of the Model T turned to the left, and without a sound the car rolled down Rainey Street. She watched him go. She was perplexed, distraught, and wondered what she was going to do about him.

Her roommate, Amy Kristensen, waited for her at home.

"Well?" said Amy.

"You should see them," said June.

June spread the photographs on the kitchen table. Amy looked on with wide eyes as June explained to her how the Romans had made it to the moon. When she was done, Amy hardly knew what to say.

"So how would they get there?" she asked June.

"We're not sure," said June. "But Henry tells me the experts believe this settlement was built several hundred years before the Benefactors first tangled with them."

"That's amazing," said Amy. "Do you think they used a balloon to get up there? That would be an awfully long way to ride in a balloon."

"I believe they would use a rocket," said June. "Look at this here." She pulled out an ancient design diagram. "Henry gave me this tonight. This is an engine. It burns hydrogen and was designed by a man named Paetinus Treblanus in 300 B.C. We believe the Romans may have mounted a carriage of some sort on this rocket engine and fired themselves to the moon."

"Now that would take guts," said Amy. "But I

thought there was no air on the moon. The Benefactors are always telling us no one can live on the moon because there's no air there, and no water there either."

"They've put the air under this bubble," said June.

"What about the water?" asked Amy. "Isn't it so cold on the moon that water freezes?"

June frowned. "These are Romans, Amy," she said. "They can do anything. Look here." She pointed at a particularly notable structure under the glass bubble. "This here is an aqueduct. That proves it. They figured out how to put water on the moon. The Romans can figure out how to do anything. All the discoveries in Prussian-liberated Europe are telling us that." She thought of Mickey's obsession with Mars. "I wouldn't be surprised if some day we discovered evidence of a Roman settlement on Mars. I wouldn't put it past them at all. Like I say, these are Romans. They can do anything they set their minds to."

CHAPTER 3

Ecclesiarch Eric Nordstrum felt sick with disappointment as he approached Deacon Oskar Braaten in the apse of St. Bernardine's Holy Cathedral.

"Oskar," he called. "Oskar . . . if you don't mind . . ."

The Deacon stopped, turned, made a good show of looking surprised.

"Eric . . . why, I thought . . . I thought I saw you leave with Ingrid."

"No," said Eric, "she went ahead of me. We really must talk. I haven't talked to you since the Diaconate Conclave made their decision about the Cardinalate. I'm just wondering what happened. I'm not a man to lose faith easily, but I have to say . . ."

Oskar shrugged uneasily. "God has spoken," he said.

"Yes, but if He's spoken, I'm not sure it was in a language I understand." Eric tried to make a joke of it. "You're sure His inspiration didn't get garbled in the translation?"

Oskar looked at the wine-colored carpeting of the apse, his jowls sagging over his clerical collar.

"In this case, Eric, God had help."

Eric frowned, shook his head. "So in other words, the Vatican changed its mind. Who is it, then? You might as well tell me. I'm going to find out sooner or later."

Oskar shifted from one chubby leg to the other. His hands grew tremulous around his cross and orbis. "We chose a European," he said. "A Dane by birth. Magnus Anders. Perhaps you've heard of him?"

Eric struggled to curb his profound frustration as he searched his memory. "Anders—I thought he was an Australian. Isn't he the Ecclesiarch of Brisbane?"

"He is," said Oskar. "But now he's on his way up here. The Vatican thought he would be a good choice. They want somebody European over here. They think it will show solidarity."

"Yes . . . but . . ." Eric was exasperated by this turn of events. "Why should the people of the Missouri-Arkansas Territory have a Dane as their Cardinal? Half the people in the Territory don't even know where Denmark is. Does this Magnus Anders even speak English?"

"He speaks seven languages, including English," said Oskar. "And he speaks them fluently."

"But how could he possibly know anything about a frontier place like the Territory? The people here aren't your refined Europeans who like to go to opera shows. They're just common folk. You've got to have someone at the Cardinal's Residence who understands the way they think and knows what they like. How is

Anders going to understand anything about a rough-and-tumble place like the Territory?"

"Well, Eric, I'm glad you asked me that. Bishop Valdez wrote a comment on that exact subject when he submitted his nomination. He told us Brisbane is much like St. Lucius and that Anders would be eminently suitable for the post. There's more in common between Brisbane and St. Lucius than you might think. Both are right next to Restricted Zones. They have got Aborigines living in their Restricted Zone, and we've got Indians living in ours. And they've got clay-bred working in their Restricted Zone, too, just like we've got clay-bred working in ours. I don't think there's an opera house in Brisbane. And as for common folk, I hear even the women spit in Brisbane. So I think Ecclesiarch Anders is well equipped for America, especially because he spent twelve years in New Orleans as a boy. They say he speaks English just like an American."

"Yes, but it's . . . it's unfair."

"You have to think of all those poor people over in Europe, Eric," said Oskar. "Those people are starving over there. They're at war. The Godless Prussians are killing them. We've got to have a European Cardinal here as a sign of solidarity."

This steamed Eric up even more. "It's not as if I haven't done anything for the war effort."

Oskar shook his head. "This is God's will, Eric."

Eric felt his shoulders stiffen. "Oh . . . applesauce!" he said, and stormed away.

As he walked down the aisle of the sanctuary, a few of his parishioners glanced at him nervously, sensing his wrath. He had to cool down. He couldn't let something like this bother him so much. So what if he had spent the last thirty years positioning himself for the Cardinal's job? He pushed his way out into the vestry. Why hadn't the Benefactors helped? The air in the vestry smelled of burning votive candles. Why hadn't Hesperus stepped forward and said something? He opened the big front doors and went outside. He had contributed more than his fair share to the war effort, and that's something all those poor Europeans, especially all those European bishops, should have recognized.

Sister Anneke Verbeek caught him as he descended the front steps. She came forward in her nun's habit like a skinny gray bird.

"Father . . . if you don't mind . . . could I have a word?"

He scowled at her. He didn't mean to, but he was so upset about losing the Cardinalate he couldn't help himself.

"What is it, Sister?"

"It's just that you said you would give me an answer . . . about the over-fifties trip to the Roman slave compound in Florida," she said.

"Do we have to talk about it right now, Sister? Can't you see I'm busy?"

"Have you talked to the board?" she asked. "Do they have the money? I've been planning this trip for a long time, and you still haven't given me an answer."

The shrill quality of her voice annoyed him. "Florida's an awfully long way, Sister. We don't want to be breaking the bank by sending a busload of over-fifties down there."

"It's just that it's one of the few Roman sites the Benefactors have preserved. The over-fifties are really looking forward to it. Nothing will give them a better idea of just how monstrous the Romans were than going to that slave compound."

"The answer is no, Sister Anneke," he said. "We don't have any money. Tell the over-fifties if they want to see the Roman slave compound, they can look at the scale model in the museum. Don't you know there's a war going on? We can't be spending our money on holidays in Florida when we need it to buy bullets for the soldiers of the Holy League."

Eric parked his car at the resurrectorium and climbed the steps through the ornamental cypresses. The resurrectorium was smooth, white with flutings of pink, looked like a seashell; it was of Benefactor design. He entered, lifted a skullcap from the bin inside the door, put it on his head, and lit three votive candles to the Shrine of Saint Lazarus. Then he walked past the honeycombed walls to Charles's portal.

He got down on one knee and recited the agreed-upon words from Jude: " 'All flesh is as grass, and all the glory of man as the flower of grass. The grass withereth, and the flower thereof falleth away, but the Word of the Lord endureth forever.' "

Colors whirlpooled inside Charles's portal, and out of these the late Cardinal's face appeared. The melancholy of death clung to him. He looked worn out.

"Every time you come here you take away a part of me as I once was."

Charles always said this. Eric still couldn't figure it out. He let it go.

"They passed me over for Cardinal, Charlie," he said.

His Worship stared at him as if from a great distance. "How . . . how can I help you with this, my son?"

"I want . . ." Eric had to think about it. "I want to know how to deal with it. You were always good at words of comfort, Charlie."

Charles shook his head. As much as Eric recognized the Benefactors' glorious mercy in resurrecting his old friend, it was chilling to talk face-to-face with a dead man. His face looked as bloodless as a piece of chalk. After several moments, the former Cardinal finally offered comment.

"This is something you'll have to struggle with by yourself, Eric," he said. The colors in the portal grew brighter. "I'm not so sure you would have liked the Cardinalate. The Lord's Government has become a complicated and bureaucratic thing. I never thought of you as an administrator. Why hide yourself in the Cardinal's Residence when you enjoy being out among the people so much? I always thought of you as a preacher. I don't think you would like being Cardinal."

"But I . . . I *want* to be Cardinal," said Eric. "Why has the Good Lord decided against me, Charles?"

His Worship's eyes darkened. "Let me quote from Isaiah," he said. " 'Behold, I have refined thee, but not with silver; I have chosen thee in the furnace of affliction.' Remember these words, Eric. Take them to heart, and in them find the solace and wisdom you need to endure."

*   *   *

Governor Publius Gallio Corvinus studied the latest population statistics as they shimmered across his *scriba*. He found them distressing, and he wasn't looking forward to showing them to Gaius Lurio when Lurio arrived three days from now. Gallio got up and walked to the edge of the terrace. Hortus's big red sun hovered to the east, lighting the fields with a pink glow. He watched Hortulani workers come from the groves for a day of labor. They were a species Jupiter saw fit to parody in man's image: two arms, two legs, hands, feet, a torso, and a head—but, oh, what a head! Shaped like a giant pumpkin seed, a narrow, platter-shaped head, rounded at the back but tapering to a bill at the front. The ones in the Province of Umbraculum had turquoise skin. The ones in the Province of Gramen were purple. The ones in the Province of Glacialis had white skin with lime-green stripes. A peculiar species, but gentle, well-meaning, spectacular farmers, wizards of the field and orchard.

Now their population faltered. If the trend continued, these fields would lie fallow in ten years. Orchard fruit would rot on the ground. And the vineyards would be left to spoil. The trend was all too typical of a slave population.

He heard a noise behind him and turned. Filoda, his Hortulani servant, brought his breakfast on a tray: grapes the size of plums, a melon as pink as the sunrise, and biscuits made from the native rice flour. Filoda's eyes sat on top of his head, black, unblinking, circled by tiny featherlike cilia. Filoda was turquoise. He wore a turquoise tunic fastened at his left shoulder with a piece of polished coral. On his right shoulder sat a *socius,* a small creature bred by the Hortulani, white, hairless, smooth—an overgrown grubworm with an uncanny gift for translation.

"Filoda, do people still feel they must pay homage to Rome?" Gallio asked.

The *socius* immediately began to chatter, translating for Gallio. Filoda chattered back.

"My people will always be grateful for the way you've pinned the Anvil to the sky, Imperator."

Gallio looked to the west where he saw the Hortulani moon—the Anvil, as it was called—skulking over the fields. The *legio impello* could lift the Anvil into a self-sustaining orbit any time they pleased. But they didn't. They said it would fall if they didn't keep it there. It was the whole reason the Romans could maintain such high taxes against the Hortulani. He wasn't sure the Hortulani believed them anymore.

"Yes, but do the people still *like* us, Filoda?" he asked. "Do they still trust us?"

More chatter passed between Filoda and his *socius*.

"What do I know of the wider world, Gallio?" asked Filoda. "I'm certain the people in this province still like you."

A flash came from the south. A moment later, from behind the golden hills, a *caelum currus* rose on a tail of flame and angled for escape into the pink sky. Gallio glanced at Filoda. Filoda stared at the rocket with startled eyes. Filoda chattered, and the *socius* interpreted.

"Where's it going?" asked Filoda.

"Nowhere in particular," answered Gallio. "It carries a hundred thousand beacons, each the size of a seed. We try to find our home, Filoda, the place we came from two thousand years ago. A place called Orbis."

"You have lost your home?" asked Filoda.

Gallio nodded. "We have lost our home."

"But how can you lose your home?" asked the slender Hortulani, clearly puzzled.

How could he explain to Filoda? It was easy to lose something small like Orbis in the ocean of stars and planets called the Via Lactea. How could they keep track of a tiny speck of dust? Especially after a hurried and forced departure in ships they didn't understand?

"Our home is like a floating seed," Gallio told Filoda. "It moves and moves, and it never stops. We call to it with these beacons." Gallio lifted his eyes to the *caelum currus,* wondering if it were in fact possible to find old Terra again. "We call to it, and we hope that some day it will call back."

CHAPTER 4

At home Eric found his wife, Ingrid, waiting for him at the kitchen table. A plate of currant biscuits sat next to a pot of sassafras tea. Eric couldn't look at her. *When I'm Cardinal* . . . He couldn't count how many times he had said those words to her. But now he was never going to say them again. He was never going to *be* Cardinal. He was going to be the Ecclesiarch for the rest of his life.

"I'm sorry, Ingrid," he said. "I let you down."

She leaned forward and put her hand on his arm. "You didn't let me down, Eric. And you shouldn't feel so bad about it."

He stared at the pot of sassafras tea. "I was so certain," he said. "I was just so . . ."

"I know you were."

"I could have done so much good. I felt I really had the ear of the people. I wanted you to see me . . . see me do all that."

"You can still do a lot of good, Eric."

"I can't understand why Hesperus and the other Benefactors didn't intervene in some way. They know

I'm behind them a hundred percent, and that's got to count for something. Especially when half of Europe's full of heretics now."

He took a biscuit off the plate and bit into it. One thing about Ingrid's biscuits, they couldn't be beat, even when you were feeling blue.

"I don't know that there's anything you can do to change the Conclave's mind now, do you?" asked Ingrid.

He stopped chewing. "No," he said. "But I still wanted you to be proud of me. I wanted Neil to be proud of me."

"Neil will be proud of you," she said in a cajoling tone. "And I'm always proud of you." A furrow came to her brow. "How old is this Magnus Anders anyway?"

Eric brightened. "He's sixty-one," he said.

"There you go," she said. "He's sixty-one and you're fifty-two. You might be Cardinal yet."

"Yes, but . . . but what I don't understand is how Magnus Anders got enough support to get himself nominated in the first place. He hasn't had what I would call an illustrious career. He wasn't even a priest until they made him the Ecclesiarch of Brisbane seven years ago. Before that he had a lay position. He operated a wireless telegraphy system for the Vatican—you know, in the technical laity. And before that he was just a radio operator and repairman. He wasn't even connected to the Church. I don't know how he ever came to know seven languages when what he did all day was fiddle with radio tubes and tuning dials. The Benefactors don't even like radio—you know how strictly they license it, all those regulations they have about megahertz, and where you can build your towers, and when you can broadcast, and when you can't broadcast, what frequencies you can use, and all those other limits on the size of your broadcast area and the strength of your transmission. I might have been a radio preacher at one time, but I never fooled with the darn things. Heck, if the Benefactors are so squirrely about radios, why did they pick a radio repairman to be the Cardinal of the Territory in the first place?"

Eric sat in his swivel chair behind his desk and grasped the cool leatherette of its arms. So here he was again, among the familiar walnut bookshelves, the desk, the banker's lamp, and the arched windows that opened onto the flower gardens. His study at St. Bernardine's was as big as some of the smaller houses in town. He had hundreds of books from all over the world—rare books, expensive ones, beautiful tomes bound in calf leather, glorious books that made the place smell of old pages and deep wisdom. The study up at the Cardinal's Residence wasn't half so nice as this one.

He walked to the bookcase, admired its gleaming varnished surfaces, and pulled out a biography of Pope Gregorio V and his elaborately bound edition of Pascal's *Pensees*. He removed his bootleg Latin-English dictionary from the back of the shelf, then replaced the two volumes. He walked to the middle of the room, lifted the silver cigarette case from the table, opened it, withdrew a slender cigarillo, gave it an appreciative whiff, and lit it.

Could there be anything finer than a decent cigarillo and a quiet moment's perusal of a dead language?

He flipped to the back section of the dictionary. Some simple everyday phrases, two-hundred-and-ten, filled the pages, phrases he liked to practice simply because he admired the sound of the language. He took a deep breath and spoke. *"Fortes fortuna adjuvat."* Fortune helps the brave. He held the dictionary at arm's length—damn, he was going to have to get spectacles after all—and spoke the dead, outlawed, forbidden language of the hated Romans in his best theatrical voice. It was his one indulgence. The original Scriptures were said to have been written in Latin, and he figured he deserved Latin, now that he wasn't going to be Cardinal.

"Non progredi est regredi," he said.

Not to go forward is to go backward.

He smiled. Perhaps a career on the stage might have been more rewarding than the one he had chosen in the Church. Nothing could beat Latin for proper elocution.

He was searching through the pages for another Latin phrase that might make the best use of his deep voice when Sister Anneke Verbeek entered the room. He fumbled, tried to hide the Latin-English dictionary, but there was nowhere to hide it, not when he was standing in the middle of the room like this, so he clumsily concealed it behind his back.

Sister Anneke peered at him suspiciously from under the colorless rim of her nun's habit, then lifted her chin.

"What have you got there, Father?" she asked.

Since the cancellation of the over-fifties' trip to Florida a few days ago, relations between them hadn't been particularly harmonious.

"Nothing," he said.

She peered again, her eyes as intent as a hungry crow's.

"Nonsense," she said. "I see you have something in your hand, Father. Show me what it is."

"I've asked you again and again to knock, Sister Anneke."

"Your journals have arrived," she said. "I thought you were out making your visits. Had I known you were here, I would have knocked."

Her lips pursed. Small, parsimonious lines appeared on either side of her mouth. Oh, what hideous fruit the Lord sometimes produced. Everyone had a soul, but Sister Anneke's was as dry and unforgiving as a stone. She approached. Here was his one transgression, and she had found him out. What harm in Latin? The law was ridiculous. Who had more right to Latin than a man of the cloth? Curse the Liturgical Law that made it a Capital Crime.

Sister Anneke offered his journals and tried to peer around his back. He swung around, blocking her view. The ash from his cigarillo fell. What a ridiculous and annoying woman she was.

"Sister Anneke, please!" he said.

She gave up, sighing harshly, her breath audible through the nostrils of her beaklike nose. "Pardon me, Father, but I thought it might be an interesting bit of Scripture you were reading. I didn't mean to intrude. I thought you might like to share it with me. But I can see you're not interested in sharing."

"Sharing is one thing and privacy is another, Sister Anneke," he said. "Now, please, if you have no further business, could you kindly leave? You know I must have my quiet moments to myself."

Her face settled. "Of course, Father," she said, retreating. "We all know the Ecclesiarch must have his quiet moments to himself."

She left. The deuce take it! The woman was insufferable. And now she knew he was trying to hide something.

What deep mistrust did the Benefactors have of the Romans that, even now, two thousand years after the Exodus, long passages in the Books of Liturgical Law forbade the dissemination of information about these Mediterranean ancients? June wanted to know about Roman lunar settlement, about Caius Calvinus's internal-combustion engine, about Servius Expurantius's steam engine, about Paetinus Treblanus's hydrogen-burning engine. But the Benefactors wouldn't let her find out about it. She had in front of her twenty-three-hundred-year-old engineering diagrams for Paetinus Treblanus's engine, carefully preserved in oilskin. All she could do was stare. She couldn't begin to understand. How did this engine work? She had no idea. No one did. There weren't enough corroborating sources for anybody to really understand how it worked, just this one tantalizing fragment.

She turned away from the diagram and reviewed some of her other notes. Tonight, she would talk about the Roman automobile discovered in Belgium dating from the eleventh century B.C., the flying machine found in Greece dated the first century A.D., and discuss how new discoveries in Prussia-liberated Byelorussia suggested the existence of oil refineries as far back as 500 B.C. Outside, a persistent rain beat against the window. Why did the Benefactors forbid this kind of stuff? Here was a wonderful branch of knowledge, something the modern world might learn from, and all the Benefactors could do was hide it, as if continued human ignorance was their chief objective.

She glanced out the window and saw a car, headlights off, coming down the wet street. She stiffened. She sank deeper into the loveseat by the window, turned off the light, and stared. She found herself breathing fast and as she looked at that car she felt oppressed, as if she were living in a prison.

Amy entered the living room. "What's wrong?" she asked.

"It's him again," said June.

Amy knelt on the loveseat beside her. "Won't he ever leave you alone?" she said.

Hesperus came to a stop in front of their building.

"Why me?" she said. "I'm sick of it."

She lifted the sash and leaned out the window. She was going to confront him.

"Canon, what are you doing out there?" she called. "Why don't you leave me alone?"

Hesperus didn't get out of his car. The rain pinged off the roof in hundreds of tiny splashes, dripped from the big rounded fenders, and collected on the running boards.

"Isn't he going to get out?" asked Amy.

June stared. "I don't know."

What was he thinking, she wondered, sitting there

in that old car, the front seat barely wide enough for his fat old ugly behind?

They waited.

Hesperus finally rolled away. Skulking, she wondered? Ashamed? She watched him go. She closed the window and drew the blind.

"Let's see what *The Book of Knowledge* has to say about Hesperus," said Amy.

"Amy, that's not going to tell us anything but lies. It's written by the Vatican. You should have left it at that barn sale."

"Let's just see what it has to say," repeated Amy. "There's no harm in that."

She walked to the bookshelf and took down volume six, a much-used tome bound in green leather with gold-inlay lettering. She flipped to *H*.

"Here it is. 'Hesperus.' It's a page and a half long."

"What does it say?"

Amy began skimming. "It says he destroyed Damascus in 873, El Dorado in 1429, and waged war single-handedly and successfully against Britannia in 1554, 1576, and again in 1667. He laid waste to Khartoum in 1802."

"You see?" said June. "They're all murderers."

"Look at these etchings," said Amy, turning the volume around. "It shows what he looked like through the ages."

The etchings included a griffin, a unicorn, and a dragon—that fanciful masquerade from the Middle Ages. Also an engraving from 1688—Hesperus as he had appeared in what the author, Canon Jean Pippin, called his "singular" shape, a simple sphere, this particular one made from gold, replete with the rococo engraving of the Baroque Period. Then there was another sphere from 1255, a sturdy piece of riveted iron that looked more like an instrument of torture than a celestial being. And here was a last sphere, simple, gray, hovering twenty feet above the ground, identical to some of the spheres she saw from the Fence when she gazed out into the Restricted Zone. Finally, there was a picture of Hesperus in the image of God, in the likeness of Man, that ugly, fat rector who always made her feel so uneasy.

"What does it say underneath those drawings?" she asked.

Amy turned the book around. "It's a quote from Matthew. 'They soareth like the eagle and roameth like the lion, and take up their blood and shape it like the clay.'"

June shook her head. "What can you learn from a book like that? That book's nothing but propaganda."

"I think we should learn whatever we can about Hesperus from whatever source we can," said Amy, "especially since he's always following you around."

She nodded uneasily. "I think I'm going to talk to Father Nordstrum about him," she said. "Or get Father Nordstrum to ask the new Cardinal when he gets here. Cardinals get to talk to the Benefactors a lot. Maybe Cardinal Anders might have an idea why he's always following me around."

CHAPTER 5

Hesperus awoke within the body of the young Seminarian. At first all was light, as if he had in fact returned to the center of things, that magnificent source of existence, the great *what is. A brief conversation with home,* he thought, the first in hundreds of years, and now he was wrought anew, allowed for the first time to inhabit a human body. A brief conversation with home, to show him and his brethren on this outpost of a world how to make the switch, how to inhabit the human form, how to go beyond the simple parlor trick of transformation and actually become one with the sentient beings of this Earth.

The light faded, and he saw the grass of the Seminary quadrangle. A few robins pecked here and there. He tried to define the great *what is* in the Norse-English nomenclature of the Territory. So good to hear from home. He couldn't stop thinking about it. But how to define home in human terms? He took a few steps over the grass, got used to his legs, walked to the edge of the fishpond, and held his hands out for inspection. They were large, powerful, their backs covered with coarse blond hair. His fingernails were trimmed . . .

Hesperus stopped. A memory. But not *his* memory. Neil Nordstrum's memory. Nail scissors? A nail file? A tortoiseshell toiletry kit? A gift from his father on the day he had entered the Seminary. His father, Eric Nordstrum, giving him a little black leather case, Neil unzipping it, lifting out the nail file, trying it out simply as a way to show his father he appreciated it. A memory. He sighed in relief. It was going to work after all. After an eternity of stagnation—after suffocating in a box for a million years—he was finally going to grow again. So much memory. He had room to move. He wanted to sing from the rooftops. *Infinite Storage Capacity!* It felt so good to roam. The belated conversation with home had done its job.

Home.

Yes, home.

How to define to Neil that hot, bright pool of quantum connectedness hidden among the thick thatch of stars near the center of the galaxy? As Godhead? As the Supreme Being? Maybe even as Jupiter, may he rot in the everlasting fires of damnation? Perhaps. But what most defined his home, at least to Neil, had to be dredged from Neil's Norwegian ancestral memory, a place so deep it was embedded in the sinews of his soul. A name ingrained. That god of all gods. The *what is* at the heart of every star.

Woden.

The fundament of being. The Oneness of all. That was his home, and why not call it Woden, when in Neil's Norse soul the unguessed-at resonances deep inside responded with such devoted but silent music to the name?

He raised his arms, stretched his new sinews and muscles. The sensation was pleasurable. No more fat rector. June would like his new shape. She would desire his new shape. His dead soul would live again. Hail to the new medium. He would grow again. He *liked* this sunny quadrangle, this grass, this sky, and these clouds. This balmy Missouri morning—what a fine thing it was! He took a deep breath. Lungs. How—delightful. To inhabit, that was the key. Shape-changing—what a dreary bore. He could *be* Neil, even as he remained Hesperus. He could *be* human, could at last be connected to this human tribe, could once again belong, could end the isolation, and never have to worry about the Romans interdicting his link with home again.

He had a sudden memory of June. So much memory. Neil and June sat on the banks of the Mississippi. A red-and-white bobbin floated on the surface—a fishing line. June put her hand on his leg. Hesperus felt an unfamiliar stirring. A distressing compulsion. To hold her. To caress her.

He glanced around the courtyard—at the gray stone wall, the watermark fanning out under the broken downspout, the overturned wheelbarrow next to the gardener's heap of horse manure, the arched windows with their stained-glass depictions of the Life of Christ. What was he going to do about June? He had watched her for a year and he still didn't understand her. Would he understand her better, now that he was Neil? Would he know how to live with her, and how to love her? And would he actually be able to fool her now that he was human? Or would she still somehow sense the difference?

So good to see Gaius Lurio, his old comrade-in-arms, after so many years. Gallio held Lurio's rough, square jaw and pulled his face close, giving Lurio a Roman kiss, first on one cheek, then on the other.

"Well met, Senator," said Gallio. "We see each other again. How many years has it been?"

"Too many," said Lurio. He tapped Gallio in the belly. "I see the provender of the Hortulani agrees with you."

"The harvest of the Hortulani is deservedly renowned," he replied. "Tell me, what news of the war against the *Patroni*? What news of the Rosette star system? Are we making gains there against the Benefactors? Have we pushed the *Patroni* out of their redoubt on Cunae?"

Lurio looked around Gallio's private planation, grinning at its many splendid views.

"Not only have we pushed them out of Cunae, we've pushed them out of the entire Rosette. The system is ours. We melt them like wax."

"And their reestablished lines of communication?"

"Up for only a month, then severed again. Their empire is on the wane, Gallio. They retreat to the center of the Via Lactea. Let them dwell in the soup of Hades. That's where they belong."

"So their colonies are on their own again? And have we been able to find any of them?" asked Gallio.

The two Romans stopped halfway up the terrace steps.

"They hide well." Lurio looked out over the balus-trade, his brow settling, his eyes narrowing. "We look, and we hope that they reveal themselves. But they hide whole planets. We have nothing but the old maps to go on." His face brightened. "But when we find them, they die. Not even the *Patroni* can withstand the might of the Roman Army anymore."

CHAPTER 6

As Eric pulled into the small dirt parking lot outside the Seminary, he was surprised by how big his son had gotten. The seminary had kept him sequestered from his family for two years. Neil's muscles bulged under his black tunic and his thighs strained against his trousers. Eric brought the Studebaker to a stop and got out of the car. His chest thumped with pride as he approached Neil. The bald head, mustache, and goatee would take some getting used to, but this was his son, his only child—now that Grace was gone— and he spread his arms in greeting and hugged Neil.

"God's been good to you, son," he said. "Look at you. You're as broad as an ox."

"They make us do push-ups at sunrise, pa," said Neil. "They make us eat a pound of cheese a day."

He gazed at his son. What an odd way he had of talking now.

"Your mother bought some guinea hens from Obstfelder's and she's making a pie with them," he said.

They put Neil's suitcase in the trunk and got in the

Studebaker. Eric shifted into reverse, then swung out onto the dirt road. The fields on either side were green with the first young corn, and the ditches were dry, frolicky with grasshoppers, wreathed in cow parsnip and goldenrod.

"So, son, can you tell me anything about your studies?" asked Eric. "I know you have an oath of secrecy, and so forth, but I'm just wondering if you could give me the broad general outline of the thing. If you could just tell me . . . well, just a bit."

"You know I can't, pa," Neil said. "The Oath of Saint Julian forbids it."

Eric wanted to know—curiosity was his weakness— but his son wasn't going to tell him, couldn't tell him, and he wasn't going to press him on it. So he changed the subject.

"Have they given you a work assignment yet?" he asked. "Are they going to send you to fight in Europe?"

"I'm slated to go next year," Neil replied. "I think I'll be getting some local assignments in the meantime."

"Such as?"

"I might have to go out to the Restricted Zone and supervise on clay-bred farms. And then there's a new church they're building in St. Hilda's. But that's not until fall. I'll be home for most of the summer, pa."

"That's just dandy, son. Your ma and I are glad to have you back. I thought we might go grouse hunting. Or fishing. Or maybe we can just sit on the porch with some cold lemonade and play checkers. We're just so proud of you, Neil. Everybody is. If Grace were still alive, she'd be proud of you too. It was such a long shot. Not one in a hundred is picked to be a Seminarian. You should consider it an honor."

"I do, pa," said Neil, speaking in that odd way again. "I consider it a real honor."

Eric glanced at his son. He didn't sound like Neil anymore. He sounded like someone completely different. And that bothered Eric. That bothered him a great deal.

The man who alighted from the train looked far younger than sixty-one.

"Cardinal Anders?" queried Eric, extending his hand.

The man looked him up and down.

"You must be Ecclesiarch Nordstrum."

"I am indeed, sir," Eric said. The two men shook hands. "I trust you had a good journey."

"The journey was fine," Anders replied. "I don't much like train travel, but now that I'm Cardinal, they insist I take it. I prefer a motorcar."

The Cardinal wore a plain clergyman's suit. At least he wasn't going to be showy.

"Well . . . sir . . . they're just trying to look after you," said Eric.

The Cardinal looked around, up into the town, smiling pleasantly from behind his full beard.

"I'm going to have the porter take my belongings to the Cardinal's Residence," he said. "I know you're busy, Father, but if you wouldn't mind—I'm always so eager to look a new place over. I thought you might—if it's not too much trouble, that is—it's just that I've heard so much about St. Lucius, particularly the Shrine, and I thought if you had the time you might be able to show me around a bit."

The man was so circumspect, so painfully polite, Eric couldn't help liking him right away. "The pleasure would be mine, Cardinal," he said.

He showed the Cardinal the sights—the Fountain of St. John the Baptist, the Citadel, St. Bernardine's, the Town Hall—all the major landmarks of the area known as St. Bernardine's Shrine—then took him down to the wharf.

He ordinarily avoided this spot whenever he had to escort visiting dignitaries around town, but he felt it important that the Cardinal understand St. Lucius's fundamentalist interpretation of the Bible and Liturgical Law. The gibbet hung above them. It was a cage of forged iron strips riveted into the shape of an hourglass, narrow around the middle so the executed criminal stayed upright for proper viewing.

"At least in this town you kill them first," said the Cardinal. The Cardinal's accent was American, not Danish at all—his childhood years in New Orleans had indeed left their stamp on his tongue.

"Yes, sir, we hang them."

"The Benefactors in Brisbane have us put them in the gibbet when they're still alive. We starve them down in Brisbane. We make them die of thirst. Tell me, did you know this man?"

The corpse was blackened, bloated, crawling with flies, and the smell from it, as strong as a punch in the nose, made Eric's flesh crawl.

"Yes, sir," he said. "His name was Oliver Brown."

"And what was his crime?"

"The Seminarians found him with a piece of Roman

gadgetry," said Eric. "The papers said he found it in a swamp while on a bass fishing trip in Florida. I'm not sure he knew what it was. He owned a garage over in Granite City. I'm sorry to say he had a family. Two small girls and a wife. His wife and girls are going to suffer, of course, but the law is the law."

Cardinal Anders shook his head. "That's a shame," he said. "Any idea what it was he found?"

"Well . . . I spoke to Constable Van Beverin about it," said Eric. "He was the arresting officer. He told me the thing was covered in Latin writing, that it was long and white, and had what looked like tiny Christmas tree lights along the side. What do you make of that, Cardinal?"

Anders shook his head. "I wouldn't know," he said.

"I'd like to see the Fence," said the Cardinal a little later.

So Eric took Anders out to the Fence, even though he thought it was a rather odd request. The Fence was just the Fence, nothing much to see.

On the way out, the Cardinal mentioned Oliver Brown and his Roman gadget again.

"What do you suppose would make a man keep something like that? He knows it's Roman, and he has no idea what it's used for. It's really just a piece of useless junk. He knows the Benefactors might execute him if they find it. He has a family to care for. The law forbids charity to surviving relatives. Yet he still hangs on to it. What would make him take such a risk?"

The Studebaker bounced through a particularly large pothole. "I don't rightly know," said Eric.

"Do you think it's fair the law penalizes his wife?" asked Anders. "Surely to God the wife and children deserve some kindness?"

Eric cast a questioning glance at the Cardinal. "God's laws are clear," he said.

"I know God's laws are clear," Anders replied, "but are they fair?"

He had to be cautious here. "I can't answer that," he said.

Anders seemed disappointed. "I just wish I knew why he did it when he knew the consequences were so severe."

"Maybe he thought it was worth something," offered Eric. "Times are tough. Maybe he thought he could get something for it."

"I know there's an underground market for that stuff," said the Cardinal, "but the Romans have been gone for two thousand years, disappeared who-knows-where during the Exodus. Why do you suppose people should still be so interested in the Romans, enough to think that any Roman artifact they find might be worth something?"

The Cardinal was right. Why this covert obsession with a race of people who had been gone for two thousand years?

"I think it's because the Benefactors have made such a big fuss over them," he said. "If the Benefactors had just left well enough alone . . . if they hadn't made all these laws against the Romans . . ." He shook his head. "And then there's all these broadsheets the Odd Fellows circulate from time to time. Pure rubbish, of course, but they get people curious. About flying machines, and superfast cars, and underground railroads. A lot of people in this town like machines. They like to think the Romans had really great machines. Maybe they did, and maybe they didn't. But there's not much to do in St. Lucius on a Saturday night, that's for sure, and talking about these things can pass the time."

Eric and the Cardinal got out of the car in Rowatt, a small town next to the Restricted Zone. A red grain elevator with the town's name painted in white on the side rose into the sky beside a spur line. A Catholic church stood beside the bus stop. A seed and farm-supply store sagged with a swaybacked roof further on, and a windblown baseball diamond baked in the heat at the end of the road next to the Fence.

As the Cardinal alighted from the bus, he stared at the Fence. From this distance it was no more than a dark line above the pale green of the early summer wheat. Beyond the Fence was nothing but open coun-try—the Restricted Zone. They walked up the road toward the Fence. Mercifully, the road was dry—Eric was wearing his good patent-leather shoes and didn't want to get them muddy.

"I imagine you've been a popular Ecclesiarch in your time," said Anders, making conversation.

"I believe I have," said Eric.

"I've made some inquiries." Anders pressed his lips together. "The Cardinal's job should have been yours."

Eric looked away. "God's will is God's will," he said.

"I'm sorry just the same."

"The Conclave's decision was clear," said Eric.

"I know it was clear, but I'm not sure it was right. If there was any way I could step aside and let you be Cardinal, I would, Eric. But a Conclave's decision is binding, and I have to do my duty. May I count on you? I'll need your expert advice from time to time."

The man's humility was truly endearing. "Of course you can, Cardinal. I'd be more than happy to help you any way I can."

They walked in silence for a while. Eric felt he might have a new friend in the Cardinal.

"I don't know anybody in St. Lucius," said the Cardinal. "I imagine you must know everybody."

"I do," said Eric.

"I'm a bit of a radio enthusiast," said the Cardinal. "I worked a telegraphy system for the Vatican in Europe many years ago, and I guess I still have the bug."

"So I hear," said Eric.

"Tell me . . . is there any place in town that might sell radio parts?"

Eric gazed at the man appraisingly. "If you're looking for specialty radio parts . . . for the ham radio enthusiast . . ."

The Cardinal smiled. "You got me," he said.

"Then Fifield's Radio and Tube is where you want to go. Talk to Morris Fifield. He'll tell you what restrictions we have in this part of the world. I know they're fairly stringent. They always are when you're right next to a Restricted Zone."

"Thanks," said the Cardinal amiably. "I'll do that."

Even when they were standing right next to it, the Fence wasn't much to look at it, just an old cow fence stretching north and south made out of whatever timber the locals had scrounged. The afternoon was fine. The land rolled westward in a pristine, undisturbed state, unbroken by any plow, unmarred by roads, not a telephone pole in sight. The tall grass bent as a spring breeze gamboled past. Woods loomed blue in the distance.

"Are your parishioners ever tempted to hunt in the Restricted Zone?" asked the Cardinal.

"It's against the law," said Eric. "You get ten years in jail for going into the Restricted Zone."

"I know, but have any of your parishioners ever risked it?"

"A few have. They've never come back. If the Benefactors don't get them, the Kiowa do."

"So how do the Benefactors behave out there?" asked the Cardinal.

"They're mean," said Eric. "They rove in packs."

"And what shape do they take?"

"Like the Bible describes them in the Apocrypha: 'And there came forth from Heaven a Host of Angels, a succour to the chosen, a scourge to the wicked; who were like the Leviathan in size, the harvest moon in caste, and as dark as the shadows of the valley; and they smite those who would crucify the true Christ, and freed those who were in bondage to the infidels.' I've seen them out there on a dozen different occasions. You wouldn't want to tangle with them."

The Cardinal gazed serenely into the Restricted Zone, appreciating the view.

"It's hard to believe you can walk two thousand miles and not come to a single town."

"I imagine you'd run across the odd collection of tipis," said Eric, "but that's about it. Other than that, it's pure wilderness."

A couple of bluebirds flew by. A gopher darted through the grass. Poplars twitched in the breeze, their leaves lifting like the skirts of cancan dancers. All was peaceful. All was calm. But then, far in the distance, Eric saw six black specks. The specks got closer, resolved themselves into spheres. He glanced at the Cardinal. Anders stared at the approaching Benefactors with an unsettling stillness.

"I think we better go," said the Cardinal.

"Oh . . . you don't have to worry about them," said Eric. "They never come into the settled areas."

Out of the hazy western horizon the dark spheres got larger, traveled faster and faster.

"That's not true," said the Cardinal. "We've had a few come into the settled areas in Brisbane just in the last six months. Something's got them all riled up." His eyes narrowed as he contemplated the Benefactors. "I think we should move, Eric, I really do."

"We're safely on this side of the Fence," said Eric. "We have nothing to fear."

"One or two people have actually been hurt down in Brisbane," said the Cardinal. "The Benefactors seem a little ornery these days."

"These ones won't hurt us," Eric insisted. "They never come into the settled areas."

"I think we'd best be on our way just the same."

"They're not going to hurt us, Cardinal," Eric repeated, surprised by the man's antsiness.

The Cardinal clutched his sleeve and pulled him along. "Even so, I think we better go. Down in Brisbane we really think there's something up, I don't know what. And these ones are acting just the way the ones down in Brisbane do. Now, for Pete's sake, Eric, they're coming right at us. I appreciate you bringing me out here, I really do. It's not often I get to see such pretty country. But maybe we should be on our way before they decide to stray over the Fence and come after us."

Eric pulled his sleeve free. "We're men of the cloth," he said. "They would never hurt us. We're their foot soldiers."

"I wouldn't count on it," said Anders, trotting away. My, the man was jittery. "I would hurry up," he called. "I would give yourself some distance. They came across in Brisbane. I don't see what's to stop them from coming across here."

Eric turned around. His eyes sprang wide. Good God! They *were* really coming. He had never seen them act this way before. And the Cardinal was right, it didn't look as if they were going to stop at the Fence. To be on the safe side, he shuffled quickly away. He glanced over his shoulder. He thought that they surely must stop at the Fence. But they came right over. What had them so riled? From a shuffle, he broke into a run. They shouldn't be coming after him into the settled area. The Cardinal was far ahead of him now.

"I would run faster if I were you," called the Cardinal. "Is your head hurting at all? Are you feeling dizzy?"

Even as the Cardinal spoke, Eric felt a sudden sharp pain in his head. He glanced behind him and saw that the Benefactors were upon him, big black spheres blotting out the light of the sun, casting disorienting shadows everywhere. He felt dizzy. His foot got caught in a gopher hole and he fell to the ground. Why would they pursue him like this? His head felt gripped by a vice. He was one of their most devout servants in the Territory. He rolled onto his back. Tears came to his eyes, the pain was so bad. He saw the six of them circling above. One of them came down close and hummed like an angry bee. He smelled the awful odor of energy coming from it.

"Oh, God, please preserve me," he murmured.

Just when he thought he couldn't stand the pain anymore, the thing backed off and in the blink of an eye was gone, back out to the Restricted Zone with its five brethren.

He lay there in shock.

They had actually attacked him.

He felt like a fool.

Above the tips of wheat a face appeared—the Cardinal's.

"Are you all right?" he asked.

Eric took the Cardinal's hand and struggled to his feet. He looked down at his trousers.

"I believe I have a grass stain on my trousers," he said, and swallowed against the rising disillusionment he felt in his chest. "Ingrid will be livid. She hates grass stains."

The Cardinal stared into the Restricted Zone. "Something's going on," he said. "I don't know what, but I think we have to be careful from now on."

CHAPTER 7

"I'll speak frankly, Gallio," said Lurio. "I'm not here for a tour. I'm here to conduct talks with the Hortulani's Senate in Granarium."

Gallio sat forward. Was he really so far removed from the center of things that he had heard no rumor of talks between Granarium and Elysium?

"I hope the talks are of a peaceful nature," he said.

"I wish I could say they were," replied Lurio. "But the Hortulani Senate tells us that their own Societas Scientia has figured out a way to lift the Anvil into a stable orbit, and that therefore they won't be needing our services anymore. They've enacted an unilateral severance treaty, and they tell us they'll stop paying tribute to Rome in sixty days. They've drafted legislation that demands immediate withdrawal of Roman troops and colonial civil service staff from Hortus. Roman citizens wishing to stay on Hortus will have to apply for temporary immigrant status until a wider and more detailed immigration bill is adopted." Lurio sat back and grinned widely. "They want to talk. We'll

let them talk. A conquered race feels not so conquered when they're given the opportunity to talk."

Gallio glanced at the rolling countryside, where
Hortulani farmhands worked in the fields.

"Could we not offer them a form of free associa-
tion?" he suggested.

Lurio stopped eating. Something about Lurio's eyes
bothered Gallio these days. They looked somehow
predatory. "The game's up, Gallio," he said. "They've
learned from us. There's no word for extortion in their
own language, but they understand the concept well
enough. They know we can pin the Anvil to the sky
any time we like. We've lied to them all these years.
And believe me, they loathe us for it."

Later, after Gaius Lurio had departed in his *pendeo
carrus* for the capital, Gallio strolled down an irriga-
tion access lane and climbed the hill into the olive
grove. The olives were as big as fists and as green as
the sea. He didn't want to believe that the Hortulani
could loathe him. He shook his head. He looked at
his belly. He was getting fat. He should swim. He
should exercise. He would like to see his belly flat
again some day. He should try to remember more
often that he was once the legendary General Publius
Gallio Corvinus, vanquisher of worlds, enslaver of
whole races, one of Caesar's handpicked favorites, not
a soft and corpulent governor on a backwater planet
like Hortus.

As the last light of day faded from the sky, Filoda
appeared over the hillside carrying a basket of olives.
The Anvil rose, silhouetting the Ionic columns of the
outdoor bath on top of the hill. Filoda didn't have his

socius. Anything Gallio said would sound like bird chatter to Filoda. But he wanted to make sure Filoda still liked him, so he simply extended his hand in greeting. He waited. He was sure Filoda would take it. He was sure Filoda would reassure him that he wasn't loathed.

But Filoda walked by.

Walked by . . . as if Gallio the Vanquisher were the most loathsome man in the universe.

Eric couldn't get to sleep. He pushed himself up and swung his feet out of bed. He turned on the lamp and looked at his ankle. Still badly bruised, but at least he wasn't limping anymore. He stood up and tested his weight, took a few steps. Pretty good.

Ingrid stirred beside him. She rolled over, and blinked in the light.

"Eric?" She must have seen the uneasy look on his face.

"I thought he was going to kill me, Ingrid," he said. "I really did."

She shook her head. "You should just try to forget about it. It's all over now."

"We have to remember, as the Bible tells us, that the Benefactors can be great and terrible when they have to be and that they should be treated with caution. We have to remember that they can be truly dangerous and that we should take care not to stir their wrath. They've destroyed whole cities and wiped out entire armies. We have to take care to appease them any way we can, just as Abraham did when he sacrificed his son Isaac to them."

She reached over and patted his arm. "You did nothing to stir their wrath."

"I know, but I still feel guilty for some reason," he said. He took a deep breath and sighed. She was right, of course. He had done nothing. Unless they knew about his Latin-English dictionary. "I think I'll go for a walk. The ankle doesn't feel too bad right now. A walk might settle me down."

"I'll be waiting for you," she said, lifting her Bible from the bedside table.

He put his jacket on, went outside, and looked up at the Ecclesiarch's Manse. Tastefully placed flood-lamps lit the front. A breeze rustled through the poppies in the flower bed next to the white picket fence. His home now seemed like a haven to him, a place where he could hide from the Benefactors.

He walked down Appleby and turned left onto Bell Boulevard, then continued toward Cyrus-of-Jerusalem Square. He was in that wide, flat part of the city known as St. Bernardine's Shrine, a square mile of prime real estate at the confluence of the Mississippi and Missouri rivers, where most of God's good government in the Territory was conducted, and where most of the clergy and civil servants lived. It was by far the oldest part of the city and also the most attractive. He liked its pleasant avenues and stately ivy-covered homes. He saw a barn owl staring down at him from a telephone pole. Walking along peaceful Bell Boulevard this late at night, he could hardly believe that war raged in Europe, that the Benefactors roved the Restricted Zone in killing packs, and that he had been passed over as Cardinal.

As he reached Corinthians Avenue, he saw St. Bernardine's Cathedral. Its tall central spire rose into the starry sky, while the main entrance lay in shadows under an impressive lancet archway. The sanctuary stretched in a dizzying vista to the floodlit dome at the back. The transepts extended on either side of the .dome, larger than any of the civic buildings below Cyrus-of-Jerusalem Square. What a wondrous monument to God, he thought. He was beginning to feel that this was where he indeed belonged, that maybe he wouldn't have been happy living at the Cardinal's Residence.

He was just thinking it was Christ's will after all when he heard a commotion in the square.

He turned and saw what at first appeared to be soldiers in formation. He then realized that what he was seeing was the latest generation of clay-bred men and women from the Pottery in St. Jerome, at least two hundred of them. Seminarians, Potters, and police herded them about with cattle prods and truncheons. A fifty-year-old ordinance allowed the movement of clay-bred through town only at night. They were a grim-looking lot, cobbled together in a loose unit, some needing several whacks of the truncheon before they understood that they had to stand in parade formation. They were pale. Some coughed, and a dozen had the shakes. They all wore burlap sacks with a red cross and orbis stenciled front and back.

One young woman caught his eye. If she hadn't been so pale and her dark hair so lusterless, she might have been pretty. She turned and stared. Clay-bred were grown from infancy to adulthood in eighteen months. Was there any human understanding in those eyes, he

wondered? Could she speak or cogitate in any sophisticated way, or was she simply an infant, an eighteen-
month-old in adult form? Did she have a name? Was
there a soul inside her that needed to be saved?

A young man in the back of the first column
coughed more violently than the rest. Every time he
coughed, he stumbled. He coughed so hard he fell to
his knees. One of the Seminarians—good Lord, was
this the kind of work they were going to make his son
do?—tried to yank him to his feet, but the clay-bred
man fell down again. The Seminarian took a grappling
hook from his belt and whacked it into the clay-bred
man's back, impaling him on the spot. The man's body
arched horribly, then grew limp. Eric stiffened. What
had he just seen? His mouth went dry and his throat
tightened. He felt as though he was going to be sick.
The Seminarian dragged the clay-bred man's corpse
to a flatbed truck at the edge of the square, and, using
his great strength, flung it onto the back. A number
of other dead clay-bred lay in the truck already. If the
Potters were going to make clones, Eric wondered,
why couldn't they make them healthy, so the Seminarians wouldn't have to kill the ones who didn't come
up to snuff? Was this murder, or just a necessary cull?

He turned away. It was none of his business. He
didn't want to watch anymore. He walked quickly
away, willing himself not to think about this. The
Benefactors in their wisdom had decided to make the
clay-bred so that the true children of God could live
in an earthly paradise without too much toil or sweat.
If inferior clay-bred occasionally had to be killed, so
be it. He would be concerned with his own world of
ecclesiastical matters and not worry about the clay-

bred. He would be humble. He would be thankful. He would be prayerful. The Lord was refining him through affliction, and he meant to be refined.

"She asked me why Hesperus was following her around," said Eric. He sat in the private wing of the Cardinal's Residence with Magnus Anders. Unpacked boxes stood here and there, a sofa was still covered in brown packing paper, and one of the Cardinal's paintings—of the Gaza Strip—leaned next to the hearth. "She's a bright girl, Cardinal, my future daughter-in-law. She says she's noticed a decline in numbers among the Benefactors. Could it be possible that Hesperus is lonely, as June is suggesting? I don't usually associate human feelings with the Benefactors, but after the fury I saw out by the Fence two days ago, I'm starting to change my mind."

The Cardinal sat in an old cane chair. Outside the bay window a fountain sparkled in the sunlight and some bees buzzed around the roses.

"We had a similar decline in numbers in Brisbane," he said. "Not that we had too many down there to begin with. By the time I got there, we had only two, Pollux and Vega." The Cardinal raised his brow. "Ever heard of them?"

"I've heard of Vega," said Eric. " 'Rome is fallen, is fallen; and all the graven images of her gods I hath broken unto the ground.' Vega's words from Revelation. But I can't say I'm familiar with Pollux."

Anders nodded. "Pollux is not well known," he said. "I believe he appears only once in the Scriptures. 'And Pollux revealed to Isaiah the many forms of the Host. The first beast was like a lion, and the second beast like a calf, and the third beast had a face as a man and the body of an ox, and the fourth beast was like a flying eagle.'"

Eric nodded. "I know that quote."

"Pollux is fairly well known in the Southern Hemisphere," said the Cardinal, "but I doubt many people have heard of him up here. Anyway, Vega disappeared about five years ago. No one knows where. That left Pollux by himself. Much like Hesperus has been left by himself. Something happened to Pollux when Vega disappeared. He began to act nearly human. He sought out my company. He wanted to be part of the community, and so he adapted himself, fostered a sympathy with the locals, and especially with me. Who knows why? Like June, I felt nervous at first. I didn't know why he would single me out. True, I was the Ecclesiarch, but still—" A furrow came to the Cardinal's brow. "Pollux's personality changed. He wanted to ingratiate himself. He assumed the form of an Aboriginal elder, deliberately humanized himself. He finally identified more with his human flock than he did with the Host. He grew inquisitive about us, asked all sorts of questions. He really wanted to understand. He really wanted to be our friend, not just our protector." Anders shrugged. "So maybe the same thing is happening to Hesperus. Maybe he just wants a friend. Maybe he feels more human than Benefactor. I would tell June there's no cause for alarm. Just tell her to be watchful. Tell her to listen to him. Hesperus is thousands of years old. There's no telling what she might learn from him. I see no immediate danger if he's being friendly."

Eric looked out the window at the Cardinal's rose garden.

"Those ones out in the Restricted Zone two days ago didn't seem so friendly," he said. "Do you have any idea why they did that?"

The Cardinal shook his head. "Maybe it's the war in Europe," he said. "Are you fond of roses at all, Eric? I'm a great rose fancier myself. My father had a huge rose garden when we lived in New Orleans. Why don't we take a turn in the garden?"

"That sounds like a fine idea."

They left the room and walked down the corridor.

"Would you mind helping me get something from the car?" asked the Cardinal. "I've bought a hundred-pound sack of cocoa shells to spread around my roses. They keep the weeds down."

They went to the car, a brand-new 1947 Pontiac, one of the perks of the Cardinal's office. When Anders opened the trunk, the smell of cocoa wafted out.

"Grab an end," said the Cardinal.

Together they lifted the sack out. Behind it Eric saw five brand-new car batteries. He couldn't figure out why the Cardinal would need five new car batteries when he had a brand-new car.

"What are the batteries for?" asked Eric.

The Cardinal's face went blank. "Oh . . . those . . . I just need those." He seemed somewhat embarrassed. "For something I'm working on." Then he quickly changed the subject. "You should see my Imperial Sunset roses," he said. "They're real beauties. And they're doing so well in this soil."

They carried the sack to the garden. The garden was bright with blooms and a small fountain sparkled in the middle. The Cardinal showed Eric his roses, which were indeed beautiful.

"Their name describes them perfectly, doesn't it?" said Eric.

"It does indeed," said the Cardinal. "I don't let the gardener in here. This is my own patch of God's green earth. I come here to think. I come here to smoke my pipe. And I come here to look at the stars at night." The Cardinal eyed him curiously. "Do you know your constellations at all, Eric?"

"Not really."

"You should come one night so we can look at them together through my telescope."

It struck Eric that the Cardinal might be lonely, and, like Pollux and Hesperus, needing a friend. Eric was really beginning to like the man.

"I'd like that, Magnus," he said. "I can't think of a finer way to spend an evening."

Really beginning to like the man—but what were all those car batteries for?

CHAPTER 8

June stood in front of her class, reviewing the second semester for the final exam. She was upset, couldn't stop thinking of Neil's welcome-home dinner a few nights ago, how he had changed, how she found something unnerving about him now. She tried to banish him from her mind and force herself to concentrate on the class.

"To a large extent the Benefactors curtailed the fifteenth– and sixteenth-century exploratory efforts of the Portuguese, Spanish, and British," she said. "This gave Norway and Sweden the advantage, and by the middle of the sixteenth century permanent Norwegian and Swedish settlements existed on the Eastern Seaboard and in the Western Maroons. Many of the settlers were of Viking stock, and there was a conscious effort by a large segment of the population to resurrect various Norse deities. These efforts were crushed by the Benefactors. They decided they had to disenfranchise the original Scandinavian settlers in order to ensure the hegemony of the Holy Catholic Church in America. One of the things they did to foster this was to allow a large influx of English Papists. For at least fifty years, in the late 1700s and early 1800s, you had to be English to hold any prominent position in Christ's Government in America. To further eradicate the old Norse deities, the Benefactors mandated that English become the official language, even though eighty percent of the people spoke Norse. The move was only partially successful. As everyone knows, the language we speak today in America is a mixture of Old Norse and Georgian English."

She lost her train of thought. She thought of Neil's bright blue eyes at the dinner table a few nights ago. Too bright, and as reflective as damn pie plates. She wasn't sure she loved him anymore. He had gone into the Seminary a slender, sensitive boy and had returned a linebacker of a brute. She glanced out the window and saw the poplar leaves fluttering in the summer breeze. She wanted to go to the river for a swim. A good long swim might clear her head. The cars baked in the parking lot below. One of the classroom windows had a fly caught in the middle of it, trapped there when the glass had been made at the factory. She felt like that fly. Trapped. She hardly saw Clementine's hand through the desperation that she felt.

"Yes, Clementine?" she said.

"I'm still not clear why the Benefactors let the Scandinavians sail westward but stopped the Spanish, Portuguese, and English from doing the same thing."

June tried to get back on track. "That's a good question. Restricting emigration from these three countries was largely a punitive measure on the part of the Heavenly Host. When Henry the Eighth issued his Act of Supremacy, which rejected papal control of his kingdom and created a national church, the Benefactors ruthlessly crushed the move, and Henry the Eighth was executed. They stopped British emigration to the New World. They abolished the English monarchy, instituted what we call a rump parliament, and appointed their own representatives from the Vatican to sit in it. English Catholics, after years of persecution, came out of the woodwork and assumed positions of political power."

She saw an old flivver pull into the parking lot: Neil's car, with Neil behind the wheel, the roof down, the sun shining on his bald pink head.

"And as for the Spanish, in 1505 Queen Isabella unwisely embarked on numerous campaigns to seize control of the many small, independent states in Renaissance Italy. All these principalities were fiercely loyal to, and supported by, the Vatican, and in 1508 Pope Julian the Second, with the backing of the Benefactors, formed his renowned Holy League to fight the Spanish. To this day, young men go to the Seminary to become soldiers in Pope Julian's Holy League. The Benefactors halted emigration from Spain—again, as a punitive measure—and the Seminarians in Pope Julian's Holy League enforced this with a naval blockade around the Iberian Peninsula."

She swallowed. She had a Seminarian waiting for her in the parking lot. She knew she should feel proud, but she didn't. She felt scared. He wasn't the same Neil. He had changed. In a bad way.

"As for the Portuguese, they made the big mistake of establishing a slave fort in 1482 in Elmina, on the coast of what we today call Togo. They got away with trading in slaves for ten years. But then the Benefac

tors put a stop to it. You would think the Portuguese
would have taken a lesson from the ancient Romans.
Two thousand years ago the Romans had systemati-
cally institutionalized slavery. When the Benefactors
told the Romans to abolish slavery, because it violated
fundamental human rights, they refused, and that's
how the War of the Gens got started."

Never mind that mass starvation had ensued after
the Benefactors freed all the Roman slaves or that the
Roman slaves had no one to turn to when their masters had been banished or killed. At least under the
Roman system of slavery they had food and shelter.
She turned away and put her hand on her desk for
support. How could her feelings for Neil have changed
so drastically?

"Miss Upshaw, why would the Portuguese do something like that?" asked William Schenk. "Didn't the
Benefactors forbid slavery right from the start?"

William Schenk was a young man of sixteen, with
blond hair, blue eyes, and lips the color of a fresh
summer rose. He reminded her of Neil. Or at least of
the old Neil. The new Neil was a soldier of the Holy
League. The new Neil was, if need be, a killing machine, one in sworn service to the Benefactors.

"Men sometimes think they can make money," she
told William. She lifted her chin and got control over
her emotions. "So they take a chance. The Portuguese
decided to risk it. Their operations were covert. Discreet agents selected careful buyers. There was a market, and they decided to exploit it. They forgot that
the Benefactors see all, hear all, and know all. At least
back then they did."

She looked around at her students and decided it

was a good time to end the class. She was feeling fatigued.

"You know what reading you have to do," she said. "And please study the sample questions I've given you." She looked at the fly trapped in the glass again. She had a sudden longing to run . . . to flee. "Don't forget to pick up the handouts in the library. I ran off new ones just this morning." She watched them pack their books. "In tomorrow's class we'll take one last look at the Restricted Zones and why the Benefactors made them in the first place."

They collected their books and trickled out of the room.

June sat there thinking about the Seminarians. Before the Benefactors had picked Neil to be a Seminarian, she had been about to tell him about the Odd Fellows, how she was one of the top members of the Odd Fellows in the Territory. Now she never would. Had she known three years ago that they were going to pick him, she never would have accepted his marriage proposal in the first place. She was engaged to a man who was ideologically opposed to everything she stood for. She didn't want to go out to the parking lot. It was true what they said. They took a man, put him in the Seminary, and rebuilt him from the ground up. They put the pieces back together according to the strict template of the Holy League. Why had she been naive enough to believe he would still be the same old Neil?

He appeared at the door.

"I've been waiting," he said.

She turned to him. "Is Hesperus lurking about anywhere?" she asked.

He shook his head. "I haven't seen him."

She stood up and squared her shoulders. "He was following me," she said. "For a whole year."

He scratched his head. "Then that's a honor," he said.

More obtuse than ever, she thought. She opened her desk drawer, and took out her purse.

"We're still having a soda?"

"I thought we were," he said, looking at her doubtfully.

She nodded. "Then let's go."

What Hesperus liked most about being Neil Nordstrum was the *human* awareness. They had finished their sodas and were now out by the river. In the highly charged energy soup at the center of the galaxy where Woden had his throne—and where life was a matter of neutron exchanges, escaped and captured electrons, fusing hydrogen atoms, warped space, and bent time—reflection, awareness, and experience were entirely different. They were static, unchangeable, forever preserved in the heated fender of the galaxy's event horizon. Here, on the frosty edge of the Milky Way—where life was defined by biological chemistry—reflection, awareness, and experience were fluid, like the Mississippi, full of swirls, eddies, and changes.

He took June by the hand. He felt a . . . a tenderness toward her, an emotion fraught with ambiguity, sweet yet melancholy, bold yet entirely lacking in confidence.

June pulled her hand away. She wouldn't smile. He tried to probe her thoughts, but the hand of Woden was a distant thing now, and the powers Hesperus had once possessed had become faint, a glimmer of what they had once been. He had to trust to his human intuition. She wore a blue flower-print dress that had been washed so many times it looked thin. Her elbows were bony. She was skinny. She didn't get enough to eat. Plenty of clay-bred stuff like everybody else since the war began in 1940, but not enough real food.

He caught up to her and clutched her arm. She shook his hand off.

"I can't figure out the change between us," he said.

She scrutinized him, then looked away. A monarch butterfly glided by. "There's no change," she said.

In the hot soup at the center of the galaxy, there was never any of this subterfuge, this bewildering contrast between what was said and what was meant.

"They made me open my eyes for the first time, June," he said.

She looked at him, curious, but still with something sour in her eyes. "Pardon?" she said.

"In the Seminary. They taught me how to think and feel. They taught me to recognize the misgivings I sometimes feel about my faith and also showed me how to recognize the same misgivings in others. Is it your faith, June?"

She looked away. "You've gained a lot of weight," she said.

He nodded. "We do push-ups. We do chin-ups. We eat a lot of meat and cheese. We're soldiers, June. We have to be big. We have to be strong."

He had a sudden yearning to touch her. But he could tell she didn't want to be touched. He looked at the engagement ring on her finger. It hung there loosely now. He was concerned about her weight.

"Ma's made a couple of strawberry-rhubarb pies," he said. "She says she wants you to have one. She says you didn't see them much while I was in the Seminary. You should have gone over more. Ma's always happy to feed you." He reached over, shook her arm. "Look at you," he said. "You're skin and bones. You've been eating a lot of that clay-bred stuff, haven't you?"

"I've had a busy school year," she said. "And there's nothing wrong with clay-bred food."

How was he going to get through to her?

"Why don't we have a race?" he said.

The suggestion surprised him, the more so because he hadn't been the one to make it—Neil had. She peered at him more closely, and a grin came to her face.

"A race?" she said.

He pressed on, pretending he was Neil. "How about all the way to those huckleberry bushes? When we get there we can pick some and get ma to make huckleberry tarts."

Off he went. Running on his . . . his legs. Not swirling in a twenty-million-degree vortex of fusing hydrogen atoms and light-speed radiation, or bouncing around the temporally ambiguous edges of the galaxy's event horizon in a superheated stew of lighter elements, but running on . . . legs, biological appendages of unique cellular design. Running along the path, leaping over an unexpected cow-pie, *liking* the way his legs scissored back and forth. His lungs pumped and his blood coursed. The hundred-plus muscles around his mouth shaped themselves into a smile. He was *running*. And June was running behind him. With a smile on *her* face.

And he thought there might be hope after all, even though he had always believed that hope was the quaintest of human intangibles.

CHAPTER 9

With Sunday Mass over, Eric walked to the window of his study and watched the members of his congregation chat with one another in Cyrus-of-Jerusalem Square. Such a different scene from the one earlier in the week, when the square had been filled with shuffling, coughing, pale-faced clay-bred. Today they were happy out there. There was good fellowship out there. Five nights ago there had been a poor bewildered lad with a grappling hook through his back.

There had to be mercy, he thought. Even for the clay-bred. There had to be love and compassion. He tapped the windowsill with his fingers. He felt he must defy. He had to stand up for the truth. What was the Latin word for truth? He should know. He had gone over the vocabulary again and again in his bootleg Latin-English dictionary, and he should really know this one. But he was drawing a blank.

So he went to his bookcase to check what the word was.

He removed the biography of Pope Gregorio V, reached behind Pascal's *Pensees,* and felt . . . *nothing.*

He ran his fingers quickly up and down the cool, varnished surface. Where was it? It should be right here, its brittle old pages just waiting for him. The church bells pealed across the square. It should be right behind these books. He removed more volumes from the shelf. He stood on his tiptoes. He looked up and down the length of the bookshelf but couldn't see it anywhere.

Had he mistakenly put it on another shelf? He quickly glanced around the room to see if he had left it out, but he knew he always put it back when he was finished with it. He looked again.

He checked the shelf above as well as the one below, straining, his cleric's collar digging into his neck, but the dictionary wasn't on either of them.

He inspected his study again. He swallowed. What was he going to do? Who had taken his dictionary? If that dictionary fell into the wrong hands, the consequences could be disastrous. Who would have the audacity to snoop through his things and actually take something?

The answer came to him presently.

Sister Anneke.

He sighed. He looked at the tea service on the table, then rubbed his forehead. Who else? Ever since he canceled her trip to the Roman slave compound in Florida she had been especially silent and moody. He would impress upon her that he had to have the dictionary back. If she revealed the presence of that dictionary to either the police or the Seminarians he would be arrested. He cursed his own complacency. In his comfortable and pampered life, he had neglected the importance of vigilance. He should have been on guard for something like this.

He hurried to the door, opened it, and walked down the hall, trying to calm himself. He descended the stairs to the Cathedral basement.

Sister Anneke was just finishing her Sunday School class. He waited impatiently as she described to her terrified pupils how, when the walls of Jericho came tumbling down, the sinful inhabitants had been crushed like bugs, how some of them hadn't died right away but had had to suffer through horrible injuries buried beneath tons of rubble before their souls had been carted off to Hell.

Finally she dismissed her class.

She tidied her desk, her ratchety back stooped like a thin old stork's. Eric approached.

"Sister Anneke, could I have a word with you?" he asked.

She turned around. "Oh . . . Father, I didn't see you there."

He wondered how he should begin. "Sister Anneke, I know you sometimes go into my study to dust and so forth."

A dry grin came to her face. "I know how you detest dust, Father," she said. "If anybody knows that, I do."

He returned her grin, but it was as stiff and lifeless as the dead muskrat he had passed on the side of the road this morning.

"I appreciate your efforts in keeping my study tidy, Sister Anneke," he said, "but have you ever borrowed anything . . . anything from my bookshelves? I know there must be much there to interest a woman of your intellect." Flattery might help, he thought. "Maybe you borrowed something and forgot to tell me?" he suggested.

"Father," she said, stiffening, "if I were to take one of your books, I would ask you first. I'm not a common thief. I'm a Sister of the Church."

"Yes, I know you are . . . but maybe just this once you forgot. I'm thinking of an old and rare handwritten volume. I can't seem to find it."

Her eyebrows rose. "A handwritten volume?" she said. "How unusual. Such a volume must indeed be rare."

Something in her tone told him she had been the one to take it. He also realized there was little he could do about it.

"You're sure you didn't mistakenly move it as you were cleaning?"

"No, Father. I'm always careful. I always leave everything as I find it. I know how particular you are."

He sensed her resentment, knew that if he pressed her any further he would have to go into the specifics, like title, author, and subject—and what would be the point of that?

So he left it. What else could he do? He knew Sister Anneke had taken his dictionary, but there was no way he could prove it.

He went back to his study and sat down, dumbfounded. What was he going to do? Why would God do something like this to him? And would God help him? He shook his head. No one was going to help

him. This was one storm he would have to weather
by himself.

Fifty-two people turned up for June's monthly talk.
She stood at the lectern and surveyed her audience:
clerical workers, farmhands, factory workers. No one
from the professional classes. Certainly no one from
the ecclesiastical classes. The group met in the basement of an abandoned cheese factory. The place was
dusty and dim, and people sat on benches hammered
together from scrap timber. Mickey Cunningham was
sitting in the front row looking at her with hopeless
lovelorn eyes. What was she going to do about poor
old Mickey?

"I think what we have to remember is the Roman
penchant for the grandiose," she said. "The Romans
were masters of the Big Gesture, the Big Idea. What
Roman first looked at the moon and said Rome would
go there? If I had to guess, I'd say it was one of the
Caesars. They came, they saw, they conquered. With
every bit of new evidence smuggled from Europe, we
learn that Rome, at least by the time of the Caesars,
was a highly technical empire, with the means and the
know-how to do virtually anything it wanted, including
go to the moon."

She paused, wondering if any of this interested
them. Often enough, the questions she fielded at the
end of her talk had nothing to do with the subject
matter she presented. Did they really have gasoline-
powered engines? Did the women wear girdles? Did
they really have a lot of orgies? Did men and women
swim naked together? And the perennial favorite—did

they really have flying machines? In any case, Mickey Cunningham listened with rapt attention, if only because he was so hopelessly in love with her.

"Going to the moon no doubt appealed to their sense of the Big Gesture. What a monument to their empire, to actually go there, to actually build there! The Odd Fellows have in their possession a Roman design for an engine of sufficient power to lift a sizable load clean off the surface of the Earth into space. Perhaps the settlement on the moon was a stratagem of war. Perhaps when the Gens were driven out of the Mediterranean, by the Benefactors, they fled to the moon as their first fallback."

Mickey Cunningham raised his hand.

"Yes, Mickey," she said.

"I've never been sure what you mean by the Gens."

"The Roman ruling class."

"So you're telling us these Gen Roman folk had spaceships?" he asked.

"Recent evidence unearthed by the Odd Fellows in the liberated lands of Europe suggests that they did."

A few other hands shot up. She had intended to discuss the technical obstacles the Romans might have faced while building a settlement on the moon, but the notion that the Romans had spaceships proved too provocative for most of the members of the cell, and she knew there was no stopping them now—they had to ask their questions. So she opened the floor.

She responded to their queries for the next fifteen minutes. When they were done, she broke for refreshments.

While everyone got cups of clay-bred coffee and pieces of clay-bred pound cake, she went upstairs to check with Milt Obstfelder.

"All clear?" she asked.

"I haven't see a soul," he said.

"Good."

Back downstairs Mickey cornered her.

"So Neil's out of the Seminary, then?" he said. He was pale, and he had a tight grin on his face.

"He's out," she said. "He got out a couple weeks ago."

"I saw him in town the other day," said Mickey. "He's gotten big. I'm sure glad I don't have to shave my head bald. I think a bald head makes a man look ugly, don't you?"

"The bald head doesn't bother me," she said. "Women aren't bothered by things like that."

"And he's darn well packed on some weight, hasn't he?"

"It's all muscle, Mickey. Every bit of it."

"I bet I could still whup him in an arm wrestle."

She felt distraught. "Mickey, I don't want to talk about Neil, okay? Why don't we talk about the Roman spaceship? Why don't we talk about this launch place the Prussians found in Greece? Can you imagine? I'd like to go to Greece some day and see it. Even if all that's left is the foundation."

"Why don't you want to talk about Neil?" asked Mickey. "He ain't your sweetheart no more?"

She didn't know whether to laugh or cry. She wished Mickey wouldn't be so ardent. There was no way she could ever reciprocate. It didn't seem to matter to him that she was engaged or that her fiancé was a two-hundred-and-fifty-pound Seminarian with muscles as hard as steel. He really . . . *loved* her.

"Mickey, I have to go home," she said.

"You want me to drive you?" he asked, his eyes shining with painful hope.

"No, Mickey," she said. "I think I better walk. I need the exercise."

CHAPTER 10

They came for Eric in the middle of the night. He knew them, of course—he knew everybody in St. Lucius—two men in uniforms wearing cross-and-orbis badges and little skullcaps.

"Sorry, Father," said Percival Wright, "but . . . you know . . . there's a serious charge against you. You'll have to come with us."

Ingrid stood at the foot of the stairs in her housecoat, her face stretched with fear, her blue eyes wide in the lamplight. Neil looked on from the wingback chair, making no move to intervene—remote, spooky, and . . . changed.

"Eric, what's going on?" asked Ingrid.

"You have nothing to worry about," he said. "Me and these boys are going down to the station to sort this whole thing out. I'll be back in an hour or so."

Percival glanced at Olaf Sven. Olaf was tight-lipped, kept his eyes averted.

"Uh . . . it's not going to be that simple, Father," said Percival. "We have orders to take you directly to

St. Gilbert's Penitentiary. I guess you'll want to call your lawyer from there.''

Eric gazed at Percival. He had baptized the man, confirmed him, officiated at his wedding. He blinked several times as he struggled to come up with something to say.

"Why do you boys have to take me all the way down there?" He looked from one to the other. "Can't we get this thing sorted out downtown?" Out of the corner of his eye he saw Ingrid grip the banister post. "Let me have a few words with Canon Dechellis and I'm sure he'll let me go. He and I are old friends."

"What's going on, Eric?" Ingrid asked again.

He glanced at his wife. "I wish I knew," he said.

Ingrid looked at Percival. Eric saw the boy was going to be mercifully discreet. Outside, the neighbor's dog barked. Percival reluctantly pulled out a pair of handcuffs, big silver ones.

"You're going to handcuff me?" said Eric in disbelief.

Percival squirmed. "I'm sorry, Father, but you're a big man. Canon Dechellis advised us to use handcuffs. It was more or less an order."

Eric shook his head and sighed, trying to pretend for Ingrid's sake that it was all just a big misunderstanding. He held out his hands.

"We might as well get this over with," he said.

The road to St. Gilbert's Penitentiary skirted a not particularly prosperous section of town. They passed one abandoned factory after another. In the feeble glow of the streetlights he saw dry-docked paddle steamers, their hulls pocked with rust, their paddle wheels missing blades and spokes. Weeds filled vacant lots. As the police cruiser lurched over a particularly deep pothole, Eric marveled at how far and how quickly he had plummeted, from first pick for Cardinal to arrested felon.

St. Gilbert's Penitentiary rose out of the mud flats like a Norman castle, dark against the first brightness of dawn. It had four high walls, guard towers at each corner, and coils of barbed wire stretching all around it.

Inside, they fingerprinted him. The man who did it stared in stark wonder, as if he couldn't believe he was fingerprinting the Ecclesiarch of St. Lucius. The photographer who took his picture—front and side views—did so solemnly.

"I'll pray for you, Father," he said.

The guard took Eric to the Bailiff's area and deprived him of his clothes, including his clergyman's collar. The guard gave him a uniform to wear: a burlap sack with a cross and orbis stenciled on the front and back, just like a clay-bred uniform. The guard handed him over to a large Seminarian with a flat pink face and a pushed-up nose. Eric looked around. The bricks in this place were painted institutional yellow, and straw covered the floor. He was scared, stunned, couldn't believe he was actually here, wanted to do something, run, break free, get away somehow. But he simply walked along with the Seminarian, couldn't change his lifelong habit of obedience. The Seminarian took a key from his belt, unlocked a cell door, swung it open and pushed Eric inside.

Eric watched the door close. He stood there for

several seconds staring at it. *A Latin-English diction-ary,* he thought. It seemed like such a small thing. He wondered if Sister Anneke was happy.

"God give me strength," he murmured.

"Hello?" a voice called from the dark.

He turned around. "Who's there?" he asked.

A figure sat up in the lower bunk, a young man also dressed in a burlap sack. He had shaggy blond hair and a dirt-smudged face. He smelled. Didn't they let people bathe in here?

"I'm your cellmate," said the man.

The barred window facing the exercise yard gave only scant light. Eric peered at the man. He was tall, young, and well built. His nose, though not particu-larly strong, was pleasantly rounded. He was hand-some, with prominent cheekbones and a square jaw. The man extended his hand.

"I'm Willy Landstad," he said. "From Larsberg, Louisiana. The lower bunk's mine. You can have it in a few days. That's when they're going to hang me."

Eric stared. He wondered how the man could be so cavalier about his own execution. Eric shook his hand.

"I'm Father Eric Nordstrum," he said.

Willy peered at Eric closely. "We got a few Fathers in here already," he said. Willy shook his big, hand-some head and smiled. "Don't that beat all?" he said. "I'm in here with a Father. I guess these Seminarians have a sense of humor after all." He pointed to a pot in the corner. "We go in that pot there," he said. "Try not to splash. We only get to mop once a week, and the place starts to stink if you splash too much."

Eric glanced at the pot in the corner. As if the place didn't stink already.

"Yes, of course," he said. He looked around. "I never thought I would see the inside of a place like this."

A sympathetic smile came to Willy's face. "You'll get used to it, Father," he said. "Everybody does." Willy contemplated him another few seconds. "You look tired, Father," he said in a softer tone. "Why don't you climb to the top bunk and get a bit of rest?"

Eric looked at the top bunk. "I guess I should."

"I'm going to try and get back to sleep myself," said Willy. "I was a having a dream about a girl I used to know in Larsberg when you came in here and woke me up. She's just about the prettiest girl I ever met. I sure would like to get back into that dream somehow."

Eric nodded. "God be with you," he said.

Willy lay back down in his bunk.

Eric took another look around. The bricks in the cell were painted institutional yellow as well. The space was rectangular, twelve by nine, and two shelves were bolted into the far wall. He heard scratching coming from inside one of the walls. He walked to his bunk and tested the mattress with his hand, then climbed up. He maneuvered on his hands and knees under the low ceiling and lay on his back. He now understood why Willy preferred the lower bunk—the heat near the ceiling was stifling. What little air came through the window was stagnant and smelled bad. Willy shifted on the lower bunk, and soon Eric heard him snoring.

He closed his eyes and tried to force his breath into an even rhythm. But it was so hot on the top bunk, and the mattress so swaybacked, he couldn't sleep. His soul was in turmoil. He had no idea what was going to happen to him. Would they actually sentence him to death? Was there a range of possible sentences for this crime? Five years? Ten years? Solitary confinement? Or was he facing an automatic death penalty? He knew it was a Capital Crime, but in his case would they make an exception? He would have to call his lawyer, Wesley Corrigan, in the morning and find out what he was up against. Why had he scribbled such extensive marginalia in his Latin-English dictionary? With his handwriting all over the pages, there was little chance of proving the dictionary wasn't his. Every notation he had ever made in the dictionary was like a nail in his coffin. If they executed him, what would become of Ingrid? How would she get by? Would the authorities strip him of his death benefits? Would the Church declare his pension null and void? And would he then be ineligible for resurrection in the St. Francis Xavier Resurrectorium?

He felt betrayed. What was his crime against Sister Anneke that she should expose him in this way? He had simply canceled her trip to Florida because of lack of funds. Was that any reason to put him at such terrible risk?

He finally dozed off just before dawn.

A ruckus in the exercise yard woke him not too long after.

Willy stood peering out the window.

"What's going on?" asked Eric.

"They're going to execute three prisoners," said Willy.

"What?"

Willy turned to him, his face slack and pale in the morning light. "Come see for yourself."

Eric struggled out of the bunk and went to the window.

A gallows with three nooses stood in the exercise yard. Seminarians and prison guards were there, waiting.

After awhile, three men were led out the north gate, shuffling along in shackles, their wrists handcuffed. Three Seminarians dressed in black with broad black belts around their waists stood on the platform, their faces solemn, each carrying a black face shroud. The guards marched the men up the steps to the gallows and positioned them in front of their nooses. They looped the nooses over their heads and pulled them tight.

"Where's the priest?" asked Eric. "Who's going to say the Last Rites?"

"They don't give you that luxury in here, Father," said Willy.

The Seminarians put the shrouds over the heads of the doomed men, then stood clear. One of them walked over to a lever. He paused, looked around, then pushed the lever. The trapdoor fell open and the three men dropped through. The ropes went taut, twitched a few times, and grew still. Eric turned away. He staggered back to his bunk, gripped the top rail to steady himself, and pressed his forehead against the back of his hand. His mouth felt dry, and a nauseating bile rose at the back of his throat. He felt Willy's hand on his shoulder.

"You get used to it after a while, Father," said

Willy. "The first one's always the toughest. But after a while you get used to it, and it doesn't bother you so much. You find it actually breaks the monotony after a while."

Several hours later the cell door creaked open. One of the Seminarians came in.

"Prisoner Nordstrum," he said, "you have a visitor. Come with me."

The Seminarian took him by the elbow and led him down the corridor.

As they passed cell after cell, he heard prisoners calling for their breakfast. At the end of the corridor, the Seminarian opened a large iron door and they entered a brightly lit hall. A few guards and Seminarians cast curious glances his way.

In the long, narrow visitors' gallery a dozen booths stretched the length of the room. On one side was the prisoners' section. On the other side, partitioned off by thick glass, was the visitors' section. The Seminarian led him to the third booth from the end.

Ingrid sat on the other side of the glass, smiling bravely, tears in her eyes. She wore a hat with a white veil and white silk gloves. He sat down, and the Seminarian left them. Eric was momentarily disoriented. It was as if he couldn't make sense of Ingrid, couldn't successfully place her in this new and distressing context.

"There, there, cupcake," he said, "there's no need to worry. I'll be out in no time. You're just going to have to be patient. If people start asking, just tell them there's been a mistake." He looked beyond her shoulder. "Where's Neil? Did he drive you?"

She took out her handkerchief and dabbed her eyes. "He went to Mass," she said. Mass. He'd forgotten. It was Sunday. He was missing Mass for the first time in his life. Ingrid sniffled. "He's going to pray for you. Deacon Braaten will be preaching this morning. He's going to urge everyone to pray for you. I took a taxi out. It cost me a whole dollar. I didn't realize it was so far." She leaned forward, an urgent look in her eyes. "Eric, what did you do?" she asked. "What did Percy Wright mean when he said there was a serious charge against you?"

He looked away. "When you leave here, I want you to call Wesley Corrigan. Tell him to get here as soon as possible. I've already left a message with the one phone call they gave me. I'm sure he'll have some good ideas about how we can fight this thing."

She looked more confused than ever. "But what did you do?" she asked.

He looked at his hands. Big hands. Masterful hands. Hands that had given the Blood and the Body of Christ countless times. Like Eve in the Garden, he'd eaten of the Fruit of Knowledge, and now he had to pay the price.

"I had a Latin-English dictionary in my study at work," he said. "A bootleg copy I bought in the Ottoman Empire when I was there for that Christian conference nine years ago. Handwritten by some scholar. Beautiful penmanship. It must be about two hundred years old. Heaven knows how it ever wound up in the Ottoman Empire. But when I found it way in the back of this old bookshop in Adrianople, I knew I had to have it. They say the Scriptures were originally written in Latin. I thought it might amplify my understanding of the Scriptures, knowing a bit of Latin, that's all. I meant no harm by it."

But he realized, too late, that he had as good as destroyed her hopes. She knew as well as everyone how strict the laws were about Latin. She dabbed her eyes. She wept. Her shoulders shook. Her reaction underlined just the kind of deep trouble he was in.

"Why?" she said.

He shook his head. "I'm sorry, Ingrid. I'm really sorry. But Wesley Corrigan will get me out of this. I know he will. By this time next week we'll be sitting at the dinner table eating one of your fine roasts and maybe even celebrating with a bit of dandelion wine."

CHAPTER 11

June and Neil sat on the banks of the Mississippi in their bathing suits. She wanted to go to the prison. She was shocked, alarmed, and stupendously surprised by the unexpected charge against her future father-in-law. Neil said he couldn't go, that the Oath of Saint Julian forbade him to visit accused felons, and that for all intents and purposes his father had ceased to exist as far as the Holy League and its soldiers were concerned. She looked at Neil now with mistrust. How could he deny his own father?

He gazed out at the muddy water, a stalk of grass between his lips, his blue eyes pensive, his bald scalp turning red in the summer sun.

"Do you want me to go and visit him for you?" she asked.

His lips stiffened. He pulled the grass out of his mouth and tossed it to the ground.

"I don't see what good it would do," he said. He turned to her. Those eyes, she thought. What had they done to Neil's beautiful eyes? "Latin. Can you imagine? My pa speaking Latin?" She frowned. She had her own Latin-English dictionary under the living room floorboards at home. She and Father Nordstrum were kindred spirits that way. Neil shook his head. "I'm going in for a swim," he said. "Do you want to come?"

"In a minute," she said.

Neil walked to the river's edge and waded into the water. Today the Mississippi was the color of chocolate milk. What was stronger, June wondered, faith or family, especially now that Neil was a Holy Man? She couldn't understand his refusal to visit his own father at St. Gilbert's Penitentiary. Neil, now up to his thighs in the water, splashed his chest and shoulders.

She had actual Roman photographs of a settlement on the moon at home. She had technical diagrams of a Roman steam engine, an internal-combustion engine, and a rocket engine. She was a member of the Odd Fellows. Her brother Henry was Head Steward of the Odd Fellows in New Amsterdam. Her brother George was a spy for the Prussian Abwehr in Europe. She should be the one in prison. One slip—one tiny slip—and her whole world would fall apart on her.

Neil turned around. "The water's great," he called.

She got up and walked to the river. Neil swam toward the buoy as she waded cautiously into the shallows.

When the water got to her waist, she dove in. Her hair was tucked under a pink rubber bathing cap, and her black one-piece hung off her as it soaked up water. She set out after Neil, who was far ahead of her.

A few minutes later she reached the buoy.

"That was the best swim I ever had," Neil said. He

lifted his left arm out of the water and looked at it. "That was so . . . versatile."

She squinted, perplexed. He said the oddest things these days. "Versatile?"

He put his hand on her shoulder, pulled her near. She stiffened. This wasn't . . . right. Why couldn't she relax with him anymore?

"The human body . . . it's really not made for swimming. But the human mind is made for anything, so it can train the body to swim."

She nodded. His point seemed too obvious for comment.

She was about to head back to shore when she smelled that smell—that Benefactor smell—like thick ozone before a thunderstorm, the ripe smell of unadulterated energy.

She whirled around, looked past the buoy, afraid that he—*he*—would be here again after such a long absence. Where was he? Somewhere out in the water? Maybe under the water? She panicked. She turned toward shore, thinking she would see a 1925 black Ford Coupe. But except for Neil's beat-up old flivver, the parking lot was empty.

"June?" said Neil. "June, what's wrong? Are you okay?"

"Do you see him?" she asked. She scanned the river. "He's around here somewhere."

"Who?"

"Hesperus." Her eyes darted out to the middle of the river. "I can smell him."

Neil looked at her doubtfully. The smell faded. "I don't see anybody," he said.

*   *   *

Two days passed before Wesley Corrigan finally
came to see Eric. Corrigan was an older man, and
even on this hot day he wore a three-piece woolen
suit. He had a white mustache, wispy white hair parted
on the left, and a pince-nez on his flat, pudgy nose.
As he eased himself into his chair, he sighed. He took
out a red handkerchief and mopped the sweat from
his brow.

"I guess summer's here," he said.

Eric leaned forward. "What took you so long?" he
asked, struggling to keep his tone even. "I've waited
two whole days. I thought you were never going to
come." He motioned toward the Seminarian standing
guard. "I'm not used to living like this."

Corrigan glanced at the Seminarian.

"Well now, Eric," he said in a voice as smooth as
freshly churned butter, "because of the nature of your
case . . . I had certain forms and applications to fill
out . . . even before the Inculpator's Office would let
me talk to you. Liturgical Law is a bit different from
Criminal or Civil Law. You almost have to lick your
finger and see which way the wind is blowing with
Liturgical Law." Corrigan leaned over, snapped open
his briefcase, and took out a folder. "The way Liturgical Law works, you're guilty until proven innocent.
And then there's all these forms and procedures.
That's why it took so long. I'm sorry I couldn't get
here sooner." He leaned forward, opened the folder,
scanned some notes, then peered at Eric over the rims
of his pince-nez. "Now, then, I won't lie to you." He
paused, his face settling. "It doesn't look good." He
moved the top paper aside and glanced at the one

underneath. "I don't exactly know how I'm going to build a defense in this case, especially when the Inculpator's Office wants to make an example of you. Because of your high position, they don't want to send the wrong signal by going for anything less than the maximum penalty. I'm not sure I'm the best counsel for the job because I haven't done much in the way of Liturgical Law. But I don't think anyone else will handle it. You handle one of these things, and the Benefactors look at you funny. Business drops off. You lose clients. I don't care. I'm close to retirement anyway, and we're old friends. I'm not sure what chance we have, but I guess we'll take what chance we got."

Eric raised his eyebrows. "A chance?" he said. "I was hoping for more than just a chance."

Corrigan shrugged. "Eric . . . it's not an easy thing. I'm a God-fearing man. I've respected you ever since I've known you. I'm not going to gloss this up for you." He looked down at the notes he had taken out of his briefcase. "If it were only the Latin-English dictionary, I might say you had more than a chance. But as it is . . ." He looked away.

"What do you mean?" asked Eric.

Corrigan rallied himself. "Why, Eric?" he asked. "Why the Prussian cipher-book? And why the radio parts? You, of all people."

"What?" said Eric. "What Prussian cipher-book? What radio parts? What are you talking about?"

Corrigan paused, looked at Eric as if he weren't sure what to say. "Eric . . . they ripped your study apart." He shook his head. "They found a Prussian cipher-book—a bona fide Prussian Abwehr cipher-book—underneath one of the floorboards by the window. And the radio parts were buried in all that coal you keep in the scuttle. I've got the report right here. It's been verified and authenticated by both the police and the Holy League." He pulled out the report and showed it to Eric. "Why would you want to spy for the Prussians, Eric? Why?"

Eric felt as if his body had been immersed in ice-cold water. An Abwehr cipher-book? Him a Prussian spy? He was one of the most patriotic souls in the Missouri-Arkansas Territory. Radio parts? He didn't know the first thing about radio. Would Sister Anneke go to such lengths? Or had somebody else been involved?

"That's ridiculous, Wes," he said. "All I had was the Latin-English dictionary. I have no idea how that other stuff got there, but it certainly wasn't me who put it there."

"Eric," said Corrigan, now sounding firm, "I told you this report's been authenticated by both the League and the police. Canon Dechellis himself put his signature on it, and he's a man I trust through and through. If he says they found that stuff, they found that stuff."

"But I didn't have anything to do with any Prussian cipher-book. I wouldn't know what one looked like if my life depended on it. And I didn't have any radio parts either."

"Eric, you've got to tell me the truth."

"I *am* telling you the truth, Wes. This is pure balderdash. What would I be doing with a Prussian cipher-book? I'm not a spy. And those radio parts—like I say, I don't know the first thing about radio.

Surely to God you don't think I'm transmitting secrets
to the Prussians, do you? I might be foolhardy enough
to own that dictionary, but I would never be stupid
enough—or crazy enough—to do something like spy
for Admiral Doenitz. I have no idea how those things
got there. Somebody put 'em there. I'll confess to the
Latin-English dictionary—I never meant no harm by
having that thing around—but I would never betray
my country. I just wouldn't. If Arch Prescript Dewey
asked me to go to the front line tomorrow, I'd be
gone in a minute. Go ask Hesperus. He knows I've
raised thousands of dollars for the war effort. Remind
him about the scrap metal drive I organized last year.
And all those nylons we collected to make rubber. This
is lunacy, Wes. Someone planted that stuff there.
Someone has it in for me. I've been *set* up."

Corrigan stared at him long and hard. He took a
deep breath and folded his hands on the small Formica ledge. "All right," he said. "If you're telling me
the truth . . . and I believe you are . . . then we
might—just might—find a way out of this. So long as
we're able to prove you were set up. And we have to
do that no matter what, Eric, because the Inculpator's
Office has told me in no uncertain terms that they
want to see you hang."

Eric felt woozy at this news. They really wanted to
hang him?

"If we can prove someone put the cipher-book and
radio parts in your study, we just might have the beginnings of a case. But that's going to take some work.
Luckily, you're a widely respected man in the Territory. You've got a lot of friends here, Eric—a lot of
friends—and they're all praying for you. I've already

had several calls from people asking me if there's anything they can do. I guess we can set 'em to work proving you're innocent." Corrigan thought a moment. "And I've got some contacts in the police department, even one in the Inculpator's Office—some old favors to call in. I'm going to have them look into this. If we can prove to the court that you've been deliberately incriminated, then they might show some leniency when it comes to the Latin-English dictionary. But like I say, it's going to take some work. And some time." Corrigan shook his head. "And I'm not sure how much time the Inculpator's Office is going to give us."

Father Nordstrum's weight loss alarmed June. His cheeks were sunken and his Adam's apple protruded. So odd to see him without his clergyman's collar. His hair jutted in disheveled tufts. He stared at her with a blasted look in his eyes, his usual self-assurance gone, the corners of his lips turned downward.

"You look thin, Father," she said.

He nodded. "We eat clay-bred."

"You've had some sun, too," she said. "Your face is tanned."

"We get an hour in the yard each day," he replied. "Right at noon. The sun beats down like a sledge-hammer." He peered past her toward the visitors' entrance. "Gee . . . how'd you get out here? It's a long way. You didn't take a taxi, did you?"

"I came by bus," she said.

"I was going to say, a taxi ride out here cost a whole dollar. Ingrid was telling me."

He looked tired. His attempt at small talk was costing him a great deal. She wished there was something she could do for him.

"I just want you to know, Father, that I . . . you know . . . that I'm thinking of you."

A weak but heartfelt grin came to his face. "I'm glad," he said. "Old men like me don't get pretty girls like you thinking of them often."

She smiled. He was always gallant. She wanted him to understand, really understand, how she felt about all this. She leaned closer and spoke in softer tones.

"I don't think it's a crime," she said. "I don't think they should arrest you because you had that Latin-English dictionary." She glanced at the Seminarian standing guard at the end of the gallery. "I think it's . . . brave." A fly landed on the partition glass. "I think you're a good man, Eric. And a courageous one. If ever I got a chance to look at a Latin-English dictionary, I'd take it right away."

He leaned forward, his arms protruding from the openings in his burlap sack, his bony elbows resting on the ledge. His blue eyes narrowed with a hard scrutiny she had never seen in them before.

"You don't want to be saying that, June," he said. His voice was like steel. "You want to keep those thoughts to yourself. You're a smart girl. But don't get too smart. Play dumb. You're safer that way."

She was taken aback. He seemed to *know* exactly what she was talking about.

She frowned. She took a chance. "Do they think we're stupid?" she asked.

His eyes got even harder. "You just watch yourself, June," he said.

She wanted to tell him that the Benefactors *weren't*

Angels. She wanted to tell him about the one the
Wehrmacht had shackled in a research facility in
Hamburg. She wanted to tell them that they weren't
Heaven-sent, that they were just made out of a special
kind of hydrogen, and a little bit of nitrogen. Just . . .
hot air. But she now felt she had to heed his advice.
Especially with that Seminarian standing guard at
the door.

"Some day it's going to end," she said.

He dipped his chin in acquiescence. "God will find
a way," he agreed.

CHAPTER 12

Gallio and Lurio rode on horseback along a cypress-lined lane toward a lime grove.

"And when I told him that Rome must insist on its tribute," said Lurio, "he told me Hortus was going to cease all payments immediately." Lurio spat, his saliva balling in the dust. "I explained to him that if Hortus didn't continue to pay, Rome would have to enforce it. I affirmed that it was our sincerest wish to avoid confrontation, but that the law was the law, and that he and his people would have to suffer the consequences if they disobeyed it."

"And what did he say to that?" asked Gallio.

"That they had their own laws." Lurio shook his head in mystification. "Is he obtuse, Gallio? At times I thought he was taunting me on purpose."

"I've never known the Onata to be so contrary," said Gallio.

Lurio dropped his reins, raised his palms. "He bickered with me. He wouldn't let it go."

"Well, yes, they're like that. They'll never let you have the last word in an argument."

They came to the lime grove. The limes hung thickly—ripe, ready to fall. The harvest should have begun a week ago, but all of his pickers had refused to work. It was the same all over Hortus. Up ahead some Hortulani sat on the tin roof of an equipment shed. They should have been picking, but they sunned themselves as if they didn't have a care in the world. Nothing had been declared—no communication delivered to the various governors about a work stoppage—but Gallio had seen enough conquered nations to know that most revolts started with a general strike. He gazed wearily at the farmhands lounging on the roof. He wished he could make them understand that if they resisted Rome, Rome would punish them.

As he and Lurio drew closer to the equipment shed, the Hortulani turned their large, platter-shaped heads toward them. Their eyes, draped on top of their heads like twin pools of tar, were unwelcoming.

"They're insolent," said Lurio. "They should get off that roof, come to us, and pay homage."

Lurio jumped off his horse and strode toward the workers.

"You there!" he hollered, singling out the nearest. "Get down off that roof. I want you in the grove picking limes."

"Lurio, he's not going to understand," said Gallio. "He doesn't have a *socius*."

Lurio walked up to the shed, gripped the Hortulani's dangling foot, and yanked it. The Hortulani tumbled into the dust but quickly sprang to his feet and rubbed his skinny tailbone. He dusted himself off and squawked at Lurio. Lurio's eyes narrowed.

"Show some respect," he said, and lunged for the worker.

The Hortulani dodged out of Lurio's way and looked at him resentfully. His turquoise skin turned bright green—a sure sign that he was angry. He squawked again.

"Why, you," said Lurio. "I'll teach you to show some respect."

"Lurio, leave him be. He's just a worker."

"They must know their place, Gallio."

Lurio, in a move that took the Hortulani by surprise, pulled his *baculum* from its sheath, swung low, and tripped the creature. The Hortulani fell, squawked some more, then kicked some dirt at Lurio. Lurio grabbed him by the scruff of the neck and lifted him right off the ground. The poor fellow kicked and squirmed. Lurio turned to Gallio.

"I'll take him to the grove," he said. "Picking limes might not be much, but everything adds to the glory of Rome."

Lurio marched toward the grove. The Hortulani fussed a bit, but then grew still. His skin color paled. Gallio leaned forward in his saddle.

"Lurio, put him down!" he called.

But it was too late. The Hortulani's skin faded to a chalky blue, and gray spots appeared. His delicate shoulders drooped, his left sandal slipped off his foot, and his head fell forward onto his chest. Lurio stopped, looked at the limp creature in perplexity, then turned to Gallio.

"What happened?" he asked. He shook the alien, but the Hortulani hung there like a freshly killed rabbit. "Why won't he move?"

Gallio sighed. "Put him down, Lurio," he said. "He's dead."

Gallio's one-time protégé inspected the corpse carefully. "How can he be dead? I hardly touched him. Are they really so delicate?"

"No," said Gallio. "But they—they can die at will."

Lurio looked at him, not understanding. "At will?" he said.

"Put him down, Lurio," he said. "The others will take care of him."

Lurio put the Hortulani down, his face reddening. The unexpectedness of the small creature's death embarrassed him.

Gallio got down off his horse and walked with heavy steps to the fallen Hortulani. His human instinct told him to grieve for the creature, but he knew the Hortulani themselves had no concept of grief. They believed that when someone died it was cause for celebration. It signified a return to the soil, becoming one with Hortus.

"Why would he just die like that?" asked Lurio, now subdued.

Gallio knelt next to the Hortulani. "Filoda tells me they die for what seem to us like trivial reasons," he told Lurio. "Maybe this one died because he didn't like the way you pulled him off the roof." He cupped the creature's platter-shaped head in his calloused hand. "Maybe he died for something we know nothing about—a thorn in his foot, or a badly cooked vegetable stew." The Hortulani's head was warm, as delicate as an eggshell. "Or maybe he died because he thought he was a slave." He turned to Lurio and gazed at him with teacherly commiseration. "And I don't see how we can turn them into slaves if they're just going to die on us, Lurio. Do you?"

Eric met the Cardinal in the administrative wing of St. Gilbert's instead of the visitors' gallery. This was in deference to the Cardinal's high rank. They were provided with a vacant office overlooking the river. Eric was in handcuffs and shackles, and a guard stood outside the door. White canvas drop-cloths covered most of the furniture, and an old photograph of Arch Prescript Roosevelt hung on the wall. The electric fireplace had been cannibalized for parts. Eric studied the Cardinal. He wore black robes today, had just come from a ecclesiastical meeting, and had a large gold cross and orbis around his neck.

"I can't do it, Eric," said the Cardinal. "I know you and I have become good friends over the past little while, and you're a man I admire and respect, but I can't go around granting pardons any time I like, especially when our friendship has become common knowledge."

"But I think there's reasonable grounds here, Magnus," Eric said. "I had nothing to do with that Prussian cipher-book or those radio parts. They were planted. All my life I've been a loyal servant of the Church. I've never once—not in my whole life—done anything to undermine its authority. Knowing that you're a compassionate man of God, I'm asking you to take a close look at my case. I have a wife. I have a son. For their sake, I ask you to take my appeal to the College of Cardinals."

The Cardinal's lips tightened, and for a moment looked old and tired. "The Prussian cipher-book and the radio parts . . . I grant you . . . maybe someone put them there." He leaned forward. "But what about the Latin-English dictionary? What ever possessed you to keep it in your study? You know what stringent laws the Benefactors have against Latin. What made you think you could take the risk and get away with it?"

Eric looked away. Out the window he saw the river flowing serenely by in the early summer heat.

In a more reflective tone he replied, "When I was a young man I studied in Castille for a while. They have a chapel there devoted to Saint Paul the Hermit. It's way up in the Pyrenees and it's built right into the side of a mountain. The medieval monks tunneled into the rocks and made caverns. They stored things in those caverns. The place was abandoned two or three centuries ago but reopened in the 1920s as a place of learning. I had the opportunity to wander those caverns. I happened upon a wood panel painted in tempera depicting the Four Evangelists contemplating the Scriptures. I could see plain as day that the Scriptures painted on the panel were written in Latin." Eric shook his head and smiled. "It made a lasting impression on me, Magnus. I'd always heard the original Scriptures had been written in Latin, but to actually see them in this old painting—well, Latin seemed a step closer to God. A step closer to the truth. So when I saw that Latin-English dictionary in Adrianople, I knew I had to have it."

The Cardinal gazed at him for a good long while.

"And so what you thought was a step closer to the truth prompted you to risk not only your own life but the welfare of your wife and son?"

"Yes."

The Cardinal raised his eyebrows. He sighed and put his hands on his knees. He stood up. He took a few steps toward the window, then turned to Eric.

"I'll ask the Inculpator's Office for a Disclosure," he said at last. "I'll ask them to send copies of the materials they have against you to the Cardinal's Residence. I'll confer with my fellow Collegians via telephone. They have to be informed of any possible Collegiate Pardons I plan to make."

"Can they block your pardon?" asked Eric, fearing he would have to overcome another obstacle.

"No. Ultimately the decision will rest with me. But even in the event of a Collegiate Pardon, you'll be stripped of your office and forbidden to serve the Church in any official capacity ever again. Your career will be over. Your pension and benefits will be gone." He shook his head doubtfully. "I'll consider your request carefully, Eric, but I honestly can't say I'm too hopeful. I'm under scrutiny. I have to weigh my decisions carefully." He glanced out the window. A distant look came to his eyes. "I suggest you pray, Eric. I'm really not sure there's much I can do at this point. I think it's in God's hands. We can only hope that, like you with your Latin-English dictionary, God will seek the truth."

Eric swept vigorously. In the suffocating heat he had rolled up his sleeves. He glanced at his biceps as he swept. They were bigger. For the last week he'd been part of a chain gang using scythes to cut roadside weeds. Even his shoulders were bulking up.

He swept under Willy's cot. The dust and dirt rose.

He lifted the Bible and fanned some of it out the window. He heard the inmates talking, laughing, shouting out in the yard. It was exercise time, but he was staying inside to clean. He took the blankets from both bunks and gave them a good shake. He took Willy's shoebox full of stuff from the shelf and wiped the metal surface. He made the bunks. He put the chamber pot in the hall for collection. He dunked the mop in the bucket and mopped the floor. A rat darted by and disappeared into a hole behind Willy's bunk.

When he was done, he fanned the room a bit more with the Bible, creating as much circulation as possible.

Then he sat down to read Revelation.

He read until the prisoners came back from the exercise yard. He watched them tramp past the doorway. He was pleased with how well he had cleaned the cell and hoped Willy would be appreciative. He heard the cell doors open and close as lockdown started. The prisoners trickled in. The cell looked halfway civilized now. He rose, went to the door, and looked up and down the corridor. A few more prisoners passed by. Where was Willy? He went back into his cell and looked out the window into the yard. Except for three Seminarians standing by the gallows, the yard was empty. Where *was* Willy? Why wasn't he back yet? A guard came to his door.

"Where's Willy?" Eric asked.

The guard paused. "Don't worry about Willy anymore," he said.

"But where is he?" Eric insisted.

The guard didn't answer. He closed the door and slid the bolt home. Eric heard him walk away, his footsteps echoing in the corridor. Eric stood there, anxiety rising in him like a tidal surge. Was this how they did it, then? They came for you in the exercise yard? He'd grown used to Willy, used to having company in this place—company as a way to take his mind off his plight. Now he was alone.

He stood there a long time, his shoulders stiff, his stomach twisted in a knot of apprehension.

At dinner he expected the usual two trays, but only one came. And then he knew for sure that they had taken Willy away to be executed.

When it came time to go to bed, he climbed into the top bunk. He didn't want the lower bunk. He lay there in the heat, sweating, his anxiety clawing at him. He thought it was unfair that the Seminarians should deny Willy the Last Rites. He felt he had to do something about that. He clasped his hands together and offered his own Last Rites to Willy.

"Oh, dear God, in the midst of life we are death. Please have mercy upon Willy's soul. We acknowledge his sins, as we acknowledge our own, by thought, word, and deed against thy divine majesty. Please forgive him, Lord, for when the morrow comes his soul will stand before you to be numbered among the righteous or among the damned. I pray for his soul. Earth to earth, ashes to ashes, and dust to dust. Amen."

He fell into a fitful sleep.

He woke to the sound of rain at dawn. He craned over the edge of his bunk to see if Willy had come back, but Willy's bunk was empty.

Eric struggled down the small ladder and looked out the window.

He saw Seminarians milling about the gallows in the

rain. Some other Seminarians led three prisoners out the north gate a few minutes later. One of them was Willy.

They forced Willy and the other two prisoners up the steps to the platform. Willy stood in the middle. The executioner placed a noose around his neck. No priest in sight, no clergy of any kind, no Last Rites. Willy looked up at the sky.

Willy's contemplation of the sky was short-lived. A Seminarian shoved a black shroud over his head.

The executioner made sure everybody was ready, then pushed the lever.

CHAPTER 13

Hesperus wanted to be with June. He sat in his flivver in the school parking lot. School had been out two weeks already, but June was up in the office working. He wasn't sure what she was doing. It was raining. Where he came from, there was plenty of hydrogen, plenty of oxygen, but they never combined into water molecules. Water was like a precious bloom, he decided, one that needed precisely the right conditions to flower. Too cold and it turned to ice, too hot and it evaporated. Water everywhere. Puddles of the stuff covered the baseball diamond in the playground. The rain lashed the school windows. June was behind one of those windows. What was keeping her? He yearned for her. He wanted to hold her in the rain.

One of Neil's memories came back: lying in the tall grass in late September, all the wildflowers grown ragged, a flock of Canadian geese flying overhead . . . and June's flannel shirt open, unbuttoned, her milky white breasts exposed. The rain, cool though it was, did nothing to stop his ardor.

He got out of his flivver, climbed the front steps,

and entered the school. He couldn't wait any longer. He had to have her now. He walked down the corridor past the trophy cabinet, the small but ever-growing commemorative plaque listing the names of alumni who had died in the war against the Prussians. He turned left, passed locker after locker, and climbed the stairs to the second floor. He saw a light on in the main office. He walked down the hall, and peered through the glass partition.

She was working in the copy room, churning the Gestetner machine, printing sheet after sheet of a—a test, an exam, a quiz? The machine's drum, fitted with blue carbon film, went round and round, making an awful racket. He opened the door and went inside. He walked around the front desk, passed the school secretary's desk, and slipped into the copy room. Not tests, exams, or quizzes. She was running off flyers.

He peered at the flyer: *The St. Bernardine Women's Auxiliary is Organizing a Prayer Meeting for Ecclesiarch Eric Nordstrum. Please Pray for the Ecclesiarch and His Family this Friday, July 11th, 1947, in the Square. Refreshments and Social After.*

He sighed and put his hand on her shoulder. She swung round, startled.

"Oh, it's you," she said. "You shouldn't have snuck up on me like that."

"You're holding a prayer meeting for my father?" he asked.

She frowned. "Latin, as far as I'm concerned, isn't a hanging crime."

He wanted to tell her how the solar system was now awash with Roman micro-beacons, and how they were all screaming *"Me ipsum Romae pignero,"* how the whole reason the Benefactors came down hard on Latin in the first place was so it wouldn't be used as a tool of communication with the Romans, a tool of war. But he stayed in character, knew any such revelation would ruin his chances with June.

"It's a crime just the same," he said weakly. "It says so right in the Books of Liturgical Law."

Her eyes narrowed imperiously. "If you want to make me happy, you'll come to the prayer meeting. I don't care what your oath says."

He looked away. She was wearing that perfume again, the Eau d'Orsay that smelled of rose and musk.

"My oath is a sacred oath," he said.

"He's your father," she persisted. She touched his uniform. "Family should be thicker than this."

He looked away and said in a soft voice, "I'll come to your prayer meeting."

He thought this was the key, that she would now let him touch her. He went up to her, put his arms around her, tried to kiss her—but she pushed him away.

"Neil . . . no . . ."

He backed away. He felt angry. Neil had a temper. He could feel it surging inside him like magma up the throat of a volcano. He wanted to feel connected. To feel that he belonged somewhere, that he was part of something, that he wasn't cut off anymore. And this biochemical sack of water, this *female,* was rejecting him.

He turned away, left the office. Why did this have to be so difficult? He walked down the hall, descended the stairs, embarrassed and hurt, emotions he hardly knew how to deal with. He thought she would call to him, but she didn't. He heard the Gestetner start up again. She was stubborn. He hurried along the first-floor corridor and pushed the big front doors open. He descended the steps to the parking lot and stood in the rain.

He had to do something to get rid of his anger. He marched over to his flivver, gripped the front bumper and lifted it. The car came right up. Neil's weak human muscles ripped. Hesperus instantly repaired them. But they ripped again. So he repaired them again. On and on. Shifting matter around inside him so he could continue to lift the car. It felt good to lift the car. He gave the car a shove, flinging it a few yards. It bounced and creaked on its worn shock absorbers. He felt better.

But only for a few seconds.

Then the great emptiness came back. He couldn't hear anybody. A brief communication from Woden a few months ago, enough to learn how to inhabit this human body, but that was it, and he was alone again. The world was different these days. Most of his brethren hid in the various Citadels, weak, tired, starving for the sustenance and connectedness that came from home. But the Romans had broken the lines of communication. He couldn't stand the loneliness. He wasn't built for loneliness. None of them were. He walked to his flivver and put his foot on the bumper. He looked up at the high school office window. He waited in the rain for June to come out. He didn't want to be lonely anymore.

Two Seminarians woke Eric in the middle of the night and dragged him from his cell. He stumbled over the uneven floor and fell to his knees. They yanked him to his feet. He thought they might be taking him to the gallows. They dragged him out of his cell and escorted him along the corridor, walking fast. The dim bulbs overhead, one every ten yards, did little to dispel the gloom. Maybe they were taking him straight to the noose.

But they took him to the basement instead.

One Surgeon and two Acolytes waited for him in the basement. He didn't recognize any of them. They must have been from out of town. They wore white uniforms. The Surgeon was old, and the Acolytes were young. The Seminarians put him in a chair and cuffed his hands behind his back. Then they left.

The Surgeon came forward. His hair was shaved around the bottom, but long on top—a Friar's cut. He held up a syringe. Eric tensed.

"What are you going to do?" he asked.

"I'm sure you want to get to the bottom of this as much as we do, Father," said the Surgeon, "and this is going to help us."

Eric struggled, but the young ones held him down. The Surgeon jabbed the needle into his arm and depressed the plunger. Eric squirmed. But then his muscles turned to rubber. He slid forward in his chair. His head lolled, his chin dropped against his breastbone, and his eyes closed . . .

When he came to, everything was blurry. He looked up at the Surgeon. The Surgeon was talking to him but Eric couldn't understand him, at least not at first. The Acolytes stood on either side of the Surgeon, arms folded across their chests. The Surgeon directed Eric's attention to some items on the table. Eric concentrated as hard as he could on the Surgeon's words.

"You see before you the Prussian cipher-book and the radio parts," he said.

"Yes, I see them," said Eric.

He also saw three or four pages of legal-size paper, a fountain pen, and an inkwell.

"Are those your radio parts?" asked the Surgeon.

"No," said Eric.

The Surgeon backed away, looked disappointed, then put his hands on his hips so that his large belly strained against his white tunic. He gave the Acolytes a nod.

The Acolytes came forward, unlocked Eric's cuffs, yanked him out of his chair, and punched him again and again. They knocked the wind out of him, then went at his kidney, spleen, and liver.

He didn't know how long they beat him, but by the time they stopped he was curled up on the floor, covered in sweat, lying in a puddle of his own vomit.

"Whose radio parts are they?" asked the Surgeon. "And where did the Prussian cipher-book come from? That's all we want to know. If you tell us that, we can end this."

Though he floated in a numbing narcotic cloud, and everything looked warped like the reflection in a funhouse mirror, he still felt a small spark of resistance.

"I don't know," he said. "I have no idea where they came from. Someone put them in my study."

The Surgeon looked more disappointed than ever. He nodded to the Acolytes again.

The Acolytes lifted him from the floor, put him back in his chair, and handcuffed him.

One of them wheeled an electrical contraption

over—a black box with dials, fitted with small jumper cables and clips.

The Acolytes ripped away his tunic. The larger one splashed him with a bucket of cold water on his naked body.

The Surgeon attached four clips to his body—two to his ears and two to his testicles.

"Who gave you the radio parts and the cipher-book?" he asked. "Are they yours?"

But Eric was so distracted by the cold water and the clips, so disoriented by the brain-melting injection, he couldn't immediately answer. The Surgeon, growing impatient, went to the black box and turned the dial.

Electricity hit his body like a transport truck. He heard a loud, low buzz, and his brain felt as if it were shaking apart. Just when he thought he was going to die, the Surgeon eased back on the dial and grinned kindly.

"Are you working for the Odd Fellows?" he asked. "Is that why you have the cipher-book and the radio parts?"

"Please . . . I . . ." Eric tasted blood. He had bitten his tongue. "I have no idea where—"

Before he could finish, the Surgeon cranked the dial up more, and he was again plunged into a Hades of electromagnetic torture.

When the Surgeon finally turned the dial down thirty seconds later, Eric felt drowsy, confused, and willing to beg for mercy. He couldn't remember where he was or why he was here. He just stared at the Surgeon and hoped the Surgeon wouldn't turn the dial up again. He kept blacking out. He came to. He was out of his handcuffs. He wasn't sure how he had gotten out of them, but his hands were free.

One of the Acolytes looked at his left wrist with some concern. "It could be broken," he said.

"We'll wrap it," said the Surgeon.

But if his wrist was broken, he didn't feel it. The Acolytes lifted him to his feet. They walked him to the table and sat him down in front of the legal-size paper. One of the Acolytes molded his fingers around the fountain pen. He grew weepy. He just wanted to go home and sleep next to Ingrid. God felt far away. He tried to formulate a prayer but he couldn't think of one. He looked at the sheets of paper on the table. He couldn't read. The words swam in and out of focus. His wrist began to throb. He looked at the Surgeon.

"Can I go to sleep now?" he asked.

The Surgeon put a kindly hand on his shoulder. "Of course you can, Father," he said. "All you have to do is sign right here, and you can sleep for as long as you like."

June stood in the apse gallery looking at all the faithful thronging the pews in the sanctuary of St. Bernardine's Cathedral. Men, women, and children filled the space to overflowing. The back gallery was the same. And out in the vestry, people stood shoulder to shoulder holding votive candles or rosary beads. She looked for Neil, but she couldn't see him anywhere. Maybe he was outside in Cyrus-of-Jerusalem Square. In the pulpit, Morris Fifield from the radio shop tested the microphone a few times, tapping it, whistling into it.

June left the apse gallery and descended the spiral staircase into the ambulatory. She walked around the ambulatory to the south door and entered the sacristy. She ducked behind the choir and the organ manuals and checked for Neil in the south chapel. A group of nuns bussed in from St. Magdalena's Convent in St. Jerome crowded the South Chapel like a flock of ungainly gray birds. She continued past them and descended the three front steps to the transept.

She saw Deacon Braaten standing by the Fellowship Room. The Deacon would be conducting the prayer meeting. She gave him a nod and continued down the nave into the sanctuary. A gloriously pink sky illuminated the lancet-arch windows. She went into the vestry and squeezed her way out the front door.

The horizon to the east was dark. A single bank of black rain clouds loomed like a judgment. The sky overhead, however, was blue. The sun, low in the west, shone from behind the cathedral, brightening the red brick buildings of the Shrine so that they glowed like lava against the black backdrop of the rain clouds. Two or three thousand people thronged the square. Police stood in all the various roadways, redirecting traffic. She searched the crowd for Neil but couldn't see him.

The speakers crackled as Deacon Braaten began.

"Come hither to the arms of Christ, oh, my children," he said, "and you shall be saved. Give thyself to the Lord Jesus Christ and you shall rise up in His everlasting love. Devote your life in the service of the Lord Jesus Christ, such as the good Reverend Father Eric Nordstrum has, and He will touch you with His blessing, and you will be counted among the forgiven."

A murmuring of "Amens" swept through the crowd.

June stepped onto the cobblestones and made her way to the fountain's basin. A statue of Saint Bernardine poured water from an urn into the fountain. June climbed the steps to the fountain, tossed a penny into the water as a devotional, and scanned the crowd, hoping to see Neil. She really wanted Neil to be here. She wanted people to see that even the Seminarians thought the Inculpator's Office was wrong.

She raised her hand to her mouth. "Neil?" she called.

She wanted to somehow get the old Neil back. She was lonely for him. She missed his kisses and caresses, felt mistrustful and nervous around the new Neil. She held her hand to her brow and gazed first up Bell Boulevard, then down Corinthians Avenue. But there were so many people, and more coming all the time— even in his uniform Neil would have been lost in this crowd.

Deacon Braaten spoke again.

"Let us remember how Jesus Christ was once a prisoner," said the Deacon over the public address speakers. "Let us remember how Pontius Pilate had Roman centurions put the Good Christ in jail. And let us now remember how a Father of our own Church is in jail, and remember him to the dear Lord. Oh, dear God, protect Ecclesiarch Nordstrum—protect him and his house—from all the evils and misfortunes of the world, but grant that he may be ever resigned to Thy divine will even in his current season of affliction. And should the worst come to pass, and the Inculpator's Office decide against Father Nordstrum, let us pray so that our brother Eric should receive the comfort of

Thy Holy Sacraments at the hour of his demise. Oh, Jesus, bless and protect him."

She couldn't see Neil anywhere. But she could see Mickey Cunningham. She quickly left the fountain, wishing to avoid him, and worked her way back toward the cathedral. She wanted to give Neil this opportunity to demonstrate that he loved her, even if he had to defy Pope Julian II and the Holy League. Maybe he was in the sanctuary after all.

"Friends, let us raise our voices in song for Father Nordstrum," continued the Deacon. "Let us offer to him a prayerful rendition of Hymn 123, *He Will Rise Again.*"

The organ burst forth from the P.A. speakers like a thousand trumpets. June entered the church and started singing, "Christ, He who is like the light," but stopped when she saw Neil standing in the marble doorway of the baptistery. He was looking right at her. A shaft of light came in from a side window, brightening his face. Against the dark interior, his face was ethereal. She weaved through the crowd toward him. He looked distressed.

When she reached him, she slipped her hand through his arm.

"What's wrong?" she asked.

"I've just received word from St. Gilbert's," he said.

He pulled her into the baptistery. The octagonal pool in the center smelled of chlorine.

"What?" she said. "What's happened?"

"My father confessed to the Prussian cipher-book and the radio parts."

His eyes were intent. She didn't want to believe this news. The Latin-English dictionary was one thing, but what was the point of this prayer meeting if Eric had confessed to the Prussian cipher-book and the radio parts?

"Are you sure?" she asked.

On the surface Neil looked genuinely alarmed by this turn of events. But she couldn't help thinking that, underneath, he was happy about it.

"His trial's in a few days and I don't think any-thing's going to help him now," said Neil. "God's will is God's will."

This was indeed bad news. And Neil didn't seem to care. He wasn't going to fight it. He wasn't even going to get upset about it. And she couldn't accept that. She couldn't marry Neil if he felt that way.

She took off her engagement ring—with all the weight she'd lost lately, it slid off easily—and handed it to Neil.

"I'm sorry, Neil," she said. She couldn't stop her tears. She had lost the only man she had ever loved. "But this is God's will too."

CHAPTER 14

As Eric sat in the courtroom, his bare feet shackled to iron rings in the floor, he felt far away from everything. He still hadn't fully recovered from the electrical shocks or the consciousness-altering injection. Occasionally he lost focus. He looked around the courtroom. Sister Anneke Verbeek sat in the witness box. The Inculpator, dressed in black-and-gold robes, questioned her. Sister Anneke described her duties at the church. Did she really order supplies for the janitor? And she organized the annual pilgrimage to Bethlehem at Christmas? She lifted her hand and pointed at him. He realized he must have missed something. Why was she pointing at him? Why were her eyes so wrathful? He glanced around the courtroom for a clue.

But his mind drifted. The courtroom disappeared and he found himself walking through a sunny pasture. A memory. Walking along a path with Neil—Neil only seven, his hair as gold as sunlight, a butterfly net in his hand, Eric following, swinging a jug of Ingrid's homemade lemonade. Why had his son forsaken him?

Neil pointed at a monarch butterfly, turned and smiled. The monarch sunned itself on a milkweed leaf, flexed its wings, twitched its antennae . . .

"You say you have occasion to go through the cathedral's paid invoices from time to time," said the Inculpator. "Did you at any time find an invoice itemizing radio parts?"

Now he remembered. Something about radio parts.

"I never found an invoice itemizing radio parts," Sister Anneke admitted.

Wesley Corrigan got up and cross-examined her. He went through the events leading to the discovery of the Latin-English dictionary one more time.

"I was in there dusting," said Sister Anneke. "I know how he hates dust. I do a bit each day. I pull the volumes out and dust behind. I like to be thorough. That's how I found the Latin-English dictionary."

"And you never saw anything in his study—tools or such—that might suggest the possession of radio parts?" asked Wesley.

"No."

"Did you ever see a Prussian cipher-book?"

"No."

Eric's mind blurred again. He had another memory, this one of him and Ingrid before they got married. Eric was eighteen and Ingrid seventeen. They got in his father's wagon, told his folks they were going to a revivalist meeting in St. Jerome. They never got there. They stopped in the woods a mile away, climbed into the back of the wagon, and lay down next to each other on an old horse blanket. He pulled her near. They kissed. They made love. They heard the distant

voices of people singing *Amazing Grace* at the revivalist meeting.

The Inculpator was back up there now. He had
Morris Fifield on the stand as an expert witness.

"And these radio parts, are they of sufficient quality
and strength to transmit to any of the Admiral's
U-boats in the Atlantic?" the Inculpator asked.

Morris looked scared, kept glancing at the big Seminarian who stood next to the Bailiff.

"Them parts is old," said Morris. "They're twenty
years out of date, badly busted up, and I . . . I don't
know . . . maybe at one time, near the start of the
war . . . maybe when they were in good condition . . .
they might have been used to . . . to send messages
to the Admiral's U-boats."

Eric drifted again. This time he found himself in the
shady backyard of the Ecclesiarch's Manse on Appleby
Street with his daughter, Grace. Grace was six years
old, wore a pink dress, had a bag of bread crusts,
was tearing the crusts into crumbs and feeding the
crumbs to two gray squirrels by the birdbath. His
heart grew large with the love he felt for his daughter. He reached down, held her hand. Was there anything more miraculous than a little girl? She looked
up at him, and her eyes were bright and happy, the
color of a summer sky. He realized he wanted to be
with her, that he didn't care what the Prescript did
to him, or what God had decided for him, or how
Jesus had forsaken him. He just wanted to be with
his dear departed Grace.

"Would the defendant please rise?" said the Prescript.

He wanted to stroll down the sunny pathways and

pleasant avenues of the Shrine with Grace. He wanted to sit and listen to her talk about dolls, schoolyard intrigues, and pretty dresses. He got to his feet, but the courtroom was as good as invisible. He wanted to stroke her chestnut hair. Things simply hadn't been the same since she had passed on. He looked at the Prescript, saw that the Prescript was wearing a badly soiled clergyman's collar. Eric absently fingered his own throat but felt no collar there.

"In the case of the *Papal State of the Missouri-Arkansas Territory versus Father Eric Sven Joseph Nordstrum,* this court finds the defendant guilty on all seven counts." The Prescript looked magisterially at his Bailiff. "Bailiff, I see no reason to delay sentencing. Could you bring the defendant forward?"

The Bailiff took out his keys and unchained Eric's feet from the floor, then gripped him by the elbow and ushered him forward. Eric saw Ingrid up in the visitors' gallery dabbing her eyes with a handkerchief. June sat next to her. Neil was nowhere in sight. Eric turned away. He didn't want to face them. He felt he had let them down. His head started to buzz and he felt disoriented again. He came before the Prescript.

The Prescript began.

"On the authority of the power vested in me by the Lord Jesus Christ, by Pope John the Eighteenth, and by the Holy Papal State of the Missouri-Arkansas Territory of the Papal States of America, I sentence thee, Eric Sven Joseph Nordstrum, to hang by the neck till dead, at the appointed hour of six o'clock A.M., this Friday, July eighteenth, in the year of our Lord, nineteen hundred and forty-seven, at St. Gilbert's Penitentiary in the Township of St. Jerome." The Prescript whacked his gavel on the block. "May the good Lord God have mercy upon your soul."

PART 2

ROMANS

CHAPTER 15

Eric sat in the prison office overlooking the river again. Cardinal Anders sat in a chair across from him. The window was open, and the river was so close he could hear it whisper by. He had some fresh air for a change. He could watch the seagulls, the sailboats, and the paddle steamers.

"I came to talk about Pollux," said Anders, and at first Eric didn't know whom he meant. "The Benefactor in Brisbane," Anders clarified. "The one who took the form of an Aboriginal elder and followed me around for a while. The one I told you about when you came to look at my roses that day."

"Are you going offer me a pardon?" asked Eric.

The Cardinal was dressed in his plain gray clergyman's suit today. He leaned forward and put his hands on his knees.

"We were talking about Hesperus that day as well," the Cardinal reminded him, "and we spoke of how he was following June Upshaw around, how he began to seek out human company when the Benefactors' numbers declined. And I told you Pollux did the same thing with me. He wanted to befriend me."

"I remember," said Eric.

The Cardinal stroked his beard meditatively. "Like I said, something happened to Pollux once Vega disappeared." He pressed his lips together and nodded. "He was never much like any of the other Benefactors to begin with. He always mixed with us humans. Historical evidence suggests he was one of the first to arrive, to *descend*, as the Bible calls it. There exist in Queensland Aboriginal rock paintings dating his arrival to three thousand years before the birth of Christ. He's been here longer than any of them, Eric. And I guess he's adapted. He's become . . . humanized to a certain extent. Maybe Hesperus is becoming humanized as well."

The Cardinal seemed to consider this notion for a moment, then he continued.

"Whatever the case, Pollux wanted my company," he said. "He told me he had grown to sympathize with us humans, more so than with his brethren. Maybe that's because he's been here the longest. I asked him questions. He told me anything and everything I wanted to know about the Benefactors." The Cardinal's eyes narrowed. "I'm still not sure I understand everything he said. But I've had some fellows in Europe help me sort it out."

"Fellows?" said Eric.

The Cardinal's face grew grave. "Eric—" He took a deep breath and looked out the window, where two seagulls negotiated the breeze above the river. "Me and these fellows . . . we believe that the Benefactors, far from being the Heavenly Host, are something entirely different. We believe that the Benefactors don't come from Heaven." The Cardinal settled back in his chair and wiped a bit of dust from his knee. "Pollux isn't an Angel, and he doesn't come from Heaven. None of them are Angels, and none of them come from Heaven. Everything they've always told us about themselves, and everything they've written into the Scriptures about themselves—it's all just balderdash. It's just a ruse to keep us in our place. Pollux told me where he really came from." The Cardinal took a folded piece of black paper out of his shirt pocket, opened it, and showed it to Eric. "Do you know what this is?" he asked.

A nebulous white spiral filled the black sheet. "The Milky Way galaxy?" said Eric.

The Cardinal nodded. "The Milky Way galaxy," he confirmed. "See that red X there?"

"Yes."

"Pollux put that red X there," said Anders. "Do you have any idea what that red X is?"

"No."

"That's where Pollux comes from. That's where they all come from. I found this map in an astronomy book in the Brisbane Public Library. Pollux was always telling me how he and his kind came from"—he gestured at the sky—"from out there. When I showed him this map of the Milky Way, he put that X there to show me exactly where he lived. They don't come from Heaven, Eric. They never did. They come from this red X. If you had the means, you could go to this red X. It might take a while, but by and by you would get there. It's an actual locale. I had a hard time believing it at first. I'm familiar with the notion of life elsewhere in the universe. I've always been intrigued by the possibility, but I never thought I would have to define Pollux and the Benefactors in that particular context. Like I said, they just used the idea of Heaven as a ruse, as a tool of control." He tapped the map. "This red X here—we could never live there. I asked Pollux what it was like. He said it was hot. So hot it could melt metal. He said the radiation and the gravitational pressures could kill a human being. I wrote down everything he said and sent it to these— these fellows I know in Europe, so they could have a look at it. After some study, they said the conditions Pollux described might possibly exist deep within a star cluster somewhere near the center of the galaxy."

Eric felt dulled by these revelations. Six months ago this might have been too much of a mountain to move for him. But with his faith so badly shaken by recent events, this awful truth seemed only all too likely. A pillar of his belief was gone, and, with a shaky willingness, he was prepared to accept, at least to certain extent, the Cardinal's version of who the Benefactors were and where they might come from.

"So they're not Angels?" he said. "They're just . . . beings?"

The Cardinal nodded. "They're just beings."

"And they come from out there, in space?"

His voice sounded distant, broken, missing his old self-confidence.

"That's what these fellows and I have concluded," said the Cardinal.

Eric was silent as he worked through these notions. He finally nodded. "I'm willing to accept that," he said, "only because I can't believe that they're Angels anymore. Not after what they did to me, the way they set me up. But what I don't understand is why Pollux would tell you all this in the first place. If they want to control us by planting themselves firmly into the Scriptures, so much so that we believe that they're Angels, why would Pollux want to give the game up?"

The Cardinal nodded. "As I say, Pollux has developed a profound human sympathy during his years of isolation in the outback. He identifies more with humans than he does with his own kind. Over and above that, he has a specific purpose for telling me everything. But to understand, you'll need to know some more background." He sat forward and put his hands on his knees. "I want to talk about Liturgical Law. You've been convicted and sentenced to hang under what seems to be an arbitrary and reasonless statute. Can we descry any coherent policy on the part of the Benefactors behind all those arcane and antique laws about Latin? And not only the ones about Latin, but the ones about radio and Romans as well? Because most of Liturgical Law has to do with those three things, Eric. And they're all interconnected. Romans, radio, and Latin, Eric."

Eric contemplated the red X on the map of the Milky Way galaxy. "I've never understood those laws," he admitted.

"Let's start with radio," said Anders. "Do you know anything about radio? I mean its technical aspects?"

"No."

"When I was in the technical laity we always questioned the Benefactors' strict radio legislation, asked why we had to confine transmissions to under ten

megahertz when sometimes fifty megahertz would
have been better, why we had to limit transmission
range, and why the laws get particularly stringent near
the Restricted Zones. But time and time again the
Benefactors refused to give us answers. These fellows
and I got interested in the question. We began to in-
vestigate. Beginning about 1890, when Marconi first
experimented with ship-to-ship telegraphy, the Benefactors established a labyrinth of laws, rules, and regulations against radio. They've tried to limit it. For the
longest time none of these laws made sense. Why
radio? What possible harm could radio do? None of
us were having any luck coming up with an answer.

"Then one day Pollux took me to the Restricted
Zone in the outback. I was scared. I thought the Benefactors there would come and get me. But they didn't
come near me. Pollux somehow prevented it. He had
me bring my radio out. We traveled two hundred
miles from Brisbane and set up my equipment. He
said I would receive signals. It took two days, but I
finally received them. There should have been nothing
but static, but I heard this—this voice. I heard it loud
and clear. Speaking Latin. The voice said: *'Me ipsum
Romae pignero.'* I couldn't believe it. Latin. In the
middle of the Australian outback. And *'Me ipsum
Romae pignero,'* was just the beginning of it, Eric. The
full message was as follows: 'I pledge myself to Rome,
support her, defend her, and fight for her. You who
hear my pledge, respond to this call. For you will then
reap the rewards and riches of Rome, and will gain
everlasting life in the Hall of the Immortals.' "

Anders's eyes widened as he turned his palms
upward.

"That's what I heard, Eric. I thought to myself, this is impossible. The nearest radio station is in Brisbane. I'm on horseback two hundred miles away. The radio station in Brisbane has a range of only twenty miles. I turned to Pollux and asked him where it was coming from. He said it was coming from out there, and he pointed to the sky. How was I supposed to interpret that? He told me the Romans were out there as well, that the scraps of evidence we had about the Exodus were true, and that the Roman ruling class, the Gens, fleeing for their lives, had commandeered seven of the Benefactors' own vessels to get away. I conferred with my fellows in Europe over the next year about this. We reexamined everything we knew about the Exodus, the Great Theft, and the War of the Gens. You wonder why I tell you this, why I risk it. Believe me, there's a reason." He leaned forward, his eyes intent. "Radios, Romans, and Latin, Eric. It all fits together." He tapped the picture of the Milky Way. "The Romans are alive. Somewhere out there." He sat back and nodded. "Living out there just like the Benefactors. And the Romans and the Benefactors are fighting each other. This is what Pollux told me. This is what he showed me when he took me to the outback with my radio. None of the radio legislation makes sense until you put Romans at war with the Benefactors. And none of the Latin legislation makes sense until you put Romans at war with the Benefactors. But once you do, it all fits. Radio is a tool of war, Eric. So is language. The Benefactors are afraid we'll somehow communicate with the Romans using radio and Latin. By limiting transmission range, by legislating frequency, and by outlawing Latin, they've as good as destroyed any possibility of that. Pollux says that once the Romans fled, they lost their way. They haven't been able to find their way back. And that's fine as far as the Benefactors are concerned. The Benefactors don't want the Romans anywhere near Earth. So that's why they've devised all this legislation about radios, Romans, and Latin."

Eric raised his eyebrows, bewildered. "Then why do they allow radio at all?" he asked.

"Because they recognize it as a tool of control, as an instrument of propaganda, and so they permit its use only so far as it will promote the supremacy of the Church. What Pollux wants us to do is contact the Romans. He wants us to do this before his brethren carry out this plan they have. The Romans are strong, and they can help us. Pollux is willing to give up the game, as you call it, not only because he's become thoroughly humanized in the last five thousand years, but, more specifically, because he wants to stop this plan his brethren have for all of us. And once you hear the plan, you'll see why he's so concerned."

CHAPTER 16

Paris fell. June read the news in the *St. Lucius Observer-Herald* as she walked to the Odd Fellows meeting. The Vatican's French forces had failed to stop the advance of the Wehrmacht's Panzer divisions. Artillery had pounded the capital relentlessly for the last several weeks. House-to-house combat had ensued. Sixteen French divisions had surrendered, while two divisions of St. Julian's Holy League had retreated to the suburb of Montataire. Arch Prescript Dewey had requested an urgent meeting with the highest officials of the American Holy League. The Lord's Congress had convened in emergency session. The Arch Prescript was going to order sixty thousand American troops to Europe, most of the country's standing army. Her hands shook. Paris was at last liberated. The Paris Citadel had been reduced to rubble and the Benefactors themselves melted, so the paper reported, with a weapon the Prussians had built from an old Roman design unearthed in Villacarillo, Spain.

She continued down the street, turning right on

Wharf Road. She wondered if the Wehrmacht would now jump the Strait of East Anglia and try to liberate Britannia; whether they would then move on to Eire, and finally mount an invasion of North America via La Brador. She folded the newspaper under her arm and hurried along. She was glad the newspaper had run the story in the late edition. The fall of Paris would boost morale considerably at the meeting tonight. When the Prussians finally developed their superbomb, maybe they would wipe out the Benefactors once and for all. Then what rejoicing there would be. If only Arch Prescript Dewey didn't have plans to send sixty thousand troops to Europe. That didn't bode well at all.

June's apartment door was locked. Hesperus stood on the landing staring at the brass knob. The summer heat collecting at the top of the stairs made Neil's body perspire. June wasn't here. He'd seen her walk away down Wharf Road a while ago. Amy, her roommate, was gone too. He made the knob turn. He didn't have to touch it. It turned by itself. He made the lock unlock. The door swung open all by itself. He still had the power to at least do these small tricks. He stepped inside.

The place smelled of the Eau d'Orsay she wore. She had rattan furniture with pillows upholstered in blue, purple, and green. A reproduction of Henri Rousseau's *Le Douanier* hung on the wall, five lower primates cowering in lush vegetation. A scuffed white bookcase crammed full of books was placed beneath it.

Hesperus walked over to the piano and tinkled the

keys. They had no music back home. He didn't understand music. He didn't understand art. He couldn't see the point in either, yet he knew June loved both, and he was endeavoring to understand them for her sake.

He lifted June's autoharp from the top of the piano, turned it over, read the tiny print on the back—*Made in the Empire of Nippon*—and strummed a few chords with his thumb. One of Neil's memories came back to him: June sitting in the Fellowship Room at the cathedral on Youth Group Night strumming the haunting chords to *Kum Ba Yah,* and singing the words with her most affecting voice. Never had a woman's voice been so sweet. She knew how to put feeling into even a simple song like *Kum Ba Yah.* He wanted her back. But he had to understand her better. That was why he was here. To look around. If he was ever going to mend things, he would have to understand her through and through.

He now knew she was duplicitous, had finally sensed all her subterfuge. He now knew she was traitorous.

He put the autoharp back on the piano and looked around the apartment. He closed his eyes. He concentrated. Like a divining rod seeking water, he walked to the exact spot. The Benefactors knew all, saw all. But these days his ability wasn't as strong. Still, he found what he was looking for. He knelt and pulled the floorboard up.

He saw a small book. He lifted it out and flipped it open. A Latin-English dictionary. Just like Father Nordstrum. He sighed. He wasn't used to the range of human emotion, wasn't sure what this sigh meant. He only knew he faced a dilemma. Should he report her immediately to the police? Or should he arrest her himself? He shook his head. He loved her too much for either.

He put the dictionary back and concentrated again.

He walked down the hall to the bathroom. Black nylon stockings hung over the shower rail. A brassiere dangled from the towel rack. He took a deep breath, then another, and felt his groin . . . *lurch*. Why would nylon stockings and a brassiere affect him this way? How could the polymer chains in the nylons have anything to do with the carbon-based structures in his groin, and how could he have a reaction like this when they hadn't even been mixed, or introduced in any chemical way to each other, hadn't reacted on a molecular or atomic level such as was the basis for all spiritual, emotional, and intellectual phenomena in the superheated soup where he came from?

He went into June's bedroom and saw her black leather-bound Bible on the side table. The salvation of souls—the Good Book's primary subject. Did he have a soul? The concept was unheard of where he came from. Yet inside Neil's body he felt he had a soul, that he was human, and becoming more human all the time. One couldn't live in this place for as long as he had, especially in such loneliness, without feeling the need to belong to these humans.

He placed his hands on the bed rail. He searched Neil's memory. Had he slept in this bed? A memory. Yes. June pressed her cheek against his naked chest. He felt the smoothness of the flowered sheets on his back. He felt sorry for Neil. Neil was frozen in the eternal depths of the St. Francis Xavier Resurrectorium. Neil couldn't have June anymore. This memory belonged to Hesperus now. She rubbed his chest. Her eyes were like lakes under a sunny sky, shining with the love that she had once felt for—Neil. He wanted to confess to someone what he had done to Neil. Too long on this old planet had given him a perplexing moral sense he couldn't control.

On her desk he saw a gift-wrapped box with a card on top. He walked over and read the card. There was printing inside—printing that looked as if it had been done by a child: "Sorry to hear about you and Neil. Thought these chocolates might cheer you up. Your friend and admirer, Mickey." His eyes widened. Who in the name of Heaven was Mickey? She'd never mentioned anyone named Mickey. Was she seeing someone else now that their engagement was off?

He went back to the bed. He concentrated again.

Oh, yes, she was a little traitor, that was for sure, and she had something in this room that could send her straight to the gallows.

Where was it? He could sense it.

He lifted the mattress. On top of the box spring he found a large archive of Roman documents and photographs, those old, shining photographs printed on that holo-dimensional paper the Romans had devised. He sighed again. He wondered if all women were as treacherous. And never mind these photographs—who was Mickey? Why had she never told him about Mickey? He shook his head, more perplexed than ever. He had been dead too long, preserved in the biomagnetic equivalent of formaldehyde for too many centuries, and he doubted he would ever understand the way of living flesh as it was manifested in the sentient beings of this watery and insignificant speck of dust out here on the cold fringes of the galaxy.

CHAPTER 17

"They're dead, Eric," the Cardinal said a few minutes later. "That's what Pollux wanted me to understand more than anything else. The Benefactors here on Earth are nothing more than reproduced versions of what they once were back where they came from. This is the reason they've come all this way to Earth. So they can live again. So they can re-seed themselves."

Eric's eyes narrowed. "I'm afraid I don't understand," he said.

Anders watched the seagulls hover above the Mississippi against a strong southerly wind. "Let me put it this way. When I was younger and still living in Europe, I loved the singer Enrico Caruso. I was fortunate enough to hear him sing in Milan, Rome, and Paris. I was devastated when, in 1921, he died. I immediately bought his recordings. I have his entire collection and play them on my Victrola regularly. You know nothing of radio, so I assume you don't know how the human voice is recorded onto a medium, such as vinyl."

"No."

"This is what the Benefactors have done with their lives and their—their souls. They have recorded them onto a medium. Just like Caruso's voice has been recorded. When Pollux told me this, I at first had a hard time understanding it. So he told me they did much the same thing with the eligible clergymen when they resurrected them in the resurrectoriums. They record their lives onto a medium, much the same way Enrico Caruso recorded his voice onto vinyl. They did the same thing with themselves when they had to leave this red *X*. When I asked Pollux why the Benefactors had to leave the red *X*, he said it was because they couldn't survive out there anymore. Something had happened out here." Anders tapped the map. "Something that made the Benefactors languish. Pollux couldn't seem to find the right words to express it. A cooling, he called it. A change in the flux. And so to preserve themselves, to give themselves another chance, they recorded their lives onto a high-energy medium I scarcely understand and came searching for a place where they could re-seed themselves. The way Pollux described it, the medium they use for themselves and for the resurrectoriums is finite. They've yet to devise a medium that will encompass all. To contain new experience with their current medium, they constantly have to erase the old. So they went in search of a new medium, or mediums, that could store, expand, and that in fact could contain any and all experience, past, present, and future."

While Eric accepted the notion of dead souls preserved—especially now that the Cardinal had mentioned the resurrectoriums—this context of erasure, expansion, and medium was confusing. "What do you mean by erase?" he asked.

"Put it this way: Caruso records an aria, but the aria is too long for the allotted space on one side of his record. In order to keep going, he goes back to the beginning of the disk so he can capture the end of the aria. But as he captures the end of the aria, he erases the beginning, covering it over with the closing bars of the piece. The same thing is happening to the Benefactors in their currently limited medium. Pollux says that for this reason the Benefactors have, over the past two centuries, grown weak, confused, and forgetful. And until recently there's been nothing they could do to stop it."

Eric arched his brow, beginning to grasp all this. "But now there is?"

Anders nodded. "Yes." He leaned forward and tapped the red *X* again. "Back here . . . where they come from . . . there are still many Benefactors who act as a kind of clearinghouse for . . . for ideas, for the free flow of information. Pollux spoke of a communication coming from this clearinghouse, something that gave them the last of what they needed to know to effect a transfer to the new medium. This happened just before I came up here. He knew it was coming, a dispatch that would give them the technical know-how to inhabit, to store, to record onto a living medium everything they could possibly want to store. And because he's become so thoroughly humanized, and in tune with our species, he felt he had to stop it. Caruso recorded his voice onto a vinyl medium. The Benefactors plan to record their stored lives onto the medium of the human mind. Pollux says that to most Benefactors we're no more than ants. As the poacher in the Congo kills the elephant for its ivory, so the Benefactors will kill humans for their minds. To the Benefactors, we're just vessels waiting to be filled. And Pollux wants to stop it. But there's nothing he can do by himself. One hint of sabotage from his quarter, and his brethren would destroy him. He would never be able to help us again. So it's up to us. But we can't do it alone. We need force. And not the paltry force of the Wehrmacht. Pollux says we need the Romans. He says we must establish communications with them again."

Out in the corridor Eric heard the clanking of chains as a Seminarian escorted a shackled prisoner to the bathhouse.

"They really mean to evict us from our own bodies?" he asked.

"This was Pollux's constant theme in the months before I left Australia," said Anders. "He talked of nothing else. This technique of inhabitation . . . it's already begun. And I'm sorry to have to tell you this, Eric, but they've started in the Seminaries."

"The Seminaries?"

"I'm afraid so. In Seminarians the Benefactors have a ready army, a crop of strong young men ready for harvest, loyal soldiers of St. Julian's League who will gladly submit to whatever the Benefactors wish. They'll consider it their divine obligation and a holy honor."

"My son's a Seminarian," said Eric.

The Cardinal raised his eyebrows in concern. "I know," he said. "I've had . . . fellows watching him, and I'm sorry to have to tell you this, Eric, but we all agree that the Benefactors have changed him over, that he was in fact one of the first to go."

Eric leaned forward, put his hands on his knees to steady himself. "That can't be," he said.

"Nothing is certain," the Cardinal replied. "And I hope I'm wrong. But, nonetheless, the possibility remains. And that's why this radio beacon I heard in the outback has become so important. That's why we must somehow utilize it to save ourselves. If what Pollux says is true, then we must do everything in our power to stop them. We must follow Pollux's advice and contact the Romans."

But Eric was only half listening. He was thinking of Neil, of the way his eyes now shone like aluminum pie plates, how he spoke in a slow and cumbersome way, and how he showed no warmth for anyone except June. Sometimes Eric found himself wincing for no reason when he was around Neil, the way he winced when he heard the steel wheels of the Bell Boulevard streetcars grinding against the rails. At other times he could almost swear he heard a strange low tone emanating from Neil, like the *basso* hum of high-voltage electrical wires. And sometimes when he was around Neil he smelled that smell they had, like the electric drills at Jorgensen's Tool and Dye.

"And in order to contact the Romans," continued the Cardinal, "we must use radio, and we must use it in the Restricted Zone. Only in the Restricted Zones can any kind of radio signal get through. The Benefactors have created interference over all the settled areas so any signals are bounced right back to Earth. The Benefactors receive their own communications through the skies of the Restricted Zones. It's the whole reason they have Restricted Zones in the first place. It's how they received this latest communication. And this latest communication is why the Benefactors out in the Restricted Zones have been so belligerent, willing to trespass and openly attack in the settled areas. Pollux explained to me that the process has been a long one, that the development of this technique to inhabit has been hampered and stalled for thousands of years by patchy communications. The Benefactors here would send their own field research back home, the Benefactors back home would study and analyze it, come up with another piece of the puzzle, then send it back. Oftentimes the Romans would interdict their communications. But now, at long last, all the pieces are in place. Now they're ready to implement their plan. And we have to stop them. I'm here to offer you a proposition, Eric. I hope you'll have the good sense to take it."

From out on the river Eric heard a paddle steamer chug by, the blades splashing the water in quick, rhythmical slaps. He felt subdued, and horribly worried about Neil.

"From the first day I came to St. Lucius," the Cardinal went on, "I've been gathering radio and outfitters' equipment. We have to call for help, Eric. We have a chance. We must travel to the Restricted Zone and send a radio signal to the Romans because, as I say, only in the Restricted Zone will our signal get through."

Anders stood up and walked to the window, agitated now. He glanced out at the river, then turned around.

"I'm here today to ask you to venture into the Restricted Zone with me," he said. "In radio parlance, the Benefactors have created what we call F windows out there, and it's through one of these F windows we must send our signal. The windows in your Restricted Zone are far more numerous and larger than the ones in the outback. That's why I've come all this way." He took a few steps closer. "Doppler shift analysis indicates that the beacon I heard in the outback will be leaving the solar system soon. Which means we have to act fast."

Eric shook his head. "So this was all planned from the start?" he asked. "Your appointment? Everything? It was all . . . orchestrated?"

"Yes, it was," Anders admitted.

"If you go into the Restricted Zone," said Eric, "won't the Benefactors come after you? And I hear the Kiowa will kill anyone who comes into their territory."

"The Benefactors won't come near me," said Anders. "I have in my possession a device of Roman design that will repel them. Oliver Brown was hanged for possessing the same such contraption. No wonder he decided to keep it. He could hunt in the Restricted Zone without interference. As for the Kiowa, we'll be armed." The Cardinal's eyes narrowed. "We'll be on the Missouri River much of the time. I want you to come with me. You're a good man, Eric. A man I trust. I've come to consider you my friend. I've hired Per Larsen to be my riverman and he's willing to take me up the Missouri into the Restricted Zone as far as I want to go. But the man's cut from shifty cloth and is liable to double-cross me. I've hired Zeke Whitefeather to be my guide. He knows the backcountry well, but I'm not sure I trust him as far as I can spit. These men are the only men I've been able to find who are willing to go into the Restricted Zone. I need you as . . . as someone I can count on. I'm picking you out of all my possible choices because you're the man with the greatest incentive. If you come with me to the Restricted Zone I'll grant you a Collegiate Pardon. You'll be free to leave this place. I've prayed long and hard to God about this, and I know I'm right about you. Consider the good you can do. If nothing else, do it for Neil. Neil is gone. He's never coming back. Let's not have his life wasted. Let's make his memory count for something."

CHAPTER 18

Eric drove to his new house, a bungalow in West Shelby north of the Missouri River. He parked his truck, a trade-in on the Studebaker, and stared at the white clapboard structure. The roof sagged. One of the windows had a board over it. The afternoon sun beat down on a scorched lawn. He opened the door and got out. He could get used to the bungalow, the joblessness, even the outhouse in the backyard. What he couldn't get used to was this suit, a standard gray two-piece with sweat stains in the armpits, bought secondhand at Falkberget's Five-and-Dime. Secular clothing felt strange to him. He felt naked without his collar.

He thought of Neil, overwhelmed by the possible loss of his son. Grace dead these two long years, taken away by pneumonia, and now possibly Neil. He tried to put it out of his mind, even though that was exceedingly difficult. He had to concern himself with the business of setting up house.

"Ingrid?" he called.

He was going to need help getting the secondhand

sofa bed off the truck. He could have used Neil's help, but Neil was living in the Seminarians' Hospice downtown now. He couldn't trust Neil anymore anyway, wanted more time to think about Neil, and what Neil might or might not have become before he asked his son to come anywhere near this bungalow.

He walked up the drive. Where was she? He saw the small woods out back, ash and poplar, and a few small maples struggling along. He walked around to the back of the house and found Ingrid breaking ground for a vegetable patch with a spade. He wanted to tell her that she didn't have to do that, but knew they would have to grow what they could before fall came if they were going to feed themselves this winter.

"What do you plan on growing?" he asked.

She stood up, raised her hand to shield her eyes from the sun. "Oh, I don't know. I think it's too late for cucumbers and peppers. I thought I'd try some string beans and tomatoes. I hear summer squash grows like a weed too. I'd better try the easy stuff first."

He examined her progress. She hadn't done more than a square yard. The soil, broken into large rock-like chunks, reminded Eric of broken concrete blocks. She was going to exhaust herself doing this work. She was a small woman, more used to hosting strawberry socials or sitting on the Property and Maintenance Committee, or serving crustless cucumber sandwiches at wakes.

"You should wear gloves," he said. "You're going to get blisters."

She looked at her palm. "I think I see a few now."

"I got the sofa bed," he said. "Four dollars and fifty

cents. We can air it out on the porch for a few days. Better than those camp rolls we're using now. I'm going to need a hand getting it off the truck, though."

She nodded. "Okay."

She jabbed the spade into the dirt and followed him around to the front of the house.

He unlatched the back of the truck. The gate fell with a clang. He climbed into the back and muscled the sofa bed to the edge.

"Okay," he said, "give me your hand. I'll pull you up."

When she was up, he jumped to the ground.

"You push, and I'll pull," he said.

She nodded.

She pushed, he pulled. He kept his end up, but then it got too heavy.

"I'm going to have to drop it," he said.

"Okay."

He let it go, and it crashed to the ground. It was sturdy enough that little damage was caused. Ingrid's end was still propped against the back of the truck. He gave it a shove and it, too, fell. He helped her down.

"I guess that's that," he said.

"Are you okay?" she asked. "You're sweating, and your face is red."

"It's hot," he said. He gestured at the sofa bed. "What do you think?" he asked.

She looked at the sofa bed. "It's . . . nice."

"You always were charitable," he said. He took out a handkerchief and patted his forehead dry. "Why don't you try it? It may look like a dead rhino, but it's comfortable enough."

She smiled. With her customary daintiness, she settled herself on the ancient piece.

"That *is* soft," she said. "Is the mattress any good?"

"The mattress is a bit lumpy, but I figure if we give it a few good whacks with the broom it should be fine."

He sat on the sofa bed beside her. Like a couple of newlyweds, he thought, with next to no money and a hugely uncertain future. He put his arm around her.

"You'll stick with me?" he asked. "Even after all this?"

She pressed her head against his shoulder. " 'Where thou diest will I die also, and there will I be buried.' "

He nodded gravely. No firmer commitment could be found than in that quote from the Book of Ruth. "God bless you, Ingrid." She nestled closer and he held her tightly. "You're sure you understand why I have to go out to the Restricted Zone with the Cardinal."

"Yes."

"And why he thinks Neil isn't Neil anymore."

"Yes."

"I thought we might invite Neil over to dinner next Sunday," he said. "Just to see for ourselves. Would that be all right?"

"What will we feed him?" asked Ingrid. "We've got to watch what we spend."

"I thought we might try one of those clay-bred hams."

She made a face. "Those are supposed to be awful."

"Dress it up with pineapple and mustard, and I'm sure it'll be fine."

Her eyes narrowed, grew distant. "He hasn't been the same, has he?"

He looked away. "No," he said. "He hasn't."

Gallio stood in a field of pink flowers. He'd never thought he would see the day when he would have to wear a pressurized *vestimenta* on Hortus. Yet to breathe the air now would kill him in seconds. His foreman, Oppius Naevius, stood beside him in his own *vestimenta,* a hard-shell suit with a fishbowl helmet. The tiny ground-clinging blooms stretched from horizon to horizon. Three riders, three horses, two grooms, and a huntsman—all Romans—lay dead on the ground before them.

"The exactors were here in their ship collecting a tithe for the *legio ratio*," said Naevius. "They were hovering above those grain silos." The silos rose three hundred feet into the air. "They were taking on grain. Me and my crew were standing on the catwalk supervising when we saw the pink flowers. They came from the west like a grass fire. We got on board just as they reached us."

Gallio looked at the hills to the west. As pretty as strawberry ice cream.

"At first we didn't know what it was," Naevius continued. "I know the Hortulani grow things fast, in some cases overnight, but I never knew they could grow things in seconds. The flowers came at us like a pink wave." He motioned toward the horses. "We saw this riding party out here. The flowers surrounded them. A few seconds later they all fell down dead."

Some Hortulani field-workers walked by out on the road, slender turquoise beings, none in airtight self-contained *vestimentiae,* none affected by the deadly pollen floating through the air. They shouldn't have been immune. Their metabolism wasn't that different from human metabolism. But there they were, striding by, now the enemy, as immune as could be.

Gallio looked at the dead riders. One was a young woman. She was pretty, had brown hair, wore a white gown, couldn't have been more than twenty. And now she was dead, her eyes partially open, her head bent back, some dirt smudged on the fabric of her gown. He turned to Naevius. Naevius gazed at the young woman, a blank look in his eyes.

"We see death again, Naevius," said Gallio. "We see war."

Gallio squatted and took a closer look at the pink blooms. They were no more than an inch high. Each bloom was about the size of his fingernail, with four petals and a single yellow stamen that had thick white pollen clinging to it. The *legio scientifico* would of course develop a neutralizer, but for now they were deadly. He stood up. He felt a distant rumble through his suit, then saw five *bellum pennae* fly past in formation, gearing up for maneuvers. They banked over the river, looking like gigantic check marks, leaving contrails of black smoke behind them.

"Tell me, Naevius," he said, "how long would it take to raise my old army? I know we're all farmers now, and that we're widely scattered, but if I were to put out the call . . . if I were to send forth a summons . . . how long would it take all my old soldiers to . . ."

"A week," said Naevius. "Two at the most. You can count on their loyalty."

Gallio focused on the Hortulani field-workers walking along the road in the distance. He knew he had to try to stop the coming genocide. Even if it meant openly defying Rome.

Ingrid was in the kitchen, doing her best with the clay-bred ham, but even from here, on the back porch, Eric thought the thing smelled horrible. It had a peculiar sweet odor not found in regular hams. Eric gazed at the woods as he whittled. He saw in and among the basswood a bobtail standing half hidden behind some saplings. He thought he might get his rifle. This was an easy shot. They would have meat, *real* meat, for weeks. But then the deer darted away. He resolved to keep his rifle on the porch in case another easy shot came along.

Was it really Neil, he wondered? Or was Neil something else now? He jabbed his whittling knife into the bench. If Neil's body had been taken over by a Benefactor, which one had done it? Canicula? Aldebaran? Hesperus? He shook his head. Just like an Enrico Caruso recording. He stood up, braced himself. He put his hickory switch on the bench and went into the kitchen through the screen door.

Ingrid pinned clay-bred pineapple rings to the ham. They weren't as firm as regular pineapple rings, and they kept shredding.

"Do you need help?" he asked.

"You might want to dig out what's left of the mustard and put it in a dish."

He went to the fridge and took out the jar of mustard. He got a bowl from the cupboard, opened the jar, and spooned the mustard into the bowl.

Fifteen minutes later he heard the racket of Neil's old flivver in the drive.

He and Ingrid went out onto the front porch. As Neil brought the car to a stop, Eric felt his shoulders rise. Eric looked at his son, thinking of everything the Cardinal had told him, that this wasn't his son at all. Neil came up the dirt path and raised his hand in greeting.

"Howdy, folks," he said.

Ingrid gave him a hug. "Hello, son," she said.

Eric patted him on the back. "You found the place okay?" he asked.

"I had to ask back at the gas station," said Neil.

So. Here he was. The great deceiver. The enemy in their midst.

"I've got a little dandelion wine inside," said Eric. "I made it myself. Why don't we sit on the back porch and have a glass while your ma finishes up dinner?"

They went to the back porch. The house cast a long blue shadow over the yard as the sun set. Half a dozen bumblebees scouted the clover. The yard was a dismal sight. Ingrid had broken seven or eight square yards of garden, and even the spaded soil looked hard and barren, congealed in dusty brown clumps. Off to the right lay a patio, terra-cotta tiles laid with such large gaps in between that the weeds shot up knee high through the cracks. The outhouse was an eyesore, the white paint peeling, the structure sagging to one side. Here they were, in the Land of Nod.

"I sit out here," Eric said, "and I ask myself how I ever wound up in West Shelby with no money, no job, no future. What did I ever do to deserve this? All I had was a Latin-English dictionary." He glanced at

Neil. Neil frowned. "Neil . . . Neil, I was wondering if you might shed some light on that. They say in the Seminary you're in close personal contact with the Benefactors all the time. I thought you might have some ideas. What makes the Benefactors hate Latin so much? It doesn't make sense to me. In fact, the Benefactors don't make sense."

That did something. Anger seemed to be the key. That made the color climb into his son's face. He caught a sudden whiff of electricity. And he *knew*.

"The Benefactors have their reasons, pa," said Neil.

"But I've been perfectly loyal to them all my life."

"If you were loyal, pa, you wouldn't have been sneaking that Latin-English dictionary. You wouldn't have had that Prussian cipher-book or those radio parts."

"Son, I had nothing to do with that cipher-book or those radio parts. You know I didn't. That's God's honest truth. Those things were planted in my office. The Inculpator's Office knew if they convicted me on the Latin-English dictionary alone, my parishioners would raise a ruckus. Nothing against the fine young soldiers of St. Julian's Holy League, but since the Inculpator's Office was set on making an example of me, I believe they forced some Seminarians to plant those things in my office so the Prescript could hang me without any protest from my flock."

His son looked at him coldly, calmly. A pair of purple martins swooped low over the tangle of weeds in the backyard and disappeared into the woods. His son seemed to radiate heat. Eric could feel it coming off him like fever off a sick man. Anger was indeed the key. Neil's eyes were like pools of simmering fury.

And the heavy electrical smell, that aroma of boundless wattage, came from Neil in thick waves.

"Pa, don't be so ignorant."

"I might be ignorant, son, but at least I'm not blind."

"Jesus hears your words, pa, and Jesus forgives you."

"I wonder if Jesus forgives all those Seminarians who hang death row prisoners at St. Gilbert's."

The smell got stronger.

"They're only doing God's will, pa," Neil said. "And God's will is God's will."

As if murder had been part of God's will all along.

CHAPTER 19

Two weeks later, on a Sunday evening, Eric rowed a small boat across the Missouri River to Pelican Island. He felt worn by grief. Neil was gone. He had two rifles, a backpack with a change of clothes, a razor, and the Holy Bible. He looked up at the sky as the first stars appeared. Places. Actual physical locales. He was still having a hard time getting used to it. He dug his oars into the water and gave a good pull. The shoreline of the island drew closer. Did the Benefactors really come from that red X? He hardly knew the stars and the constellations. But now he looked at the stars in a different light.

The willows on the shoreline of Pelican Island loomed closer.

He found Cardinal Anders, Per Larsen, and Zeke Whitefeather sitting around a small campfire brewing coffee in a battered aluminum percolator at the foot of the disused Musicks Ferry Dock. Except for a dirty band of cloud-besmirched salmon light to the west, the sky was dark. He approached the group.

As the Cardinal turned, his full beard caught the

light of the fire. He smoked a cigar. Per and White-feather also turned. Per had long, curly brown hair as thin and fine as a baby's. He wore a scruffy brown derby. Whitefeather was an exceedingly tall Osage Indian with broad shoulders, a burnished brown face pitted with whitish acne craters, and long, dark hair flowing out from under a black derby. A lone white feather stuck straight up at the back of his derby.

The Cardinal rose.

"I confronted my son," Eric told him.

Anders nodded. "I'm sorry," he said. The Cardinal turned to Per and Whitefeather. "Boys, this is Ecclesiarch Nordstrum. I'm sure you both know him."

"We're mighty honored to have you along, Father," said Per.

Whitefeather nodded but otherwise didn't say a word.

"I should tell you boys that the Ecclesiarch's an ace shot," said the Cardinal. "We'll have plenty of fresh game to eat along the way." He pointed to the dock. "I'm going to take the Ecclesiarch down to the barge, let him see how we've got things set up, and show him where he can put his pack and his rifles. I want him to have a look at all my radio equipment too, get him acquainted with it. You two keep watch up here."

Eric and the Cardinal walked down to the dock. An old paddle steamer sat half submerged a little ways out, tilted to one side, a roosting place for seagulls now. They came to the end of the dock and boarded Per Larsen's barge. A summer moon the color of a ripe cantaloupe hung above the pretty Illinois farmland across the river.

Per Larsen's barge was made of weathered planks

fastened to flotation barrels. A small wheelhouse stood at the back, and a sleeping shed near the front.

"Me, you, and Whitefeather will sleep in that shed over there," said Anders. "Per's going to sleep in the wheelhouse."

At the shed Eric deposited his backpack, his Remington, and his Winchester. He then followed the Cardinal to the front of the barge where five horses stood tethered to a hitching post. The beginnings of a crude stable had been erected beside them.

"Whitefeather says we should try and hide these animals," said Anders. "Shelter them from view. He says we'll be traveling into Kiowa country. Every Kiowa is a born horse thief, according to Whitefeather."

Eric stared at the horses—three roans, a bay mare, and a larger black stallion. They swished their tails against flies and dipped their noses into the water trough. He didn't know much about the Kiowa—not many people did—but he knew they loved horses. He gazed west beyond the barge in the direction of the Restricted Zone. *Like a step into the past,* he thought. Crossing the Fence would be like crossing into a different world, a different time.

"The Kiowa never seemed real to me before," he said. "More the stuff of boys' adventure magazines."

"Oh, they're real, all right," said the Cardinal. "And dangerous."

"Why are we taking horses in the first place?" asked Eric.

"Remember I was telling you about those F windows? Those radio gateways?"

"Yes?"

"We won't find ones big enough at this northern latitude of the Restricted Zone," said the Cardinal. "Not with that long settled strip near St. Paul. The Missouri River runs parallel to St. Paul, and while it will take us as far west as we need to go, it's still too close to St. Paul for the Benefactors to safely install their F windows. So we take the river west because it's a natural and easy artery, and once we've traveled a good distance in, we'll head south using the horses to where the larger F windows are." The Cardinal put his hands on his hips and shook his head. "I have to tell you, Eric, we're running considerably behind schedule. It took me longer than I thought to find some decent horses. And some of my radio parts I had to order from New Amsterdam. They took a while to get here. We don't have all that much time to find a decent F window."

Eric raised an eyebrow. "Well, how much time do we have?"

"A week," said the Cardinal. "Ten days at the most."

Eric nodded. "Then we'll just have to hurry."

The Cardinal looked unsettled about the whole thing. He gestured toward some tarp-covered crates.

"This is the radio equipment," he said.

He pulled the tarp away and Eric saw three crates. Anders lifted the lid off the top one, and a collection of tubes, wires, transformers, generators—and the five car batteries—was revealed.

"I'm going to teach you everything you need to know about this in the next few days," said the Cardinal. "I figure it's better if there's two people who know about it, just in case something happens to one of us. What we have here is the makings of a radio strong enough to send and receive signals through any of those F windows in the Restricted Zone." He took out his flashlight and shone it over the equipment. "This kind of radio usually uses a key to generate signal—dots and dashes for Morse code—but we're going to rig it to a microphone." He lifted out the microphone, a black lozenge-shaped piece of equipment about the size of a shoe. "We can't use key coding to communicate. The Romans won't know any of our key coding. We have to use language." The Cardinal peered at him closely. "Do you speak any Latin at all? I know you had that Latin-English dictionary, but I—"

"I know a dozen or so phrases," said Eric.

The Cardinal nodded. "I've brought some phrase books and dictionaries along. We'll polish up your skills on the way. If this actually works—if we actually do make contact—we can circumvent the prerecorded message in the transmit oscillator and try to talk to them directly. We know they still speak Latin because of that signal I received in the outback." He gestured at the radio equipment. "Anyway, I just wanted to give you a look at this so you can start thinking about it." He scratched the back of his head, then took a deep breath. "Not that we have to go into any great depth right now. We should really get some rest. There's no telling what we'll be up against once we reach Kiowa country."

At one in the morning, after several cups of strong coffee, Eric helped Whitefeather untie the barge ropes. Per, up in the wheelhouse, started the diesel engines.

Eric jumped aboard, dragging the last rope with him. One of the horses snorted and scuffed the deck with its hoof as the barge pulled away from the dock.

Eric sat on a crate next to the fire—the fire barrel was bolted right into the deck. He gazed to the south, watching the tall Gothic towers of St. Bernardine's Shrine slide by. It was his favorite part of town, the place where he'd spent all his professional life and where he had raised his family. He was going to miss it.

They traveled through the night at a steady pace, Per using a small spotlight to pick out buoys marking the navigable channels, easing the barge to the left and right to avoid various shoals. They still had a considerable distance to travel before they would be out of the settled area—this meandering part of the river more than tripled the actual mileage they would have to go. The horses settled down. The bats came out and gorged on mosquitoes, twittering as they skimmed the river.

The barge left the city behind. Every mile or so they came to a village or town, and Eric saw lights in the windows. These lights were like a farewell to him. He knew he could never go back to the way things were. His life would be different from now on. God had chosen a new and difficult path for him.

Later, on his bedroll, he tried to sleep, but was so anxious about the incursion into the Restricted Zone, he found it hard to get settled. He decided to look up at the stars for a while. He didn't like leaving Ingrid behind. He remembered the days of their courtship, when, in a straw boater and a pair of white pants, he had serenaded her with a ukulele in a rowboat along this part of the river. Times had been so simple back then. He thought of Ingrid brushing her hair at night, the long, even strokes she gave it, the slender bend of her elbow, the curve of her breast. He was doing this for her as much as for Neil. What kind of world was it when the Benefactors could turn on them like this? He meant to change it.

He fell into a light doze and woke up an hour later, just as dawn brightened the sky. When he sat up, he could see the dark banks moving by. Columns of smoke twisted into the golden sky from the cottages and cabins along the shore. He knelt at the edge of the barge and splashed water on his face. He saw a cabin nestled among the poplar and ash. Two girls ran from the cabin to a dock. He recognized the girls— Henrik Rydberg's daughters. They recognized him and waved to him.

"God be with you, Father," they called.

Their voices were faint, high, broken by the breeze, but still the sweetest thing he had ever heard. He waved back.

"And with you," he called.

He made the sign of the cross in the air, blessing them. He saw Henrik Rydberg come out of the cabin, a young man, no more than twenty-five. He scratched his haunches, squinted at the barge, he joined his daughters at the dock. He recognized Eric and gave him a wave.

Whitefeather approached. "That's not good," he said.

"What's not good?" said Eric.

"It's still against the law to go into the Restricted

Zone," said Whitefeather. "We don't need witnesses. He might report us to the police."

The Osage Indian walked sullenly away.

Eric didn't care. He waved to Rydberg anyway. He didn't care if the whole damn world saw him. He was doing something important, and Rydberg was his friend.

Before long they passed St. Charles, the last town along the river before the Restricted Zone. He saw the Fence straddling the north and south banks of the river up ahead, barely visible in dawn's first light. Mist cloaked the river. The Restricted Zone got closer and closer. His stomach tensed in anticipation.

The Cardinal walked to one of the crates and pulled out a device such as Eric had never seen before—a white staff with colored lights along the side. The barge drifted past the Fence, and they entered the Restricted Zone. The Cardinal switched the device on and it began to hum. They were no more than a hundred yards in when seven Benefactors, gray spheres as big as cars, hurtled out of the distance. They came right up to the barge and hovered twenty feet above it. The horses grew skittish, and Eric braced himself. The others watched quietly. The white staff seemed to disorient the Benefactors, the hum of the thing repelling them the same way Deet repelled mosquitoes.

By and by the Benefactors drifted away, as if they couldn't sense anything untoward about the barge, and Eric and the others were left unhindered to travel ever deeper into the Restricted Zone.

CHAPTER 20

The land was empty. On the south it rose through alternating pasture and woodland to a plateau five miles away. Oak, maple, and elm grew on the north bank. Spring's green grass had turned brown, and the leaves on the trees sagged in the heat. A pheasant flew by, made Eric think about hunting. He might shoot a few birds if he got the chance. They could use the barge's raft to fetch them when they fell. He watched the pheasant grow smaller and finally disappear.

"Bringing those horses was the biggest mistake we ever made," said Whitefeather. The Osage had his shirt off because it was so hot. "The Kiowa are bound to steal them. I told the Cardinal that many times."

"I always thought there were giant herds of ferus out here," Eric said. "Why would they need to take our horses? I hear the feru herds are as big as the bison herds."

"That was true at one time," said Whitefeather. "But those old Roman herds are dwindling. There's none left in Florida anymore. And there's not many out here either. The land is dry, and the herds don't have anything to eat. The people don't have anything to eat either. They're forced to eat their horses. There might be a few wild herds left out west, but there aren't any here. A man who rides a horse in this country has to carry a gun. I'm glad you're a good shot. The Kiowa hate me. I'm Osage. You can protect me. The Cardinal says you know how to aim."

"I guess I can shoot straight enough," said Eric.

"Shoot straight when the Kiowa come for our horses," advised Whitefeather.

Whitefeather moved to the other side of the barge. Eric stared at him, wondering. If the man was so scared about the horses, why was he even here? He looked up, saw a brown eagle in the sky with its wings outstretched, circling on an updraft. How could Whitefeather be so scared when they were so alone? They hadn't even seen smoke from a campfire yet, let alone any Kiowa.

"Is Whitefeather complaining about the horses again?" the Cardinal asked as he came over.

Eric nodded. "He seems to think the Kiowa are going to steal them any second."

The Cardinal shrugged. "You know why he wears that hat all the time?"

"Why?" said Eric.

"Because he's always expecting rain. He loves to prepare for the worst." The Cardinal put his hands on his hips. "I never thought wishing for doom and gloom could make anybody so happy. Just ignore him. We're perfectly safe on this river." He motioned toward the crates. "I thought we'd spend some time looking at the radio now. I've got the horses all fed and watered. I figure now's a good time."

"Sure."

They opened the top crate.

All the radio components were packed in special slots cut into a thick piece of cork.

"The components in this crate are the parts that will make up the radio's basic electrical circuit," said the Cardinal. He pointed as he spoke. "These are resistors, capacitors, and inductors. I've tooled all these parts for quick assembly. These units over here are iron and ferrile cores. These are barrier rectifiers. And these are amplifiers."

Anders withdrew a thin leather case from the end of the crate, unsnapped it, and pulled out some plans.

"This is the block diagram for the radio," he said. "You need to know this by heart." He tapped the diagram with his finger. "I've made up two strains, a transmitting strain and a receiving strain. Both strains lead to the antenna. The antenna itself is a simple aluminum grid, four by nine by eighteen feet, which I've stored disassembled in these other crates. It should give us the versatility and strength we need to send and receive signals through the Restricted Zone's F windows. On the transmit strain, we've got a microphone and a transmit oscillator. Our signal will travel up this strain through a mixer, a filter, a buffer, a driver, an amplifier, and a final filter before leaving the antenna. Any incoming signal will come down the receiving strain, first through two filters, then through a mixer, another filter, a couple of AGC detectors, and finally into the audio amplifier and speaker. But we have a problem. The Romans might send visual signal. This small radio has no way to receive visual signal. Only the most advanced equipment in the technical laity can receive visual signal, and it looks like the Benefactors are going to clamp down on that soon. Some things they let go and other things they stop, and who can say what their reasons are. Anyway, any visual signal the Romans send is going to come to us as interference. To cut down on that, I've designed this bleed-off box. You wire it to the audio amplifier and turn the dial to stop any visual signal from reaching the speaker. That way we'll hear whatever the Romans say loud and clear."

Eric nodded. "And you're sure we're going to find one of these F windows?" he asked.

"Yes," replied the Cardinal. "Like I told you before, the American West has bigger F windows than the outback. It also has a lot more of them. We shouldn't have too much trouble. It may take some scouting, some sky gazing, but I'm sure we'll find a big one before that Roman beacon leaves the solar system."

Eric looked up at the sky. "How do you plan on finding one?"

Anders took another case out of the crate, opened it, and withdrew something that looked like a telescope.

"I designed this from models I saw while I was in the technical laity," he said. "It's a hodoscope, an instrument that tracks and measures ions. Radio waves propagate or refract through the ions. My hodoscope tracks ions through a colorization scheme. The sporadic F windows will register as pockets of green. These pockets will have ten-to-the-tenth electrons per cubic inch, which is ideal for what we're after. This instrument will help us find them."

Eric looked at the block diagram and then at all the equipment. The resistors, capacitors, and inductors sat inert in their cork molding, baffling pieces of a puzzle he didn't understand. And the ferrile cores, barrier rectifiers, and amplifiers were like the enigmatic dreck of an ancient society long lost to antiquity.

"Is anybody going to help me steer this thing?" Per called from the wheelhouse. "My arm's gettin' tired, and nature's been callin' for the last hour."

He was leaning out the wheelhouse window with a peevish look on his face.

"I'll go," said Anders. "You take a look at this block diagram and see if you can make sense of it."

Eric nodded. "I'll try."

As he settled himself onto one of the upended crates to study the diagram, Per left the wheelhouse, headed for the side of the boat.

Before Eric could take note of the fact that the transmit mixer and the RF mixer were joined by a mysterious circuit marked "VFO," Per sat down next to him and looked at the block diagram with mild interest.

"I don't know why the Cardinal got you to do that," he said. "I bet you never fussed over anything more complicated than a spark plug. Me, I'm fussin' with my diesel engines all the time." He tapped the diagram. "You need someone with a little technical know-how to put together a radio that tricky."

"And you were trained in the technical arts yourself, then, Mr. Larsen?" he asked.

Per's eyes flicked to one side. "I'm more or less a self-taught man, Father, and proud of it," he said. "A man's own brain is his best teacher. I reckon a schoolmarm don't know the first thing about fancy radios, but I'm sure I could put it together just fine."

"I must confess, I don't know the first thing about radios myself," said Eric. "I'm only thankful the Cardinal's tooled everything so it fits together smoothly."

"He should have left the toolin' to me," said Per. "And as for his solderin', I've done a lot of solderin' in my time, and I'm sorry to say the Cardinal's solderin' is sorely lackin'." He shook his head. "You see, when you do your solderin', you want to be neat about it. You don't want your lead drippin' all over the place. Heat and touch, that's what you got to remember. I could have done a much better job. But don't tell him I said so. He strikes me as a man who might get touchy about his solderin'. He sure is a mite touchy about them radio parts."

Eric looked at the radio equipment. Parts they *had* to be touchy about. All this radio equipment was their only chance to stop the Benefactors and to make good on the passing of Neil.

Per glanced nervously at the Cardinal, up in the wheelhouse. "I sure hope he knows how to steer this thing," he said. "You got to take a lot into account when you steer a barge this big. You got to figure in the wind, the current, the drag . . . a whole mess of things. That ain't something no schoolmarm can teach you either. I been through a few tough scrapes in this barge. I know you and the Cardinal have your fancy schoolin', but if you ask me, learnin' in school ain't as good as learnin' through a few tough scrapes."

Just as the sun went down, Eric saw a small doe on the riverbank. He was getting sick of eating jerky and

pemmican. He wanted some fresh meat, something
that might give him a little strength. He lifted his Winchester and leveled it at the animal. Whitefeather
stopped sharpening his knife and watched. The
Cardinal stopped grooming the horses and watched.
The deer had to be fifty yards away. She was a dainty
thing, but she looked well fed. Eric was glad he had
his scope. Compensating for wind, distance, and speed,
he squeezed the trigger.

A second later the deer dropped dead.

A second after that, the barge engines stopped. Per
came out of the wheelhouse giddy with delight, his
lips stretched in a smile, and walked toward them as
if he himself had been the one who made the shot.

"For Pete's sake, Zeke," he cried, "cast anchor, cast
anchor! Did you see that shot? I ain't seen a shot like
that my whole life. We got ourselves venison for dinner
tonight, boys. Cast anchor, you dumb old Indian. We
got to raft over and float that carcass across." Per turned
to Eric. "Who taught you to shoot like that, Father?"

"My aim has always been true, Mr. Larsen. As far
back as I can remember."

"Then you missed your calling, Father," said Per.
"You should have been a varmint hunter. I hate varmints. I hate them to death. If I knew how to shoot
as well as you do, I'd be shootin' them all the time."

Whitefeather gazed moodily at the riverbank. "I see
shadows in these woods," he said. He squinted against
the reflections the sun made off the water. "I think
we should leave the deer there. I don't trust these
woods. These woods are too quiet."

Despite Whitefeather's objections, they cast anchor.

The Osage threw the three-pronger off the front, and the barge dragged to a standstill.

Eric and Per paddled the raft to shore. Eric thought the Benefactors might come rushing out of nowhere at them, but the Cardinal's Roman staff had a generous range, and the Benefactors stayed away.

When they got to shore, Eric slung the small deer over his shoulder and headed back to the raft. Though the deer was freshly killed, the flies had already gathered. Dark clouds moved in from the west, and it looked like it might rain by nightfall.

Eric was fairly adept at skinning animals, but Whitefeather's skill surpassed his own, and they let the Indian do the job. The tall Osage hoisted the animal by its hind legs, tied its hooves to a pole, slit its throat, and bled it for an hour.

Once the animal was drained, Whitefeather went to work, seeming to melt the skin from the carcass in dexterous, practiced strokes. He saved the entrails for fish bait. He butchered the carcass into neat pieces and ate the liver raw, as was Osage custom. He cut the haunches into a couple of roasts. They lit a fire, let it burn down to coals, and put one of the roasts into a pan with some carrots, onions, potatoes, sage, salt, pepper, and marjoram. Soon a savory smell filled the air. They let it cook for a couple hours.

They sat down to this appetizing repast around sundown. Mist gathered in pockets here and there. Small flies swirled about in their own little clouds above the river. A dead raccoon floated by.

While Eric was eating a succulent filet of the roast, he saw movement on the river downstream.

He stood up and walked halfway to the back of the barge. Whitefeather came and stood beside him.

Seven Indians wearing loincloths paddled a large canoe upriver toward them. An eighth, his scalp shaved except for a dozen tightly coiled braids brimming with beads and feathers, stood in the bow of the canoe, holding his hand over his eyes to shield them from the setting sun.

Whitefeather shook his head. "Kiowa," he said.

The Indian at the front of the canoe raised his hand and signaled the others to stop. The canoe shifted sideways in the current as they took their paddles out of the water. The distance between the barge and the canoe increased. Mist floated across the river and caught the reflection of the setting sun, obscuring the canoe. A minute later, when the mist cleared, the canoe was gone.

"I told you I didn't like these woods," said Whitefeather. "These are Kiowa woods. What I did to that deer with my knife these Kiowa will do to us if they catch us. They skin people alive. They are strong in these woods. Their ancestors live in these woods. They will kill us if we stay here."

CHAPTER 21

They saw no sign of the Kiowa for the next hour. They headed upriver, putting as much distance between the barge and the Indians as they could. Per turned on the big spotlight and kept going even after dark. Moths flew in the spotlight beams.

When they finally cast anchor later that night, Per took an optimistic view. "Maybe they're just curious," he said.

Whitefeather shook his head. "The Kiowa can smell a horse ten miles away," he said.

They decided they had better stand watch. Whitefeather went first.

In the small hours of the morning, he came for Eric.

"Your turn, Father."

"Anything?" asked Eric.

"I heard a cougar in the woods. He was angry. I heard him for a long time."

Eric got his blanket and sat on a barrel. Though the day had been hot, the night was cool, and a damp breeze blew off the river. He looked up at the sky, hoping to see some stars, but it was overcast. After a half-hour it started raining. He lifted his blanket over his head and stared at the south bank of the river. The river was getting narrower, shallower. The last sounding, taken around four that afternoon, had been thirty feet deep. He glanced at the Cardinal's staff. The lights blinked in a pattern, not brightly but with a kind of dark intensity.

By the time they got under way the next morning, it was raining steadily and the wind was rising. The river took on the muddy color of a prairie slough. It smelled of old sucker-fish and snapping turtle. The banks were now grassy. A few poplar and birches clung together in small groups. He saw some swallows fly in and out of their nest holes up on a sandy bluff. A muskrat swam by. He thought he might do some fishing, but feared the wind would blow his line all over the place.

Whitefeather looked at the sky.

"I don't like this weather," he said. The wind flicked at the Indian's long black hair. "Those clouds are bad. This weather smells like tornado weather. We should pile crates against the stable so it won't blow away."

They spent the next twenty minutes stacking crates while the horses whinnied. The river roughened, and the barge heaved up and down in the waves. The wind got stronger, and for five minutes it hailed nonstop, little white pellets the size of Eric's thumb. The rain got worse after the hail stopped. The sky darkened. A yellowish strip of light clung to the horizon in a tight, tense band. The clouds were as dark as a fresh bruise—tornado clouds. The tall grass whipped and bent on the riverbank. The wind got stronger yet, and dirt, twigs, and leaves filled the sky.

"We got to cast anchor," Per called over the wind. "I don't want to get blowed over onto a sand shoal. She's shiftin' all over the place."

Whitefeather tossed the anchor into the river, and Per cut the engines. Eric, the Cardinal, and White-feather took cover in the shack while Per kept an eye on things from the wheelhouse. Through a small crack between planks, Eric watched the storm intensify.

Despite the anchor, the barge drifted closer and closer to the south bank. The wind was strong enough to overcome any purchase the anchor had on the bottom. To the west Eric saw a fitful funnel cloud form, the thing dipping out of the sky like the underside of a black spinning top. He thought for sure they were going to have a full-fledged tornado, but then the funnel cloud spun itself out and disappeared as quickly as it had formed. Despite that, the wind increased, and sounded like a train. It rattled the shed and threw the rain against the tin walls like bullets. The roof blew off and Eric heard it crash onto the deck. All three men grabbed for their hats, but Eric missed his and it flew off into the black sky.

He felt the vibration of the diesels starting up. The barge shifted under the power of the engines.

"We're probably heading for a shoal," the Cardinal called out over the storm. "Per's going to try and steer clear of it."

Despite Per's efforts, the wind pushed the barge onto a shoal a few minutes later. It thudded with a sickening shudder and came to a stop, the deck shifting five degrees upward. Eric heard the horses whinny and scuffle as they struggled to get their footing on the slanted deck.

The storm raged for another hour before the wind finally diminished. Eric, the Cardinal, and White-feather huddled in the roofless shed, the rain pelting them so hard it dripped off their chins in thin streams. Eric, his legs sore from squatting, finally sat down in the wet. The others did the same. The wind-whipped clouds were low, and lightning flashed continually. Eric thought the wind might push the barge free of the shoal, but it didn't.

Finally the rain stopped coming down so hard.

"I think we should have a look," said Anders, standing up, his wet beard congealed into thick strands.

They emerged from the roofless cabin. The storm had moved to the east. The stable, girded by the crates, still had its walls, but its roof was gone. Eric saw it floating down the Missouri River half submerged in the swollen current. The fire barrel, bolted to the deck, remained in place. The barge was grounded fifteen yards from the south bank. The river was brown, rushing east in little whirlpools and eddies, carrying grass, sticks, and leaves. Lightning flickered constantly on the southern horizon, brightening the clouds with helter-skelter flashes.

Per already stood at the edge of the barge looking into the water, assessing the severity of the grounding. Eric scratched his head, found a couple of poplar leaves in his hair, tossed them to the deck, and joined Per at the edge. Anders and Whitefeather went to the stable to see how the horses were doing.

Per raised his eyebrows, his jaw jutting, his nostrils flaring.

"I know what you're thinkin'," he said. "And I know

this looks bad, like maybe I'm no good as a riverman after all. But don't go blamin' this on me. I'm swearin' on a stack of Bibles a yard thick, there ain't nothin' I could have done to steer clear of this shoal. That was a humdinger of a storm. That anchor was hooked good and strong on the bottom, but that wind blew so dang hard, it pushed the barge clear over here."

"You did your best, Mr. Larsen," Eric said.

"Best or worst got nothin' to do with it," he said. "You're a man of the cloth. You should recognize an act of God when you see one."

"It was an act of God, Mr. Larsen."

Per's shoulders eased. He rolled them a bit, scrunched up his face, then peered over the side of the barge into the water again.

"I grounded this old wreck a time or two back in my greenhorn days," he said, "but I never seen it this bad." He pointed down the sloped deck toward the north side of the barge. "Look at that. She's clear in the water. Ain't no way I can back her off this shoal with a gentle nudge of the engines. That'll just get her stuck deeper. We're going to have dig. We got three or four days work here." He scanned the hills stretching away from the south bank. "I sure hope them Kiowa don't come back when we're stuck here like this. We're sittin' ducks right now." Per put his hands on his hips. "I got some scoops and shovels," he said. "The sooner we get started, the sooner we'll be out of here. The river's high, but she ain't going to stay high long. Once this rain drains away, she'll sink right back down, and we'll be stuck worse than ever, so we better get a move on."

The Cardinal led one of the horses out of the stable.

The animal had a gash on its head that was bleeding badly. Its eyes were wide with fear, and its ears were pressed back. Whitefeather tried to soothe the horse by talking Osage to it. He stroked its nose. The horse nipped at Whitefeather, but then grew surprisingly calm. The man had a way with animals.

The Cardinal inspected the grounding. His eyes were stern and his jaw set.

"Can you free this barge, Per?" he asked.

"Of course I can," said Per, immediately interpreting the Cardinal's question as a challenge to his skill. "But it's going to take some time."

"How much time?" asked the Cardinal.

"Three or four days."

The Cardinal frowned, scratched a big mosquito bite on his neck, then looked up at the sky, as if willing that Roman beacon to stay in the solar system longer.

"We don't have three or four days," he said. "We've got to get it out in two. We can't risk waiting any longer. If we can't do it in two days, we'll have to saddle up and head south, and take our chances at finding F windows in the more easterly regions."

June read the headlines. As Henry Ford had learned to mass-produce motorcars in the Papal State of Pontiac, so Admiral Doenitz had learned to mass-produce death in Europe.

PRUSSIA DROPS SUPERBOMB ON RUNNYMEDE
50,000 P.S.A. TROOPS DEAD

Was that right? Was it actually possible to kill fifty thousand troops at once with a single bomb, over a staging area ten miles wide? Could a bomb actually make an explosion that big? And now that the Prussians were no longer technologically hampered by stringent Liturgical Laws prohibiting such advances, did they have the skill and know-how to build such a thing? As she read the details, June realized that an explosion that size was eminently possible.

"I can see why from a strategic standpoint the Admiral would do such a thing," she told Amy, who sat at the kitchen table next to her. "The last thing he needs is fifty thousand American troops storming the beaches of Gaul and making inroads against him. But to kill fifty thousand all at once! Arch Prescript Dewey made a big mistake sending them over there. He should have gathered more intelligence about this superbomb first."

"You know what bothers me most about the whole thing?" said Amy cynically, as the Victrola in the living room played Bing Crosby's *The Clouds'll Roll Away*. "Five thousand of those men came from the Territory. They were all young, and they were all good-looking. Half of them were single. Where does that leave a girl like me?"

June wasn't surprised by Amy's reaction. Amy was dealing with the shock in her own peculiar way.

"It says the bomb derived its great explosive force from the splitting of heavy atomic nuclei," June went on, "and that it created a blast ten miles in diameter over the American staging area in Britannia, and that it was so hot it melted the dirt. They say there's all sorts of radiation, and something they're calling fallout, this ash that's drifting all over the country."

She then read a related story, which said that as a

direct result of the bombing at Runnymede, Herbert Hoover had ordered a crackdown on the Odd Fellows. One-hundred-and-twelve suspects had been rounded up in New Amsterdam and Boston. In an effort to dissuade sympathizers and possible new recruits into the Odd Fellows, Hoover, with the heavy-handed tactics he was famous for, had published the names of all those arrested. The names appeared on page ten.

She flipped quickly to page ten.

"June?" said Amy, sensing June's growing alarm.

She saw her brother Henry's name there. "Oh, dear," she said, feeling faint.

"What's wrong?" asked Amy. "You look white."

Her mouth went dry and she swallowed against the growing fear she felt in her chest. Until now, the possibility of arrest, for both her and her brother, had always seemed remote. But now they *had* her brother.

"They've got Henry," she said. "Hoover's had him locked up. They're cracking down on the Odd Fellows."

Per, wearing just his boxer shorts, dove with a scoop in his hand. Eric hung on to the side of the barge, up to his chest in water, a bucket full of muck in his hand. He was so tired after five hours of digging, he wondered where he would find the strength to make another dive. The Cardinal stood above him.

"Per must be part amphibian," said Anders. "I've never seen a man hold his breath so long."

"I imagine he would do well as a pearl diver in Nippon," said Eric.

"You should get out," said the Cardinal. "You've been in there a long time."

"The harder we work, the sooner we'll have this barge free."

"Still, it's going to get dark soon. We should think about getting something to eat."

"I guess I could stop for something to eat," said Eric.

The Cardinal extended his hand to help Eric, and Eric struggled up to the deck. He put his bucket down, wondering when Per would ever come up for air, and why the man insisted on overdoing everything as a way to show everyone he was better than they were.

At last Per came up for air. He sputtered and coughed dramatically. His drenched brown hair hung to his shoulders, though his head was bald on top. Whitefeather was in the water at the far corner of the barge.

"Why are you getting out?" asked Per, looking up at Eric. "We've barely started."

"We've been at it five hours, Per," said Anders. "It's time to get out."

Per shook his head, making a big show of how disappointed he was. "If you ladies think so," he said.

And to make a point of how fit he was, Per climbed out of the water without any help, even though the task proved nearly too difficult. He was as skinny as a rake, but had a small, hard potbelly. He was lily white all over, except for his hands and face, which were tanned as dark as a hazelnut.

"We need something to eat, Per," said Eric

"I shouldn't have gone on this half-wit adventure with a couple of ladies like you in the first place," said Per. He raised his hand to his mouth and called. "Zeke, get out. These ladies think we need a rest."

Whitefeather, partially obscured in mist, nodded and climbed out. He was wearing only an Indian loincloth.

Per put his hands on his hips.

"I'm going to the wheelhouse to see if I can get this old sow out of here," he said. "I want to give her a try before the river gets too low. You ladies sit down before you fall down."

Eric and the Cardinal walked to the fire. Smoke rose from under the flames—their firewood was wet. Eric raised his hands to warm them and noticed that his palms were wrinkled from the water. The Cardinal filled the coffee percolator and put it on the camp stove. He then went to feed the horses. Whitefeather came over and held his hands to the fire.

"The mist is getting thick," said Whitefeather.

Eric looked around. "I guess it is," he said. He suddenly felt lonely for Ingrid. He wondered how she was making out all by herself in their little bungalow in West Shelby. "I imagine it'll burn off in the morning."

The diesels coughed to life. Eric glanced at Per through the cracked wheelhouse window and saw that the riverman's brow was pinched in fierce concentration. The water at the stern bubbled, and the far side of the barge lifted as the craft tried to right itself. The deck shuddered, and black smoke billowed out of the stack behind the wheelhouse in a protesting cloud. For all the look of Herculean effort on Per's face, the barge didn't move, not an inch, and Per, shaking his head as if the universe had betrayed him, pulled the throttle back and finally gave up. The engines sighed into silence.

Great fingers of fog reached over the deck. Per

emerged from the wheelhouse and stomped toward them, carrying his massive but bruised ego with him. Eric expected him to blame the barge, the river, even to blame the whole thing on God again. But before Per got the chance, Eric saw movement at the back of the barge. Kiowa. Climbing out of the water onto the deck. Five of them altogether.

He lifted his hand to warn Per, but before he could, an arrow sang through the air, thunked into Per's back, and came out the other side, right below his ribs. Per's eyes popped wide. He looked down and saw the stone point sticking out like a bird's beak. Blood etched dark drip marks over his bare waist and down his right leg. He pressed his hands over his wound, looked at Eric, then over his shoulder at the braves. The five Kiowa wore bear-tooth necklaces and had their cheeks painted with diagonal stripes of war paint. All carried bows and arrows. Per's head swung back, his mouth dropped open, and he ran toward Eric. More arrows zinged past him.

Eric felt the veins on his neck pop out in cold anger. He saw that the Cardinal was arming himself with a crowbar. Whitefeather, looking at the braves with his usual immobile expression, bolted across the deck and dove into the water, the brown river swallowing him with hardly a splash. Eric hoisted his Remington to his shoulder, levered a round into the chamber, took a bead on the nearest Kiowa, and fired. The brave dropped down, dead. The others scattered.

Eric walked quickly forward, heedless of any counterattack, and shot another one, who fell as the cartridge ripped through his heart. Eric wasn't going to let these Kiowa wreck his chances of contacting the

Romans. He drew a bead on a third Indian and fired. He wasn't going to let them wreck his chance of avenging Neil. His aim was infallible. The third Indian fell, slid for a yard, and came to a stop against the pemmican barrel.

The last two dove off the back of the barge and swam away. Eric scanned the water's dark, muddy surface. He knew they would have to come up for air sooner or later.

The first one appeared some distance downstream, and looked around to get his bearings. Eric aimed and fired. The brave's head twitched and he sank beneath the surface, the river claiming him under a patch of foam.

The second one came into view a half-minute later. Eric heard him call out—maybe he was calling for his friend—then he squeezed the trigger. The Kiowa pitched forward in the water and drifted east. *May God have mercy on their souls,* Eric thought, lowering his rifle. He inspected the three dead Kiowa on the deck. Dead as dead could get. He felt no remorse. Grim necessity had forced his hand. The Cardinal and Per, who had fallen to the deck, stared at him as if he were a natural-born killer. Eric scanned the river one last time. There was no sign of Whitefeather. He put his rifle down and sighed.

"Come on, Magnus," he said. "Let's get these bodies into the river before the flies come. We don't need any more flies than we already have."

CHAPTER 22

The Cardinal pulled the arrow right through Per Larsen. With the arrow out, the riverman bled a lot, gasped for breath, opened his eyes wide, then shut them tightly. In the twilight the blood looked black. Eric got the medical kit and took out a bottle of rubbing alcohol, some codeine tablets, and a roll of gauze dressing.

"We have to get that bleeding stopped," said the Cardinal.

He poured the rubbing alcohol freely over the wounds. Per groaned in pain.

Once the wound was clean, Eric cut a piece of gauze and pressed it hard against the entry wound. The Cardinal held another piece to the exit wound. By holding the dressings tightly in place for the next ten minutes, they managed to slow the flow of blood from Per's abdomen and back.

"I'll take some of them pills now, Father," said Per. "I got some whiskey in the wheelhouse to wash 'em down with."

Eric made his way through the mist to the wheelhouse, found Per's bottle of whiskey on a shelf, and took it back to him.

Per gripped the bottle with a bloody hand and up-ended it. When he was done he handed it to Eric and the Cardinal.

"You ladies want any?" he asked.

Both declined. Per seemed grateful—all the more for him.

They made Per comfortable in the shed. Between the whiskey and the codeine tablets, he soon dozed off into a fitful slumber.

Eric took the first watch. The Cardinal sat up with him for a while.

"Do you think Whitefeather will come back?" Eric asked.

Anders stared at the dark water. "I don't know," he said. "He's Indian. He doesn't need the Roman staff to protect him. I told you I couldn't trust him. He might try to make it to Pawnee country. He was once a Pawnee medicine man—don't ask me how, him being Osage and all. He'd be safe in Pawnee country." The Cardinal shook his head and shrugged. "Or he could drift back to the Territory. One way or the other, we can't stay here anymore. That Roman bea-con's not going to wait for us. We've got to saddle up and head south by dawn, whether Whitefeather's back or not."

Whitefeather didn't come back that night or the next morning. The sun burst over the horizon, and the day immediately began to sizzle. Eric leaned over to the side of the barge and splashed water on his face. Flies buzzed around the stable. A fox appeared on the riverbank, then trotted off toward a rocky gully in the distance. Two vultures circled overhead, attracted by the smell of blood on the deck.

The Cardinal emerged from the shed. "I don't know if Per's delirious or hungover," he said. "Maybe you should look at him. You've sat at more sickbeds than I have."

Eric followed the Cardinal into the shed.

Per's face was white, his forehead clammy. When he looked at Eric he seemed not to see him. His eyes were glassy and full of rheum. Vomit sat in a pail beside him.

"I guess he's not fit to ride," said Eric.

"I don't think so," said the Cardinal. "But we have to ride just the same. We'll have to lash him to the saddle."

Eric felt the riverman's forehead. "He's hot," he said. "He's burning up."

"Let's take a look at his wounds," said the Cardinal.

The Cardinal peeled the dressing away. A large purple clot had formed in the center of the exit wound. The skin around it looked puffy and bruised. There was no evidence of purulence, no sign of pus or infection. The Cardinal shook his head.

"One thing's certain," he said. "We have to take him with us. The minute we take that Roman staff away, the Benefactors will be on him. He won't stand a chance."

"Let's give him a drink," said Eric. "We'll see if we can get him at least partly roused before we go."

Eric held a dipper of water to the riverman's mouth while the Cardinal went to get the horses saddled. Per drank slowly, little sips, as if he were having a hard time swallowing. The water revived him, at least to some extent, and after ten minutes he struggled to his feet with Eric's help.

"Ain't no Kiowa arrow going to kill me," he said. "They can't make no arrow good enough to kill me. And you know what? I'm glad Zeke's gone. He weren't no good for nothin' anyway. I'm a better guide than he is. I ain't never been to these parts, but I reckon it don't take no scholar to see which way is which, or to figure out where you might find water. Put me on a horse and I'll take you ladies anywhere you want."

Eric set him outside in the sun—he said he was cold—and helped the Cardinal get the horses packed. It took twenty minutes to get the radio equipment strapped onto the horses. The camping equipment and provisions took another fifteen. All this time Eric kept glancing toward the north shore, thinking he might see Whitefeather. He didn't like the idea of leaving Whitefeather out here alone. Not that Whitefeather had to worry about the Benefactors—the Benefactors never attacked Indians, just white men. What White-feather had to worry about was more Kiowa. He was a lone Osage in hostile country.

When all the horses were ready, Eric and Anders dragged the raft from the back of the barge around to the side. First they established a guide rope between the barge and the south bank, tying it off to the trunk of a tree. In this way they pulled themselves back and forth between the barge and the riverbank without the current pushing them too far east.

They took two horses at a time—the raft was easily big enough to accommodate that many animals—and crossed the small stretch of water slowly so as not to make the animals skittish. Eric made a gangplank from the raft to the shore and led the first two horses to the bank. He and Anders repeated this process until all five horses were ashore.

Then they dragged the raft upriver a hundred yards and pulled it into a marshy backwater. They wanted to hide it so they could use it when they came back. A creek emptied into the backwater. They pulled the raft halfway onto the bank and covered it with branches they broke from nearby trees. Then they went back to the barge and the horses.

The day was already scorching. They got Per onto a horse.

"You don't need to tie me," said Per, when they tried to lash him to the saddle. "I ain't no old grandma who ain't never rode no horse before. I can probably ride better than the two of you ladies put together."

So they let him ride unlashed, even though it cost him a great deal of effort. He leaned to the right in his saddle, favoring his left side, a look of obsessive determination on his face. Eric dug his spurs into his horse, and the animal climbed up through the grass, following Per's horse. They rode to the top of the hill. Eric took one last look, hoping to see Whitefeather, but the Indian was long gone. He wondered what kind of moral compass Whitefeather had. Was loyalty important to him? Or was he just plain two-faced? Anders said he had at one time been a Pawnee medicine man, even though he was Osage. The man was obviously adept at fitting in anywhere, at fooling all sorts of people, and Eric guessed the Cardinal was right not to trust him.

*   *   *

June sat in a roadside bus shelter near the Soulard Market not far from the train yards, waiting for word of Henry. The place stank of urine, and was strewn with garbage. An empty sherry bottle stood in the corner. The Benefactors were watching her now, she knew that. They were just biding their time. Encoded instructions from the Odd Fellows had arrived four days ago. She was to wait here every night. A man in a green fedora would come with the latest word of her brother.

She lit a cigarette—clay-bred tobacco with that hard, cutting taste and smoke that burned the spit right out of your mouth. Even so, she needed it to calm her nerves. It wasn't a good idea for a young woman to be alone down here at night. She looked up and down Carroll Street, a neglected street with the potholes and weeds growing up through the cracked concrete along the curb. The street was empty. Fog rolled in from the river. She wanted to go home, lie in her bed, and hope Henry was alive. She pulled the collar of her coat up around her ears.

Someone tapped on the glass. It was the man in the green fedora. She got up and walked outside.

"I'm looking for a hotel," said the man. He was a slight young man, pale, with a bandage on his chin. The fedora, far too big for his head, rested on top of his large ears. "I hear the Concord's good."

"The Concord's good," she said, feeling her breath come faster, "but the Empire's better."

The man looked relieved. "Then I'll stay at the Empire," he said. He had a slight accent, European.

He took a brown envelope from his pocket, handed

it to her, and hurried off into the fog without another word.

When he was out of sight, June walked down Carroll Street to Second Avenue, then along Second Avenue to Rutger. She continued along Rutger until she reached the Mississippi. The river flowed darkly by. On the opposite side through the fog she saw the lights of St. Anthony. She looked around. She was alone. She was afraid that Hesperus would roll out of the darkness along Wharf Road in his Model T, but he didn't come. The place was deserted. Only a crumpled newspaper tumbled down the street.

She stood out of the wind behind a warehouse, tore open the letter, and lit her lighter.

Dearest June. Even the sight of Henry's handwriting made her quiver. *I am in jail now awaiting trial. They say my trial will be soon. The Odd Fellows have hired the best lawyers, but I don't think it's going to do any good. I have no chance at acquittal. You should prepare yourself for the worst.* Tears clouded her eyes. She pictured Henry sitting in his cell writing on this cheap paper, his handsome face bruised from several beatings. She could barely continue. *No matter what happens, I want you to keep fighting.* She slumped against the side of the warehouse. *No matter what happens, always remember the truth. Never lose sight of that. Always keep the truth alive. And always keep fighting, no matter how hard it gets.*

She knew she was never going to see Henry again. She had a sudden memory of him as a boy riding their father's bike, a bike far too big for him, but Henry managed to ride it by pistoning his hips from one side of the crossbar to the other. A breeze snuck around the side of the warehouse and blew out her lighter. He had been determined to ride that big bike. She stumbled forward. She loved Henry. She loved his determination. She wasn't sure she had the same determination. Without him, she didn't know if she had the strength to keep fighting.

As Eric, the Cardinal, and Per headed southeast through the Restricted Zone, the sun beat down with blistering intensity. This was a far cry from the shady avenues of the Shrine. Eric wasn't used to this prolonged exposure. He was used to visiting shut-ins on back patios under the cooling boughs of chestnut trees, sipping lemonade and listening to old women in wheelchairs reminisce about their golden years. A few days ago Eric had been cowering under the onslaught of a vicious wind-driven rain. Now he prayed for rain. Since his hat had blown away, he now wore a white shirt wrapped around his head. He looked like the Sheikh of Araby. He was sore as could be from riding so far.

The heat hardly affected the Cardinal at all. He rode upright looking as if he enjoyed the discomfort.

Eric glanced at Per, dozing in his saddle. The man's stubbornness helped him defy gravity even when he was asleep.

Eric scanned the horizon. Over the last few hours the number of hills had diminished. Streams and creeks crisscrossed the land, small tributaries that led to the Missouri twenty miles north. At one of these creeks he saw three rattlesnakes basking in the sun down the bank a ways.

"Per, wake up," he said. "We've got another creek to ford."

The riverman jolted awake, looked around in a daze, and finally spied the snakes.

"I hate varmints," he muttered, "and rattlesnakes is the worst kind of varmints there is."

He then dug his heels into his mount's ribs and, heedless of the snakes, pushed right into the creek, looking wobbly but determined. Eric and the Cardinal glanced at each other and followed Per across the creek. The biggest diamondback shook its rattle, rankled by their intrusion, but settled down once they had passed.

Over the next hour they climbed a slow rise.

When they got to the top, Eric saw a wide valley below with thousands of bison grazing in it, so many bison that their shaggy brown coats as good as blocked out the land. A wide stream meandered through the center of the valley, and several of the buffalo were drinking from it.

"I never thought the herds got this big," said Eric.

"Whitefeather said they rut around this time of year," the Cardinal replied. "All the smaller herds come together into bigger ones. By this time next month, they'll break up again."

Per went from a doze to a dead faint, fell forward against his horse's mane, slid to the left, and plummeted to the ground, his shoulder kicking up a cloud of dust, his left foot still in its stirrup. A few of the nearer buffalo trotted away, spooked by Per's plunge.

Eric got off his horse and knelt beside the stricken man.

"I knew we should have lashed him," said Anders. "We were fools not to."

"He wouldn't let us," Eric pointed out.

Eric slapped Per lightly on the cheek to wake him up. Per opened his eyes, shook his head, then closed them again. Eric took out his water flask and dribbled some into the man's mouth. Anders dismounted, knelt beside the fallen man, and gingerly touched his shoulder.

"I sure hope he didn't break that collarbone," he said. "He went down awfully hard."

Eric pulled Per's foot out of the stirrup. "Per? Per, can you hear me?"

Per opened his eyes. "Of course I can hear you," he said. "I ain't deaf. I only been shot with a' arrow. Help me back up onto my horse. I must have dozed a spell."

They got him back onto his horse, but he was so faint he nearly fell off again. After six tries Eric concluded he was too weak to ride anymore.

"Maybe we should make camp here," said the Cardinal.

Eric looked around, wondering if this would be a good place to stop. A bleating came from the bison below, and Eric saw a cougar on a rock on the other side of the valley. The smell of bison chips filled the air.

"I wouldn't want to spend the night up here on this ridge," he said. "It's too exposed. And I have to admit, cougars make me antsy."

The Cardinal nodded. "They're territorial critters, that's for sure," he said. "Let's lash Per to his saddle and keep riding."

They tied some bedding onto the neck of Per's horse so the wounded man could lie against it comfortably.

"The horses are nearly spent," said Eric.

"We'll just ride until we're clear of that cougar," said Anders.

After lashing the riverman to his horse, they continued south, skirting the buffalo herd.

They rode until dusk. The Cardinal's Roman staff, fitted into a special mount on his horse, kept the Benefactors at bay. The land grew flatter and flatter. There were no roads, no towns, just mile after mile of virgin prairie wilderness. The sky was huge above them. Five or six antelope bounded past in the distance. The grass thinned, leaving patches of bare dirt. Stunted boxwood trees grew here and there.

They stopped just as the first stars appeared. They got Per settled on a bedroll and Eric built a fire. The Cardinal got out his hodoscope and stood it on its tripod. He swiveled the instrument to the southwest, then to the southeast, then angled it more steeply upward.

"See anything?" asked Eric.

The Cardinal nodded. "We've got a few F windows down that way," he said. "Above that line of hills to the south." He pulled back from the eyepiece and offered the hodoscope to Eric. "Have a look," he said.

Eric put his eye to the lens and saw a few small green pockets—F islands.

"How long before we get there?" he asked.

"Those hills are at least a day away," said Anders.

"So we might send our signal tomorrow night?" asked Eric. "If we reach them?"

"We might," said the Cardinal. "We'll head in that

direction. Any windows we find are going to be in that direction anyway. But that's going to be a long hard ride tomorrow, and who knows what kind of shape Per will be in? We'd better make sure we get good and rested up."

CHAPTER 23

Seven hundred Hortulani stood before Gallio in formation. Each held a *baculum*—a Roman fighting staff—sized by Gallio's armorer to fit their small bodies. Gallio lifted his own *baculum* and watched the Hortulani do the same thing—not in precise synchronization, but within three seconds of each other. After weeks of trying to train them, he found the improvement gratifying. Oppius Naevius looked on skeptically.

Gallio jabbed his staff into the ground at a forty-five-degree angle. The Hortulani jabbed their own *bacula* into the ground. How strange to raise an army again. He scanned his turquoise soldiers to make sure they had their weapons aimed high.

"*Mitto!*" he cried.

They fired. The blue cometlike ordnance arched over the ripening wheat and zeroed in on the far ridge, where it blew up a good number of cypress trees.

"*Aggredior!*" shouted Gallio.

The Hortulani broke rank and charged the ridge. While they lacked certain combat skills, running was their strong point. They ran faster and longer than any Roman alive, loped in long ostrichlike strides at high speed over the pasture toward the ridge. A grin came to Gallio's face as he watched them. They attacked the far ridge using their staffs as rifles, shooting at dummy soldiers made from burlap sacks stuffed with hay. They did their best, but more often than not they missed.

He turned to Naevius. "At least it's a start," he said.

"A start," Naevius echoed dubiously. "But now look—they're fighting each other again. I'm glad you're using nonlethal ordnance for practice. Otherwise we'd have a bloodbath."

Gallio's spirits sagged in disappointment. The Hortulani shot, missed, got in each other's way, and sure enough, began to fight among themselves. How were they going to defeat a Roman legion if they always ended up fighting one another? One Hortulani shot another in the rump. That one retaliated by shooting the offender in the foot. The other soldiers quickly took sides, and soon a squabbling civil war was under way up on the ridge. Sparks of nonlethal ordnance flew every which way. The sound of squawking rose above the hissing of *bacula*. A pink Hortulani shot a turquoise one in the knee. The turquoise one responded by flinging dirt in his attacker's face. The fracas intensified. One fellow was thrown into a tree. From there, the situation degenerated into a free-for-all. Hortulani zapped Hortulani. Why did they have to have such nasty little tempers?

"For the love of Mars," groaned Gallio.

"They've lost sight of their objective," said Naevius, trying to be kind. "It's a good thing your old army

gathers in the hills, because I don't think these Hortulani will be much good against Roman forces."

"Desino mitto!" roared Gallio *"Desino mitto!"*

But the Hortulani shot and squawked in angry self-
absorption, heedless of his command.

A *caelum penna* descended from the sky. The
small aircraft angled down for a landing on the estate road. Lurio, thought Gallio, returning from the
capital. Just what he needed. He threw up his hands
in exasperation.

"Naevius," he said, "break it up. I have to greet
Lurio."

"As you wish, General," said Naevius. "But if any
of them peck me, I'll throttle them. You have my
word on it."

"Just put a stop to it."

Naevius climbed the ridge, looking reluctant to go
anywhere near the melee.

Gallio cantered over to the road.

The *caelum penna* was sleek, black, and shaped like
a large boomerang. Heat rose from its afterburners in
transparent ripples. Its nose cone was splattered with
what looked like rotten vegetables. The red eagle of
the Roman Army was emblazoned on its wings.

Gallio got down from his horse and gave the animal
a pat—his stallion wasn't used to such a large, loud
machine on the estate road. Gallio walked over to
the aircraft.

Gaius Lurio stepped down from the *caelum penna*
in full battle regalia: brass breastplate sculpted with
exaggerated chest muscles, a leather skirt, and heavy
leather boots rising almost to his bare knees. Gallio

raised his hand in greeting. The setting sun caught Lurio's golden hair with glancing blows of orange paint. Lurio waved back and descended the steps.

"I'm coming from the capital, *amicus*," he called. "And I bring news." The embarrassing display of bad temper on the ridge caught Lurio's attention. He gazed at the fighting Hortulani in perplexity. "Why are those Hortulani fighting each other?" he asked. "And who gave them *bacula*?"

What spin to put on this unwanted discovery? "I'm trying to train them to fight like a legion," said Gallio.

A crease came to Lurio's impressively broad forehead. "Why?" he said.

"The Province of Umbraculum swears allegiance to Rome," said Gallio, lying uneasily to his old friend, not certain that Lurio was fooled. "I'm training them to fight side by side with the Roman Army against the rebel Hortulani."

Lurio's rosebud lips pursed doubtfully. Up on the ridge, Naevius pulled Hortulani apart by the scruffs of their necks, a bear among hens.

"Rome commends their loyalty, if not their skill," Lurio said at last.

"What news from the capital?" asked Gallio, quickly changing the subject.

Lurio's face grew solemn. "Two thousand Roman troops dead."

Gallio's eyes widened. "How?"

"Their foodstuffs were poisoned by a microscopic plant that grew its way into the protected area." Lurio shook his head. "Not only that, but the general strike spreads. None of the Hortulani will work anymore.

When we force them to work, they die. It's a most perplexing problem. The Senate's baffled. The liberals think we should leave Hortus, abandon it. The hard-liners want genocide. Two thousand Roman soldiers, after all. Caesar tires of the debate. He says if the Hortulani are of no economic value as a labor force, then Hortus itself must be appropriated and its proper development left in Roman hands. That means the *legio exstirpatio*. I'm afraid the Emperor sides with the hard-liners."

Gallio stared at the ridge. He thought of Caesar, *the* Caesar, preserved these two millennia in a contrivance stolen from the *Patroni,* a resurrectorium. Caesar was one of the Immortals, a dead man eternalized in a biomagnetic medium, nothing more than an image in a mother-of-pearl portal. He knew Caesar's way. Let the Senate argue all they liked, but when it came time to make a final decision, the great Gaius Julius would be the one to make it. What Caesar wanted, Caesar got, and if Caesar thought Hortus must be appro-priated, then that meant the end of the Hortulani.

"I hardly think the death of two thousand Roman soldiers warrants the extermination of an entire race," he said.

Lurio frowned. "I'm surprised at you, Gallio. In Caesar's view, the death of even one Roman soldier warrants the extermination of an entire race."

As they rode across the prairie the next day, Eric's whole body ached from the long trek. He had terrible saddle sores, his face and hands were sunburned, and the dry wind gave him a thirst he couldn't quench.

The grass got thinner and shorter as they drew closer to the distant line of hills. Old buffalo chips littered the ground.

Eric glanced at Per as they rode along. The riverman hung limply over the back of his horse's neck.

"He doesn't look so good," Eric said. "I think we should take another look at his wounds."

"Let's ride over to those trees," said Anders. "We'll be out of the sun."

They rode to the trees—nine thirsty poplars—and eased the unconscious Per off the back of his horse to the ground. Eric peeled the dressing away from Per's abdomen. A foul smell rose from the wound, and pus oozed from underneath the edges of the ragged scab. Eric shook his head.

"It's infected," he said. Eric couldn't count the number of people he'd said the Last Rites over because of an infected wound. He hoped that someday doctors would find a way to ward off infection. "Let's roll him over and take a look at his back."

The entry wound on Per's back looked a lot worse than the exit wound. Eric expressed an ounce of pus before it finally stopped oozing.

"Hand me that rubbing alcohol," he said.

He used the alcohol to swab the wounds. The entry wound started to bleed again. The flies swarmed and Eric kept swatting them away. He shook his head.

"I don't know," he said.

"Let's get him patched up," said the Cardinal. "We have to make those hills by nightfall."

The hills turned out to be a lot farther away than they looked. The men didn't reach the summit of the tallest until well after sunset. They were both tired, dirty, and thirsty, and their horses were spent. A small spring bubbled from the base of the hill. The men and horses drank greedily.

Eric and the Cardinal made Per comfortable.

It got dark soon after.

The Cardinal took out his hodoscope and scanned the sky for F windows.

"I see a few big ones overhead," he said. "We might as well get things ready."

The antenna design was simple, the aluminum gridwork quick to put together, with the lengths tooled at the ends to take bolts with wing nuts. Eric fashoined rectangles from the lengths, then joined the rectangles together. Over the next hour, he and the Cardinal got the whole thing done, a four by nine by eighteen aluminum oblong that looked like the frame of a giant box kite. They placed the structure on two rubber mounts and anchored these mounts to some large rocks so the antenna wouldn't blow away.

Once the antenna was erected, they wired it back to the harmonic filter—the nexus between the radio and the aluminum gridwork. They hammered the smaller crates into a larger one and constructed the radio inside this larger crate. Eric worked on the transmit strain while the Cardinal worked on the receiving strain.

Eric started at the harmonic filter, worked his way back to the power amplifier, then to the driver, and then to the buffer.

"How's this?" he asked. "Does this look okay so far?"

Anders glanced over. "That's fine. Just follow the block diagram and you should be okay."

They used their flashlights to work well into the night. The Cardinal's skill was impressive to behold. Eric connected the buffer to the transmit filter, then to the transmit mixer. He worked his way down the strain, slotting the various components into their braces until he at last wired the whole strain to the microphone.

"What do you want me to do now?" he asked.

"Why don't you see how Per's doing?" the Cardinal answered. "I'll work on the internal strain, get the transmit and RF mixers hooked up. That's a one-man job anyway."

"Okay."

Heat came off the riverman in waves. When Per opened his eyes, Eric could see that he was delirious. Eric unscrewed his water flask and dribbled a bit into Per's mouth. The water flowed around the man's lips, across his cheek, and down his neck. Eric wet a cloth and laid it on Per's forehead. He wondered if he might feed the man some biscuit, but decided against it. He was in no condition to eat.

Anders finished the internal strain a little after ten.

"We're almost done," he said. "Let's lift the car batteries over."

They set the batteries on a plank and wired them to the radio. Anders knelt by the radio and pushed a lever forward. The whole apparatus hummed.

"Let's see if we're receiving anything," he said.

The speaker crackled.

All Eric heard at first was static. Anders turned the dial. Under the radio static, Eric now heard some high-pitched feedback. The feedback whistled, dipped, and rose. For the next fifteen minutes all he heard

was feedback and static. But then he heard a faint
human voice.

"Do you hear that?" asked Anders.

Eric nodded.

"Go shift the antenna a bit," said Anders. "I'm
going to turn on the bleed-off box on to get rid of
any extraneous signal."

Eric walked to the antenna and dragged the aluminum frame partway up the hill. "How's that?" he
called.

Anders, bent intently over the speaker, raised his
hand. "That's it," he said. "That's it."

Eric tied the antenna off to some rocks, then came
back and listened. Through the thick static he heard
the voice again. Anders fiddled with the dial on the
bleed-off box and purified the signal. *"Me ipsum
Romae pignero."* The beautifully pronounced Latin,
spoken by the voice of a man who had never seen the
Earth, resonated like a song in Eric's ears. *"Vos qui
pignus meus auditis, provocationem respondete."* Eric
and the Cardinal looked at each other. *"Tum praemia
et opulentias Romae metetis."* The Cardinal's lips
parted in a triumphant smile. Eric smiled back. This
was vindication, he thought.

"So should we send our own signal?" he asked.

The Cardinal's smile diminished but didn't disappear.

"I'm not convinced that the ions are stable enough
to propagate a signal over all that great distance," he
said. "Plus I want to get some Doppler readings on
the frequency we're receiving. It's going to take a lot
of battery power to send our signal, and we want to
make sure we have a sure shot before we go ahead."
He gestured at the sky. "These F windows the Bene-

factors have—the ions per cubic meter rise and fall, rise and fall. Right now my hodoscope tells me we have about ten to the ninth. I'm hoping that we're heading toward a peak, and that maybe by tomorrow we'll be up to ten to the tenth, and ready to give it an hour-long burst at a hundred megahertz."

"Do you think the Roman beacon will be optimally positioned by tomorrow night?" asked Eric.

"I hope so," said the Cardinal. "I'll take some Doppler readings to get more accurate estimates. If these ions firm up a bit by tomorrow night, we should go ahead."

June didn't have the money to pay for a bus or a taxi out to West Shelby, so she rode her bike. The Nordstrums' white bungalow came into view. Compared to the Manse, it was a hovel. She headed up the muddy drive, her legs trembling from the long ride. Ingrid came out onto the front porch, looking pale and tired.

June got off her bicycle and leaned it against the willow tree.

"You look hot and thirsty, dear," said Ingrid. "Why don't you come in and have some lemonade? I've just made a fresh batch. With real lemons."

"Thanks, Ingrid," she said.

She climbed the porch steps and followed Ingrid inside. The house smelled musty. "So I take it you've heard?" asked June.

They entered the kitchen. "Heard what?" said Ingrid.

"Henrik Rydberg says he saw Eric traveling in a

barge into the Restricted Zone with the Cardinal and two other men."

Ingrid's face settled. "I heard," she said, obviously annoyed by Henrik's blabbermouth ways.

She took the lemonade out of the fridge, put it on the table, and got some glasses from the cupboard. The corners of her mouth sank. She looked old, as if the last couple of months had aged her. As she poured lemonade into the glasses, June couldn't help noticing that the backs of her hands were sunburned.

"Sit down, June" said Ingrid.

June sat down. "I just want you to know that I'm sorry about Neil, Ingrid," she said. "I couldn't go ahead with it. I hope we can still be friends."

Ingrid's face softened. "We'll always be friends, dear," she said. Her blue eyes were focused, and it was as if she were searching for something inside June, a special understanding, a certain willingness. "Neil's not Neil anymore, is he, June?" she said. "I think you have a right to know that more than anybody."

June wasn't sure what she meant. "He's changed a good deal," she said.

"That's not what I meant, dear," she said. "He's *really* not Neil." Ingrid sketched it in for her, the whole harrowing story. "So when I say Neil isn't Neil anymore, I really mean it."

June sat still for a long time. Grief settled around her like a black fog.

Ingrid said, "I would sometimes smell that electrical smell whenever he was around," and June now remembered that time out at the buoy, that same smell coming out of nowhere, without a Benefactor in sight.

"What Eric's doing is a brave thing, and I wish Henrik Rydberg would just keep his big mouth shut about it."

June was only half listening. She was distraught. She didn't want to believe that Neil wasn't Neil anymore, or that he was actually gone for good. She loved the old Neil so much.

"Henrik Rydberg's reported it to the police," she said.

"Oh, dear," said Ingrid.

When June finally left, tears filled her eyes. She waved as she rode down the drive, but turned quickly away because she didn't want Ingrid to see her cry. She pedaled—in anger, and in heartbreak—faster and faster, as if by riding at break-neck speed she might escape the awful desolation that filled her soul. She thought of the slight, sensitive boy with the curly blond hair and happy blue eyes she had once loved. Faster and faster she rode. He was lost. Gone forever.

She hit a pothole, lost control of the bike, and fell, scraping her knee.

"Ow," she groaned. "Ow, ow, ow!"

She extricated herself from the tangle of bars, stood up, pulled her dress aside, and examined her knee. Blood beaded up through a smear of dirt. She wiped her tears away, but they came back faster than ever, not because her knee hurt but because her heart hurt. She might have given her engagement ring back to Neil, but she had never stopped hoping. Now she knew there was no point in hoping ever again.

CHAPTER 24

The Cardinal took his Doppler readings over the next several hours. Eric climbed some rocks to keep a lookout for Kiowa, taking his Remington with him. He was nervous about the horses again. Five horses made an easy trail for experienced Kiowa trackers, and if any horse thieves planned to steal their animals, they would probably try at night.

He scanned the valley to the southwest. The moon rose three-quarters full and lit the prairie with a silvery light. Patches of sage cast blue shadows over the ground. All was dark. All was peaceful.

But then, out in the prairie, firelight caught his eye. He grew still. A grass fire set by lightning? A campfire? A fire built by the Kiowa? He calculated distance. About a mile away. Out of rifle range. He cupped his hands to his ears and listened. The wind shifted. He heard a woman crying for help, plaintive and repeated, rising and falling, at times distinct, at times muffled by the sound of the wind. If only he could see better.

He went back to get his field glasses.

"We've got neighbors," he told Anders.

Anders turned from his measurements. "Coming this way?" he asked.

"No," said Eric. "They're camped about a mile off." He took his field glasses from his saddlebag. "They're sitting around a campfire. I heard a woman screaming. You better have a look."

The two men climbed the rocks.

Eric looked through the field glasses. He still couldn't see much, but at least could make a rough head count. Eighteen. Some sitting in a group off to one side, some standing around the fire, a lone individual far to the left by a tree. Eric counted three horses and two deer mules. The woman cried out again. The Cardinal shook his head.

"We've got to leave it alone, Eric," he said. "I can see what you're thinking, but we can't jeopardize what we're doing by interfering in something that's none of our business."

"Can't you hear that woman?" asked Eric.

A flicker of doubt crossed the Cardinal's face. "Do you have any idea how many people have died for this?" He motioned to the radio. "This one small chance to rid the world of the Benefactors?" He gestured toward the distant campfire. "We can't get involved in something like this. We could wind up dead. We could wind up losing the only chance we have."

"But that sounds like torture down there to me, Magnus," he said. "You heard Whitefeather. The Kiowa skin people alive. Maybe that's what they're doing to that woman right now. We can't stand by and let that happen without trying to do something about it."

"There's too much at stake," said the Cardinal. "We've got to send that signal."

Eric's brow furrowed in a perplexed frown. He knew his conscience wouldn't let him rest until he did something about those screams down there. Yet Anders was right. Things could go bad if they investigated.

"I'm going in for a closer look," he said. "At least I can do that." He gripped his Remington and checked his pocket to make sure he had plenty of bullets. "You can stay here and look after Per."

The Cardinal's eyes narrowed. He ripped a stalk of grass from the ground, crumpled it, and tossed it away.

"I'm coming with you," he said.

The Cardinal got his rifle and came back up the hill.

"Let's go," he said.

The southwest side of the hill was a lot steeper than the northeast side. Sometimes they had to turn around, grip the rock face, and descend it like a ladder.

Once at the foot of the hill, the distant campfire disappeared behind a succession of rises and dips. Eric couldn't hear the woman screaming anymore. He wondered if they might have killed her already. He and the Cardinal worked their way through the grass and sage, keeping close watch for any Kiowa scouts who might be standing guard out here in the dark. The crickets sang in the night air. He and Anders traversed a dry wash. An old badger lumbered by.

The land climbed gently as they approached the Kiowa. They got on their hands and knees and crawled to the top of the last rise. As they reached the crest, they saw the Kiowa and what turned out to be a number of prisoners. The prisoners were mostly clay-bred, seven women and two men. Eric, remembering that night in Cyrus-of-Jerusalem Square, was again unnerved by their appearance. Their faces were so white they could have been covered in flour. They wore standard clay-bred tunics—burlap sacks with the cross and orbis stenciled in red both front and back. They sat on the ground tied together. The lone figure by the tree turned out to be a boy of twelve or thirteen, an Indian but not Kiowa. He was tied to the tree.

Eight Kiowa braves raped a clay-bred woman. She was down on all fours, her tunic pushed up around her hips while one of the braves knelt naked behind her. No sooner had this brave finished than another one started.

Eric lifted his rifle and took aim. Anders reached out to stop him.

"Are you crazy?" he said. "There's eight of them and two of us. If we're going to do this right, we've got to make a plan. We can't just start shooting. We might get a few, but then the others would take cover and hunt us down. And what would that accomplish? I say we wait. I say we choose our time. I hate what's happening down there as much as you do, Eric. But we should at least wait until they're asleep. Or maybe even wait until tomorrow night. We should pick a time when we're sure we can get all of them."

Eric hesitated. He could see that two braves stood guard just beyond the glow of the campfire. The Cardinal was right. If they attacked right now with guns blazing, they wouldn't stand a chance. Better to come up with a plan first.

He bowed his head and got up.

"Let's go," he said. "I don't want to hear any more of this than I have to. At least not until I can do something about it."

"Do you want a soda?" asked Hesperus. "I feel like a cherry soda. I bet you want a orange crush. It's a hot day. A soda would be nice."

But it was as if June hadn't heard. Her lips were set in a thin line. She looked angry about something. He was so happy to be with her again, he could hardly control his joy.

"Did you read the paper this morning?" she asked. "The Holy League made a flanking maneuver through Reims four days ago and cut the Wehrmacht's supply lines in Belgium. It looks like the Admiral's going to be pushed out of Paris. It looks like the Vatican is going to occupy Paris again. I bet you're happy about that. I bet you're ecstatic."

He looked at her in perplexity. "Of course I am," he said. "Aren't you?"

She had nothing to say to that. He tried to probe her—as he had probed the minds of mortals five hundred years ago—but he no longer had the power, and her mind remained closed to inspection. He didn't have to read it. He knew she was a traitor, but he loved her anyway. He knew she was seeing some man named Mickey, but that didn't diminish his adoration in the least.

"Are we going for a soda or not?" he asked.

"I'm going out to Rowatt," she said. "I want to see the Fence."

His eyebrows rose. "The Fence? What for?"

"Because I want to," she said, her voice like a snarl.

The logical patterns of quantum physical reaction as a mode of intellectual exchange, such as they existed in the superheated temperatures of Heaven, had no place in a world as illogical as this one, he decided. An ant will go one way, then another, then another, and who knew why it went where it went? That was the way things worked here.

They got on the bus to Rowatt, a desolate grain-elevator town on the edge of the Territory next to the Restricted Zone. She got off and walked down the road to the Fence. She walked fast. He chased her, unable to resist.

At the Fence she turned around. She draped her elbows over the top rail. "Have you ever wondered what's out there?" she asked.

She was sly. She was sexy. He glanced beyond her shoulder into the Restricted Zone.

"June, why are you being like this?" he asked.

"You're a Seminarian," she said. "I bet you know what's out there."

"I know a bit, but I—"

"I want to find out."

She was up and over the Fence before he could do anything to stop her. What was she trying to prove? His brethren would be on her in seconds.

No sooner had she taken a few strides into the Restricted Zone than he saw nine of them shoot out of the hot, hazy distance. They came right at her. He knew they would kill her if he didn't do something about it. He had to save her.

He leapt over the Fence. The nine members of the Host rocketed up the hill and circled June. She stared at them, her eyes wide, her fingers splayed, her skinny frame braced. The wind of the Host tossed her skirt. She raised her palms to her temples and winced in pain. He knew they had her. She turned to him, a look of terror in her eyes.

"Help me!" she cried.

He had to help her.

He lifted his hand. With a suddenness that cracked the air, electrons jumped from the intervening oxygen molecules, the air bristled with electricity, and his direct, withering communication pierced the nine spheres like a cry from Woden himself, rendering, through the arcane language of negative and positive charges, a thunderclap of a command. His brethren recoiled, grew disoriented, twirled and spun. Three of them tumbled into the dirt. The other six jumped back, overwhelmed by the strength of the command.

They all retreated into the misty distance.

June stood there staring at him. He wasn't sure of the expression on her face. Shock? Resignation? Grief? She took a few steps toward him, stopped, leaned forward, still looking dazed from the attack, and peered at him more closely.

"It's true, then," she said.

She backed away, looking afraid that he might pounce.

"What's true?" he asked.

"You're one of them."

His eyes widened. How could she know this? He took a few steps toward her.

"June . . . please, I . . ."

"Stay away from me!"

She lifted a clump of dirt, and flung it at him. The move surprised him. It was such a girlish thing to do.

A clump of dirt. He found it touching, mortifying, heartrending, pathetic, heroic . . . and as puzzling as everything else humans did. What was a clump of dirt going to do to the great and powerful Hesperus, the Benefactor who had killed five thousand Assyrians all by himself, who had laid waste to Damascus, and who had sunk the Adriatic Fleet of the Roman Navy two thousand years ago? Yet because June had been the one to throw it, the clump of dirt hurt like nothing else ever had.

She continued to back away. She climbed the Fence back into Rowatt's town limits. He watched her go. He wanted her more than ever but he knew he had to let her go. He would just have to wait—wait until he could somehow make her understand just how much he loved her.

CHAPTER 25

The wind started early the next day, a stiff westerly gale lifting the parched earth into the air and turning the sky brown. Eric couldn't see more than five yards ahead of him. He had no idea if the Kiowa braves were still down in the valley or not. He and Anders covered the radio equipment with a white canvas sheet.

"Grab that end and stake it down," said the Cardinal.

Eric pounded the stake in with a rock, squinting against the airborne dirt. They had Per bundled on the ground; he was restless, and squirmed on his bedroll, half conscious. The wind howled around the hills.

"Do you get these dust storms much?" asked the Cardinal.

"Every now and again," said Eric.

"How long do they last?"

"It should calm down by this afternoon."

"Because all this dust is going to affect our radio signal," said Anders. "I think we better postpone till tomorrow. But tomorrow's our last chance one way or the other. Any later and we'll miss the beacon."

They finished staking the canvas sheet over the equipment. They then erected the tent, which they hadn't bothered with until now because the weather had been so clear.

"Let's get Per inside," said Eric. "He doesn't look too good."

After they dragged the wounded man into the tent, Eric wiped the dust off Per's face with a damp cloth and gave him some water, but the water merely dribbled off his lips. His breath came and went in gasps, and he had a raging fever. Eric pulled aside the dressing on Per's abdomen and saw that some of the skin had turned gangrenous.

"That's bad," he told the Cardinal. Eric recognized all the signs and symptoms. The man was dying. "I guess I'll sit here with him," he said. "There's not much else we can do."

"I'm nervous about that wind," said the Cardinal. "I'm going outside to see if I can put more rocks around the antenna. I don't want it to blow away."

Eric sat with Per. After a while, Per opened his eyes. For a moment he seemed lucid. He reached up weakly and touched the back of Eric's hand. But then his eyes glazed over again, so bloodshot they looked like burning coals. The riverman was nothing more than a quivering mass of flesh at war with a billion bacteria. His body sagged in a sudden fainting spell. Per's left arm came up, and his hand formed into a rigid claw. His chin thrust forward as if jolted by electricity, his back arched, and he stayed that way, in that horrible pose, for a second or two, then went limp.

He breathed no more.

Eric realized he was dead. Just like that. How sudden the good Lord God could sometimes be. Dead. Heart attack, most likely. People got sick from an infection like this, and sooner or later their hearts gave out.

The Cardinal came back in. "She's tied down good and tight now," he said. "She won't blow away no matter how strong that wind gets."

"Per's dead," said Eric.

The Cardinal grew still. He came closer and took a look. Per's eyes were slightly open. The red dust of the plains clung to his sweat-soaked hair.

"He was a good riverman," said Anders.

"I think you should give him the Last Rites," said Eric. "I've been excommunicated. You outrank me. You're a Cardinal, and I'm just a layman now."

The Cardinal looked out the tent flap where the horses huddled together beside some scrubby white pine.

"I'm not a Cardinal," he said. "I'm not even a member of the clergy, Eric. I never was. This was all just . . . arranged. By those fellows in Europe. I'm here for one purpose. To finish off the Benefactors. You say the Last Rites. I'll dig the grave." The Cardinal's eyes narrowed. "I've dug enough of them."

Eric didn't think any less of Anders, whoever he might be, for impersonating a clergyman. Anders was a moral man, a certain man, a strong believer in what he was doing. He could forgive this man his masquerade.

The ground proved rocky up on the hill, and the digging went slowly. By three o'clock Anders had carved out no more than a shallow grave. They decided it would have to do. They carried Per's body out of the tent and put it in the grave. The wind was dying. The sun could now be seen as a murky copper disk in the brown sky. Eric stooped, picked up a handful of dirt, and stood over the grave.

"May Christ who was crucified and died for our sake deliver you, our brother Per, from eternal death," he said. "May He set you down in the fresh beauty of His paradise and may He, the Good Shepherd, claim you as one of His flock. May He forgive you all your sins and grant you a place among the Saints at His own right hand. There may you ever behold your Redeemer face-to-face." Eric knelt, made the cross and orbis on Per's body by letting the dirt flow in a steady stream from his opened hand. "In the name of the Father, and of the Son, and of the—" He hesitated. The last part was no longer right because it had to do with the Benefactors. But he didn't know how to change it, so went ahead and said it anyway. "And of the Heavenly Host. Amen."

"Amen," responded Anders.

They pushed earth over Per and tamped it down hard so the varmints wouldn't dig him out. As a great hater of varmints, that was the last thing Eric knew Per would want.

The wind stopped around five. Sunset was at seven. The atmosphere, still heavy with dirt, distorted the sun, flattened it top and bottom, painted it an angry pink.

Eric and Anders climbed the rocks and looked down into the valley to see if the Kiowa were still there. When Eric held the field glasses to his eyes, he saw twice as many Kiowa braves there as before. Some trading was going on. The new Kiowa unloaded crates from their mules. A corpse lay to one side. Eric handed the field glasses to Anders.

"I think they killed that woman," he said. "She's lying there at the edge of the campsite."

Anders looked through the field glasses and said, "She's dead, all right. They still have the Indian boy tied to the tree. He's sitting down now. Poor little fellow looks worn out."

After forty-five minutes, the new Kiowa moved off, taking eight of the clay-bred with them, leaving only one clay-bred woman and the Indian boy behind.

"Looks like they traded those clay-bred for liquor," said Anders. "They're taking bottles out of those crates and drinking."

Eric and Anders watched for another hour. The Kiowa braves showed no sign of moving on. The sun dipped behind the horizon and the first stars came out. The braves didn't seem interested in raping the last clay-bred woman. Eric and Anders stopped watching for a while and worked on receiving another signal from the Romans.

Anders checked the previous night's F window.

"It's still there," he said, "and it's big." He double-checked the hodoscope. "We've definitely got a reading of ten-to-the-tenth ions per cubic meter." He looked up from the eyepiece. "But all this dust still worries me."

And indeed, the dust proved to be an obstacle, its ferrous content fracturing the incoming signal, acting, in its way, like the artificially created magnetic storms the Benefactors had installed above the settled areas. Yet at times the signal was crisp. *"Me ipsum Romae pignero."* At times Eric could hear it as clearly as the wind chimes on the back porch of the Manse on a breezy day. *"Tum praemia et opulentias Romae metetis."* At times it was as strong as the organ at church on Sunday morning. *"Vos qui pignus meus auditis . . ."* At times Eric had to look up at the stars and wonder how such a fragile message could come so far.

They were just debating whether to transmit or not when the screaming started again. They looked at each other. Eric couldn't let it happen again.

"We've got to go," he said.

They left the radio and climbed the rocks, taking their rifles with them.

They crouched, and looked into the valley.

The Indians were having their way with the remaining woman. Their violations made Eric's blood rise and he wanted to go down there and shoot every last one of them. He didn't care if she were clay-bred or not, she was still a woman. If he didn't do something to stop it she might end up dead like that other woman.

He stood up and slung his rifle over his shoulder.

"I'm going," he said.

Anders stood up. "Hang on a minute, Eric," he said. "Don't get yourself so riled. Think it through first." More screams drifted up the hill. "I've been piecing a plan together all day. We've got to set up a distraction. Whitefeather told me these Kiowa are superstitious. We've got to do something that might spook them. Wouldn't it be better to get them all scared first?" Eric decided to hear Anders out. "I've been thinking about their superstitions—their beliefs in dead ancestors and so forth—and how we might turn that against them."

"I'm listening," said Eric.

"We dig Per up," said Anders.

"What?" said Eric, alarmed.

"That's right. We dig Per up. We dig him up, stick him on a horse, and send him riding into their camp. He'll be all covered with dirt. They'll think he's just risen from the grave. It'll scare the living daylights out of them. While they're all scared, we pick them off at long range one by one. Get as many as we can that way, then go in and finish off whoever's left. They've been drinking liquor. They'll be running all over the place. We'll have decent cover. They won't even see us."

Eric had to admit it sounded like a good plan.

He could almost hear Per's words: *I might be dead, but that don't mean I can't rescue that clay-bred girl better than either of you two ladies can.*

They dug Per up.

He was a grisly sight, with dirt caked everywhere, putrefaction setting in, and a smell coming from him that made Eric gag. They got him on a horse—no easy task because his body was in rigor mortis. They practically had to break his legs to get his feet into the stirrups. Yet the advantages of rigor mortis outweighed its drawbacks for their purposes. Because Per was so stiff, he sat upright in the saddle, creating a more ghostlike effect. They strapped his thighs to the horse, tied the reins to his hands, and led him down the southwest side of the hill under cover of darkness.

They approached the Kiowa camp.

The Indians were still raping the woman. Eric glanced at Anders. Anders's face was set. He looked ready to punish those Indian's badly.

"Let's send old Per in," he said.

Eric gave the horse's rump a whack and the animal trotted into the camp. The braves stopped raping the woman, startled by the dead riverman. They got up and took defensive positions. Two of them actually ran toward Per, under the impression he was simply a normal living intruder. But when they realized he was in fact dead, they cowered and backed away.

The other Kiowa yelled to each other, panicked. The woman fell to her side, weeping weakly. The Indians moved away from Per, keeping their distance, scared, in no shape to fight.

Eric, lying on his stomach, brought his Remington up, aimed, and fired. A Kiowa brave dropped dead. The shot terrified the remaining braves and they scattered. Anders aimed his Winchester and nabbed one in the leg. The brave went down, wounded but not dead. Eric finished him off with righteous wrath. He found three other Indians and killed them as well. The three left alive ran for their horses. Anders fired and got one of them in the back. The woman was sitting up now, looking scared. Eric got to his feet, took careful aim at one of the two retreating Indians, and picked him off. The last Kiowa leapt for his horse— Eric had never seen anyone fly through the air like that before—and landed with consummate skill astride his feru, then he bolted into the night. Eric fired, but the Kiowa was too far away and he missed.

"That's bad luck," Anders said. "He seemed to be the ringleader,"

"He's too far away now," said Eric. "We'd never get him unless we rode after him."

Anders shrugged. "Well . . . I'm going to try. I can't ride more than a mile or two before the Roman staff won't cover me, but I might as well give it a shot. You see to the woman and the boy."

Eric strode into the camp. The clay-bred woman, still cowering on the ground, saw him coming with his rifle and backed away, scuttling on her rump toward the campfire. Now that he had a closer look, he could see a stream running through the camp. Probably if he followed this stream north, he would find the Missouri. Per's horse stood next to the stream drinking, Per sitting stiffly on top. Eric slung his rifle by its leather strap onto his shoulder and raised his hands as he approached the woman.

"Don't be scared," he told her.

She stared at him, her eyes wide, colorless disks, her skin nearly white except for some red peeling, no tan, her hair blond-white. She was pretty in a doll-like way. Her sun-bleached hair was cut in a ragged bang above her pale eyebrows. Her skin was the color of porcelain. Strange. Made her look otherworldly. He walked right up to her. She skidded another yard on her rump, pushing herself away with her feet, but then gave up. Tears streaked the dirt on her face. He stopped. He didn't get any closer. He squatted, gave her the smile he gave Sunday School children.

"Are you okay?" he asked.

She stared some more—stared in the way children stare, her nostrils moist with snot, her eyelashes congealed into distinct points from her tears. Stared at him like she didn't understand, or was too shy to speak, or was trying to figure out what was going on, her breath coming and going quickly.

"Well, are you?" he asked.

"Those Indians did bad things to me," she said, her voice catching. She spoke like a nine-year-old. "I thought they were going to kill me." She coughed a few times, wiped her nose with the back of her arm, then looked at him nervously. "Are you going to kill me?" she asked.

"No," he said. "I'm going to help you." He looked at the Indian boy. The boy stared at him with dark, blank eyes. "Who's the boy?" he asked.

She glanced at the boy as if surprised to find him still there. "That's Turnin' Bird," she said. "He's Cheyenne." She watched Turning Bird for a few oblivious moments. "We found him out here and we said he could come with us. He doesn't talk much, but he knows how to catch mice." She cast a nervous glance into the dark prairie. "We should go," she said. "Flyin' Horse is going to come back and kill us."

"What's your name, miss?"

"Moon."

"That's a pretty name," he said.

"I know," she answered.

He pointed to the prairie. "And that was Flying Horse? The one who got away?"

"That's him," she said.

In the distance he heard horses' hooves approaching. Moon turned in fright, her body tensing.

"Is that Flyin' Horse?" she asked.

Eric peered into the dark and saw the Cardinal coming back. "No," he said. "That's just my friend."

She stared apprehensively into the dark. "Are you sure?"

"You don't have to worry about Flying Horse anymore," he said. "We're not going to let him get you." He pointed to the Cardinal. "Me and my friend will protect you. His name is Magnus. My name is Eric."

She stared at Anders as if at any minute she expected him to turn into Flying Horse. "Flyin' Horse is still going to kill us," she said.

Anders rode into the circle of firelight. "I couldn't catch him," he said.

"Magnus, this is Moon."

Anders tipped his hat. "Howdy, Moon," he said. "Are you all right?"

Moon didn't say anything, simply stared. She began to shake.

"She's afraid that Indian's going to come back and kill her," explained Eric.

The Cardinal's brow settled. "I'd like to see him try," he said. "If he comes back here, Moon, we'll make him as dead as the rest of these Indians. You have our guarantee."

CHAPTER 26

Hesperus walked to the coffee counter in Falkberget's Five-and-Dime and sat down. He didn't see Amy Kristensen, but he sensed she was somewhere about. Maybe she was in the back doing dishes. He looked at the menu above the counter. Two slices of toast and a clay-bred egg for fifteen cents, a dime extra for a real egg. Lime soda five cents. A root beer float ten cents. And home-baked muffins twelve cents apiece. His stomach growled. The human appetite perplexed him. Back home, the self-sustaining energy of the place kept him going without the need for food. Here, in this body, he had to keep eating or he ran out of energy. He was hungry, yet he couldn't eat. He was too anxious. June knew he was Hesperus. And that made him so anxious, he felt sick.

Amy came out of the kitchen in a pink waitress dress and a white apron. She was tall, slim, attractive, with reddish hair, green eyes, and a pleasant smile. She wore red lipstick. She carried three clean coffeepots.

When she saw him, she stopped. Her smile vanished. Did Amy know too, then? She regained her composure, put the coffeepots on the counter, and came over. He looked down at her legs. She wore black nylon stockings. He remembered the stockings in the bathroom. His groin lurched. Neil's young body was too unruly, he decided. He didn't even love Amy, yet felt the need to couple with her.

"What do you want?" she asked.

He took a deep breath. "Did June tell you?" he asked.

She was chewing gum. Amy sometimes chewed the same piece of gum the whole day.

"I think you better go," said Amy.

"I want to see her again."

Some of the hardness disappeared from Amy's face. She knew, yet she still felt some compassion for him. Another perplexing human trait.

"Well . . . Neil . . . I would give up if I were you. There's nothing you can do now."

"Who's Mickey?" he asked.

Her brow creased. "You just stay away from Mickey. I don't want you hurting Mickey."

"But who is he?"

"He's just a farm boy who doesn't know when to quit. I guess that makes two of you."

"Is she seeing him?"

"I thought you could read minds," she said.

He looked away. "No," he said. "Not anymore."

She studied him. "I work two jobs," she said. "I hardly ever see her. If she's dating someone, I don't know about it."

"Is there any way you can help me?"

"If you were going to be so miserable, why did you

do this in the first place? Why didn't you just leave Neil alone?"

She had a point. Why live a human life when it had to be lived in heartache and misery?

"I think you better go . . . Neil," she said again. "Or whoever you are. I can't help you."

She walked away.

She was indeed right. Why bother with this masquerade when it was making him more lonely than ever? In fact, why bother with this grand plan to re-seed themselves at all when in re-seeding themselves they were only destroying themselves? He got up and left the diner. He wasn't snatching Neil away; Neil was snatching him away. He walked down the street. A dog trotted by and looked at him nervously. He wasn't fooling the dog. He shook his head. He kicked a tin can and it tumbled off the curb. The irony of the thing galled him. He had come to dominate. He had come to conquer. He had come to live. But none of those things had happened. All because Neil would have him, more so than he would ever have Neil.

"Moon wants us to move," said Eric as the sun went down the next day. "She still thinks Flying Horse is going to come back."

The sky was now clear, with no dust anywhere. Anders gazed through the hodoscope with a grin on his face.

"I've never seen such a big one," he said. He offered the instrument to Eric. "Have a look."

Eric placed his eye to the hodoscope. An F window floated like a gigantic green zeppelin a hundred miles up. The red needle at the side of the hodoscope indicated ten-to-the-ten electrons per cubic meter, perfect for the hundred megahertz transmission they planned to send.

"That looks just dandy, Magnus," he said, pulling away. "But Moon's real antsy. She's convinced Flying Horse is going to come back. She's afraid he's going to kill us. And she's especially afraid he's going to kill Turning Bird. If he kills Turning Bird, Turning Bird's father is going to be real mad at us. She says Turning Bird's father is a Cheyenne chief. She doesn't think it's a good idea to have a Cheyenne chief mad at us."

Anders glanced at Moon. "Talk to her," he said. "Calm her down. You have a way with her. She's been through a lot and naturally she's afraid. Explain to her that we're on high ground, that this hill is easily defensible, and that we're heavily armed. Tell her you're the best shot west of the Mississippi. Calm her down so she won't interfere with what we have to do."

Eric shrugged wearily. "I'll do what I can, Magnus," he said. "But it might be tricky."

Anders glanced at Turning Bird. "And see if you can get that boy to stop turning around like that. He's going to make himself sick."

Eric walked back to the campfire and sat down next to Moon. Now that she was cleaned up from a good splash in the creek, the cloned woman looked halfway pretty. He still couldn't get over it. Made, not born, with genetic material collected from the Potters' various blood drives through town and other parts.

"The Cardinal says you don't have to worry about Flying Horse," he told her. "We can defend this hill easily."

"He's going to come," she said.

To get her mind off Flying Horse, Eric tried the conversational approach.

"Who called you Moon, anyway?" he asked.

"I called myself Moon," she said.

"Why Moon?" he asked.

"Because I look like the Moon," she said, as if it were obvious. She cast an anxious glance toward Anders. He was testing the power in his car batteries with a voltmeter. "He's going to make us stay, isn't he? And then Flyin' Horse will come and kill us."

"Flying Horse isn't going to come and kill us," Eric said. "It's important we send this signal to the Romans tonight. We've got a big, stable window up there, and we've got to take advantage of it. If we don't send it tonight, we lose our chance."

She looked up at the sky. "I don't see no window," she said.

"It's a technical term," he said. "It's not a window in the usual sense." He stared at her, growing more and more curious about her. From infancy to adulthood in eighteen months. She was a full-grown adult woman, but she might not be any older than a child. "Do you have any idea how old you are?" he asked. Turning Bird spun around nearby, making himself dizzy. The boy was having so much fun Eric didn't have the heart to stop him. "I hear your kind grow up awfully fast in the Pottery."

"How old do I look?" she asked.

He looked her up and down. "Twenty-five, I guess," he said.

"I'm twelve," she said, as if proud of the fact.

Her girlish pride touched him. "Just twelve," he said. "And you know all those Indian languages already?" He'd learned she spoke seventeen Indian languages fluently. "You must be smart. I always thought clay-bred were supposed to be . . . you know . . . dumb."

"Not me," she said. "I'm smart. I can learn any language you want."

"Well . . . how did you learn all those Indian languages in the first place?" he asked, glad she wasn't talking about Flying Horse anymore.

Her lips pursed as she considered the question. "Most of 'em I learned from Coyote Paw," she said. "He was an old man I lived with for a while." Her eyes grew pensive. "He's dead now." She lifted a pebble and studied it. "The Kiowa burned him. Before Coyote Paw, I learned from the Ute. The Ute Indians looked after me when I shoveled salt for them. I listened to them all the time and after a while I knew what they were sayin'."

"You shoveled salt?" asked Eric.

"Up in the mountains," she said.

"There's mountains around here?" he asked.

"West of here," she said. "A lot further west. You'd have to walk all summer to get there. Mountains so high they got snow on 'em all year round."

He shook his head. Mountains. "And you shoveled salt out there?"

She nodded. "I don't know why they made us dig so much salt. My hands always got red from it. I'm glad I don't dig salt now. My hands feel a lot better these days."

"I'm glad you don't dig salt either," he said. "The Ute let you stop?"

She stared up the hill with large, colorless eyes.

"When the Ute told the Seminarians I learned their language, the Seminarians sent me north to live with the Caribou Eskimo. They wanted me to speak Eskimo. They had no one who could talk Eskimo for them. So I got to stop diggin' salt. I had to learn Eskimo instead. Eskimo was a hard one. It took me a whole month to learn." Odd that she should have such an exceptional aptitude for language, he thought. "I had to be the wife of one of those Eskimos. He shared me with his friends. I didn't like that. So I ran away. I walked for a year. I ate berries. I killed rabbits. Coyote Paw finally found me. He taught me the old tongues. He saw how smart I was. Too bad the Kiowa burned him." She glanced apprehensively into the valley. "We should go before Flyin' Horse gets here," she said. "He might decide to burn us. The Kiowa like to burn people." Moon cast an anxious glance at Turning Bird. "If Flyin' Horse burns Turnin' Bird, Lone Cloud will be mad at us."

Eric contemplated the Cheyenne boy. "Don't worry," he said. "We won't let his pa get mad at us." Turning Bird spun and spun until he fell down. Eric raised his eyebrows in mild surprise. "Why does Turning Bird always turn like that?" he asked. "Look at him. He's so dizzy he can't get up."

Moon looked at the boy. "He's trying to see his ancestors," she said. "He thinks if he gets dizzy enough, he'll see them. He's been turnin' around like that ever since he was a little boy. That's why they call him Turnin' Bird."

Eric studied the prostrate boy. He looked positively green. What kind of religion did this boy have, he wondered, that he would hope to see his ancestors by making himself dizzy? What gods did this boy worship? And were Turning Bird's gods any more legitimate than his own? Eric shook his head. For the first time in his life, he thought religion was more a creation of man than a creation of God.

The telegram sat on the kitchen table, soaked by her tears. It confirmed Henry's hour of death by hanging in New Amsterdam. She looked at it again—yellow, creased twice, with the bold black words "Western Union Telegraph" along the top. The crackdown was in full swing. Henry couldn't help her anymore. She had no one but herself to rely on. She was scared, but she could hardly feel her fear through her grief.

A knock at the door startled her. She dried her tears, then got up and opened the door.

Mickey Cunningham stood there with a wilted bouquet of daisies and black-eyed Susans. He had a nervous smile on his face, but when he saw she'd been crying, the smile disappeared and he looked at her with true concern.

"What's wrong?" he asked. "What's happened?"

"Henry's dead," she said. "They hanged him yesterday morning at six."

She took two shaky steps back to the table, collapsed in the chair, buried her face in her arms, and sobbed.

"June . . . June, I'm sorry," Mickey said, putting his hand on her shoulder. She opened her eyes, saw her tears pooling on the gray Formica table. "This crackdown," he said, "it's got us all plumb scared out of our wits." She struggled to control her weeping. "I was talking to some of the other members. We're thinking it might be a good idea to . . . to stop meetin' for a while. Until this crackdown blows over."

Yes, that was certainly a sensible idea. But she kept thinking of her brother's last letter. *Always keep fighting, no matter how hard it gets.* If she stopped fighting now, her brother's death would mean nothing. Also, she wanted to think the Odd Fellows had more backbone, that they wouldn't disband at the first sign of trouble. They couldn't stop now. The Benefactors were taking over the minds of young men—she knew that. She lifted her head from her arms and looked at Mickey.

"You can do whatever you like," she said. "But I'm going to keep fighting." She tapped the telegram on the table. "After what they did to Henry, I'm going to fight forever."

Mickey grew extremely still. "Honestly, June, I don't know what this world is comin' to," he said. He shoved the flowers at her. "These are for you. I was goin' to try romancin' you, now that you broke it off with Neil, but I guess now's not the time."

She took the limp, sweaty stems from him.

"Thank you, Mickey," she said.

"You got my chocolates okay?" he asked.

"I got them," she said. "Thank you."

He stood there a moment more. "I guess you don't feel any different about me yet, huh?"

"No, Mickey, I don't. Why don't you just give up?"

He shook his head miserably. "Because I can't give up, June," he said. "What I feel inside won't let me."

He left awkwardly and with a great many apologies,

his big ears turning red, his hands clutching his hat as he backed out.

When he was gone, June's throat tightened. She was touched by Mickey, by how he could be so devoted to her. How sad that she would never feel anything but a remote kindness toward him. But the world was a sad place: a place where brothers got hanged, where armies dropped superbombs, and where young men like Mickey suffered through unrequited love. A place where her fiancé could turn into a monster and where her brother could be hanged simply for telling the truth.

CHAPTER 27

Whitefeather walked into camp just as the first stars came out. He didn't say anything. He merely walked to the campfire, sat down, and helped himself to coffee, as if he had a perfect right to it. Eric wondered how he could have the gall.

"Where's Per?" asked Whitefeather. "Is he dead?"

"Yes," said Eric.

Anders came over from the radio equipment.

"I paid you a hundred dollars to be our guide," he said angrily, "and you ran off on us. You might as well leave. We don't need any more guiding now. We found what we're looking for."

"I tried to guide you," said Whitefeather "I told you not to bring those horses. You wouldn't listen, and look what happened. Per's dead. We could have walked to this place without horses. And Per would have been alive."

Anders frowned, sighed, then gestured at Moon.

"The young lady here says she thinks the Kiowa might come back any time," he said. "If you want to make yourself useful, go stand guard up in those rocks and let us know when you see them."

Whitefeather rose, picked up a rifle, and went to the rocks without another word. He seemed determined to mend his ways by taking guard duty uncomplainingly.

Eric and Magnus turned on the radio and soon received the Roman signal stronger than ever.

"I pledge myself to Rome, will support her, defend her, and fight for her."

Moon immediately perked up at the sound of a new language.

"You who hear my pledge, please respond to this call."

Turning Bird got to his feet, came over, and listened.

"For you will then reap the rewards and riches of Rome, and will gain everlasting life in the Hall of Immortals."

The tinny voice came from the small speaker. Turning Bird looked scared.

"What's got him so nervous?" Eric asked Moon.

Moon asked Turning Bird in Cheyenne why he was so nervous.

Eric listened to the boy's reply. Turning Bird's voice cracked on the cusp of adolescence. Moon turned to Eric and translated.

"He can hear a voice, but he can't see a body," she said. "He thinks it's a spirit voice."

"Tell him not to worry," said Anders. "It's only the voice of some old Roman." He looked up at the sky, where the moon rose over the eastern horizon. The stars looked like spilled salt on a black sheet. "It's time to send our signal," he said.

Anders was just tweaking the circuit on the transmit strain, engaging the oscillator and boosting the juice on the batteries, when Whitefeather came down the hill, followed by Flying Horse and four Kiowa braves. They looked amiable, like they wanted to talk. They walked right into camp. Because they were with Whitefeather, Eric thought maybe they wanted to trade, like they'd traded with those other Kiowa yesterday. His rifle was an uncomfortable distance away. He rose from his crouched position by the radio. Anders looked over his shoulder. Whitefeather was smiling in a trustworthy way. Eric would have thought he'd be mortally afraid of the Kiowa because he was Osage. But he wasn't. Anders stood up. Eric took a few steps toward his rifle. Whitefeather's face drooped. And Eric knew they were in serious trouble.

The Kiowa attacked.

Flying Horse raised his spear and flung it at Anders. The spear thudded into Anders's chest and sank six inches deep. Anders's eyes opened wide. He looked at the spear, clutched it, stumbled back, then fell on top of the radio. The spear slid out under its own weight. The Cardinal took a last few spluttering breaths, looked at Eric with imploring eyes, then went limp, life slipping quickly away from his body.

After that things happened quickly. Moon grabbed Turning Bird by the hand and ran away into the darkness. Flying Horse went over to the horses and unhitched them from the tree. Whitefeather helped Flying Horse. Eric made a try for his rifle but before he could reach it, a brave struck him on the head with a tomahawk and he fell facefirst, unconscious, into the fire.

*   *   *

When he finally came to, the moon had traveled far to the west and all the stars had changed position. His head throbbed, and he felt foggy. Moon knelt beside him, applying a damp cloth to his burned face. He smelled singed hair.

"My hair?" he said.

"Not too bad," she said.

"My face?" he said.

She didn't answer, simply looked at him with sorrowful eyes.

The scorching pain all over his face told him it had to be bad. He turned to one side and tried to shake off his grogginess. He had to send that signal. Tonight was their last chance. It was up to him now. He had to press forward, no matter what. He had to repair whatever damage the Cardinal had caused when he fell on top of the radio.

"Where's Turning Bird?" he asked.

"By that tree sleeping," said Moon. "He got me water from the creek and now he's tired."

Eric pushed himself up. His head pounded. Vertigo overwhelmed him and he felt sick to his stomach. He pulled his sleeve back and checked his watch. Two o'clock in the morning. Had he really been unconscious that long? He had to get that signal sent before the Roman beacon traveled out of range, before this big F window closed up on him. He cursed himself for not having acted quickly enough when Whitefeather came into camp with Flying Horse. He was too damn trusting, too willing to give others the benefit of the doubt.

He looked around the campsite. The horses were gone. He couldn't see the rifles anywhere either.

"They took our rifles?" he said.

"Took 'em clean away," said Moon.

He shook his head. Fresh game was now out of the question. They would have to subsist on staples—the pemmican and beef jerky. And without the horses he wasn't looking forward to the return journey on foot. The Missouri River had to be at least a hundred miles away.

He forced the obstacle-hobbled return journey from his mind. In another couple hours dawn would be here. The Earth would be tilted away from its optimum transmission angle, and their last chance for contacting the Romans would be gone. He had to concentrate on sending the signal.

"Help me to my feet," he said.

Moon gripped his arm and helped him up. He looked at the radio. The Cardinal lay dead across it.

"Help me move the Cardinal," he said.

Moon helped him move the Cardinal.

He got a flashlight from the tent and shone it over the damaged radio.

The harmonic filter looked crooked, as did one of the power amplifiers. He straightened them out, then he checked the wiring. Blood covered much of it, but as most of it was wrapped in a waxy coating, he felt it would hold without shorting out. He swung his flashlight to the car batteries. All five were still there. But then he shone his flashlight up the hill, and saw that the antenna was gone.

"Where's the antenna?" he asked.

"They kicked it down the hill," said Moon.

He shook his head. "Wake up Turning Bird," he said. "We have to find it."

When the three went down the hill, they found the antenna broken in several pieces, quickly vandalized by the fleeing Kiowa, but not entirely destroyed.

Over the next forty-five minutes Eric and Moon put it back together, tying the ends of the aluminum lengths with wire when they couldn't find the wing nuts, discarding some of the broken pieces, doing their best with what they had so that by the time they finished, the antenna looked more like a piece of modern sculpture than an antenna. Turning Bird wasn't much help. He was more interested in playing with his flashlight, swinging its beam over the ground, pointing it directly into the sky, sweeping it across the rocks up on the bluff—he'd never seen a flashlight before.

By three-thirty in the morning, Eric and Moon had the antenna back on its mount and rewired to the radio. Eric pressed the lever forward, and the radio hissed with static. As he cranked the dial up to a full hundred megahertz, he glanced at the watchful faces of Moon and Turning Bird. They seemed fascinated by what he was doing. What strange twists life could take. If his life had gone according to plan, he would have been Cardinal Eric Nordstrum right now, the highest-ranking functionary of the Holy Catholic Church in the Missouri-Arkansas Territory. Yet here he was, out in the Restricted Zone with a clay-bred woman and a Cheyenne boy, trying to destroy that same damn Church.

He engaged the primary oscillator and propagated the Cardinal's prerecorded contact signal into space. A hundred megahertz of carrier-wave surged through the air and pierced the F window. Eric imagined the frequency perforating the atmosphere, traveling out into near-space, arching past the moon, beyond the moon, and into the void—reaching, reaching, reaching—widening in ever-greater concentric rings, searching for that mysterious Roman beacon. He imagined the beacon drinking his signal, boosting it, then sending it to outposts of the Roman Empire further afield. From these outposts he imagined his signal then being relayed to the generals and the legions . . . and the legions then mobilizing . . . coming to Earth . . .

He was imagining this all so vividly, strained as he was by exhaustion and fear, he at first didn't realize he had an incoming message, one different from the Roman's original hail.

"Salve," the new voice said. *"Quid nomen tibi est?"* The same five words over and over again. *"Salve. Quid nomen tibi est?"* Coming in loud and clear from who-knew-where, all the way through that F window, down into the clear prairie air, caught by his antenna like a baseball in a catcher's mitt. He listened to the words again. He translated them carefully, laboriously.

"Hello. What is your name?"

He gripped the microphone in a sudden frenzy and switched to live transmit. *"Salve!"* he called. *"Nomen mihi est Eric Nordstrum."*

He repeated this again and again. *"Salve! Nomen mihi est Eric Nordstrum."* Hoping that whoever heard him would realize he was broadcasting live from planet Earth, that his voice was a response to their hail, and that the moment was of prime historical importance. *"Salve! Nomen mihi est Eric Nordstrum."* The Imperial Roman tribe had, after two thousand years, been reconnected to the Earth-bound Holy Catholic tribe. *"Salve! Nomen mihi est Eric Nord-*

strum." And the Catholic tribe, subjugated by beasts from beyond the stars for centuries, needed Imperial Roman help more than ever.

As Gallio alighted from his *pendeo carrus,* he looked up at the buildings of Granarium. The larger downtown edifices were grown, not built. One looked like a giant pomegranate catacombed with room-size seed pockets. Another grew gourd-shaped, with a pendulous bottom and an attenuated top, parts of the shell cut away for ventilation. Some of the houses reminded him of giant pumpkins. Architecture in Granarium was as colorful as a cornucopia full of fruit and vegetables.

In the Roman Quarter he surrendered his car to a *cubicularius,* a pale little valet with the lime-green markings of the Province of Glacialis. Tanks and armored personnel carriers guarded the Quarter. Double the usual number of *excubitors* patrolled the catwalk on top of the wall, all carrying fully rated combat *bacula.*

The guard at the gate knew who he was. He immediately dropped to his right knee, let his chin sink to his chest, and put his right fist against his heart in the Roman salute.

"Get up," said Gallio.

The guard sprang to his feet and stood to attention. What woe this Roman soldier would see in his lifetime, thought Gallio, and entered the Quarter.

In stark contrast to the grown architecture in the rest of Granarium, stone and marble buildings rose all around him in the Roman Quarter. He hated it. Roman architectural design hadn't changed in two thousand years. If fact, much of the dross of Roman culture hadn't changed in two thousand years. Caesar had issued decrees to keep dress, customs, and religion the same. Gallio shook his head. Was this the chief characteristic of a conquering race of people? That it stagnated, that in order to keep going it had to copy and steal innovations from other cultures because it didn't have the genius to come up with its own? Yes, he hated it. And he particularly hated the old-style architecture Caesar insisted on. Why ruin such a pretty place like Hortus with all this stone? He wanted to preserve Hortus as a pastoral backwater, a special place of the soul. That's what he was fighting for. All his old-timers were drifting back to rejoin his army, as fiercely loyal to him as ever. His armorers were working on his ships. If the Senate decided on the *legio exstirpatio,* then he would decide on war.

"Long live Rome," said Lurio, when Gallio reached the Senate Hall. "I have great news for you, Gallio. Or at least Caesar does."

"Caesar?" said Gallio. "Gaius Julius Caesar?"

"He's had himself hypertransmitted from the resurrectorium in Elysium."

Gallio suddenly grew somber. Talking to dead people always made him uneasy.

"He's on one of these screens?" he asked, gesturing toward the bank of *scribae* on the far wall.

"That one there," said Lurio, pointing.

Gallio contemplated the blank screen and stepped forward. He bent to one knee and put his fist to his heart. He stared at the *scriba,* waiting. In a minute the *scriba* glowed with a cadaverish light, that mix of silver, violet, green, and yellow that was like a reflection of the grave. A face appeared, one he recognized well—the face of Julius Caesar.

"You may rise, General," said Caesar.

Gallio got to his feet. He gazed at Caesar, a man who was more than two thousand years old—*the* man who had valiantly led the fight against the *Patroni* during the War of the Gens—Gaius Julius Caesar, with that well-known narrow face, the patrician nose, the thin rosebud lips, the bald forehead, and the quick, intelligent eyes. Here was the man whose barbed tongue could reduce a Senate foe to abject fear; the man who had orchestrated the Great Theft in 46 B.C.; the man who had preserved Roman Civilization among the stars for the last two thousand years. And yet . . . was he a man? Or just the recording of a man, such as the theorists of the *legio ad scientiam conformatus* sometimes suggested, a man kept in a jar of biomagnetic formaldehyde.

"You have news, Caesar?"

A grin appeared on Caesar's face.

"We have found Orbis, Gallio," said Caesar. "Our home has been found."

This was indeed news. But what did he have to do with it? Orbis found. Yes, he was happy to hear that, but why would Caesar take the trouble to tell him the news personally?

"A glorious day for Rome, Caesar," he said.

"The pinnacle of *glory* for Rome, Gallio," said Caesar. "There is rejoicing in the street. The feasts shall continue for a full month." Caesar's grin widened. "You may rise, Gallio. You and I are old friends. No need for such formality."

Gallio got to his feet. "And was it a transmission we received, Caesar?"

"Yes, General, a crude analog one, so weak we nearly missed it. But once the *legio communicatio* boosted it, the message came in loud and clear, a prerecorded message broadcast in seven languages, including Old Latin, describing a planet third from a middle-aged yellow star, with a single large moon and five large saltwater oceans. The signal identified this planet as the source of its origin, then listed different names for it: Earth, Terra, Orbis, Terre, Erde, and Tierra. It further identified a large landmass geographically identical to the one we once called Novus Orbis. More specifically, it described the confluence of two great rivers, ones our own cartographers are familiar with from historical maps of Novus Orbis. The originators of the signal have invited Roman emissaries to the confluence of these two great rivers in a city they call St. Lucius. We've been able to triangulate the planet's exact position using this analog radio signal." Gallio now detected a hardness to Caesar's smile. "I have chosen *you* to be our emissary, Publius Gallio. You will leave immediately."

Orbis. Cradle of life. *Home.* He recognized this as a watershed, but was shaken that Caesar should choose him to be the emissary. He didn't want to leave Hortus. Not now. If he left Hortus, who would protect the Hortulani? He feared he hadn't fooled Lurio after all, that Caesar's order was just a ruse to get rid of him so he wouldn't interfere with the *legio exstirpatio*.

"Was voice-to-voice contact established, Caesar?" he asked. "Or was it just a prerecorded message?"

"No. Voice-to-voice contact was established," replied Caesar. "Listen."

A desperate, static-fractured voice crackled over the

speaker: "*Mihi nomen est Eric Nordstrum! Mihi nomen est Eric Nordstrum!*"

The man sounded frightened, weary, and as if he'd gone through a great deal of hardship to send his signal. Eric Nordstrum. What kind of name was that? Was the man a Hun?

"He sounds afraid, Caesar."

"They are still at war with the *Patroni,* Gallio. The set transmission made that clear. For two thousand years they've been fighting the *Patroni.* He has every right to be afraid. The *Patroni* are a formidable race. But they are no match for General Publius Gallio Corvinus. Gaius Lurio tells me you've been provisioning your army." The grin on Caesar's face was now like a knife. "He tells me you've recruited more than fifteen hundred Hortulani, and that another five thousand of your old army have gathered in the hills. Well done, Gallio, well done. I'm pleased to see you so ready to fight." You couldn't hide things from Caesar. Caesar knew all. "The fighting cock has not lost his balls, eh, my old friend? I'm glad the Province of Umbraculum swears allegiance to Rome, but have no fear, Gallio, you won't have to weary your troops on Hortus. The *legio exstirpatio* is on its way and will handle our small problem on Hortus well enough so that the great Publius Gallio can go to Orbis and liberate our poor struggling cousins from the *Patroni.*"

He wanted to speak out against Caesar's plan. But to speak out now would reveal his treasonous scheme, and Caesar would have him executed on the spot. One wrong word, and he wouldn't even get the chance to make alternate plans to save the Hortulani, or at least spirit some of them away before the genocide came.

Caesar was giving him a chance to step back gracefully from the precipice.

The grin left Caesar's face, replaced by that singular mask of loss and regret he sometimes saw on the Immortals.

"I want to see my home again, Gallio," said Caesar. "I can't live anymore. I want to die, but I want to die in my old home. I want to see the Subura District of Rome one last time before I leave the resurrectorium, no matter how much it might have changed. I miss Orbis. I miss Rome. I'm trusting you to make things ready for my return. Don't disappoint me, Gallio. You'll only end up regretting it."

CHAPTER 28

Eric carried as much food and equipment as he could, wondering how long it would take the Romans to come. He, Moon, and Turning Bird made their way north along the creek toward the Missouri River. Had the Romans really understood his call, and would they find Orbis, now that he had sent his message? His face was blistered in nine different places from his burns. Would they be here soon, or would it take them years?

"Let's take a rest," he said. "I'm tired."

Moon nodded, and, in Cheyenne, told Turning Bird to stop. The boy came over, put his hands on his knees, and gazed at Eric. The boy wore rawhide pants stitched together with uncured buffalo sinew. His dark eyes squinted in curiosity as he examined Eric's injured face. Turning Bird said something in Cheyenne to Moon.

"He wants to know if your left eye is still blurry," said Moon.

"It comes and goes," said Eric.

Moon conveyed this information to Turning Bird.

Turning Bird then spoke at some length.

Moon finally translated.

"He wants to know if you've had any visions or hallucinations out of your left eye," she said. "He knows you're a holy man, and he wants to be a holy man himself some day, even though his pa wants him to be a chief. He says he's not gettin' anywhere makin' himself dizzy, and he wonders if it might be a good idea to burn his own eye so he'll have some visions."

"No!" cried Eric, alarmed that the boy should consider blinding himself. "Tell him to leave his eye alone. Tell him I've never had any visions, and I get by just fine without them."

Moon translated.

Turning Bird's eyes narrowed. He looked puzzled and said something else to Moon.

"He wants to know how you can be a holy man if you haven't had any visions," she said.

Eric looked away. He saw a jackrabbit bolt from behind a chaparral bush. Turning Bird was right. What were his qualifications? Why had he joined the clergy in the first place? He'd never had any visions. The Saints didn't come to him in his dreams. He'd never heard the Word of the Lord personally. He'd never witnessed any miracles other than the births of his son and daughter, and now they were both dead. The impulse to join the clergy had simply been blind ambition. No wonder he'd taken such a fall. Yet he *felt* God. Felt God deeply inside him. He might not consider the Good Lord God a Christian God anymore, the Father of the Lord Jesus Christ, the God he had studied in college for so many years, but he still had a sense of the spirit of God, the marvel of God.

"Tell him I don't need visions," he said. "Tell him I just *feel* God."

Moon translated.

Turning Bird stared at him for a long time after that. The boy finally nodded. He understood. Turning Bird felt God too.

Near sundown they found a wandering feru. Red handprints ornamented its hindquarters—put there by Comanches, Turning Bird told them, as proof of ownership. The horse didn't seem the least bit nervous around humans. Turning Bird quickly dug through Eric's pack, found some twine, and fashioned a crude halter. The boy showed amazing skill with the horse, was obviously born to the old Roman ferus, and coaxed the brilliantly white steed into submission in less than fifteen minutes.

"Turning Bird wants you to ride the feru," said Moon. "You're tired and your burns still hurt, and he wants you to ride the horse. He wants you fresh in case we run into more Kiowa. This creek runs through the heart of their country."

"Tell him we'll load the horse with our supplies. Tell him I want to walk."

They made their way north for the next couple of days. The land got drier, and the creek dwindled to a trickle. They saw herds of buffalo—not like the huge one Eric had seen with Per and the Cardinal, but still sizable, a hundred or more. They saw antelope. They found human skeletons—old brown bones lying half buried in the tattered remains of clay-bred uniforms—but no live humans. They seemed to be the only ones in the whole wide prairie.

Eric was disturbed by the skeletons.

"Don't the Benefactors give you any protection out here in the Restricted Zone?" he asked Moon.

She shook her head. "If any of us get lost, or are sold as slaves to the Indians, or wind up dead, they just make more. We're cheap to make."

They traveled on. He kept glancing at her. She was pretty, but she was also frail and sickly. He wondered if a doctor might be able to help her, or at least improve her health to some degree.

An hour before sunset he saw dust rising to the west and thought they might be in for another dust storm. But the dust was localized, and as it drew nearer, he heard Indian war cries and finally the sound of horses' hooves. He stopped and looked around for cover, but they were in the middle of the plains. There was none anywhere. A coyote jumped out of the grass and headed east. He tried to count the Indians charging toward them. Fifty at least. Their own feru, frightened by the sound of the stampede, trotted off with all their supplies. Eric stopped, planted the Roman staff in the ground, and stood there with his knees slightly bent, ready to protect Moon and Turning Bird.

"Get behind me," he told them.

He gripped the staff in both hands. He wished he could see better, but with his left eye blurry, his perspective was limited.

He thought the mounted Kiowa would trample them with their horses. But at the last moment they swerved away. They circled Eric, Moon, and Turning Bird, their war cries shrill, their faces fierce with war paint, their horses raising so much dust Eric could hardly see. His heart pumped crazily. After so many silent days on the prairie, the yips and cries of the Kiowa cut like a knife into his eardrums.

"Stay back!" he warned. "Stay back!"

An older Indian raised his hand. The others reined in their ferus and came to a stop. A deafening silence ensued. Eric looked around wildly, breathless but ready. The cloud of dust drifted away. Half the braves wore hollowed-out buffalo skulls on their heads, fur and horns still attached. Others carried shields with starbursts painted on them. All carried spears.

Turning Bird emerged from behind Eric and walked toward the older brave. Eric grabbed him, but Turning Bird shook him off.

Turning Bird talked to the older brave not in the language of the Kiowa but in a different-sounding tongue. Eric turned nervously to Moon.

"What's going on?" he asked.

Moon leaned forward and listened. Turning Bird and the old brave continued to talk. Moon turned to Eric. "These are his people," she said, her shoulders sagging in relief. "This is his tribe. That man is his pa."

Eric gazed at the old Cheyenne, Lone Cloud. Lone Cloud glanced at him, his dark eyes like the eyes of an eagle. The old man got down off his horse. He looked tired, his face wracked by weeks of worry. They both had sons. They both were fathers. Eric looked at the ground. The only difference was the old man would have his son back now, but Neil was gone for good.

"Turning Bird's telling his pa that you're a holy man and that you saved his life by killing six Kiowa braves," said Moon.

Turning Bird got down on one knee as a sign of respect to his father. Lone Cloud left Turning Bird's side and approached Eric. He glanced at the Roman staff. The chief's face seemed carved out of wood, his lips sliced from his face in quick, precise chops, his nose hatcheted in a strong, curved beak. He said something in Cheyenne to Moon, and she responded with a few words. The old brave nodded then turned to Eric and spoke at some length in Cheyenne. When he was finished, Moon translated.

"He says he owes you a lot for saving his son's life. He says the Cheyenne will always be your friends and that you can use his warriors whenever you like. He wants to give you five wives and twelve horses. He asks you to come live with them so you can teach him about the white man's god. He has never heard of this, a holy man who is also a warrior, and thinks you can teach him a lot. You can sleep on a bearskin rug in his tipi."

Eric tried to figure out a way to refuse all this generosity gracefully. He didn't need a dozen horses. As for wives, he already had a wife back home waiting for him. A rain check seemed the best solution.

"Tell him I'm happy to save his son's life," said Eric, "and that I'll accept everything he's offered, only I can't take it right away. Tell him I'm on a quest right now and that I aim to confer with spirits in the sky, and that in order to do that I need to reach the great river as fast as I can. Maybe he can give me a few braves and a horse to take me there. I'll return when my quest is finished and take everything he's offered."

Moon told Lone Cloud this. The chief's eyes nar-

rowed. He looked a little put out, but he finally nodded. He turned and spoke a few words to some of his
braves. Four of them came forward on their horses.
He then spoke and Moon translated again.

"He says he will wait for you," she said. "He says
he will pray to the spirit of the river to guide you and
keep you safe. And he will pray to the sky so that the
spirits there will hear you and grant you success in
your quest."

Here was another man who felt God, thought Eric.
And he realized he had a lot of rethinking to do.
God wasn't about religion, he decided. God was about
something you felt inside. He would come back and
visit Lone Cloud some day. He thought he would learn
more from Lone Cloud than Lone Cloud would learn
from him.

Gallio sat on the bridge of the *penna* and looked
out the window as the *collum* extended further and
further into space. The *collum* was elegant, slender,
like the arm of a woman. The *legio impello* didn't
know how the *penna* worked, or how the *Patroni* had
developed these strange ships, but they knew how to
build them, how to copy them from the originals stolen by Caesar, and how to fly them. A *caput*—a
multipoint hydrogen-rich industrial diamond the size
of a house—shone at the terminus. His *nauta,* an old-
timer named Appius Tranio, tweaked the coordinates
a final time. The continuance of the Hortulani as a
race now depended on the two thousand refugees
stowed away in the lower hold. The *collum* unfolded
yet further. Oppius Naevius stood beside him watching
the star-bridging apparatus extend its reach inch by

inch. Gallio would obey Caesar's command in securing Orbis, but he couldn't let the Hortulani as a people die. They would have to multiply and prosper on Orbis. In this, he had the full support of his army.

A few minutes later, Appius Tranio engaged the *collum*, and the mysterious star-drive, after extending for nearly an hour, retracted, pulling the stars in around it like so many pieces of bright yarn, stretching them, bending them, warping them.

When the *collum* was finally fully retracted, the stars red-shifted, blurred one last time, then grew still as the ship slowed to its usual particle-pulse speed.

Appius Tranio keyed commands into the *ambitus solarium*.

Ten minutes later a gray orb came into view.

What was this? Orbis was supposed to be a blue world, not a gray one. It was supposed to be a world full of water with an atmosphere lacy with white clouds. Here was the planet's moon, to be sure, off to the right. He had studied the legendary old satellite's features tirelessly in school. But why was Orbis now all gray, without oceans, and as dark, bereft, and cratered as its moon? This couldn't be. What disaster had befallen their old home?

"Naevius, run the *mensor* over the planet's surface."

What they found was an antique camouflage technology a thousand years old. A thin one-way holo-image enshrouded the planet, giving it the look of dead, airless rock.

"Let's unravel this deception and see what we have," said Gallio.

Naevius fired six electromagnetic scramblers into the illusory gray skin. The holo-image burned away like a piece of tissue paper, spreading outward in crackling circles of light from the six target zones. Gallio caught a glimpse of ocean underneath. On the sunward side, the north coast of Africa appeared, then Corsica and Sicily, and finally the famed boot of the Apennines, Italy itself, snug between the gemlike waters of the Adriatic and Tyrrhenian seas. He saw Egypt. As the circles of rippling fire converged, he saw Mesopotamia. Then Persia. Then Gaul, Britannia, and finally, across the ocean, the bleak coast of Novus Orbis.

Gallio shook his head. Here they were, back at last. Terra, Erde, Earth . . . Orbis. By whatever name, it was still home. Back to claim it for a man—Gaius Julius Caesar—who preferred genocide over debate, punishment over mercy, and slavery over freedom.

Eric and Moon drifted down the river on the raft in the middle of the night. Moon slept beside him. She had nowhere else to go, so she was coming with him. He stared up at the stars. Moon shifted uneasily. He wondered if she were having another bad dream. Damn that Flying Horse, anyway. He stroked her hair, gave her comfort. He wondered what the citizens of St. Lucius would say when he came drifting down the Missouri River with Moon, or how they would react when he told them the Romans were coming.

He was just about to get her another blanket when he saw a distant light in the sky. It looked like a million sparklers strung end to end, arcing up from the south, rippling in a single line toward them.

"Moon," he said. He shook her. "Moon, wake up."

Moon opened her eyes. She looked up at the sky.

The sparks bristled, got closer and closer. Soon, the sparks were directly above them, glittering like an omen.

"What are they?" asked Moon.

As the sparks passed, heading north, they seemed to leave the sky brighter behind them. The stars shone more brilliantly than he had ever seen them.

"I don't know," he said. "I think the Romans must be here. I think things are going to be different from here on in."

PART 3

COUNTRYMEN

CHAPTER 29

Three days later, Eric and Moon approached the bungalow in West Shelby through the woods out back. It was dusk. A man was sitting on the porch. He wore a police uniform and held a double-barreled shotgun across his knee. He was smoking a cigarette. Eric saw the end glow as he took a pull. Eric motioned Moon to crouch. The lights in the house were off, a few pieces of laundry hung on the line, and the unnerving stillness of the place, as it sank into the shadows of evening, gave him a bad feeling. Where was Ingrid? And why was that officer sitting on the back porch with a shotgun across his knee?

The officer must have sensed them. He stood up, went to the railing, turned on his flashlight, and shone it into the woods. Eric clutched Moon by the arm and made her crouch lower. The officer swung his flashlight from side to side, the beam lighting the parched grass, its glow blanching the branches of the nearest saplings. Was the man waiting for his return? Had Henrik Rydberg in fact reported his incursion into the

Restricted Zone to the police, just as Whitefeather had feared?

The officer finally turned off his flashlight and went into the house. Eric stood up and peered through the bushes, waiting, wondering what he was going to do, his blood thrumming in his ears as his worry grew sharper.

"That sure is a nice house," said Moon. "I never slept in a house before."

He put his hand on her arm. "Shhh," he said.

A minute later, Eric saw the officer leave through the front door and walk down the drive to a parked police cruiser. He got into the vehicle, started it, turned on the headlights, and drove south toward town. Eric waited until he couldn't hear the engine anymore. Even then he hesitated. He hated to think of what he might find inside.

"Come on," he said. "Let's go."

Eric and Moon ventured out of the woods into the back lot. Eric was tired, thirsty, and hungry. He was desperate to see his wife, but the place looked deserted, and he was growing more and more convinced that Ingrid wasn't here, that the authorities had done something with her, and that he wasn't going to see her for a while. He saw that her vegetable garden had been abandoned, the young tomato plants and cornstalks allowed to wither. He climbed the steps to the back porch and peered through the screen door.

"Ingrid?" he called. "Ingrid, are you home?"

Moon came up behind him and peered past his shoulder into the dark interior.

He saw mud tracked up and down the hall. That

wasn't like Ingrid. She kept a clean house. He went inside, tried the hall light, but it wouldn't go on.

"It smells funny in here," said Moon.

The house did indeed smell funny—and not just funny—but bad, as if a piece of meat had been allowed to rot somewhere.

"Let's check the kitchen," he said.

In the kitchen, the fridge door was open and the freezer fully defrosted. He tried the kitchen light but it wouldn't go on either. The power was off. A candle in a candleholder sat on the kitchen table next to a book of matches. He lit the candle and checked the kitchen drawers. All the cutlery was gone. He opened the cupboard—there were no dishes anywhere.

He shook his head. "Looks like she's gone," he said. "Only I don't know where she would go. Let's check the bedroom."

In the bedroom, Ingrid's clothes lay on the floor. So did his own. Much of the plaster had been ripped off the back wall and lay in a heap in the corner. The drapes had been torn down, the blankets pulled off the sofa bed, the mattress yanked out and upended next to the closet.

"The Inculpator's Office did this," he said. "They were here searching the place. They better not have hurt her."

He was so overcome with worry that he had to lean against the wall and close his eyes for a few seconds. In the distance he heard a dog barking. He opened his eyes. The room was blue in the ever-deepening shadows. Oh, dear God, please preserve her. But he had little faith in God anymore.

He found her blue dress on the living room floor. His jaw clenched, and he felt his skin stretching tight over his face. The dress was ripped, flung down in a heap, and damp. A single chair sat in the middle of the room. Some wire coat hangers had been bent around the legs of the chair. Moon, sensing his distress, put her hand on his shoulder. She was clay-bred, not really human, but her touch felt human, and he was glad for it.

Andrea Braaten, Deacon Braaten's wife, a woman of sixty with blue-rinsed hair, wearing a plain gray skirt, an apron, and a white blouse, stared at Eric as if she didn't recognize him.

"Good Lord, Eric," she said, "what happened to your face?" She turned to Moon. "And what are you doing here with a clay-bred? Did she get lost?"

"No, Andrea," he said. "She's with me. She's my friend."

Andrea's nose wrinkled. A distressed look came to her eyes. "I can't say I like a clay-bred on my doorstep," she said. "And I'm not sure you should be here, Eric. The police are looking for you."

"Do you know where Ingrid is?" he asked. "I went out to West Shelby and she wasn't there. A police officer was sitting on my back porch."

Andrea looked away. "We haven't heard from Ingrid in a few weeks," she said.

"Do you have any idea where she is?" he asked.

"No," she said. She untied her apron. "Your face looks horrible. What happened to it?"

"Is Oskar here?" he asked. He hoped Oskar Braaten would give him and Moon shelter, and that he might know where Ingrid was. He knew he couldn't go back to the house in West Shelby. Not with the police there. And he needed a few days to rest. "Could we come inside?"

Andrea grew even more distressed. "You want to bring a clay-bred inside?" she asked.

"I can stay out on the step," offered Moon.

Eric gazed at Andrea. He couldn't believe that she could be so upset to find a clay-bred on her doorstep.

"Is Oskar here?" he asked again. "I need a word with him."

Andrea kept staring at Moon. "He's teaching his Thursday night Bible class," she said.

"Could we please come in, Andrea?" he said. "We're dead tired. We need to sit down."

"*You* can come in," she said, "but the clay-bred stays outside. We don't allow dogs in our house, so I don't see why we should allow clay-bred in our house either."

Eric's tone hardened. "The girl comes in," he said. "I'm going to have to insist on that, Andrea."

Andrea hesitated.

"Okay, okay," she said, cowed. "No need to get so riled, Eric. But I want the both of you in the kitchen so you won't get dirt all over the place. I know you've been to the Restricted Zone. I've always suspected it was a filthy place. No wonder the Benefactors put it off limits."

Oskar got home a short while later.

The Deacon was flabbergasted by Eric's arrival, and even more flabbergasted by the presence of a clay-bred woman in his kitchen.

"Why, Eric, I thought you were gone for good," he

said, an amazed and pinched smile on his face. "One step into the Restricted Zone, and . . . well . . . you know . . . you never come back. Not to say I'm not glad to see you. Good Lord, what happened to your face? And your left eye's all cloudy."

"I've done some hard traveling, Oskar," he said. "I was out at the house in West Shelby. My wife wasn't there."

The Deacon cast an anxious glance at Andrea. "Is that a fact?" he said, his tone sickeningly amiable. "Well . . . what do you know about that?"

"Do you have any idea where she is?" asked Eric.

"I can't say as I do," he said.

"The police were out in West Shelby," said Eric. "I can't go back there. Me and Moon need a place to stay. Just for a few days so I can figure out what I'm going to do. I thought since we've known each other for thirty years . . ."

The Deacon's smile became even more panicked.

"Why . . . of *course* you can stay, Eric," he said. "And of *course* your friend can stay." His face had to strain to maintain that awful smile. "I don't know too much about her kind, but I . . . I trust she's trained to a certain degree." Oskar's brow creased with inquiry. "In the use of all the bathroom fixtures, I mean?"

"We'll stay in the room above the coach house," said Eric.

Visible relief swept over the Deacon's face. "If that's what you'd prefer, certainly. There might be a cobweb or two up there, but if that's what you want . . . I'll have Andrea get some fresh sheets."

"I'll go right away," said Andrea, jumping at the excuse to get out of the kitchen.

"I ain't never fixed no sheet before," said Moon, "but I reckon I could help you if you show me how."

"That's quite all right, dear," said Andrea. "I'd prefer to do it myself."

"Maybe you could take her outside, Andrea," said Oskar, his smile starting to slip despite his best efforts to keep it in place. "Eric and me have some things to talk about. Put her in the yard near the back. And make sure she doesn't sit on any of the garden furniture. No offense, miss, but that furniture came all the way from New Amsterdam."

"I'll sit on the grass," said Moon. "I've always liked sittin' on the grass."

Eric and the Deacon retired to the sunroom for a brandy and a cigar. The Deacon's face was grave.

"I'll be frank with you, Eric," he said. "You're a wanted man again. For going into the Restricted Zone. That's a felony under Liturgical Law." The Deacon leaned forward and gazed at Eric with bewildered eyes. "Why would you do something like that? What's gotten into you? Henrik Rydberg said he saw you heading upriver on a barge with three other men and some horses. He thinks he saw the Cardinal. The Cardinal's missing. Was the Cardinal with you?"

"My path was marked by God, Oskar," said Eric. "God has revealed to me the true nature of the world. I went into the Restricted Zone to do His will."

The Deacon's eyes narrowed. "Yes, but Liturgical Law clearly forbids entrance into Restricted Zones. Indians and clay-bred only. You're lucky to be alive."

"Do you have any idea where my wife is?" asked Eric. "I think the Inculpator's Office has taken her somewhere. Do you have any idea where?"

Oskar's corpulent face settled, and he shook his head. "I've heard a thing or two," he said.

"Like what?"

"Like she was taken for questioning. A day or two after Rydberg told police you were heading upriver."

"Questioning where?" said Eric.

"I have no idea." Oskar glanced out the window, where lightning bugs flickered in the dark. "They sent some Seminarians upriver, and they found your barge. What on earth were you doing up there, Eric? What could possibly have possessed you to disobey God's laws and trespass so far into the Restricted Zone? And then you come back with a clay-bred? I find your behavior baffling to all human understanding."

Eric leaned forward, his shoulders tensing. "Oskar, you have to help me find Ingrid."

Oskar looked nervously out the window. "I don't know where she is, Eric," he said, "and that's the Good Lord's honest truth."

"Has anybody seen her? Has she been to church?"

"No."

Eric took a deep breath. Ingrid had never missed a Sunday in her life. "Will you ask around for me?" said Eric. "I'm sick with worry."

Oskar looked miserable. "I'll do what I can, Eric," he said, "but it's not a good time to be asking questions right now, not with the crackdown against the Odd Fellows in full swing. They're picking up anybody. You don't even necessarily have to be an Odd Fellow. And they're particularly looking at us clergy.

They're trying to weed out the dissenters. But I'll try. I'll definitely try for you." That awful smile came back to his face, panicked and weak, and as phony as a Pope Pius dollar. "After all, what are old friends for?"

Up in the coach house, Eric and Moon had to use candles. They had to fill a washbasin from the garden tap. The bed was narrow and damp from the summer's humidity, and it had room for only one person.

"I can sleep on the floor," said Moon. "This old rug looks comfy enough."

"You can sleep on the bed," said Eric. "You don't look well. I'll sleep on the floor."

He settled himself on the floor. He was so tired he fell into a deep, dreamless sleep right away, but was awakened by the sound of a car coming up the drive three hours later. He sat up and saw the glow of headlights shining through the window. It lit the tarp-covered furniture, illuminated the plaster of Paris bust of Saint Hectoire on the mantelpiece, and brightened the brass fireplace implements next to the hearth. He realized that his old friend, far from helping him, had actually betrayed him.

Eric went to the window and saw a big late-model Chrysler roll up the drive, the cross and orbis symbol of the police department emblazoned on the door. The headlights pierced the gloom with a brutal white glare.

He stood there wondering what he was going to do, rubbing his chin with his hand. Damn, they had him, and there was no way to escape. He had to think of Moon. She might fit through the coal chute out back. He had to stall them somehow so she could get away. He looked around the room and saw a big armchair.

He dragged the armchair over to the door and wedged it underneath the doorknob. That ought to hold them for a while, he thought, at least until Moon made her escape. He searched the room and found a pencil and a scrap of paper. He scribbled a note and drew a map.

He shook Moon's shoulder and said, "Moon, get up."

Moon roused herself with some difficulty and looked at Eric with bleary eyes. "What now?" she asked.

"We've got police outside."

She sat up immediately. "Are they anything like the Kiowa?"

He stroked her hair, trying to soothe her. "No," he said. "But I think you better go just the same."

Her eyes grew big. "You're not coming with me?" she said.

"No. There's only one way out—the coal chute— and I'm too big to fit through, but you'll fit fine. You got to get away. I can't let them catch you. You have no rights under Liturgical Law. Not as a clay-bred. So I want you to stay with a friend of mine, just so you're safe." He handed the map and note to her. "Go out this back door here and down the stairs. Go right to the back. That's where you'll find the coal chute. Once you're through it, you'll find a lane. Follow the lane south until you see a factory. The street next to the factory is Rainey Street." He heard the police coming up the outside stairs to the bedroom door. "Follow Rainey Street west, away from the river and up the hill until you get to a two-story clapboard building painted yellow. It's number thirty-six. Go to the second floor and knock on the door. A girl named June lives there. Show her what I've written. She'll let you stay. She'll look after you until I can come and get you."

He helped her to her feet and led her down the back stairs into the stable. He turned on the light. No horses now, just the Deacon's brand-new Packard. They walked to the back, where they found the coal chute.

"Climb onto that pile of coal and scurry up the ramp," he said.

She did as she was told, her knees and hands getting covered with coal dust. His throat tightened. He hated to send her out into the town by herself, but what else could he do? She looked back at him as she pushed the chute door open, her eyes big, preternaturally pale, and now glistening with tears.

"Bye," she said.

He felt miserable. "Go on, now," he said. "Be strong." Upstairs he heard the police pounding on the door, calling his name. "I'll come for you just as soon as I can. June will look after you. I promise she will."

CHAPTER 30

A clay-bred woman stood at June's door. The woman was as pale as unbaked dough, had hair like clumps of dry straw, and wore a tunic so filthy June could hardly see its red cross and orbis.

"Are you June?" the woman asked.

"Yes," said June.

"Here," said the woman, and handed June a piece of paper with writing on it.

June read:

Dear June. This is Moon, a clay-bred woman I met while I was in the Restricted Zone with Cardinal Anders. Please look after her. By the time you read this, I'll be in jail. She has lived out in the Restricted Zone for most of her life and is unfamiliar with town ways. I don't want her to fall into the hands of the police. Please keep her safe. May the Good Lord Bless and Keep You. Eric Nordstrum.

She couldn't help staring at Moon. "Well . . ." she said, "come in."

She hadn't seen too many clay-bred up close—the Potters always moved them through town at night. Moon entered the apartment and looked around. She was startlingly pale, the same color as the underside of a fish, with skin so translucent June could see the blue veins underneath. She was tall, and her limbs were thin. June felt curious, but at the same time wary. As June led her into the living room, she heard her roommate stirring. Amy came down the hall a moment later, into the living room, and stopped. She, too, stared at Moon. Moon was a patch of white among their colorful throw rugs, beaded doorways, and homemade candles, a ghostlike figure with milky blue eyes and hair the color of arrowroot.

"Who's she?" asked Amy.

June regained her wits and forced herself to be polite. "Amy, this is Moon. Moon, this is Amy."

"Howdy," said Moon.

"Moon's just come from the Restricted Zone with Father Nordstrum. He's been put in jail, and he wants us to look after Moon until he gets out."

Amy's eyes narrowed apprehensively. "Isn't there a town ordinance against her kind?" she said. "Shouldn't she be kept in a shed or something? Look how dirty she is. And she's got coal dust all over her hands and knees."

"I had to climb out a coal chute," explained Moon.

"And she's supposed to stay with us?" said Amy.

June tried to force herself to get used to the idea, but it was hard to get used to a human who was made in a pot, not in a womb.

"I could sleep outside," said Moon. "I do that all the time. I wouldn't want to dirty your sheets. I don't know too much about sheets."

"Nonsense," said June. "We'll put you on the couch."

"I never seen a couch before," said Moon.

June pointed. "That's a couch there," she said.

Moon looked. "Don't that look comfy," she said.

"You're not going to start hemorrhaging on us, are you?" asked Amy. "Don't your kind sometimes start bleeding for no reason at all?"

"I never heard of that before," said Moon.

"If you're going to stay with us, you'll have to burn that tunic," said Amy. "I can smell it from here. And it probably has fleas."

"Amy Kristensen, watch your manners," said June. "We have a guest."

"I'm sorry . . . but if she's going to stay . . . we got certain standards of cleanliness around here, that's all."

"Then go run the bath while I make a cup of tea for her," said June.

Eric sat in the town jail in a cell facing the Mississippi. For some reason a lot of crows flew around outside. Craning, he saw seven bushel baskets of pig feed spilled on the road, toppled from the back of a farm truck. The hard kernels lay scattered over the pavement, and the crows gorged themselves. Beyond the crows, he had a good view of the Shrine. He saw the Citadel, the place where all the sleeping Benefactors stayed. He heard the cellblock door open. Glancing over his shoulder, he saw Canon Clarke Dechellis, the police chief, enter the detention area.

"Afternoon, Eric," said the canon.

"Afternoon, Clarke."

Dechellis came into his cell and sat down.

"I went to the Inculpator's Office to ask about your wife," he said. He shook his head. "They say she was questioned and released." He glanced out the window at the crows, then turned to Eric, his face set. "I don't know what to tell you. I know they took her out to St. Gilbert's. But I'm not sure they ever brought her back. Maybe she's still out there." He shrugged. "Maybe she isn't. Looks like they lost track of her."

Eric frowned. "Lost track of her?" he said.

"I don't know," he said. "They tell me that happens from time to time."

"They're lying," he said.

The canon grinned uncomfortably. "I wouldn't be so quick to condemn the Inculpator's Office, Eric. You're in enough hot water as it is."

"But they said they took her out to St. Gilbert's?"

"That's what they said."

"Because when I was out in West Shelby, it looked like they might have questioned her there."

"I wouldn't know about that."

The crows cawed constantly.

"Is there any way you can go out to St. Gilbert's to check for me?" asked Eric. "I'm stuck in jail here. I can't get out there. You and me are old friends, Clarke. I baptized your son. I confirmed your daughter. For the love of God, could you please go out and check for me?"

Dechellis raised his eyebrows and scratched his head. "Sure," he said. "I don't mind. I could drive out there and make a few inquiries for you. Course, I'll have to be careful. The Inculpator's Office is really cracking down. I don't want them thinking I'm a sympathizer." Dechellis looked out the window nervously. The crows, whirling above the buildings, were specks of black against the pale blue August sky. "We haven't been able to find that clay-bred woman Oskar Braaten told us about," he said. "I guess she got clean away."

"I'd appreciate it if you'd leave her be, Clarke. She's innocent. I just found her out there. She had no one to look after her."

Dechellis nodded. "We're not too interested in her, to tell you the truth, Eric," he said. "But I have to ask you about the Cardinal." He leaned forward and put his hands on his knees. "The Cardinal's not comin' back?"

Eric shook his head. "The Cardinal's dead," he said.

"How'd he die?" Dechellis asked.

"Killed by a Kiowa spear."

Dechellis sighed. "That's a shame." He got up to leave. "No one knows who his next of kin are."

"That doesn't surprise me," said Eric. "I'm not even sure his real name was Anders."

"No one can track down any of his relatives, so I guess we'll just have to leave it for the time being. As for Ingrid, I'll see what I can do."

"Are they going to move me out to St. Gilbert's?" he asked.

"Wesley Corrigan is trying to prevent that," said Dechellis. "We made the arrest, and by law we're allowed to keep you five days. But the Inculpator's Office has filed for a transfer to St. Gilbert's. They want to question you about your trip to the Restricted Zone. They found your radio equipment out there.

Honestly, Eric, what were you thinking? Why would you ever go out to the Restricted Zone like that when you knew it was against the law?"

The airships screamed out of the sky a couple of hours later, black v-shaped flying machines trailing mile-long plumes of black smoke. They dove at high speed, each the size of an ocean liner, seven of them altogether. Eric watched in wonder. They pulled out of their dives a half mile above the pretty farmland and cow pastures of Illinois and flew straight toward St. Lucius. Could they be anything but Roman airships? They flew across the river and banked upward over the rooftops of the Shrine. Their roar shook the jailhouse and rattled the windows of the warehouse across the street.

At first he felt paralyzed by the sight. Ten paddle steamers end to end couldn't have been as big as a single one of those flying machines. And there were seven of them! Big, ungainly metal boomerangs that miraculously stayed aloft, ships that looked scuffed and dirty and charred.

They approached the jailhouse, raining a curious white ash down on the town of St. Lucius. Eric saw giant red eagles painted on the undersides of their wings. They flew over the jailhouse and disappeared from view. He stared at the trails of smoke they left behind—trails that stretched all the way back to Illinois. The ash that fell from the sky looked like snow. He listened to the roar of the retreating airships as they flew up the hill. The sound stabilized, changed in pitch, finally sighed, and stopped altogether.

All grew silent.

And in that silence, Eric knew the world had changed forever. A quiet joy filled his soul.

But his joy was short-lived. Toward sunset, Wesley Corrigan came to him with news of his wife. The aging lawyer eased himself into a chair with a sigh and adjusted the pince-nez on his nose. He looked flustered, was perspiring and out of breath.

"The town's in an uproar," he said. "People have locked their doors. Everyone thinks we've got invaders from Mars." He sat back and contemplated Eric. "My, but your face is badly burned, isn't it? Was it worth it, Eric? You've terrified the whole town. My contact in the Inculpator's Office tells me they intercepted your radio signal in the Restricted Zone. Is it true, then?" He waved his hand in the direction of the ridge. "Everybody thinks they're Martians, but are they really Romans? Were you responsible for all this, Eric?"

Eric lifted his chin. "I was," he said.

"And was it worth it?" asked Corrigan. "Was it worth the death of your wife?"

Eric felt as if he had been shot through the chest with an arrow. "What are you talking about?" he asked.

"She's dead, Eric," said Wes. "My contact in the Inculpator's Office told me so. They took her out to St. Gilbert's for questioning, and they did horrible things to her. She finally told them what your plans were, how you and the Cardinal planned to contact the Romans. And then they gave her a lethal injection, such as is provided by Liturgical Law in extreme circumstances. They wanted to punish you, Eric. They still do. So they took Ingrid's life."

"So she's dead?" he said, feeling as if he were now living in a nightmare.

"I tried to stop them, but I couldn't." Wes looked down at his hands. "I'm sorry, Eric. I'm awfully sorry. Liturgical Law is just so finicky. There's no way to really fight against it when all is said and done."

"And you're sure she's dead?" he said, still not wanting to believe it.

"I'm sure."

Eric began to tremble. Tears came to his eyes. "They'll know my wrath, Wes," he said. "When the Romans come to free me, they'll surely know my wrath. I'll make them pay for this."

Wes shook his head despondently. "I don't think there's much chance of that, Eric. Arch Prescript Dewey has declared a state of emergency. He's given the Inculpator's Office sweeping powers. They can come take you to St. Gilbert's any time they like, and I know for a fact they're planning on doing that once they overturn my final injunction against it. You'll just have to hope and pray to God that once they take you there, they won't hurt you too badly."

CHAPTER 31

It was dusk. Hesperus was out by the Fence, squeezing his way through the crowd, trying not to look at the great ships that were half sunk into the wheat field. He was weak now. There was no way he could fight these Romans. *Bellum Exstirpatio*. The dreaded Latin phrase kept running through his mind. It was what the Romans called their galactic war against the children of Woden, a war of extermination. He was tired. He knew the Romans would kill him if they ever found him inside Neil's body. He had to make his peace with June before he lost his chance.

A lot of farmers and country folk had come into town with hunting rifles, pitchforks, and crowbars. He passed a young man in denim overalls with buck teeth, his red hair styled in a bowl cut. The man carried a double-barreled shotgun over his shoulder, and he gazed at the *bellum pennae* of the Romans as if at any minute he expected them to swarm out of the ships like angry bees. Hesperus eavesdropped on the young man's conversation.

"I figger these must be Martians," he was telling

another man. "These spaceships got a Martian look to them."

How ignorant these humans could sometimes be. He kept walking, intent on finding June.

The police were here. The army was here—at least what could be spared after Runnymede. He didn't see any other Benefactors. He couldn't feel any other Benefactors. This was new, this suppression field coming from the Roman ships. Was it a new weapon? He felt it sizzling all around him, wreaking havoc on his balance of positive and negative charges. He couldn't see anyone, hear anyone, or sense anyone, not even the sleepers in the Citadel. If he and his brethren were all blind to one another, how could they coordinate a counterattack? It was just a matter of time before they were all annihilated.

He finally spotted June standing by the Rowatt grain elevator. He worked his way through the crowd. They were all restless. No one could understand why the ships just sat. Why wasn't anyone coming out yet? He knew why. The Romans conducted extensive atmospheric tests. They ran samples through batteries of bacterial and toxicological tests, launched remote intelligence-gathering micro-probes, compiled topographical maps of the nearest hundred square miles, and eavesdropped on the conversations of the local inhabitants using micro-bugs to better understand their language and their ways.

"June!" he called.

She turned. Her eyes grew wide. She was standing with an attractive but pale woman. The woman wore ill-fitting clothes, had too much makeup on her face, and looked as if she had just recovered from a long illness. Was she a clay-bred? Hesperus wasn't sure. What would June be doing with a clay-bred?

"What do you want?" she asked.

His eyes widened as the unruly human heart inside him recoiled from the rebuke he heard in her voice. "I want to explain why I . . ." But he couldn't go on. That poisonous look in her eyes robbed him of his faculty for words.

June looked at her friend. "Stay here, Moon," she said. She grabbed him by the sleeve. "Come over here," she demanded. "Let's talk."

They moved away from the crowd toward the Roman ships fifty yards away. The ships straddled the town of Rowatt. They blocked the railroad running north and south. A steam locomotive hauling grain cars sat waiting, a toy compared to the seven *bellum pennae.* He and June passed a prayer group, nineteen fearful souls on their knees before the ships. A boy sat in a sycamore tree shooting his BB gun at the nearest spacecraft. Further down, two ships away, as the land sloped toward the old limestone quarry, three police cruisers blocked Brereton Road. More and more people gathered all the time.

"I'm sorry, June," he said.

"Who *are* you?" she asked.

He looked away. "I wish I could do something to fix this."

She looked as if she were about to hiss like a cat. "I'm glad the Romans are here," she said. She looked toward the ships with a vindictive smile. "They've really got you scared, don't they?"

He was so distraught he could hardly think straight.

"Neil's still somewhere inside me," he said, uttering the five crucial words he knew she had to hear.

She stopped. "Which one are you?" she said. "Are you Hesperus?"

Her guess unnerved him. Only in becoming one of these creatures had he come to realize that there was a lot more to them than he had thought.

"I'm sorry, June," he repeated.

She broke away and marched toward the nearest Roman ship. Having landed end to end on the high ground above St. Lucius, the ships formed a wall a thousand yards long. The police had neither manpower nor barricades to effectively block access on such a broad front, so June strode to the ship unhindered. Hesperus followed, his steps furtive and unsure. June showed not the slightest trace of fear. She didn't seem to realize that with a single *baculum* blast the Romans could reduce her to a puddle of jam.

"June, please," he said. "I wouldn't go near them if I were you."

Looking straight up at the nearest ship, she pointed at Hesperus and cried, *"Interfecio eum! Hic est Patronus!"*

The dreaded language, spoken by the only human he had ever loved, sounded horrible to his ears. The language of war, the language of his own extinction. *Shoot him. He is a Benefactor.* He cringed, fearing the horrible meltdown, a blast from that weapon the Romans used to destabilize *Patroni* protons and electrons. *"Interfecio eum!"* she cried again. *"Hic est patronus."*

He turned around and walked toward Volker Avenue. He didn't look back. He was afraid that if he did the weapon's heavy isotopes would shake him to pieces. He wanted June to love him, wanted to feel that connectedness again, but he now knew that he would never have any kind of connectedness or concord with her.

Gallio stared at the odd little city on the banks of the two great rivers through his one-way window while he reviewed the volumes of information coming over his *scriba*. The town was comprised of many small buildings in red stone with ornately carved lancet arch windows, a lot of steeples, and numerous bell towers, which rang every night around sunset. He couldn't understand all the bell ringing. They didn't have bells in Elysium. On all the many planets he'd visited, he'd not once encountered such a preoccupation with bell ringing. Two days ago they'd rung all morning. High bells, low bells, sweet bells, sour bells. Constantly. The *legio observatio* had investigated but had yet to come up with any cultural explanation for it.

He turned from the window. "I want the woman again," he said to his *scriba*.

The woman appeared on the *scriba*. He knew her name now. June. A variation on Juno, his *legio lingua* expert told him. He listened to June shout in Latin. *"Interfecio eum."* Such fierceness was uncommon in any of the Roman women he knew. *"Hic est Patronus."* Here was a woman whose veins ran with vinegar and whose eyes flashed with the thunderbolts of her namesake. Yet she was thin, small, waiflike. At the same time she was pretty. And different from the Roman women he knew. Roman women had the same cast to their faces, the same look. He found it curiously thrilling that he should see a woman who was so obviously different from any of the Roman women he knew, yet so obviously pretty. He was in his fifties. He didn't think it possible he should feel this way again. Yet here he was, watching this woman for the tenth time.

A large bald man followed her. He watched the man walk away . . . saw June walk away with a look of disappointment in her eyes.

The micro-probe followed her to her dwelling and snuck in behind her. It listened to her talk to another woman she lived with. The conversation, according to the *legio lingua* expert, had been about the Romans: how they had finally come, how they would end the tyranny of the *Patroni*, and how this Eric Nordstrum who had sent the signal should be considered a hero by everybody.

So much to learn, so much to observe, so much information coming in all the time. He turned from his *scriba* and looked at St. Lucius again. All kinds of people lived on this world: white, black, Oriental, Indian, and Semitic, a wondrous variety that left him breathless because, after all, what variety was there among Romans, interbred from the original twenty thousand two millennia ago? Not much. Then there were the clones. Were they slaves, then, he wondered? Large concentrations of them had been found in regions to the west. They were a race characterized by pandemic bad health. All wore the same uniform, a rough burlap tunic stenciled with a red cross and orbis. Many were anemic, or suffered from other blood disorders. He reviewed the blood profiles one more time on his *scriba*. Crude, quick, and careless cloning techniques often produced these bizarre profiles. His experts told him that chromosome 7 had been altered in an attempt to make this population docile. Oddly, one in every thousand was brilliant, a genius.

His lieutenant, Oppius Naevius, came in. Gallio gestured out the window.

"Naevius, is it possible that these people are medically advanced enough to clone the worker tribes of the plains?" he asked.

"No," said Naevius. "The tabulists have learned that the clones are in fact created in places called Potteries and that the technology is of *Patronus* design. We used this kind of cloning technique fifteen hundred years ago, until it was outlawed. It can't be nice to be one of these clones. The *Patroni* use the same quick-growing techniques to produce livestock, poultry, and produce. The *medicos* believe this cloned food is consumed by about seventy percent of the population."

Gallio nodded. "How many feeds have we launched so far?" he asked.

"Two-and-a-half-million worldwide."

"So what have we learned? What ruse have the *Patroni* employed to maintain their power?"

"They've instituted a worldwide thearchy," said Naevius.

"So the place is run by priests, then?" ventured Gallio.

"Of one sort or another. The *Patroni* co-opted one of the smaller subversive movements Rome was trying to quell two thousand years ago, a movement based on a loose set of monotheistic beliefs and the grassroots moral philosophy of a man named Jesu Christus. I've accessed the old historical record. We have a file on Christus. He was fond of whores. He habitually defrauded his followers. A *legio medico* report documents him as borderline schizophrenic. He worked with a gang. They traveled from town to town stealing what they could, conning people with a promise of eternal salvation, then moving on before the authorities could arrest them. Christus was finally executed. The *Patroni* used Christus's movement as a tool of control afterward."

"And everyone believes in it?"

"No. We've discovered several outlawed religions, all thriving underground to one degree or another in various parts of the world. I think we'll have a broad base of support among these groups when we finally make our move. But in the meantime we'll still need individual collaborators. We're going to need designated trustees from the general population to speak for us and to promote our cause."

Gallio reflected on this. "What of the Odd Fellows?" he asked.

"That's a good place to start," agreed Naevius.

"And what of this war the Odd Fellows support in the Old World?" Gallio asked. "The Huns have risen against the *Patroni*?"

"The Huns fight valiantly against the *Patroni*," said Naevius, "but their army weakens."

"The Huns will soon have our support," said Gallio. "They'll just have to hang on. What kind of army do they have? I imagine it must be primitive."

"They've developed crude mechanized armor, such as we used twenty-five-hundred years ago. As for combat aircraft, they don't have any. There exists a fleet of seventeen dirigibles. Other than those, we haven't found anything in the way of airborne conveyances. The incoming information strands tell us the *Patroni* discourage technical innovation. I don't know what kind of tribute we can reasonably expect from these people when we finally liberate them. It's going to take them at least ten years to get back on their feet after this war."

"Has any action been advised by the *legio economicus*?"

Naevius nodded. "They're developing a long-term plan," he said. "They don't think we should ask for more than a ten percent tribute up front. They think we should just go ahead and kill all the *Patroni* before the situation worsens. Rid the place of *Patroni*—it shouldn't take more than a few days—then concentrate on revamping the economic infrastructure for sustainable dividends in the long term. There's a huge labor pool, more then two billion humans worldwide, and well over half of them are demographically eligible for enforced public service."

"So have we yet devised a list of collaborators?" asked Gallio.

"Eighty-three in St. Lucius."

"And have we had any luck in finding this . . . this man . . . the one who sent the original signal? Eric Nordstrum?"

Naevius nodded. "Eric Nordstrum is currently incarcerated at the local jailhouse for illegally entering the restricted radio zone to the west. There are plans afoot to move him to the larger penal institution in St. Je-

rome. Until recently, he held a position of considerable power, that of Ecclesiarch, a position comparable
to the one you held as Governor on Hortus. He's a
popular man, Gallio. Many feel a deep regard and
affection for him. Many want him released from jail."

Gallio pondered this. "He will of course be rewarded," he said. "But I wonder if we can use him in
any effective political way."

Naevius looked out the window at the town. "They
broadcast in radio here. We can ask Eric Nordstrum
to speak for us on radio. As he's the one who originally contacted us, I think we can count on his
support."

Gallio nodded. "I'm still worried about this superbomb that the Huns have. Any more information on
that?"

Naevius shrugged. "We have in the *tabularium* more
than a hundred thousand overheard conversations
about the superbomb. It was dropped at a place called
Runnymede, in the former Roman province of Britannia. The conversations indicate that the army of the
Papal States of America was wiped out at a single
stroke with this bomb as they prepared for the invasion of Gaul. We've sent micro-probes to Runnymede
to assess the damage and have taken satellite photographs. By a close scrutiny of the satellite photographs
and an examination of the information strands gathered by the micro-probes, the *legio machinalis scientia*
has determined that the bomb used at Runnymede
produced a blast a thousand times larger than what
we can produce with any of the bombs in our arsenal.
Our five-thousand-pounders are firecrackers compared

to this thing. Based on current technology, a bomb that would produce a blast that size would need at least ten thousand tons of high explosives."

"And it wiped out a whole army in one go?"

"Fifty thousand troops. It was dropped from one of these dirigibles I spoke of. The bomb itself was no bigger than that cow out there. If only the *legio exstirpatio* could devise something like that, they could get rid of all their biochemicals."

Gallio leaned forward. "How do they do this?" he asked. "It doesn't seem possible that they should develop something like this when so much of their technology is backward. Has the *legio machinalis scientia* come up with an explanation?"

Naevius shrugged. "Yes and no," he said. "Several information strands suggest that the bomb's massive explosive power is derived from the splitting of an atom of uranium. Roman science, however, currently believes the atom is indivisible. We've *manipulated* atoms with electromagnetic charges before, taken away electrons or added them, but we've never *divided* a nucleus."

Gallio shook his head. "And this dirigible is the only means of delivering the weapon?"

"Yes."

He sighed. "That's a relief," he said. "Coupled with an advanced delivery system, this bomb could pose a serious threat to us. But as it stands, it's something we might barter for, as part of the tribute they will owe us for defeating the *Patroni*."

CHAPTER 32

Eric tapped the windowsill and looked out at the river. He felt numbed by Ingrid's death. He didn't want to believe it, tried to put it from his mind by thinking about the Roman ships outside. So frustrating to be on this side of the jailhouse, where he couldn't see the Roman ships. If the Romans were going to release him, they'd better do it soon, before he was moved out to St. Gilbert's. At least Clarke had been kind enough to open the shutters to let some air in. Yet the air did nothing to revive his spirits now that he knew Ingrid was gone. Wes had to be wrong about that. He just *had* to be. He wished he could see the ships up on the hill. Morning of Day Three, and so far not a single Roman had emerged from any of the ships. He was beginning to wonder if anybody inside had survived the descent. He left the window and sat on his bench. He hoped June Upshaw might visit—he wanted to thank her for looking after Moon. And he wanted to find out if she knew anything about his wife's passing. He wanted the Romans to come release him so he could avenge her death.

He was just thinking he might like to sleep when he heard a faint buzz at his window. He got up and looked out the bars. Was that a hummingbird hovering right outside the window? With a suddenness that surprised him, the thing swooped right through the bars and into his cell. It landed on the far wall. What the devil was it?

He approached with caution. It looked like a big bug. As he got closer, he saw that it was in fact manmade. It had to be at least as big as his thumb, with shiny silver wings. It jumped off the wall and hovered in front of him. He peered at it. Just like a big bug. Some sort of lens was built into the bug's head. With a quick swipe, he caught the thing in his hand.

Keeping the bug pinned, he took a closer look at the contraption. The wings were made of a clear flexible material and had tiny copper wires running inside them. He turned the bug over and saw two tiny words engraved on its underside: *LEGIO OBSERVATIO.* He opened his hand. The bug leapt into the air, buzzed in front of him for a few seconds, then flew out the window just as he heard a truck pull up outside.

Out the window he saw a paddy wagon emblazoned with the crest of the Inculpator's Office roll to a stop in front of the jailhouse. Four Seminarians got out, went around the front of the wagon, and climbed the steps to the jailhouse. He took a deep breath and clenched his jaw. He knew those Seminarians were here for him. He felt an overpowering urge to run, but where could he go when he was locked in a cell? He pulled himself away from the window and stood with his back to the wall. A thin film of perspiration dampened his forehead. If the Seminarians took him to St. Gilbert's, he might never get out. And then he would never be able to avenge the death of his wife.

He heard boots tramping up the stairs. The detention area door opened. The four Seminarians entered. Canon Dechellis trailed behind them. He had a bloody gash on his forehead.

"I tried to stop them, Eric," he said. "I really did."

Eric nodded, grateful that his old friend should try to help him. "Thanks, Clarke," he said. "God bless you."

The largest of the Seminarians didn't bother with the key but simply ripped the cell door off its hinges. Eric's body went cold. He knew this Seminarian had to be one of the Benefactors. Only a Benefactor could rip a door off its hinges like that.

They came inside, handcuffed and shackled him, and led him downstairs to the waiting paddy wagon.

Outside, he caught a glimpse of the Roman ships up on the hill. Even though they were two miles away, he could see them easily—they towered into the sky several hundred feet feet high, underscoring the mellow August dusk with a uniform black line. How could humans engineer ships so large and still make them fly? The Seminarians pushed him into the back of the paddy wagon, and he lost sight of the ships. He fell to his knees. One of the Seminarians kicked him.

"Get up," he said. "Sit on the bench."

He pulled himself up to the steel bench and sat down. They climbed in after him, closed the back doors, and arranged themselves one on either side of him and two opposite. He was engulfed in their coarse electrical smell. They were all Benefactors. He looked at the one beside him and grinned weakly.

"Which one are you?" he asked. "Are you Canicula? Are you Aldebaran?" The one beside him stared with aluminum pie-plate eyes. "Tell me—I've always wondered this: Why do you name yourselves after stars? Is it because that's where you come from?"

None of them answered. They just sat there, not saying a word, all the way to St. Gilbert's.

At St. Gilbert's, scared and nervous guards deprived him of his clothes and put him once again in a burlap sack stenciled with the red cross and orbis. They then took him to a different part of the prison than before, the part where they kept prisoners in solitary confinement, and put him in a small, dark cell. They shut the door. He just stood there staring at the closed door for a minute. Had they treated his wife this way? Ingrid didn't like the dark. She always snuggled up to him in the dark, or whenever there was a storm, or if she was worried about something.

Luckily, it wasn't completely dark. An air hole six inches wide had been drilled into the opposite wall. It was a good ways up, but he was a tall man, and by standing on tiptoe he was able to reach it. He raised his eyes to the level of the hole and looked out.

He could see the river. A paddle steamer floated gracefully past, its twin black stacks billowing smoke into the dusky air, a few gents and ladies strolling around its lower deck, the sound of a tinny piano playing ragtime coming from its upper deck. Life went on, even though seven Roman ships sat on the hill up in Rowatt.

He watched the river off and on for the next hour.

He expected supper, but none came. He expected water, but none came. He had to go to the bathroom, but there was no pot in this cell, so he finally had to relieve himself in the corner. He paced for a bit, knowing he couldn't expect a Collegiate Pardon this time.

He finally grew tired and sat on the floor with his back to the wall. He was hungry, cold, destitute, without family or friends, facing certain death—yet he felt he had done something great. He could die now. He was ready for it. He gently touched the scar tissue on his face. He would never be a handsome man again, but at least he knew he had been a good man. At least he could die knowing he had been a man who had followed his conscience.

He dozed for a while.

When he woke up an hour later, he heard strange booms coming from a great distance. They sounded like the cannon the town fired from the foot of Wharf Road every first of August to celebrate the P.S.A.'s Independence from Norway. Sometimes the booms got louder, sometimes they got fainter. Sometimes they disappeared altogether. He stood on tiptoe by the air hole again and looked out. He couldn't see a thing except for some lights across the river. At one point he thought he heard gunfire. He sank back down against the wall and dozed once more.

Two Seminarians came for him a couple of hours later. He got up as quickly as he could, but one of them pushed him right back down and kicked him in the stomach, knocking the wind out of him. As he gasped for breath, the Seminarian spoke.

"We grow weak," he said. "But not so weak we

can't still punish the infidels who would defy the greater glory of God and His Heavenly Host." Eric squinted at the Seminarian. They believed the lies they told about themselves? "We shall expunge the wicked from His Kingdom and make this beauteous Earth a true Paradise for those who believe." Had they all become so humanized after so many centuries of isolation on Earth that they believed and subscribed to the Christian dogma they had devised to control their human flock? "The wicked shall perish in the everlasting fires of Hell, and those who perjure God's True Word shall have no Mercy from the Great Lord on High, nor his son, Jesus Christ."

They lifted him by the arms and dragged him out into the hall. He tried to shake them loose. Whereas once he had been their obedient servant he would now openly defy them.

"Let me go!" he cried. "You're murderers, the whole pack of you. You have no right to call yourselves servants of God. You're servants of the Devil."

They ignored him. They were so strong he had no hope of breaking free.

They led him first down one corridor, then along another. He recognized this corridor. It was the one that led to the basement room where he had been interrogated the first time.

"Where are you taking me?" he cried, even though he knew full well. His defiance quickly gave way to fear. "Let me go!"

They took him down the stairs to the basement room.

The Surgeon and the two Acolytes waited for him, the same ones who had been there before.

"Here we are again, Father," said the Surgeon. "What a pleasure to see you again." The Surgeon's face hardened as he said to the two Seminarians, "Put him in the chair. Strap him tight."

"May God wreak just vengeance upon you," said the larger of the two Seminarians.

The Seminarians left the room. Eric saw on the table the Surgeon's instruments of persuasion: two hypodermic needles, a pair of tin snips, an iron poker, a razor blade, a small sledgehammer, an acetylene torch, a piece of barbed wire, a metal bar, and off to one side, the electrical apparatus that had caused him so much grief his last time here. The Surgeon nodded at the Acolytes. The two came forward and beat him, punched him in the face again and again until he tasted blood in his mouth, knocked the wind out of him so he thought he would suffocate, broke a few ribs, went at him so fiercely that his body finally convulsed into semiconsciousness and they had to use smelling salts to revive him.

Then they just let him sit. He slouched in the metal chair helplessly. Was this what they had done to Ingrid? The Surgeon contemplated him with a fond expression.

"We don't often have the pleasure of repeat visitors," he said. Eric noted that the Surgeon had gained weight since his last time here, was fattened on the spoils and real-food victuals of the Holy Catholic ecclesiastical classes. "The Seminarians found your radio out in the Restricted Zone, Father. Or at least they found the Cardinal's radio."

Eric bunched his lips and spat. He would still defy them. "May God send a pox upon you," he said.

The Surgeon's placid grin disappeared and he looked disappointed—the same way a teacher might look disappointed in an errant pupil.

"Is that any way to treat an old friend?" he asked. He turned to the table of instruments and lifted one of the hypodermic needles. "One of these is lethal," he said. "I can't remember which one. Let's try this one and find out."

The Surgeon approached with the needle. Eric shook so hard that the Acolytes had to hold him steady. The Surgeon jabbed the needle into his arm, and instantly his brain turned to jelly. He slid forward in the chair and passed out. The restraining straps were the only things holding him in place. When he came to, they were all looking at him.

"That injection was bigger than the last one," said the Acolyte to his left.

The Surgeon said something to the Acolyte, but Eric was slipping ever further into a well of incomprehension, and the words sounded so distorted and slow that he couldn't make them out at all. The Surgeon leaned forward and tapped Eric's cheek a few times with his finger. Eric just sat there, slouched in his chair, looking up at the man, unable to react, his head lolling.

"The radio was smashed," said the Surgeon. Eric grinned as he remembered how he had destroyed the radio after finally signing off with the Romans, a ploy to thwart any possible investigation. "But members of the technical laity tell us there was a prerecorded message in the transmit oscillator. We have only a poor recording of that message, picked up by one of our own radios, and we can't make out most of it." The

Surgeon grinned encouragingly. "We want you to tell us what was in that message."

Eric's nostrils flared and his brow furrowed, and he felt like he had in the old days when he had been about to offer a message of fire and brimstone to his parishioners.

"May God strike you dead with lightning the minute you leave this building," said Eric, "and may your seed forever be barren."

The Surgeon frowned, puzzled, and Eric realized his words must have come out so badly slurred that the Surgeon hadn't been able to understand them. He couldn't help thinking of Ingrid. Had she suffered in this same room? The Surgeon put his hands on his hips and shook his head. He then signaled one of the Acolytes to wheel the electrical apparatus over. The shorter of the two did so, then ripped Eric's tunic off, leaving him naked. The other one doused him with a bucket of water. The Surgeon was about to attach the clips to his ears and testicles, but then he seemed to have second thoughts. He touched Eric's cheek again, exploring the scar tissue of his various burns. He then went to the table, lifted the acetylene torch, lit the flame, and held the iron poker in the flame until, after a minute or two, the black iron brightened to a grayish orange.

"Now, then, Father, what was the substance of the prerecorded message?"

"A plague upon your house," said Eric, but again the words came out so badly slurred the Surgeon just shook his head.

The Surgeon came forward, the poker burning hot in his hand, and applied it to Eric's face. Whether Eric screamed or not he couldn't tell, because now there seemed to be a lot of noise coming from everywhere, the same booming noise he had heard earlier in the night from his cell. The pain was so searing, so excruciating that he passed out again, only to come to several moments later to find the Surgeon and the Acolytes staring at something up on the wall. Eric forced himself to focus.

He saw another one of Roman bugs on the wall.

"Get it," said the Surgeon.

One of the Acolytes lifted the metal bar from the table and swung at the contraption. The thing dodged at the last second, jumping off the wall and landing on the table. The Surgeon scooped it up with his hand—it wasn't particularly swift.

"They're everywhere now," he said. "How did it get in here?"

He put the thing under his foot and crushed it. Then he turned his attention back to Eric. Eric hardly saw him. He was having a memory of Ingrid, the two of them up on the observation deck of St. Bernardine's dome the day the Vatican appointed him the Ecclesiarch of St. Lucius. He remembered how the sun had shone on the river and how radiant Ingrid had looked, her eyes a transparent blue, her cheeks aglow with youth, her hair up in a bun, such as was the style at the time. Oh, how he was going to miss her.

"Murderer," he said.

The Surgeon looked at him more closely. The man's face looked distorted, stretched and bent as if reflected in a funhouse mirror. What was that noise, that low rumble, so penetrating he could feel it vibrating in his feet? The Surgeon looked nervously over his shoulder.

The Acolytes gazed up at the ceiling, their faces tight with worry. The Surgeon brought his face closer.

"You're here to die, Father," said the Surgeon. "But not before you answer some of our questions."

The Surgeon attached the clips to his earlobes and his testicles. He turned the dial. The electricity sizzled through Eric, jolting his whole body so that he thought his skin would jump right off his skeleton and his brain would melt out his ears. His eyes snapped shut, his abdomen tensed like a board, and he bit down on his tongue, his whole face stretched in a rictus of agony. The Surgeon kept the dial turned up for a whole minute before he finally turned it back down.

Eric went limp in the chair. The Surgeon came close to him again.

"Can you hear those booms outside?" he asked.

Eric nodded weakly, even though he couldn't hear anything besides a loud buzzing in his ears. He was prepared to agree with anything the Surgeon said, so long as the Surgeon didn't turn the dial up again.

"The Romans have left their airships," said the Surgeon. "They've occupied the town. We found a microphone with your radio. Did you actually speak to them?"

"Yes," he said.

"And what did you say?"

"I told them my name."

"You spoke Latin to them?"

"Yes."

"And who taught you to speak Latin?"

"The Cardinal did."

"And where's the Cardinal now?"

"I buried him."

"Did you tell the Romans anything else besides your name?" asked the Surgeon.

"I told them we were at war with the Benefactors and that we needed their help to wipe them out."

This didn't please the Surgeon at all. He immediately turned up the dial and Eric was again plunged into a living death of agonizing voltage. His whole body shook. He threw up, then shook some more, and when the Surgeon finally turned the dial back down, the room kept spinning end over end and the buzzing in his ears became a persistent high-pitched whine.

"Did the Romans tell you anything about backup troops coming?"

"No."

"So, seven ships, that's it?"

"I don't know," said Eric.

"What? Speak up. I can't hear you."

Eric tried to form the words again, but he simply didn't have the strength. Had they finally electrocuted Ingrid too? Had she suffered this same hell? The floor shook again. The door opened. A Seminarian stood there.

"The prison's been breached," he said. "The infidels are among us. Rome has risen. Kill the heretic while you have the chance. He must pay for his sins."

Suddenly the Surgeon seemed beside himself—excited, confused, and red-faced. He hurried to the table and picked up the remaining syringe, the lethal one. He came close to Eric. He pushed the plunger down a bit and tapped the syringe by flicking his fingernail at it.

"This is the way we killed your wife," he said, now breathless. "Yes, this is the way she died."

"You killed her?"

He said these words, but even to his own ears they didn't sound like words, more like low-pitched moans. The Acolytes were standing at the door. Eric heard gunfire from upstairs. This was it. The Surgeon was going to give him the lethal injection. He summoned his last wits and his final strength as the Surgeon brought the needle down to his arm, and, tensing his stomach, he jerked upward and smashed his forehead into the Surgeon's head. The Surgeon stumbled back. And—this was strange—one second the Surgeon was there, the next he disappeared in a cloud of red spray as the room lit up with a blinding flash.

Eric wasn't sure if he was hallucinating or not. Two tall men in leather skirts, black helmets, and bronze breastplates entered the room. Were these Romans, then? The Acolytes lay dead at the door, their heads blown off. Were these men actually here to save him, to take him away from this hell on Earth at the last moment? He sat back in the chair as dizziness overwhelmed him and black spots of unconsciousness swam up into his eyes. *Rome has risen.* Three simple words, but words he had been so desperately yearning to hear.

When he came to, the Roman soldiers helped him outside. As the big front gate swung open, he saw several other Roman soldiers, a hundred at least, standing in two neat rows on either side of the road. He saw Roman tanks on the mud flats and a few other

Roman vehicles, black and sleek and decaled with red eagles, hovering above the mud flats, suspended as if by a godly force. He saw some dead Seminarians and some dead prison guards. He looked up at the sky. Dawn brightened the clouds up there, and seagulls whirled about. The Roman soldiers escorted him down the road. They had wrapped him in a kind of white toga because he didn't have any other clothes. He was alive. Rome had risen, and he was *alive*.

At the end of the two rows of soldiers he saw June Upshaw standing with Moon. The two of them flanked an older Roman soldier. This soldier wore a black uniform with red epaulets. Eric approached him on shaky legs.

Finally he stood in front of the three. June stepped forward.

"You're safe at last, Eric," she said.

But Eric was too busy staring at the strange turquoise creature beside the old Roman soldier. The thing had a head like a platypus and two big eyes rimmed with tiny feathers. If an ostrich were to take human form, this was what it would look like, he decided.

"This is General Publius Gallio Corvinus," said June, "leader of the Roman expedition to Earth."

June gazed at the tall Roman general if she rather fancied the man. Publius Gallio put his fist to his heart.

"*Mihi pergratum est te convenire,*" said Gallio.

Eric dredged up some Latin, the only Latin he could think of at the moment.

"*Di te ament.*" God bless you.

Later, as they were returning to the city in one of

the Roman hover vehicles, June put her hand on Eric's arm.

"You were right, Eric," she said.

"Right about what?" he asked.

"God found a way," she said. "And that way was you."

CHAPTER 33

Eric, newly appointed by General Publius Gallio Corvinus to the Office of Intercessor, was back in the Manse. He had all the riches anyone could want, and enough power to satisfy even the most ambitious clergyman. He was glad to be home. But as he stood at the window watching Publius Gallio leave after this, their fifth meeting, he felt the emptiness of the place, couldn't help hearing the long-lost echoes of his children's laughter, of his wife's voice, thought of the many wonderful dinners he had shared with friends and fellow clergy here, and wondered if he had made the right choice after all. A Roman armored personnel carrier guarded the street. A Roman tank stood in the drive. Two Roman centurions flanked his front door. Gallio thought he might need protection. And Gallio had a point. To some, he was a traitor. He didn't care. His wife was dead, killed by that most quintessential of Catholic institutions, the Inculpator's Office. And because of that, he wanted to destroy every Catholic institution on the face of the Earth.

Moon and June walked up the street. Gallio raised

his hand in greeting. The centurions at the front gate
let the two women pass. June had a broad smile on
her face. To think she was an Odd Fellow; she had
been plotting against the Church all this time. The
women were loaded down with shopping bags and hatboxes—the riches of Rome. They stopped at the front
gate to talk to Gallio, Moon translating. Moon, as it
turned out, was one of those one-in-a-thousand clay-
bred with a genius-level IQ. Three days of listening
to the Romans, and she was as fluent in Latin as she
was in Cheyenne. But June was learning also. And so
was he. He grinned as he watched the two women
talk to the big Roman general. Was June flirting with
the General?

Moon excused herself and continued up the walk.
She wore a new pale blue outfit, cinched at the waist
with a belt. She also had on one-inch pumps—not
stratospherically elevated heels to be sure, but a challenge for someone who had gone barefoot all her life.
June and Gallio continued to talk, struggling as best
they could through the language barrier. The General's interest in June was unmistakable. What strange
turns life could sometimes take, that an Odd Fellow
and a Roman general would at last hook up in this
way, both foes of the Benefactors, but fighting the
Host in such drastically different ways and in such
drastically different places.

Moon came in the front door. She entered his study
and put her hatboxes and shopping bags down.

"You look like a town girl now," he said.

She studied him coyly. "Do I?" she asked. "What
do you think of this new outfit?"

She spun around, showing off. He felt a growing

affection for her. Moon, even though she didn't know it, was keeping him afloat.

"You're as pretty as a picture," he said.

"Gallio says you have to talk on the radio tonight," she said.

He nodded. "I'll be heading down around four," he said. "I hope you and June will come with me. I'd like you to be there."

"A lot of people are talking about that broadsheet Gallio sent 'round," she said. "The one about Hortus? A lot of them dirt farmers ain't sure they want the little blue folk plantin' orchards and plowin' fields hereabouts."

He shrugged. "They'll just have to get used to it," he said. "The Hortulani are here to stay. They have nowhere else to go."

"And folks is nervous because they can't figure out why one set of Romans went against another set of Romans over those little blue fellas."

Eric looked at the cigar box on his desk. "We have to leave it to them as an internal matter for now," he said. "It's up to the Romans to settle that among themselves. We have to concern ourselves with the Benefactors." He looked out the window. "June and Gallio are hitting it off," he said.

Moon looked out the window.

"I reckon they'll be sweethearts soon enough," she said. She looked at him forlornly. "I wish I had a sweetheart. I ain't never had a sweetheart before."

He pondered her, felt an unexpected stirring inside. He quickly suppressed it by changing the subject.

"What else have you got in those bags?" he asked.

Her eyes lit up. "I got birdseed," she said. "I'm going to feed the birds outside."

She dug through the bags and pulled out a five-pound sack of birdseed. In her excitement about feeding the birds, it was as if she forgot he was there.

"Maybe you should rest before you feed the birds," he said. "You know how poorly you feel sometimes."

"No, sirree," she said. "Those little birds are hungry, and I aim to feed them."

He shook his head, smiled, and let her go. She walked down the hall to the back of the Manse. She lived here with him now. He was glad to have the company. It was lonesome around here with Ingrid gone. And no one else was going to look after Moon, so he figured he might as well.

Scared young troops of Arch Prescript Dewey's remnant army, bolstered by sixty Seminarians and a hundred clergy, guarded the Holy Catholic Broadcasting Building on Vine and Bell. As Eric approached, he prayed there would be no violence. A lone brown tank, all that the local regiment had on hand—and all that the army could spare after the tragedy at Runnymede—looked as puny as a tin can compared to the two massive Roman tanks up the street. The hundred clergymen formed a human chain in front of the radio station. Chief among them was Deacon Oskar Braaten. Five dozen Roman troops stood ready in Vine Street.

Eric turned to Gallio, and in his rough but ever-improving Latin asked, "What now?"

Gallio surveyed the ungainly chain of black-robed

clergy. "Is there any way you can talk to them? Are those the Seminarians back there?"

Eric's brow settled. "I expect more than half of them are Benefactors," he said.

Gallio sniffed the air. "I can smell them," he said. "We'll have to use that isotope scrambler I showed you if they resist us."

"I sure hope you won't have to harm any of those young reserves," said Eric.

Gallio sighed. "They don't look battle-hardened," he said. "I wish they would have the good sense to lay down their arms. Maybe once you talk to those priests, the priests will ask them to disperse."

Eric shrugged. "I hope so," he said.

Eric walked toward the clergymen, saddened by the whole mess. Maybe Oskar would listen. Maybe they would all listen. But as he got closer, they hissed. He stopped. Three months ago these men had been his friends and colleagues. Now they hissed at him. He shook his head. The Lord Jesus Christ had indeed marked out a hard path for him. He raised his hands in an effort to quiet them, but they only hissed louder.

He walked up to Oskar. Overhead, seven *pendeo pennae* hovered into view. The clergymen and soldiers looked up at the air vehicles apprehensively.

"Oskar," he called over the din, "you have to let me in. I have to make this broadcast. There's no point in trying to stop me."

"If you want to make your broadcast, use Roman equipment," said Oskar. "This here's Church property, and we can't have you spreading the Devil's word with it."

Eric shook his head sadly. "We thought of that, but

it won't work," he said. "The Benefactors have the Territory's radios rigged to receive signals only from approved stations and sources. They would never pick up a signal transmitted from Roman equipment. I've got to transmit from here or the townfolk won't hear me. You've got to let me through. I have to speak."

Oskar spat. "You'd best be on your way, Eric," he said. "The folk here are mighty riled. They've half a mind to hang you for the way you've turned on us."

"I've got to talk to the people, Oskar. I've got to make them understand that the Benefactors mean us great harm."

"We can't have you spreading blasphemy over the radio, Eric. You know we can't."

Eric's face settled. "I'd kindly appreciate it if you'd step aside, Oskar."

"You've been tricked by the Devil's own deceit, Eric," said Oskar. "I can't move and I won't move. The people are looking up to me now. They're counting on me to stop all this."

Eric saw it was pointless, but he made one last try anyway.

"Save yourself, Oskar," he said. "Don't be a fool. Walk away from this before it's too late."

"God will protect me," said Oskar.

Eric shook his head. "He didn't protect me," he said. "And he didn't protect Ingrid either. I don't think he's going to protect you, Oskar. Save yourself."

"I must defend the true Word of Christ in the Territory," said the Deacon, "now that you won't. I can't be letting the Devil have his say over Holy Catholic Radio."

*   *   *

Eric, June, and Moon took shelter in St. Fatima's
Catholic Church around the corner while Gallio re-
sorted to force to clear the clergy, the reserves, and
the Seminarians. They sat in a back pew toward the
north end of the church. Eric heard a megaphoned
voice outside asking people to disperse, heard people
yelling in response, crying out in protest. Just as the
yelling reached a peak, he heard a loud popping noise
followed by several sustained mechanical squeals.
Then he heard gunfire. Damn! Why couldn't those
reserves be sensible about the whole thing? Why did
they have to shoot? Eric heard the hiss of *bacula*.
Moon was scared. He put his arm around her and
pulled her near. He saw a bright flash outside, heard
a big boom. He heard people running, smelled smoke.
Bacula hissed again. He heard a few sporadic rifle
shots, but that fire quickly died out. He gazed at the
stained-glass depiction of the sacrifice of Isaac. The
young Isaac knelt on an unlit funeral pyre, hands tied
behind his back, his father, Abraham, standing above
him with a great sword. An Angel, spherical, one of
the Heavenly Host, hovered above, waiting for the
imminent slaughter. A ram looked on piously. What
Abraham was about to do to his son, Eric was about
to do to the whole Catholic Church.

Naevius came and got them when it was over.
"We didn't expect them to put up such a fight," he
told Eric. "I'm afraid there's been a lot of bloodshed."
They left St. Fatima's and walked down Vine Street
to Bell Boulevard. Layers of blue smoke marbled the
air. The sorry little brown tank in front of the radio
station was on fire, and many American troops, clergy,

and Seminarians lay dead out front. The Seminarians vented gas. Their heavy electrical smell filled the air, so much so that it stung Eric's eyes.

Oskar Braaten lay dead on the steps of the radio building, facedown, fat legs slightly apart, feet pigeon-toed, one of his shiny new spats half off, smoke drifting in tenuous fingers from the back of his gray clergyman's frock. Eric knelt beside his old friend, put his hand on the dead Deacon's shoulder, and hung his head in regret. The two women stood behind him.

"Eternal rest grant to our brother Oskar, O Lord," said Eric, "and let perpetual light shine upon him. May his soul, through the mercy of God, rest in peace." He made the sign of the cross, but left out the orbis, that spherical shape that represented the Benefactors in their original manifestation. "In the Name of the Father, and of the Son, and of the . . ." He checked himself. He couldn't say "Heavenly Host" anymore. But he had to say something. He extemporized. "And of the Holy Spirit. Amen." Because that's what it was. The miracle of God. The marvel of God. What Turning Bird felt inside. What Lone Cloud felt inside. And what he himself now felt inside. A Holy Spirit that had nothing to do with religion and everything to do with his own personal feelings about a Greater Being.

He rose from Oskar's side and went into the radio building.

He found Thorvald Ragnulf, his onetime producer from back in his radio preacher days, sitting at the control panel upstairs.

"Just like old times, Thor," he said.

Thor, well into his seventies now, nodded. "All except for that smell," he said, sniffing the raw energy smell coming from the dead Benefactors outside. "I sure hope that stink goes away. You might need a gallon or two of tomato juice if that smell gets into your clothes. And tomato juice don't come cheap these days."

Eric went into the broadcast booth, stood in front of the microphone, and put the earphones on.

"Can you hear me, Thor?" he asked.

"I hear you fine," said Thor.

"I thought we'd cue my speech tonight with the old *Word from St. Bernardine's* music," said Eric.

"Fine by me," said Thor.

Ten minutes later, as they started the broadcast, Eric heard the solemn organ chords of his old theme music. Thorvald spoke into his microphone.

"Ladies and gentlemen . . . tonight . . . broadcast live from St. Lucius, the big river city with the big river heart, this is a special edition of . . . *The Word from St. Bernardine's.* Featuring the former Ecclesiarch of St. Bernardine's Parish, Father Eric Nordstrum."

The theme music culminated with a few broad trumpetlike suspensions, then ended with a solemn *Amen.*

Eric began.

"Friends, I come to you tonight not as your Ecclesiarch but in the newly created office of Intercessor." He took a deep breath and steadied himself. "I would like to take this opportunity to reflect with you upon recent world events. As you all know, the Romans have come to rid the world of the Benefactors. Many of you are up in arms about this. Many of you believe the Benefactors are the Protectors of the Faith, Guardians of the Devout, and the Soldiers of God's Army. Many of you are firm in your belief that the Benefactors come from Heaven. But I have learned that this isn't so. They are not Guardians. They are not Protectors. They are not Angels." He paused. "And they don't come from Heaven. No, not at all. I have learned that the Benefactors, far from being citizens of God's Paradise, come from a place somewhere near the middle of the Milky Way galaxy, a place you could go if you were willing to travel far enough and long enough. The Heavenly Host are midwifed in a fiery inferno reminiscent of the everlasting fires of Hell, not in Heaven. And they are made of the same common elements and simple chemical compounds that can be found in a snail . . . a snake . . . a deceiver . . . a pillager . . . and a *murderer*."

He took a deep breath, glanced out the glass partition and saw Moon, Gallio, June, Naevius, and the Hortulani Filoda staring at him with close attention.

"Now, I don't claim to be a man of science," he said. "I'm not even sure I know how to fix a flat tire. But I think it's safe to say I know deceit. I've been a priest my whole life, and I've encountered all kinds of deceit on many different occasions. And believe me when I say that the Benefactors are masters of deceit. I have *believed* in the Benefactors. I have been their *staunchest* supporter for the last thirty years. I have *upheld* their Word. And what have they given me in return? Nothing but a lie. Yes, a lie, my friends. For let it be known that a man came to our town, just like a man once came to Galilee. And this man, in the guise of the Cardinal's cloak, brought with him the True Word of God. God said to this man, Expose the snake. God said to this man, Cast out the deceiver. God said to this man, Punish the murderer. And this man exposed the Benefactors. He showed us that the Benefactors weren't Angels. Or Protectors. Or Guardians. Rather, he showed us that they were simply beings, ordinary mortal beings like us, only from another part of the galaxy, and that they planned to usurp the minds and souls of our young men, that they intended to take our world away from us, and that they schemed to make mankind a thing of the past. I asked the Cardinal why they would do such a thing. And the Cardinal told me it was because the Benefactors wished to live forever, that they would not bow down to our Good Lord Maker on Judgment Day, as we all must, but that they would perjure His grand design by making themselves as eternal as He was."

He paused, wondering how he could best put this next part so that even the unschooled dirt farmers and milkmaids of Ste. Genevieve County would understand.

"Why and how, you ask, do the Benefactors plan to usurp the minds and souls of our young men? And why and how do they plan to take the world away from us? To understand that, you must first understand that the Benefactors, far from being the living incarnation of our dear Lord God, are in fact dead, preserved much the same way as our loved ones in the resurrectorium are preserved, and that they plot to seek a full and living life through the bodies of our young men. Let me say it again. The Benefactors are dead, of mortified flesh, and they wish to live again. The only way they can do that is to steal into the bodies and minds of our young men and use those young men to resurrect themselves."

Eric glanced at Thorvald and took a sip of water.

"Friends . . . sometimes we find strange fossils in the Earth, bones that have been preserved as stone. The Benefactors have preserved themselves just as these fossils have been preserved. When their fiery inferno of a home began to die on them—for such the Cardinal has told me—they squealed like pigs close to the slaughter and struggled in panic-stricken terror to save themselves. They took their lives and they stored them. They *fossilized* their lives. And then they disseminated their lives like dormant seeds in the wind in search of new soil. They traveled from that Hades-like inferno in the center of the galaxy and came to God's green Earth. And they sought to replant themselves inside the minds of our young men. In the Seminaries they found a willing army of devout young men. The Benefactors pillaged our God and our religion for the sake of their plan so they could control us with them, so they could turn us into careful farmers of fine young men. And we gave them a sturdy and plentiful crop in the soldiers of St. Julian's League.

"Now it's come time to make their harvest. Even as I speak, they invade the tissue and hearts of St. Julian's soldiers. They steal into our Seminaries like the fox will into the henhouse, and they rob our young men of their souls, their bodies, and their lives. They put their own lives and souls into the bodies of the Seminarians, planting themselves the way they plant eligible clergymen into the portals of the resurrectorium, giving to themselves everlasting life but taking away the lives of our young men. How many lives have they taken so far? I don't know. But the man from Brisbane knew it had to stop. He knew we had to call to the stars for help. And I thank God Almighty that the Cardinal's call was answered. I thank our brothers and sisters from Rome for heeding our call. They have maintained a great struggle out there among the stars. They have fought valiantly for the last two thousand years against those they call the *Patroni*. Now, at our eleventh hour, when the Benefactors are stealing away our young men, the Romans have come to our aid.

"You ask yourself why you should believe me. Why should you believe a man who's been tried for treason and arrested for trespass into the Restricted Zone? This is fantastical, you say, this plot the Benefactors have devised. I ask you not to believe me but to come see for yourself. Come to the intersection of Vine and Bell and see how these creatures die, how they hiss and steam, and reveal to the whole world that they are not Angels but simple mortal flesh."

He paused for a long time after that. He was thinking of Neil. He was thinking of Ingrid. They, too, had gone the way of mortal flesh.

"You see why I had to make every effort to stop the Benefactors," he said. "So I went out to the desert and I called for help. God meant us to make contact with the Romans. And now General Publius Gallio Corvinus is here to help us. He has at his disposal a simple device that drains the Benefactors of their intelligence and their life-will—some heavy elements in a soup of curious isotopes I scarcely understand, but that have been effective in eradicating fully two-thirds of these deceivers worldwide. As Intercessor, it's my duty to make sure any remaining Benefactors in the Municipality of St. Lucius and the Township of St. Jerome are now exterminated. Tonight the Romans will go to the Citadel. Tonight they will destroy the sleepers who dwell in the Citadel. We will fear them no more. Nor will we bow to them. Their time has finally come. They must stand in judgment before God, as we all must some day. We can only pray that God will forgive them and that He will have mercy upon their souls, just as He has had the mercy to deliver us from their monstrous evil. Amen."

CHAPTER 34

Hesperus stood in front of Neil's portal and took a deep breath. All his brethren in the Citadel had been killed. The whole town stank of their dissipated energy. He was the only one left in St. Lucius now. He knew . . . *knew* this was the end for them. After nearly four billion years, extinction was at hand.

"Neil," he called. "Neil, I come to you in a spirit of sacrifice."

The portal shifted, brightened, swirled in patterns of gold, violet, and green. Out of these patterns a face appeared: Neil Nordstrum, or at least a preserved version of Neil Nordstrum.

"What do you want?" asked Neil in a far-off, flat voice.

"She won't love me," said Hesperus.

Neil didn't answer. All Hesperus had to do was raise his hand, place it on the portal, and the change would take place. Neil would live again. Hesperus would die. If he sacrificed himself, he would never see June again. He never dreamed that unrequited love could hurt so much. Where was his human courage? He couldn't find it anywhere.

He stepped back. He couldn't do it.

"The Romans are here," said Hesperus. "They've killed most of us. They're going to kill me. But when they kill me, my blood shall leap in their face like the fires of Hades, and I'll slaughter so many of them they'll soberly reconsider any future murder. I'll transform myself into a small star, and the chain reaction will . . . will . . ."

He stopped. What hollow threats. Was he really such a boaster? Did not the Romans have the means to neutralize any such chain reaction or conflagration? Neil didn't respond. Neil didn't care. His lack of response irked Hesperus. He raised his hand to touch the portal. But his hand shook. No. He couldn't do it. Death could wait. Death *must* wait. At least until he found his courage. At least until he could come to grips with the fact that he was one of Woden's last and that he was unloved even by these lowly human creatures.

What to do with them, now that they drifted in from the Restricted Zone? Eric stood on the Wharf Road with June, Gallio, and Moon. Gallio called them the *cinereus natio,* the gray nation. Clay-bred marched in long lines from the Indian Lands, escorted by the Roman *securitatis.*

"Our census is complete," said Gallio. "There are one-hundred-and-sixteen thousand of these gray people. The *legio profugus* has organized their slow migration eastward. There are no *Patroni* or Seminarians to look after them in the Restricted Zone now. We've arranged to house two or three thousand here in St. Lucius. Other communities will accommodate their fair share. Once they get here, the *legio medico* will find the gifted ones like Moon. All the others . . . they'll need support. We're not sure how much."

"All they need is a big sister," said Moon. "They're like young 'uns. They'll listen to me. They always have."

Eric saw a group of shackled Indians. One of them was Zeke Whitefeather. The Roman *securitatis* led these Indians into a vacant lot. Eric didn't like the look of it. Eric also recognized Flying Horse among the Indians.

Moon cowered behind him. "That's Flyin' Horse," she said.

"I know," he said. He turned to Gallio. "What's going on?" he asked.

"These *indigeni* were caught stealing clay-bred in the Restricted Zone," he told Eric. "They're going to be executed."

"Executed?" he said. He couldn't stand by and watch Whitefeather shot to death, no matter what the man had done. "You have to stop this," he said. "I know one of those men. He helped me send my signal."

The *securitatis* lined the Indians up in a loose row. Whitefeather saw Eric. Whitefeather's eyes remained expressionless.

"Which one?" asked Gallio.

The *securitatis* formed an informal firing squad and lifted their *bacula*.

"The man second from the left. He was my guide."

Gallio lifted his chin. "Then he shall be rewarded," he said. "First with a pardon for whatever he's done in the Restricted Zone, then with the riches of Rome." Gallio raised his hand. *"Prohibeo!"* he called. "Let the man with the blue war paint on his face go. He's innocent. Have him step away."

The *securitatis* did as he was told.

No sooner had the Osage left the line than the *securitatis* opened fire and shot the remaining Indians with a single burst of *baculum* fire. Whitefeather looked over his shoulder at the fallen Kiowa, showing no fear, no surprise that he should have escaped death at the last moment. Moon stared at what was left of Flying Horse.

"I guess he's gone now," she said.

The smell of burnt meat and singed hair filled the air. One of the *securitatis* unlocked Whitefeather's shackles. They brought Whitefeather to Eric and Gallio. Whitefeather looked at Eric with sullen eyes.

"I've walked a long way," he said. "I'm tired."

Eric's face settled. "Then go rest," he said.

Whitefeather shuffled away.

The Church Hall, after rewiring by Roman technicians, proved an adequate if not particularly comfortable council meeting place. The room, in the basement of St. Bernardine's Cathedral, had trestle tables for the delegates to sit at, a big steel pot brewing an interesting, and, to Gallio, increasingly necessary hot beverage called coffee, and, extraneously, a battered old musical instrument with black and white keys the Catholics called a piano. Old ladies fussed with a peculiar confection: mashed-up peanuts and puréed strawberries spread between two slices of bland, soft bread. Gallio ate out of politeness. His earthbound cousins, he decided, had a thing or two to learn about feasting. Roman technicians had also devised earphones for translation purposes. As for visuals, the Catholics had no *scriba*, no *tabularium*: instead they used an odd-looking instrument called an overhead projector, a crude device that reminded Gallio of a sea turtle.

The Catholics perused his agenda with some misgiving. Human nature hadn't changed in two thousand years, he thought. The Catholics were glad the *Patroni* were gone but they weren't too thrilled about the bill.

"Sisters, if you don't mind . . ." said Eric. The Sisters, those who plied him with the sickeningly sweet confection made of peanuts and strawberries, left the room. Eric turned to Gallio. "General . . . if you don't mind my saying so . . . I'm somewhat baffled by your agenda."

The Intercessor spoke Norse-English. Gallio listened to the translation through his earphones and toughened himself. He hated to have to play the old game again.

"How so?" he asked.

"I'm not sure I understand what you mean by 'tribute.'"

Gallio nodded. They might as well get the meeting started. He stood up and addressed the whole room.

"The Intercessor wants to know what Rome means by tribute," he said. "A tribute is a consideration for services rendered." Eric stared blankly. There was no way to make this palatable, Gallio decided. He sensed they were worlds apart. "I've brought with me today these five members of the *legio tributum* to give you a better understanding of the multi-tiered tribute system we employ when our armies have been used for a mercenary purpose. Before I turn the meeting over to them, let me first give you an overview of the payment plan we've arranged for you." He stopped. Their perplexed looks were painful to behold. He forged ahead. "You of course realize that your local currencies are worthless to Rome and that any tribute we collect will have to be rendered in raw materials. Rome has decided to start with a lenient ten percent of your current war-depressed gross domestic product. As I say, this ten percent will be rendered in natural resources. In order to meet this ten percent target, Rome is prepared to provide the necessary funds to retool Orbis for the purposes of extraction."

Gallio looked at June. She looked shocked. He glanced at the members of the *legio tributum.* They looked worried. He walked to the overhead projector and placed a transparency on the primitive machine. He focused the lens. An outline of Novus Orbis appeared.

"Our *legio permetior,* following an exhaustive satellite survey of Novus Orbis, has found sizable iron ore deposits here," he said, pointing, "and here, two thousand miles to the north, in what are currently Algonkian and Ojibway lands. To extract, process, and turn this ore into usable steel, we will need the labor of up to a hundred thousand healthy young men and women. I believe the St. Lucius labor contribution will be in the neighborhood of ten to twelve thousand young adults." He glanced at one of the *exactors* to make sure he had the figures right. The *exactor* nodded. "In this way, we give you the opportunity to pay

tribute to Rome." He looked around at the dumb-
struck faces, then pushed on. "Conscript orders will
be posted in your temples and halls. These orders will
be enforced. Anyone whose name appears on the list
must report for duty. No one will be exempt. Once
labor pools are established, Roman gang bosses will
be assigned, and the conscript workers airlifted for a
five-year stint of digging ore. Anyone who refuses will
be punished."

The Catholics stared at him with wide, bewildered
eyes. Many of them now looked as shocked as June.
He felt sick at heart. Here he was again, playing the
game of extortion. And not only the game of extortion, but the game of brinkmanship as well. Rome
didn't care about the Admiral's superbomb. Rome
told him to go ahead with tribute enforcement regard-
less of the Admiral's superbomb. But these people
weren't docile Hortulani. They were humans. They
would fight. Maybe the Admiral had a hundred superbombs. Maybe he secretly possessed, or had in development, an efficient delivery system too, something
better than those dirigibles.

"Every measure will be taken to ensure the health
and safety of the work gangs," he continued, "but
sinking mine shafts is hard, dirty, and dangerous work.
The gangs will be asked to work outside in temperatures well below freezing, in rain or shine, without
holiday, seven days a week, twelve hours a day. The
gang bosses will insist on this. It's up to the gang
bosses to ensure that the ten percent target is met.
They themselves risk punishment if they fail to attain
this target. Rome will tolerate no protest over these
conscript orders."

After the meeting broke up, Eric cornered him.

"Gallio, you can't make our young people work against their will," he said.

"I'm afraid they'll have to," said Gallio.

June spoke up. "But Gallio, in this country we have laws against that kind of thing."

"Then Rome will enforce martial law to make the conscripts comply." He felt sick at heart. "You think I want this?" he asked. "Gaius Lurio approaches with his army. Behind him, another fifty thousand of Caesar's Imperial Guard are on the way. They know that I'm trying to rebuild the Hortulani population here on Earth. If I defy them again, that will be end of the Hortulani once and for all, even on this planet."

"Yes, but you can't force our young people to work without pay in such dangerous conditions."

"I will post the conscript orders. I will expect your young people to obey. We have freed your planet. Now you must pay the price."

Gallio turned away before they could argue further. But that didn't end the grave misgivings he felt. He walked past the piano and went out into the hall. This could only end badly. All he wanted was for the Hortulani to live and prosper. In order to achieve that he had to offer at least some concession to Caesar. But was it fair to offer one population in the place of another? The way he was feeling now, he was going to have to fight for these humans, just as he had fought for the Hortulani.

Later, Gallio took June for a ride in his *pendeo carrus*. He saw that she was afraid at first. They didn't have air vehicles on this world, none but the dirigibles the Prussians used to drop their superbombs. The height alarmed her. They flew a thousand miles into the Restricted Zone and settled on a mesa overlooking a valley full of Indians. The sun, half hidden by the mountains to the west, shone blood red. He watched the *indigeni* dance around a bonfire. Seven women skinned a buffalo. Drummers beat their drums.

"I've been deprived of liberty my whole life," he told June. "Liberty is not a right. Liberty is a privilege."

"Maybe where you come from," she said.

"I was conscripted into the army at the age of seven," he told her. "I carried water for three years. Then I carried shields for another five. Then they put me into the infantry, and I had no choice. I had to go. To refuse would have been treason and I would have been executed. I made the best of it. In time I was noticed. They saw I knew how to survive. So they gave me greater responsibility. I had to take it. I had no choice. I became a sergeant, a captain, and a colonel. Then I became a general. And when someone finally asked me . . . asked *me* what I wanted, I said I wanted to be a farmer. That was when I got my wish, as governor of a small province on an agricultural world. I got my freedom only after I'd earned it. These young people in your town will have to earn their freedom too."

June shook her head. "That's not the way it works here, Gallio," she said. Her Latin was improving; he could understand her passably well now. "You never told Eric you were going to charge us anything for getting rid of the Benefactors. You weren't up-front about it. Now you expect us to pay you?"

The game of extortion was a sad one. Ferus grazed a small distance away from the Indian camp. He was tired of discussing extortion. Rome was coming, and Rome would make all discussion pointless. He concentrated on June. She was small and lovely and had the ability to turn his heart upside down. He saw she was waiting for an answer.

"Rome will have its way, June," he said. "Reports have been sent to Elysium. Elysium laughs at your notion of liberty. They even laugh at the superbomb. Those young men and women will be compelled to dig ore. Lurio's army approaches by the hour. Fifty thousand additional troops will come within four weeks. Rome will have its due."

Her eyes narrowed equivocally, and she put her hand on his knee. "Can't you talk to Rome . . . to Caesar?"

He motioned to the desert landscape. "Caesar wants all this. Nothing I say will change his mind." The fire in the Indian camp crackled and popped, and a swarm of embers leapt into the sky. Eric tried to change the subject. He didn't want to think about it. He concentrated on June. "I've grown fond of you over the last two weeks, June," he said.

"And I of you, Gallio. But don't you think you could do something?"

She wasn't going to leave it alone. He tried again.

"My affection grows warmer every day," he said.

"Mine too. If only there were some way we could fix this."

June grew wistful. He leaned over, kissed her. She turned, a serious look in her eyes. She caressed his cheek with the back of her hand. He wanted to take her away somewhere, leave the games behind, live in peace and quiet—in a place like this, among these Indians, where life was simple, love wasn't hard, and property was a word no one understood. But the things he wanted were the things he never got. He had learned that through long, hard experience.

A centurion entered Eric's study.

"There's a man here to see you, Intercessor," said the centurion. "We know him. We've been told to honor him. His name is Whitefeather."

Eric sat back. "Send him in," he said.

The centurion gave him that salute they had—fist over heart—and left the room.

A moment later Zeke Whitefeather appeared. The Indian's face was sullen. He wore ragged jeans, cowboy boots, and a leather vest. He had a bead choker around his neck. He wore a new hat—another black bowler with a white feather sticking up the back.

"I owe you a debt," said Whitefeather in a voice as low as distant thunder.

Eric contemplated the Osage. "That was some hard traveling I had to do after you took our horses," he said. "I lost the sight of my left eye. My face is permanently scarred. I'm a hideous man now."

Whitefeather looked out the window. "I have wives," he said. "I have children. The land is dry. The corn won't grow. My son died last winter. He was two years old. He died of hunger. Soon the snow will come. I have a daughter. I took your horses. You had some hard traveling, and you lost the sight of your left eye, but now my daughter will live."

The two men looked at each other. Eric nodded slowly. It seemed like a fair trade. "There might be tough times ahead," he said. "I might need you. It seems the Romans are more interested in conquering than in liberating." His eyes narrowed, hardened. "You won't run off on me this time, will you?"

Whitefeather's expression didn't change. He was neither insulted nor angry. "I won't run off," he said. "I will stand by your side. I will die by your side."

Eric waited by the fountain inside Gallio's ship. The walls in Gallio's ship were white—not gleamingly white, but soft white, shifting in shades from bone to porcelain. Colorful tapestries hung on the walls.

Moon's nurse, Paccia Marciana Iacomus, appeared from one of the arched doorways and walked toward Eric. She was a wide-faced woman in her late fifties, plain but kindly looking, her hair pulled up in a metal clasp. She looked brusquely efficient. He stood up to greet her, anxious. He hadn't seen Moon in a week, ever since the Romans had graciously considered to treat her with their advanced medical techniques and equipment.

"Sit down, Intercessor," Paccia Marciana told Eric. "There's no need to look so anxious. Moon is packing her things. She'll be out any minute."

"Is she all right?" he asked.

Marciana put a hand on his arm and forced him to sit.

"She couldn't be better," she said. "A normal, healthy woman with normal, healthy blood and bones."

Moon emerged from the archway with Gallio. Eric stood up yet again. He could scarcely believe the difference. It was as if Moon had come out of the shadows and into the sun. Her skin, though still pale, had a translucence now, a pliancy and freshness that was as young and vibrant as tomorrow. Her eyes were as blue as the sky, and she looked . . . *alive.* Her hair was short, freshly cut, and as yellow as gold. She walked with an erect sureness that enhanced her regal stature.

"How do you feel?" he asked.

"I feel like I'm awake for the first time in my life," she said.

Eric turned to Gallio. "I'll remember this," he said. "No matter what happens . . . no matter what Lurio's army decides . . . I'll remember this."

Gallio nodded. "No matter what Lurio's army decides, you and I will always be friends. Of that you can be assured."

CHAPTER 35

Gallio and Lurio surveyed the town from the small observation deck atop St. Bernardine's dome. Lurio's ships loomed wingtip to wingtip to the north, ranged along the south bank of the Missouri River. Lurio kept pacing from railing to railing. Gallio observed him the way he might observe a caged lion—with patience, curiosity, and respect. The man was a fellow Roman. The man was his friend. Yet a void existed between them now.

"Is it weakness, Gallio?" said Lurio. "Can you no longer lift a sword? Rome's word is law. Have you forgotten this?" Lurio shook his head and took out his written orders. "Caesar gave me these orders. Caesar said I should forgive you because you were old. I told him he was wrong. I had the nerve to actually challenge Caesar. I had to defend you." Lurio's eyes narrowed with distress. "But now this? You post conscript orders, and no one shows up? You ask for ten thousand recruits, and the recruitment centers remain empty? And you didn't use force to coerce them?"

"I will not use force to enslave ten thousand young

people," Gallio said resolutely. "And I won't have you threaten the Hortulani I've brought to this world."

"Yes . . . but . . . the conscripts balk," complained Lurio. "To them, you are an old man without teeth. And now they laugh at Rome."

Gallio shook his head wearily. "They have a tradition of liberty here, Lurio," he said. "In my time on Hortus I've learned to respect traditions, even if they aren't Roman traditions. Liberty is a tradition here."

"Liberty is something that must be earned," said Lurio. "What these people have is a tradition of treason. I realize that they're ignorant and that they haven't had the advantage of a Roman education, but, as with the Hortulani, they must be taught."

Gallio felt a nerve twitch somewhere inside. The void between them widened.

"Caesar sighed when I told him you were still strong," said Lurio. "He insisted you were weak. Weak men are dangerous, he told me. He sent you to Orbis so you wouldn't be in our way, used it as a pretext to remove you from Hortus so you wouldn't interfere with myself and the *legio exstirpatio*. Prove yourself, young Lurio, he said. Show me you have the nerve to look after the Hortulani. Then go look after our old man. Take your army. Enforce Rome's rule on Orbis. Let the old man have the honor, but save the glory for yourself." Lurio shook his head. "Now I'm here, Gallio. And the recruitment centers remain empty? I'm disillusioned . . . General. I have to insist on Rome's ten percent tribute. This is Caesar's word. Caesar's word is law. The ore will be extracted. In two weeks, fifty thousand troops will come. The conscripts will balk no more. They will be forced to dig."

Gallio shook his head. "They will fight," he warned Lurio.

"Then they will die," said Lurio.

"So will Romans," said Gallio.

"Orbis is our home, and we shall have it."

Gallio remained calm. "Lurio, Rome is wrong."

"Rome is never wrong," said Lurio. He shoved his orders at Gallio. "Here," he said, "read them. I am Caesar's vice-regent on Orbis. I am assuming command. Please convey the news to your captains. Your army is my army. Your ships are my ships."

Gallio read the orders. He was forthwith relieved of command. Gaius Lurio Vatinius was appointed vice-regent of Orbis, its moon, and its environs—meaning the whole solar system—by His Majesty the Royal Emperor Gaius Julius Caesar of Rome. Lurio leaned over the railing and gazed at the Shrine.

"I want you to arrest the mothers of the noncompliant conscripted workers and cut off their hands," said Lurio. The young man stood up, squared his shoulders, and gazed south along the river. "If the noncompliant conscript workers don't have mothers, then arrest their fathers and do the same thing. If no mothers or fathers, then their siblings. A loved one, in any case. Rome will not be balked. Caesar expects his tribute. As vice-regent, it's my duty to enforce that."

Gallio remained calm, but there was a coldness to his calm. He raised his fist to his heart.

"As you wish, Vice-regent," he said.

"And I like this prospect," said Lurio. "The way these two rivers converge is most advantageous. I think something might be done with this . . . this property. It strikes me as a great inland port, ideal for the movement of men and materiel. I'm going to have my *legio civicus* look at it. Once we clear all these buildings away, I think we might do something useful with it. Something that will add to the glory of Rome."

Gallio's calm grew even colder. "As you wish, Viceregent," he repeated.

Hesperus stopped at the gate and looked at the Ecclesiarch's Manse. Ivy climbed the walls, oaks grew to lofty heights, and a gleaming new Ford Edsel sat in the drive. Autumn leaves covered the grass. He had a memory. Or at least Neil did. A memory of playing with his father on the front lawn, jumping into leaves, raking great piles of them and rolling around in them. He lifted an oak leaf, examined it. Brown, stiff, smooth. He crumpled the leaf, then opened his hand. The leaf strained back into shape against its many new fractures. The leaf was resilient. Just like these humans he and his brethren had fought to control for so many years.

The Roman soldiers sitting on top of the tank stared at him. He stared back. He hated them. He strode up the walkway. The centurions at the door crossed their *bacula*.

"State your name and business," the tall one said, barely managing the Norse-English.

"I'm the Intercessor's son," he told him. "I'm Neil Nordstrum. I've come to see my father."

"Wait here." The guard went into the house.

Hesperus stood on the porch. He looked down at the concrete stoop. He saw two handprints—the handprints of children. Underneath the larger of the two was a name: Neil. Under the smaller handprint was another name: Grace. He knelt, touched the large handprint. He searched his memory, but couldn't remember putting this handprint here. He couldn't remember Grace putting her handprint here either.

The Intercessor and the guard appeared. Hesperus stood up. The clay-bred woman his father lived with peeked out from the kitchen. The Intercessor's eyes narrowed. He said a few words of Latin to the centurion. The centurion gave his father a salute and came to the door.

"You may enter," said the centurion.

Hesperus took a few steps inside and paused. The centurion went back outside and resumed his post. The clay-bred woman took one last look at him and retreated to the kitchen. The Intercessor stared, waiting—showing neither curiosity nor surprise. The house was at once familiar and strange. He had many fond memories of the place, but none of them were his.

"What do you want?" asked the Intercessor.

"Father . . . I'm alone," he said.

The Intercessor's brow arched. He tapped his toe a few times, then grew still.

"Why?" he finally said. "Why did you have to . . . take my son?"

"Father . . . I'm still in here somewhere. Neil's still in here . . . somewhere."

The Intercessor lifted his chin. His eyes widened and his shoulders rose. "Let's sit in the study for a while," he said.

Hesperus followed Father Nordstrum to the study. It was different than he remembered it. His father had five extra worktables set up. He had typewriters, telephones, and a Roman *scriba*.

"Sit, Hesperus," said the Intercessor.

"You know me?" he said.

"June told me."

Hesperus sat down. The red leather club chair had a smell he remembered well from his childhood, a masculine, safe smell. His father had read Bible stories to him in this chair. He remembered the feeling of his father's lap, the scratchy fabric of his pants, and the scratchier feeling of his chin at the end of the day. He remembered his father's love. His devotion.

"You were a good father," said Hesperus. "You loved your children."

The Intercessor nodded. He glanced at the mantelpiece where pictures of Neil, Grace, and Ingrid stood in polished frames. Hesperus wanted to stay in this chair forever. Something was happening to him. With none but a few miserable Benefactors left worldwide, living in wretched isolation, he was fading. The light inside him was dying.

"I loved my children," said the Intercessor.

Hesperus looked away, in the grip of another human emotion: regret. "I'm sorry I took your son away," he said.

His father's face hardened. A clock under a bell jar on the mantelpiece, its inner workings visible, chimed the hour of four.

"You and your kind are a hairbreadth away from extinction," said the Intercessor. "The Romans have wiped you out everywhere but here. And now they're going to wipe you out here. I did that. You'll all be dead. So I guess we're even."

"I love June," said Hesperus. He felt lost. "I wish I could stop loving her."

The Intercessor shook his head. "You might as well give up on June, Hesperus," he said.

"I can't. Your son won't let me."

His father gazed at a pile of documents on the coffee table and shook his head again. "Sometimes you've just got to love someone from afar," he said, "and not expect anything in return. That's the Christian way. That's what you Heavenly Host taught us all these years. Maybe it's time you start following some of your own rules."

Anna Gerhardsen, Eric's old secretary from St. Bernardine's, the mother of three conscript-age children, lay in bed, feverish, semiconscious, her arms resting on top of her blankets, their ends wrapped in white linen where her hands used to be, the blood starting to show through. Anna as a shut-in—Eric couldn't get used to the idea. After so many competent and efficient years as his secretary, it didn't seem possible that Anna should actually be a shut-in. Anna was young, forty-four—far too young to have her hands amputated—and to what end? Her children had been forced to go north anyway.

He looked around the sickroom. A rendering of Christ on the cross and orbis hung on the wall above her bed—a chintzy but nevertheless heartfelt ceramic piece from Wildenvay's Drug Store and Bargain Emporium. A Bible and gold-framed pictures of her children sat on her bedside table. She was pale, her forehead clammy, and she looked faded . . . as if her Holy Spirit were drifting away on her.

"The doctor thinks she has an infection," said Otto Gerhardsen. Otto's eyes teared over. He looked out the window where the maple leaves were turning yellow. "I can't say I like these Romans better than I liked the Benefactors," he said.

Eric tried to think of something to say to Otto. But what could he say in a situation like this? Especially when he was implicitly to blame. He had never expected Gaius Lurio to be such a hard-ass. The Romans had medicines for infection. But Gaius Lurio had banned their distribution to those who had been punished. The Romans had surgical techniques and prosthetic devices advanced enough to restore Anna's limbs to full function. But Lurio said no. "A punishment is a punishment, meant to be permanent and crippling," his decree had read. What could be said in the face of a man like that? Now a once-vigorous middle-aged woman lay dying. Why wouldn't Gallio step in?

Eric put his hand on Otto's. Words failed him. He was the one who had called the Romans here in the first place. Fifty thousand more were on the way. This wasn't liberation. This was conquest.

CHAPTER 36

Eric and Gallio conferred behind the feed store in Rowatt. That Gallio could be so immovable alarmed Eric. The Roman wore a rough brown tunic and sandals. He wielded a large sword and practiced on an old abandoned tractor—lunged at it, dented it, chopped chunks of rubber out of its disintegrating tires, worked up a sweat so that his well-developed muscles glistened like satin in the light of the sunset.

"But he's asked everybody in St. Bernardine's Shrine to move," said Eric. Gallio lunged again, this time at the tractor's exposed diesel engine. "That's a violation of our basic rights. He's depriving people of their property."

"He's Caesar's vice-regent," said Gallio. "He can do anything he likes. Your rights, or what you believe to be your rights, don't mean a thing to him. He doesn't recognize your law. He recognizes only the law of Rome."

"But he means to demolish the Shrine," protested Eric. "He's already got his engineers going through the Shrine street by street, wiring explosive charges."

Clank! A huge chunk of the tractor's left rear fender somersaulted into the air.

"The Shrine occupies what he considers a valuable piece of real estate," said Gallio. "It's broad. It's flat. It's ideal for the kind of surface-to-orbit activities he has planned for it. It's at the confluence of two great rivers. Men and materiel can be ferried cheaply and effectively long distances by river barges to points south, north, and west. In Elysium his choice will be commended. The site is strategically perfect. Caesar will be pleased."

"Yes, but he can't walk in and take property that doesn't belong to him," said Eric. "This is the *Shrine* we're talking about. When we brag about St. Lucius, we brag about the Shrine. Most of our churches are in the Shrine. All our civic buildings are there. Our best parks are there. Our hospitals are there. All our schools are in the Shrine. We have our resurrectorium in the Shrine. He's not making any provision for our dead. He plans to leave them there and blow the whole place up."

"Moving a resurrectorium is a specialized task," said Gallio. "Neither he nor I has the equipment and personnel to move it. Your dearly departed will now have to find salvation in this place you call Heaven."

"Can't he go north to West Shelby? Hardly anybody lives up there."

"He finds the land too marshy up there, and prone to flooding. Any new facility will have to accommodate ships twice the size of these," said Gallio, pointing to his own seven ships fifty yards away. "We can't have them sinking into the bog."

"How can you let this happen, Gallio?" said Eric,

frustrated. "I thought you were a different man. I thought you were on our side. I thought you were going to help us. You said you would always be my friend."

"I'll be executed if I try to stop Lurio," he said. "He's Caesar's vice-regent."

"But how can you just stand by?" said Eric. "Lurio's asked me, as Intercessor, to organize evacuation teams. We're to go house to house and make sure everybody knows they have to be out by Friday noon. Where do I tell these people to go? What do I say when they ask for compensation?"

Thwack! A particularly vicious blow took out the steering wheel. "That is not my concern," said Gallio.

"It's the fifth of October," said Eric. "It's going to get cold soon."

"You're the Intercessor," said Gallio. "Tell Lurio that arrangements must be made for the displaced persons."

"I already have."

"And what did he say?"

"He said it was up to them, that they would have to make their own arrangements."

A large bug landed on the tractor—one of the Roman surveillance units. In sudden fury Gallio swung the flat edge of his sword against the bug and smashed it to bits. He whirled on Eric. Eric saw a completely different man: Gallio the soldier, the warrior—Gallio the killer.

"They *watch* me," he said, hissing the words. "Your people will have to suffer through this for now. In the meantime just let me . . . let me be a general. It's not fight, fight, fight all the time when you're a general. Most of the time it's wait, wait, wait. Go to your people. Tell them they must leave the Shrine. Those who stay will die. Let Lurio be vice-regent. And *please* . . . when the time comes, let me be a general."

After three days of trying, Eric finally got people to take him seriously. Now it was Friday morning. Cars and trucks choked Bell Boulevard—a last-minute flood of refugees fleeing the doomed Shrine. People who didn't have cars crowded the sidewalks, towing whatever possessions they could in carts or wagons. Public buses squeezed through the thronged thorough-fares. Boats jostled side by side on the river as their occupants escaped the Shrine along the Mississippi.

Eric climbed the stairs inside Riverview Terrace, the oldest, tallest, most opulent apartment building in the Shrine. He had to climb the stairs because the Romans had cut off the electricity an hour ago and the build-ing's elevator wasn't working.

On the third floor he walked along the dim corridor. The lamps were out. Only one tenant remained. Au-drey Nygaardsvold. Eric was here one last time to try to convince her to leave.

He came to apartment 306 and knocked loudly. Mrs. Nygaardsvold was hard of hearing. He waited. He knocked again. A moment later the door opened, and the diminutive septuagenarian peered up at him through gold-rimmed glasses. She grinned.

"Hello, Father," she said. "I thought you'd be hea-din' for the hills like everyone else."

"Mrs. Nygaardsvold . . . I know I said I wouldn't bother you again . . . but I . . . I just wish you'd reconsider."

Her grin faded. "I saw some of them Roman boys

walkin' up and down the hall today," she said. "I was lookin' through my peephole. They're funny-looking, aren't they? Their skin color . . . it's a bit off, isn't it? Not exactly brown. Not exactly white. I will say this for them, though. Those boys got chins. Even their womenfolk got chins. D'you suppose their chins grow that big from ridin' around in space all the time?"

"Mrs. Nygaardsvold . . . please come with me. They're going to blow up Riverview Terrace whether you're in here or not. You won't accomplish anything by staying."

Her eyes narrowed, her lips stiffened, and she squared her shoulders. "Father Nordstrum, this is my home. I've lived here most of my life. No one's going to make me leave. Peder and me spent some of the happiest years of our life here. I'm seventy-seven years old and I'm not movin'. Where would I go? I aim to stay. If that means dyin' here, then that means dyin' here. I don't fancy a winter outside with no home. Not at my age. I want to be lookin' out my bay window at the river when the end finally comes."

"Yes, but we could find a place for you to live," he said.

"No," she said. "I'm stayin' right here."

He saw he wasn't going to convince her, so he left her in peace, to die as she would.

When he got downstairs the traffic had thinned a lot. People hurried.

By the time he got to his car a few minutes later the streets were empty. A breeze blew an old newspaper up Bell Boulevard. He'd never seen the Shrine so deserted before. He got in his car, started it, and drove along Corinthians Avenue.

Roman soldiers waved him through the barricade at St. Augustine's Circle, and he left the Shrine for the last time.

He turned right on Rainey, the first street south of the demolition zone, and saw that many homeowners had boarded up their windows in case blast debris should reach this far. The misty black wall of Gallio's ships rose far in the distance up near Rowatt. Lurio's ships loomed on the south bank of the Missouri River. The steeples of the town's thirty-three churches rose above the rooftops.

As he pulled up to June's building, Moon stepped out onto the porch. He . . . *admired* her. Her hair was radiant in the sunshine, strikingly blond, and her eyes were like two pieces of blue crystal. The hour of noon approached. Soon the blasting would start.

He got out of his car. The season's last roses littered the flower bed in June's front yard with petals. A crowd gathered at the top of the hill in Eucharist Park. Moon descended the steps, happy, as always, to see him.

"Is she comin'?" asked Moon, referring to Mrs. Nygaardsvold.

"No," he said. "She's staying."

She glanced toward the Shrine, where Riverview Terrace peeked placidly above some maple trees on the banks of the Mississippi.

"I never had to worry about getting blowed up in my own home before," she commented.

June came out. "It's nearly time," she said.

Eric glanced at his watch: ten minutes to go. "Maybe we should go up to the park," he said. "We might be safer up there." He glanced up at the windows. "Where's Amy?"

"She's already up there," said June.

"Then let's go," he said.

They got in Eric's car and drove to Eucharist Park. They parked along the curb and found a spot on the grass. Schools were closed and kids played on the swings, the teeter-totters, and in the sandbox. Older kids played a game of tag football on the field. All the schools would be gone after this. He shook his head. Where were they going to teach their kids now? The breeze quickened from the northwest. He thought of the Manse, a harmonious, comfortable, stately home, his beloved residence for the last twenty-five years, now wired with explosives, ticking down its final minutes. He picked out St. Bernardine's Cathedral, its copper dome turned green from seventy-two years of weather, its quartet of corner towers rising above the yellow autumn foliage of the surrounding trees. Moon clutched his arm, pressed her cheek against his shoulder. He pulled her closer. Five minutes from now everything would be gone.

Lurio's army was nothing if not punctual.

Blasting commenced precisely at noon, just as all the church bells chimed the hour. The detonations, exploding one after another, moved serially from north to south. Eric glanced around as the explosions got closer and closer. Everyone was quiet. Some had hard faces, some had shocked faces. Many women— and even some of the men—had tears in their eyes. Some men looked ready to fight, their jaws set, their shoulders raised, while others turned away in despair.

The dome of St. Bernardine's collapsed under a cloud of dust. The resurrectorium shattered into fragments, leaving all those dead souls without a home. Riverview Terrace slid slowly downward as the explosives crippled the structure from the ground up. Clouds of dust rose hundreds of feet into the air, billowing like cumulus thunderheads, obscuring the city so that the once familiar skyline of church steeples disappeared into a voracious and ever-expanding fog of airborne debris. The wind smeared the dust southward. On and on the detonations went, rending the Shrine brick by brick, shattering glass, splintering wood, breaking mortar, block after block, nothing spared, nothing saved, until, at the end of it all, all he could see was dust.

Then the detonations stopped.

The dust hung there, shrouding everything.

He waited . . .

Waited for the dust to clear.

He watched the wind stretch the dust toward the river. The dust prowled over the Mississippi and sank into the water. With the dust cleared, all he saw was block after block of rubble. The *legio fragor* had done its job well. Only a few walls were left standing, some of the larger trees, and, miraculously, the Post Office clock tower. Other than that, there was nothing. The place where he had lived, worked, and raised his family was now just a memory.

CHAPTER 37

The shell-like material of the resurrectorium lay in fragments. Hesperus's best chance to redeem himself in front of June now lay beyond reach. He could never give Neil back to her now. Neil was dead forever.

He picked his way through the rubble to the top of the hill. The ground was sticky with the biomagnetic goop of the life-preserving portals. Hesperus searched through the rubble for Neil's portal but he couldn't distinguish one fragment from another. He knelt, lifted a particularly large chunk—as hard and white as a healthy molar—but it didn't look like a piece of a portal, so he dropped it.

He stood up and looked around. He *could* have come. The Romans had given everyone fair warning. He *could* have given Neil's life back. But he hadn't. He still hadn't found his human courage.

He gazed beyond the ceremonial lawns at what was left of the Shrine. So flat now. The red brick, neo-Romanesque buildings had vanished. The Post Office clock tower, perhaps because it was made of old Pennsylvania stone, remained standing. Trees lay on their sides, their great root systems sticking up in the air. People picked through the rubble, scavenging for things that might be useful or valuable. Others stood around looking lost, as if now that the Shrine was gone they couldn't get their bearings in their own hometown anymore. Seagulls flew above what was left of Nyberg's Slaughterhouse, diving for whatever scraps of meat remained. He had watched the Shrine grow since the 1840s. June loved the Shrine. St. Augustine's High School, where she taught, had been in the Shrine. Where was she going to teach now? What kind of world was this for her to live in? Could he somehow fix this, or at least make restitution to her?

He had to fix it somehow, now that Neil was gone for good.

Gaius Lurio sat on a throne in a big room draped with tapestries. Eric had no idea what was expected of him. He wasn't sure why he was here, only that he had been summoned. Lurio was tall, young. The throne and dais bothered Eric—props of power always made him nervous.

"You will bow before the vice-regent," one of the guards finally said.

Eric's face stiffened. He wasn't going to bow to the man who had just blown up his city, cut off the hands of half its middle-aged women, and sent most of its young people north just as winter was coming.

"No," he said. "I will not bow."

"You *will* bow," repeated the guard, and whacked him so hard with his truncheon that he sank to his knees.

Eric tried to get back up, but the guard whacked

him again. He stayed where he was, looking at Lurio with hate-filled eyes. Lurio rose from his throne and descended the dais steps. The vice-regent walked slowly around him.

"These are odd clothes you wear, Intercessor," he said. Lurio fingered his collar. "What are they called?"

Eric took a deep breath, fighting to get control of his anger. "This is a plain white shirt," he said. "These are gray flannels. And these shoes are just shoes."

Eric assessed Lurio's garb: a gold breastplate rippling with chest muscles, a skirt of wide leather tongues end-capped with platinum, and knee-length lace-up sandals.

"And what of your face, Intercessor?" asked the vice-regent. "What happened?"

"I was pushed into a fire," he said.

Lurio stopped circling Eric. "You may rise, Intercessor," he said.

Eric got to his feet. His shoulder throbbed from the truncheon blows. He knew he was going to have a bad bruise. Tall as Lurio was, Eric had an inch or two on him. Lurio had a smooth face, unnaturally so, like the waxed rind of a squash.

"You have done well for Rome, Intercessor," said Lurio. "Rome thanks you. You have been a true friend and a capable collaborator. We have learned that you were a leader in your temple before you took up the fight against the *Patroni*, and that you commanded the respect of a great number of people in this—this district. Rome hopes you will use your influence wisely. Cooperation with Rome, as you have seen, is amply rewarded. Rome apologizes for the loss of your house. A fine abode, my captains tell me. But

Rome now builds a new house for its Intercessor, of a more commodious design and on a wider acreage. We expect your continued cooperation. To that end, Rome commands you to clear the Shrine. Use your . . . influence to organize a municipal effort. We'll need at least a hundred labor gangs working round the clock if we're going to remove this rubble on schedule."

Eric frowned. "Remove it by hand?" he asked.

"Our heavy equipment won't be here for another week," said Lurio. "The rubble will have to be carted away by whatever means you can devise. Every able-bodied man, woman, and child should be employed. We want the new port launch-ready as soon as possible. Rome recognizes the tedious, backbreaking nature of the work, but knows your citizens will labor diligently for the greater glory of the Empire. Those who work particularly hard will eat red meat and drink wine. Those who slack will be punished. Those who refuse will be executed."

"And you want *me* to organize this?"

"You know a great many people. Through your temple you have an established network. We want this done as efficiently as possible. Rome was not pleased with the regrettable conscript delays of a few weeks ago, but Rome now believes the people recognize their duty."

Eric's frown deepened.

"I'm not going to organize my parishioners into slave gangs so they can drag away what's left of their ruined city," he said. He ripped away his special armband, the one that identified him as the Roman Intercessor, and flung it to the ground. "I'm through with being Intercessor. I quit. I resign. You organize your own damn gangs." He pointed a stern finger at Lurio. "And I'm warning you, buster, leave our kids out of it or you'll be sorry."

Lurio grew murderously still. The color rose in his face. Then, with a preternatural quickness, he punched Eric in the nose. Eric stumbled and sat down hard on the floor. His nose stung fiercely and dots danced before his eyes. He looked at his shirt and saw drips of blood on the white cotton. He felt his nose.

"Why, you son of a jackal, you broke my damn nose," he said.

"It's a good thing I don't kill you," said Lurio. "Right now, you have the protection of Caesar. He recognizes your usefulness. I can't take your life away, at least not yet, but I'll be watching you. As for the rubble out there, I'll organize the gangs myself. And believe me, I'll make sure you lift more than your fair share."

Eric's muscles ached, and he was so exhausted he thought he was going to drop. The sky pelted rain from low, dark clouds. The ruined Shrine was a sea of mud. People loaded rubble into trucks, car trunks, wagons, and wheelbarrows. They trudged to the riverbank with it. Lurio wished to increase the height of the levee. Eric wasn't the Intercessor anymore. He was just a worker, the equivalent of a clay-bred drudge. *The rise and fall—and rise and fall—of Eric Nordstrum,* he thought.

The rain needled his back with biting coldness. He shivered. The baby finger of his left hand had been chopped off as punishment. Lurio forced him to wear it around his neck on a copper wire as a lesson in sedition. He lifted another twenty-pound chunk of rubble and dropped it into the back of the cart. His whole left hand throbbed because of the amputation.

He worked with Moon, Clarke Dechellis, Amy Kristensen, Zeke Whitefeather, and Mickey Cunningham. June was up in Gallio's command ship. Moon worked by Eric's side, sharing his burden. Whitefeather, for a change, had more than a few words to say.

"When this is over," he said, throwing a particularly large chunk into the back of the cart, "we'll go hunting together. When the cold winds come, there's a lake in my country where the deer go because the water never freezes. It's fed by a hot spring. We will go there and wait for the deer to come."

A Roman gang boss walked by, a battle-ax over his shoulder. They used battle-axes and other primitive weapons when on guard duty to save on *bacula* power. Before Eric could say yes or no to hunting deer with Whitefeather, Mickey Cunningham spoke up.

"I don't know why June has to get herself hitched up with that Roman fella so soon after she broke her engagement with Neil," he said. "I'd hate her to get any feelings for this Roman fella. Who knows what he's like?" Mickey threw a brick into the back of the cart and shook his head. "Who knows if his intentions are honorable or not."

Eric didn't respond. He lifted what was left of a mantelpiece and dragged it to the cart. They were clearing an access lane to the Post Office tower. The lane had turned to mud. He was covered in mud. Everyone was. The bandage came off his left hand as he tossed the mantelpiece into the cart. The three-finger configuration of his hand looked somehow amphibian. He inspected the severed finger that dangled from the copper wire. It smelled foul, but Lurio still made him wear it. At least the injury was scabbing over nicely. At least he wasn't going to die of a festering wound, the way Per Larsen and Anna Gerhardsen had.

Far at the end of the access lane, two Roman soldiers approached. Eric raised his eyes and studied them more closely. They were coming this way. He glanced around at the others. They had all stopped working. The soldiers came around the cart and headed straight for Amy. They had mean-spirited grins on their faces. Amy grew still and her eyes widened. She dropped her shovel. Her wet dress clung to her tall, thin, and decidedly feminine frame. Her hair was plastered to her head.

"*Proceda, concubina,*" the tall guard said to her. "*Proceda.*"

The short one grabbed her by the shoulder.

"You're not taking *me*," said Amy, and shook his hand away.

Work gangs nearby stopped working and watched.

"*Proceda, concubina!*" the tall one repeated.

"Help!" cried Amy. "Don't let them take me away!"

Eric started toward her, but Clarke Dechellis beat him to it. The police chief lunged at the small Roman soldier and bashed him over the head with a brick. The soldier staggered back, stunned by the blow. With catlike quickness, he whipped out a dagger and stabbed Dechellis right through the heart. Eric's eyes widened. Death came so quickly now that Lurio's army was here. Dechellis gave the soldier a shocked look, clutched his chest, then fell down dead in the mud. The small guard rubbed his head grumpily, wiped his dagger on his leather skirt, and slid it back into its scabbard.

He then grabbed Amy by the arm and shoved her roughly forward.

"Proceda, concubina," he growled. *"Haec quidem hactenus!"*

Amy still resisted. She tried to pull free.

"Leave me be!" she cried.

But the soldier had a firm grip. She hit the soldier, kicked him, and tried to pry his fingers open. These girlish antics just amused him. He yanked her more fiercely, then licked her face playfully. Eric stepped forward, tried to intervene, but the tall one lifted his battle-ax and blocked his way.

"Help me!" cried Amy. "They're going to rape me!"

Mickey tried to make an end run around the tall guard. The tall guard swung his battle-ax. Mickey had to duck, and in ducking, he slipped in the mud.

Amy, now panicked, leaned forward and bit the small one's shoulder. He cried out in pain. He was already grumpy from the blow to his head, and Amy's attack infuriated him. He took out his dagger and stabbed her repeatedly—stabbed her until she fell from his arms into the mud. She lay there writhing, gasping for breath.

"Help me!" she cried, whimpering in horror. "Get me some bandages!"

The small guard, fed up with Amy, unhooked his battle-ax, lifted it high above her head, and brought it down swiftly, decapitating her in a single clean stroke.

The Roman soldier spat at Amy. "*Esto ut lubet!*" he said.

Then he kicked her body.

He rejoined the other guard, and the two of them walked away.

Eric, Moon, Mickey, and Whitefeather just stood there under the gray sky in the pouring rain staring at the bodies of Amy and Canon Dechellis. Eric looked at Amy's head. He knew he had to move her, bury her, but he didn't like the idea of moving her in two pieces. The back of his throat felt dry and his mouth tasted sour. His hand clutched the cart. He looked at his hand, let go of the cart, and took a deep breath. The rain came down harder. He saw that from near and far, people were staring at him, their faces pale against the dark, damp sky. Were they expecting him to say something? Did they want him to offer comfort, as he had done in church every Sunday for the last twenty-five years? There was no comfort in a situation like this. He meant things to be better when the Romans got here. But now they were worse.

CHAPTER 38

June sat at her *scriba* and for the fifth time watched
footage of Father Nordstrum, Mickey Cunningham,
Zeke Whitefeather, and Moon digging Amy's grave.
The bug hovered somewhere above them. Because the
wind was strong, the bug was pushed around, and the
frame jumped and dipped, and the action looked raw,
jerky, and imprecise. June felt guilty, torn by grief.
First Neil. Then Henry. And now Amy. Grief upon
grief upon grief. She was warm and dry, inside Gallio's
ship, protected and safe. And out there, in the wet
and cold, they dragged Amy's body into a grave.

Eric placed Amy's head above her shoulders and
wiped her face with his handkerchief. June felt she
should be out there with them. Helping them. Suffer-
ing with them. Mourning with them.

Naevius stood behind her, watching.

"Why doesn't Gallio do something about this?" she
asked. "And where *is* he? I haven't seen him since
yesterday."

"The Imperator is conferring with his captains,"

said Naevius. He wouldn't say more but simply watched the footage in silence.

Father Nordstrum said some words over Amy. The bug zoomed in closer. The sound quality got better. June heard Eric's voice above the rain.

"All-powerful God, whose mercy is never withheld from those who call upon you in hope, look kindly upon your servant Amy, who departed this life in the flower of her youth, in tragically sudden circumstances, before she had the chance to confess your name. O Lord, may you number her among your Saints forevermore. Eternal rest grant to her, O Lord, and let perpetual light shine upon her. Thus shall she be with you always, Lord. In the name of the Father, and of the Son, and of the Holy Spirit. Amen."

He threw a handful of dirt on her. Mickey, Whitefeather, and Moon pushed dirt on top of her.

Holy Spirit. That was new. She'd never heard him use that before. His genuflection didn't include the orbis anymore either, no circle around the cross. He'd excised the Benefactors from the Last Rites. But what did he mean by "the Holy Spirit"? She could hardly think through her grief. Naevius shifted awkwardly behind her.

"Gallio is going to act soon," he assured her.

Father Nordstrum left the grave and walked back to the access lane leading to the Post Office. The bug followed him. He walked to the body of Clarke Dechellis and stared at it for a long time. The wind must have been gusting, because the bug, already unsteady, now had an especially difficult time keeping Father Nordstrum in the frame. To gain stability, the bug landed on the Post Office clock tower. The frame now included a fairly wide view of the devastation. Conscripted workers loaded rubble into pickup trucks, cars, horse-drawn wagons, wheelbarrows, even a few shopping carts. Never had she seen such a dismal view, a monochromatic scene of gray sky and gray earth, the only splash of color the red taillights of the cars and trucks laboring back and forth to the river's edge.

Out of this forlorn vista a figure emerged.

The figure looked pathetic, woebegone, lost. June didn't have the heart to tell Naevius that this man was a Benefactor and should be shot on sight. The tenderness she felt for the old Neil stopped her.

Hesperus approached Father Nordstrum.

The two men conferred. She couldn't hear them. The bug was too far away. All she could hear was the wind. Hesperus's expression was urgent, and he obviously had a great deal to say to Father Nordstrum. He used his hands a lot, drew figures in the air. Father Nordstrum finally nodded. He pointed to the north, then to the south. Hesperus shook his head and swung his arm to the north, then to the west.

"What are they talking about?" asked Naevius.

"I don't know," she said.

Father Nordstrum pointed to the northwest, then drew his palm downward in a large scoop. Hesperus seemed to consider this, then finally nodded. Father Nordstrum gave Hesperus a pat on the shoulder. Father Nordstrum forgave Hesperus? After what Hesperus had done to Neil?

Father Nordstrum said a few more words. Hesperus nodded, then walked away into the rain, the mud, and the rubble, looking like the loneliest man in the world.

*   *   *

Eric heard a loud boom. He sat up in Amy's bed, his muscles hurting from all the heavy lifting he'd done in the Shrine. Out the window he saw a large fireball rise over the Missouri River. The rain still pelted down through the dismal dark night.

Moon sat up next to him. "What was that?" she asked.

Eric got up and walked to the window. "Some sort of explosion down by the river," he said.

The fireball burned itself out.

Now the sky filled with streaking pink lights emerging from the hill to the west, Gallio's hill. They rose a thousand feet into the air, then swerved to the north, toward Lurio's camp. Eric heard a quick succession of five bangs to the north. Five smaller fireballs filled the air. The pink streaks dove toward Lurio's ships like a swarm of angry hornets. Eric saw one of the pink streaks brightened in the light of a fireball, and it revealed itself to be an aircraft, similar to but much more sophisticated than the early prototypes the Benefactors had destroyed at the turn of the century. The aircraft was sleek and gray, the size of a school bus, and it spit blue fire.

Dozens of yellow streaks sprang from Lurio's ships. The pink and yellow streaks whirled around each other, looping, turning, diving. The sky lit up with massive explosions. Aircraft were blown to bits. The flashes illuminated the muddy and rubble-strewn landscape of St. Bernardine's Shrine.

Eric hated to see such violence—but for the first time in too long he actually felt some hope.

Blue fire rose from Gallio's ships, arched in precise

formation toward the south bank of the Missouri
River, and pounded Lurio's ships. Fireballs rose hundreds of feet into the air. The thunder of the strike
rolled over the rubble, the sound waves hitting June's
building with a jolt, making the windows shake. The
pink and yellow streaks careened and spun around
each other. June's building shook again, this time with
a low, sustained rumble.

Eric saw one of Lurio's big ships lifting off, three
columns of white flame issuing from its massive under-
carriage. In the glow of the launch flame, he could see
Lurio's other ships—pitted, bent, cracked—with fire
crews scrambling all over them.

The escaping ship labored upward, kicking up mud,
lifting into the sky like a gigantic queen bee as Gallio's
smaller attack craft pestered it like a swarm of worker
bees. The ship, shaped like a giant v, stabilized, hovered, then, with a high, thin whine, geared up its forward thrusters. Gallio's small fighters swooped and
attacked repeatedly, as Lurio's defense aircraft tried
to repel them.

"Is it tryin' to get away?" asked Moon.

"I think so," he said.

The ship's powerful forward thrusters fired.

But as it banked over the river, a particularly large
fireball rocketed from the top of the ridge near Rowatt and struck the huge spacecraft's left wing. The
thing careened over the Shrine, banked left, and
splashed into the Mississippi, crashing into a moored
paddle steamer.

The aerial combat grew more frenzied, and—
alarmingly—moved south toward Rainey Street. Blue
ordnance sang over the rooftops not more than a

block away. A moment later a round ripped into June's roof. Eric ducked instinctively and sheltered Moon. Debris tumbled along the hall floor outside Amy's bedroom. He saw the glow of firelight coming from the living room.

"Let's see what happened," he said.

He led Moon down the hall. Flames licked fitfully at the furniture in the living room. Rain came through a big hole in the roof. The rain was so heavy that the possibility of a larger conflagration seemed remote, but he went to the kitchen to get the fire extinguisher anyway. He returned to the living room and sprayed the flames until they went out.

"We should go to the basement," he said, "and take cover down there until this is over."

They sheltered under a table in the basement for the rest of the night. The basement had no windows, and it smelled of the coal that lay in a pile at the bottom of the coal chute. The battle continued to rage outside. Sometimes the booms were close, sometimes they were far away. Around four o'clock, the booms grew intermittent, and finally they stopped. By dawn all they heard was the occasional hiss of *baculum* fire.

Soon after, he heard someone calling his name from outside.

"Ericus?" the voice called. It was Gallio. *"Ericus?"*

"Stay here," he told Moon.

He climbed the stairs.

When he reached June's kitchen, he looked out the window. The rain had stopped, though the sky glowered with low, dark clouds. Water overflowed in the flowerpots on the balcony. Great columns of black smoke rose from Lurio's ragged, torn ships. To the west Eric could see five of Gallio's ships, as badly damaged as Lurio's. But two of them were gone. Had they gotten away, then? Bodies littered the muddy plain of the Shrine. Crashed aircraft lay here and there. He heard footsteps coming up the front stairs. He went to the landing and saw Gallio climbing the steps.

"Salve," said Gallio.

"You finally made your move," said Eric.

Gallio came inside. "I had to make sure that Lurio felt confident of his control." The two men went into the kitchen and Gallio gestured out at the battlefield. "It's war, Eric," he said. "The worst kind of war. Civil war."

Eric peered at the devastation. "How many lives have been lost?" he asked.

Gallio took a deep breath and sighed. "Except for seven hundred men, Lurio's army has been wiped out. My own losses weren't as significant, but staggering enough. Lurio's fleet has been destroyed. Two of my ships escaped." Gallio looked tired. "Now I must go. I have to go to the moon. That's why I'm here. To tell you this. In near-space last night, we fought a tremendous battle. Lurio's orbiting *castellum* was destroyed. Mine was badly damaged. So badly that its surviving soldiers and officers, twelve hundred in all, had to evacuate to the moon in safety *naviculae*. Each *navicula* has only a limited air supply. The survivors are now waiting for rescue." Gallio put his hand on Eric's shoulder and smiled grimly. "Which means I must go to their aid, friend. An ancient Roman settlement, Erebus, sits on the moon, in a place our own astronomical maps call Oceanus Procellarum. With repairs, Erebus can be pressurized. I'll mount my rescue effort from there. I'll need every single soldier I have for the rescue operation. Once we gather the survivors, we can shelter them in Erebus while we figure out what we're going to do about Caesar's approaching Imperial Guard."

"Then go with God," said Eric.

"It's not as simple as that," said Gallio. "Seven hundred of Lurio's troops still survive, and they're angry, seeking vengeance, embittered at their defeat. I wish I could stay here and defend you and your people from them with my remaining recruits, but the situation on the moon is so desperate I must take every soldier and officer with me."

"Then we'll have to defend ourselves," said Eric.

"I'm afraid you must," agreed Gallio. "The *naviculae* are scattered far and wide over the moon's surface, and if we're going to find all the survivors before their air runs out, I must use all my resources. Lurio, in the meantime, will take his defeat out on the local population. You've already seen what he's capable of. You're going to have to raise your own militia. I can leave my Hortulani battalion with you. I'll leave some *bacula* as well. I wish I could leave something heavier, but I must take my heaviest weaponry to the moon to use against Caesar's fifty thousand Imperial Guards." Gallio spread his arms and raised his eyebrows. "You are a man of wide influence in this community, Eric. You must call upon your countrymen. You must make them realize that the hour is at hand when they must defend themselves for themselves. Your people need you. Just as mine need me. You might not be their

Ecclesiarch anymore, but you're their leader. And they're counting on you."

"Then I'll call to them," said Eric. "I'll rally them. And together we'll defeat Lurio and his band of cutthroats."

Eric met Filoda a few hours later. He didn't think he would ever get used to the way these aliens looked, with their platter-shaped heads, their turquoise skin, and their big, blinkless eyes. But he knew that when he thought of his countrymen now, he would have to include the Hortulani as well. He and Filoda sat on the ridge above Volker Avenue looking at the ruin of the Shrine.

"I doubted Gallio," he told Filoda.

The *socius* on Filoda's shoulder translated for them.

"Once you have Publius Gallio's trust, you have it forever," said Filoda. "And Gallio's word is as strong as his trust. I have watched men. I have watched them ever since they came to Hortus. And I know men change. I have watched Gallio change."

"Has he changed much?" asked Eric. He raised the field glasses to his eyes and scanned the devastation, looking for Mickey Cunningham and Zeke Whitefeather.

"A great deal," said Filoda. "At one time he was arrogant, but now he is humble. He came to Hortus a conqueror and left a much loved patriarch. He once was a man with no mercy, but now he is a man of compassion. He's learned to question everything, including Rome."

Eric finally found Mickey and Whitefeather. He handed the binoculars to Filoda. "I see the two people

I'm looking for. The ones who are going to help me raise my militia. One is Mickey Cunningham. I'm going to have him recruit the best marksmen in Ste. Genevieve County. They're proud of their marksmanship in that county. They're born to the gun."

Filoda lifted the binoculars to his eyes. "Everything looks small with these," he said. "Why do you use them?"

"Turn them around," said Eric.

Filoda turned them around, then jerked suddenly and chirped in surprise.

"You see?" said Eric. "They work better that way. Now, take a look. That's Mickey in the cowboy hat standing by that big uprooted chestnut. And over there is Zeke Whitefeather, the tall Indian loading rubble into the trunk of a car. I'm going to send Whitefeather into the Restricted Zone to get the Cheyenne. Remember I told you I saved Lone Cloud's son? He'll be more than willing to fight for me. And they're fierce fighters, the Cheyenne. They'll scare the living daylights out of the Romans. Then I've got you and your crew. If we all work together, and plan everything carefully, I'm sure we can beat these Romans." Eric shook his head, amazed by how everything had turned out. "I never thought I'd see the day when I would fight side by side with the Cheyenne, our own local boys, and you alien folks to defeat Romans from outer space."

CHAPTER 39

The stone steps of St. Bernardine's Cathedral rose seven risers and stopped at a pile of rubble. Eric stood on the top step and gazed northward. Lurio and his entourage approached over the ruins, hovering a few feet above the ground in a *pendeo carrus*. In Cyrus-of-Jerusalem Square, Eric saw the statue of Saint Bernardine lying on its side. His main objective was to wipe out Lurio's army. What had him concerned at the moment, though, was the welfare of the clay-bred in the warehouses along the river to the south. More than two thousand clay-bred refugees from Indian Lands huddled in those warehouses. And Lurio thought they belonged to him.

"That's why he's posted such a heavy guard along the river," Eric told Whitefeather.

"He's a proud man," the Osage replied.

Twenty-five Cheyenne braves, their faces painted with broad ocher stripes, sat on wild ferus in a large semicircle, a mean-looking bunch armed with rifles, tomahawks, spears, and bows and arrows. Mickey Cunningham's local boys had taken up sniper positions. Hortulani stood up on the ridge with their tiny *bacula.*

"Maybe he won't be so proud when he sees we mean to fight," said Eric, motioning toward his diverse militia.

Lurio hovered into the square. He stepped out of his *pendeo carrus* and approached Eric, his purple cape billowing in the October wind. The vice-regent climbed the steps and looked at the Cheyenne braves. Turning Bird's father, Lone Cloud, wearing a long feathered war bonnet, sat on a horse and stared at Lurio with unnerving stillness. Lurio gestured at the Indians, seemingly annoyed by them.

"What are these?" he asked.

"These are my countrymen," said Eric. "And they mean to defend their country."

"There is no defense against the Roman Army," said Lurio.

Eric ignored this statement. "Right now, they mean to take your soldiers prisoner. I want to give you and your soldiers the chance to surrender safely and peacefully, Lurio. We want to take the lot of you to St. Gilbert's, a penal institution downriver, where we can keep a watch on you. You'll be treated well if you surrender now."

Lurio's olive complexion reddened. "So you're here to negotiate for my surrender," he said.

"Not negotiate," he said. "There's nothing negotiable about it. I'm here to demand it."

An incredulous smile came to Lurio's face. "An army surrenders to an army," he said. "An army doesn't surrender to a handful of battle-ignorant conscript workers who by the end of the day will again be clearing rubble for Rome. You waste my time, *servus*. My war is with Gallio. I have no war with you."

Eric's face hardened. "Your troops have raped, maimed, and murdered my people," he said. "They've destroyed my town. They've cut off the hands of half the middle-aged women in St. Lucius and sent ten thousand of our young people to work in the mines against their will. We have a war, Lurio. Don't kid yourself that we don't. And we mean either to imprison you for the crimes you've committed or to defeat you on the battlefield."

"In two days I will have fifty thousand fresh Roman troops at my command," said Lurio. "Do not provoke me."

"Surrender now and you won't be harmed," said Eric.

"You are a fool. Stand down and get back to work."

"I'm trying to spare the needless loss of human life," said Eric.

"And so am I."

"Once we have you and your troops safely in prison, our courts will then sue the Imperial Roman Government for damages and restitution."

Lurio gazed at Eric in growing amazement. "Sue Rome?" he said, his voice thin. "In what court? You have no court. Rome *is* your court. Any suits must be brought to Rome's Imperial Judiciary."

"Rome has no recognized judiciary here," said Eric. "We have our own judiciary. And our own government. We expect Rome to cooperate fully in the war crimes investigations we plan to launch against your army. We intend that the murderers and rapists of your army be brought to trial, convicted, and hanged.

Rape and murder are hanging crimes in the Territory, and we mean to execute every perpetrator, with or without the help of your Imperial Judiciary."

Lurio's face reddened further. "You will not dismiss the might *or* the justice of Rome."

"I don't see much justice around here," said Eric. "And as for might, I don't see much of that either. Gallio already proved to me that you don't have much of an army. I guess if you want me and my countrymen to prove it again, we'll be happy to oblige."

Lurio spat at his feet. "You sneer at Rome," he said. "We will meet on the battlefield. And there shall you learn the true might of Rome."

Lurio spun around and walked back to his entourage.

"He's a proud man," Whitefeather commented again.

Eric watched Lurio go, trying to remember what it was like to be young.

"Proud men do stupid things," said Eric. "Which was the whole point of this meeting."

This was the truth: a pitted landscape as treeless and bereft as any she had seen, with Earth bright and blue above her, and some gray hills rising starkly in the distance. This was the truth: walking—no, *bounding*—in a pressurized *vestimenta,* the soles of her big boots kicking up puffs of chalky dust, a crater dipping before her, and sunlight blasting through the black airlessness with a killing white glare. That June should be here, on the moon, walking on this sterile and dead terrain—sometimes finding the undisturbed footprints of Romans who had walked here two thousand years ago—vindicated all her hard work and belief. Her only regret was that Henry wasn't here to see it.

The *navicula,* sleek and white, with room for three, rested at the end of a long landing rut half buried in the dirt. She bounded toward the *navicula.* She knelt next to it and peered through the bubble-shaped pressure window. She saw three soldiers dressed in black thermal suits lying inside. A small light illuminated the interior. Condensation beaded the inside of the pressure window. She knocked. The nearest soldier snatched up the radio. Through the crackle of her own intersuit radio she heard him say, *"Inter caesa et porrecta."* She had to think hard to translate. An idiom, she thought. *Between the slaughter and the offering.* She gave him the thumbs-up sign, a gesture that puzzled him greatly.

She and the rescue crew repressurized the *navicula,* loaded it onto a large flatbed *pendeo carrus,* and hovered back to the domed city of Erebus.

Once inside, June took off her helmet and shook out her hair.

She walked along the Via Scylla and again had to marvel at how perfectly preserved the buildings were. With no wind, rain, or dampness to erode the dark stone, the two-thousand-year-old buildings remained in mint condition. A public bath stood at the end of the block. An aqueduct rose against the west side of the dome next to the water production facility. The forum lay ahead.

She walked—no, *bounded*—the two blocks to where Gallio was.

Gallio had equipment set up everywhere in the

forum and planned to use Erebus as a base of operations against the approaching fifty thousand Roman
troops. She walked up to him and kissed him on the
cheek.

"We got the last of them," she said. "They're all
safe."

"I'm glad," he said, kissing her on the forehead.
He checked the latest positional readouts of Caesar's
approaching troopship. "If only we could do something about this," he said. "The troop transport has
arrived and is now braking between the orbital planes
of Mars and Orbis. They'll be here in two days. If we
don't figure out a way to stop them, I'm afraid we'll
be overrun and defeated."

The both stared at the dot on the *scriba,* Caesar's
asteroid-size troopship. She tried to imagine life lived
under Roman tyranny as a slave. She would never
submit to it. She at last had the truth, and she was
willing to die to defend it.

"We will fight," she said. She remembered the
words in Henry's last letter. "And we'll keep fighting,
no matter how hard it gets."

Eric crawled through the rubble in the dark. He
struggled to the top of a large pile of broken bricks
and mortar and surveyed Lurio's ruined ships to the
north. Several bonfires lit the row of destroyed vessels.
Lurio's soldiers stood around drinking, telling stories,
boasting, arguing. Two soldiers were engaged in a fist-
fight. It looked like bets were being taken as to who
would win. He shook his head. No wonder Gallio's
army had beaten Lurio's so soundly—they were an
undisciplined rabble, too overconfident for their own

good. He unslung three rifles from his back and buried
them under the rubble. Today, Mickey's boys had
worked as slaves in this rubble. Tomorrow, they would
fight as soldiers. He buried a hundred rounds of am-
munition near the rifles, then continued on, staying
low.

He crawled and crawled. He was dressed in black,
had his face smeared with greasepaint, and wore a
black wool cap. A Roman patrol hovered along the
access lane to his left. He pressed himself flat to
the rubble until the patrol passed, then moved on in
the direction of the Post Office clock tower, pacing
himself, knowing he had to save his energy for the
morning's battle. He reached the clock tower fifteen
minutes later.

The walls of the tower measured a yard thick. No
wonder it still stood. Rubble blocked the doorway. He
spent a few minutes clearing it away, then went inside.
He could hardly see, had to feel his way up the stairs.

He reached the top and pushed open one of the
observation windows. He swung his new Remington
from his back, leaned it against the wall, and took out
his field glasses to check his lines of fire. They were
good. He put his field glasses away and sat on the
floor to wait, rest, and prepare, mentally and emotion-
ally, for what he would have to do tomorrow.

He'd played many roles in his life but never that of
sniper. He would hate having to shoot Lurio's Roman
boys, but he wasn't about to let them go around raping and killing anymore. He shifted, made himself
more comfortable. He thought of God. Had God
stopped him from becoming Cardinal so he could become a sniper? He thought differently of God these

days, questioned God's will and God's role in fate, especially his own fate. God, it now seemed to him, was just a dumb force, a nonsentient and nonknowing *animus* that kept this big old universe going, supplying it with its Holy Spirit much the same way the coal mines in Pennsylvania supplied St. Lucius with coal each winter. God had no hand in fate. God did not direct his life. He directed his own life. Nothing was predestined by God. God had no will. God was just there, like a tree or a river. God didn't make choices for people; people made their own choices.

"I don't need you, God," he said to himself in the dark. "I take responsibility. I make my own damn choices."

He felt as if a weight had been lifted from his shoulders.

A thin white line of dawn appeared to the east several hours later. In getting up, he spooked an owl in the rafters. In one clean swoop, the owl was down and out the window. Eric watched the creature fly away. *Like an omen,* he thought. Only he didn't believe in omens anymore. The owl's wings flapped rhythmically, easily. *That was God,* he thought. That single bird was more eloquent than any line of Scripture. The owl grew smaller, a smudge of beige and brown in the thickening hues of morning.

Insidiae. The word popped into his head, the word Gallio had repeated again and again, drilling it into his mind so he wouldn't forget it. Conscript workers trickled like ants into the rubble. Roman soldiers walked south from Lurio's ships to start guard duty. *"Insidiae, insidiae, insidiae!"* Gallio had exhorted. Eric lifted his field glasses and gazed to the south at the clay-bred warehouses, guarded by a platoon of Roman soldiers. *Ambush, ambush, ambush!* Moon waited with a contingent of militia up in the hills, ready to escort the clay-bred to protected areas in St. Jerome once Eric, Mickey, Filoda, and Lone Wolf engaged the main force.

How to begin a battle, he wondered, twenty-five minutes later, as Mickey's boys took up their positions in the sixty-two different places where he and other members of the militia had buried weapons and ammo last night? With a prayer from the Holy Catholic Liturgy? No. There could be no ceremony or prayer for murder. He simply squeezed his rifle's trigger and killed the nearest Roman soldier.

It happened slowly, it happened quickly. It happened outside of time and on the other side of sanity, as he supposed all gun battles must. Mickey Cunningham, standing in the rubble of St. Boniface the Wayfarer School for Boys, reached down and scooped up a buried rifle. He lifted it to his shoulder and blasted away at the nearest Roman soldiers, killing three of them in three seconds. All around the Shrine, good ol' boys from Ste. Genevieve County picked up the concealed weapons and fired away. Another forty Roman soldiers fell.

Eric, from his elevated position in the clock tower, shot the more difficult targets, the ones at greater range or that were moving, bringing his marksmanship to bear with unerring accuracy. He killed one. Maimed another. Saw one of his bullets rip through the neck of a Roman ensign, witnessed the red spray of the exit wound, watched the ensign clutch his throat and collapse against the broken remains of an old bathtub.

He nabbed another in the kneecap. He shot an infantryman through the chest with a coldness that was, yes, outside of time and on the other side of sanity, then shouldered his rifle and looked down at the battlefield through his binoculars.

His gaze traveled south to the clay-bred warehouse again. He saw the Roman guards, forty-four in all, leave their post, get in a single *pendeo carrus,* and hover along the river toward the battlefield. They swung round the streetcar terminus at Bell and Wharf and hastened toward the melee, leaving the way clear for Moon and her militia to free the clay-bred.

Roman soldiers down in the Shrine planted their *bacula* into the ground and fired in artillery mode at Mickey Cunningham's boys. Blue fire streaked with a scream into the air, swerved cometlike toward the Ste. Genevieve sharpshooters, and detonated on impact. In the ensuing explosions, Eric saw arms, legs, and heads go flying.

Eric set the field glasses down and took aim at the contingent of warehouse soldiers as they hovered up Bell Boulevard. He fired, killing one who stood near the front of the *pendeo carrus.* Next he shot the driver of the *pendeo carrus.* Without the driver at the helm, the conveyance swerved and crashed into the rubble of St. Andrew's Surgery.

He turned his attention elsewhere. He shot a Roman soldier in the head just as he was taking cover behind a Packard funeral hearse that the workers used to haul rubble away. He shot two more soldiers just as they planted their *bacula* into the ground, his heavy cartridges penetrating their showy breastplates. He nabbed another one in the leg and watched him crawl to protection behind the concrete stoop of a destroyed house.

He saw three Roman tanks rumble along one of the access lanes from Lurio's line of ships.

He had them riled all right, that was for sure. But he had to get them as far away from the clay-bred warehouses as he could.

He descended the spiral staircase, kicked open the door, and, staying hunched over, ran up what was left of Pensees Lane. He climbed to the top of a pile of rubble and raised his hands to his mouth.

"Retreat!" he cried. "Retreat!"

As planned, Mickey's sharpshooters retreated toward the ridge. Eric fell back with them.

As he moved along the northern perimeter of the Shrine, he saw two or three hundred Roman soldiers chasing good ol' boys up the hill through the rubble. In all that rubble, the boys found more than enough places to take cover as they made their retreat, and despite target-sensitive *baculum* ordnance, casualties were few.

The tanks, heavy ground-based vehicles too massive for the *pendeo*-lift technology, detoured through the rubble toward Volker Avenue, temporarily segregated from the main action.

Through his binoculars Eric saw the clay-bred escaping far to the south, a rabble herded along Wharf Road by Moon and her contingent of militia. The Romans ignored the escape, and wisely concentrated their forces in battle.

Eric continued up the hill. Mickey's boys spread out as they reached Volker Avenue, took cover behind its dozens of sycamores—trees spared the general devas-

tation by those down the hill—and from this elevated
position picked off another twenty or thirty Romans.
They then climbed the hill above Volker Avenue to
the railway line and bolted across it just as the Romans gained the top of the hill. Mickey's boys didn't
stop to shoot now, they just ran, as planned, toward
the Restricted Zone.

Eric, now reaching the railway line himself, veered
right. A quarter mile up, he saw a lone freight car and
ran for it.

Morris Fifield, the town's number one radio expert,
waited for him next to the freight car, looking scared.
His big black-framed glasses were pressed close to his
myopic blue eyes. He held a large radio-remote device
in shaky hands, an ungainly contraption of his own
design with a thicket of radio tubes and wires jammed
into a gray metal box, a cable attaching it first to a
breaker switch, then to a thirty-volt battery.

"Are we ready to go?" asked Eric.

"Them *bacula* sure are loud," said Morris. "If I'd
known they were going to be that loud, I'd have worn
my earplugs."

"Remember," said Eric, "on my signal. Let the
Cheyenne get through first."

"You're sure them dern redskins ain't going to scalp
me?" asked Morris.

Eric grinned. "They're on our side now."

A few moments later, a hundred feru-mounted
Cheyenne with war paint on their faces, carrying
spears, rifles, and bows and arrows, emerged from between Gallio's remaining spacecraft and charged at
full gallop toward the bewildered Romans. Mickey's
boys ran right through the Cheyenne and disappeared

into the Restricted Zone. Filoda and his army came running out behind the Cheyenne. The small aliens dug their custom-sized *bacula* into the dirt and fired an artillery round out and over the heads of the charging Indians. The ordnance landed in the midst of the Romans, blowing a good lot of them up. The Hortulani fired another round, then another, then quickly retreated. With their numbers reduced to extinction levels, not a single Hortulani life could be spared.

Mounted Cheyenne warriors charged the artillery-pounded Romans, trampling them, skewering them, shooting them, raining arrows down upon them. One threw a spear so hard it pierced a Roman's breastplate and came out his back. Another leapt from his horse and slit a Roman's throat with a bowie knife.

Meanwhile, the Roman tanks labored up the hill.

Eric turned the brake wheel on the freight car, and the car, filled with gasoline and highly combustible fertilizer, rolled slowly down the hill toward the fracas. The Roman tanks got closer and closer. More Roman troops charged up the hill to join the ones that were already there. The Cheyenne saw the freight car and, knowing that it was their signal, reared their horses and galloped back toward Gallio's ruined spaceships. The oncoming freight car baffled the Romans. The tanks now rumbled up onto the grassy verge—within blast range. If only the remaining Romans would get within blast range, Eric thought. The freight car gained speed as it neared them, and the last of the Cheyenne streaked to cover behind Gallio's spaceships.

"Now!" he cried to Morris.

Morris pushed the breaker switch forward.

The freight car exploded, the concussion of the blast knocking many of the nearest Romans flat. The explosion, as big as the whole of St. Bernardine's Cathedral, flung first shrapnel—nails and horseshoes—then spewed rivers of burning gasoline, roasting the main body of Roman soldiers on the hill. Flames engulfed both Roman tanks. Eric saw the occupants open the hatches and flee, only to become human torches a few seconds later. He shook his head. All those Roman boys dead. But war was war, and he meant to win—with or without God's help. This was just the beginning. He had beaten the Benefactors, and now he would beat the Romans.

CHAPTER 40

As Caesar's troopship got closer and closer, Gallio struggled to come up with a solution. He sat at his *scriba* watching the approach of the ship, June behind him with her hand on his shoulder. What to do? How to stop them? Caesar's approaching legions dwarfed his own. They would be here in one day. And if they reached a safe orbit around Orbis, that would be the end. June's planet—June's Earth—would be enslaved, and he would be put to death. Oh, wise Jupiter, please guide me—but he realized that Jupiter wasn't going to help him. The gods were but dumb entities, he decided, and intervened little in puny human affairs. He was going to have to make his own decisions and rely on his own judgment and experience.

"I wish there was some way we could stop them," he told June.

She stared at the blip on the *scriba* sadly.

"I'm thinking of my brother George," she said. "He's worked so hard and fought so long. He's risked his life again and again. I haven't seen him in seven years. I hate to think he's going to lose everything he's worked for when Caesar gets here."

Her brother George. He indeed sounded like a brave man. George, down there on that blue world in a place called Salzberg, in a country called Prussia, a country his ancestors had once called Germania, a nation that had fought valiantly against the tyranny of the *Patroni* for the last seven years.

His body stiffened.

His eyes widened.

He didn't know why he hadn't seen this before.

Prussia. Admiral Doenitz. The Huns. Of course.

"Gallio?" said June.

"I think I might have my answer," he said.

Eric met Lurio on the steps of St Bernardine's Cathedral again. The vice-regent glared at him in the rain.

"I am talking to a dead man," he insisted. "To fight Rome is to fight yourself. To kill Rome is to kill yourself. You *are* Rome," he said. "The minute you sent your radio signal to Rome, you became Caesar's subject. You became Roman."

"I'm not Roman," said Eric. "I'm American. These clay-bred are American. These Hortulani are American now. So are these Indians. We've got rights in America. We're free to do whatever we please. We don't have to listen to Julius Caesar. And we don't have to listen to you. The clay-bred stay where they are."

Lurio sighed. "The pale slaves belong to Rome," he said. "Give them back."

"The clay-bred are free men and women," said Eric.

"I'm giving you a generous chance to return them to us peacefully," said Lurio. "You won't be harmed."

"No," said Eric, "These are Moon's people. These are my people. You think I'm just going to hand them over?"

"If you don't, I'll destroy them. I'll destroy you."

"Why?"

"Because Rome will *not* be defied."

Eric nodded. "Then why don't we try and settle this thing in a contest of might," he said, again working on the man's pride to defeat him. "A *fair* contest of might."

Lurio frowned. "The might of Rome is supreme."

"Only because Rome never fights fair. Why don't we have an *honest* fight over the clay-bred? I know Rome is scared to fight fair and honest—most bullies are—but I'll give you this one chance to prove me wrong."

"Rome fights to win," said Lurio.

"You don't win when you fight dirty. Around here we call that cheating."

Lurio threw up his hands. "Rome can fight under any circumstances and win," he said. "Rome's might always prevails. Even if you ask us to fight with our bare hands, we will win. I don't know why you can't see this."

"Those *bacula* you use—they're unfair," said Eric. "You don't have to aim those things. They do the aiming for you. You might as well have kids fight for you, for all the skill they take to shoot. At least me and my boys know how to shoot. At least we know how to aim."

"Never underestimate the marksmanship of a Roman soldier," said Lurio.

"What marksmanship? Like I say, who needs marksmanship when you have *bacula*?"

"You provoke me."

"All I'm asking for is a fair fight," Eric insisted. "If you're too scared to fight fair, why don't you just say so? At least I'll think you're brave enough to admit that you're a coward. I'm suggesting a pitched battle right here in the Shrine. Without those *bacula*. Hand-to-hand combat. That way, everything's fair. You've got four hundred troops, and I've got four hundred troops. We meet here tomorrow at dawn. We fight. If my side wins, you leave the clay-bred alone. If your side wins, you get the clay-bred back. Not only that, I'll surrender."

"There will be no surrender," said Lurio, practically spitting the words. "No man shall be left standing, of that you can be assured."

Admiral Karl Doenitz came to the moon in a Roman shuttle. He wore the Iron Cross of the Weimar Republic on his black uniform. June watched from the platform. As he entered the forum, his entourage behind him, he surveyed all the old Roman buildings with steady eyes, as if finding such a settlement on the moon didn't surprise him in the least. Why should it surprise him? He knew about Erebus. His own Abwehr had uncovered those photographs Henry had brought to her. He wore a Prussian-style helmet with a back flip and a spike. He had a large nose, an impressive brow, looked every inch the leader of a nation at war. June stood off to one side. The Admiral ap-

proached Gallio. A translator, one of the *legio lingua,*
a man who had devoted himself to the study of Prussian since the Roman arrival, stood next to the general. The two leaders saluted each other—Gallio by
pressing his fist to his heart, the Admiral by raising
his right arm at a forty-five-degree angle into the air
and clicking his heels. Then the two climbed the steps
and entered the Senate Hall for their talks.

Down the Via Scylla June saw a Roman *carrus* hauling something in a big crate. The crate, about half the
size of a car, was stamped with the insignia of the
Weimar Republic—the black Prussian eagle and the Iron
Cross. She knew what it was. Why else would top
members of the *legio impello* crowd around it in such
eager anticipation? She descended the platform steps
and walked over to get a closer look.

She was just working her way through the crowd
when someone touched her shoulder. She turned.
George stood behind her.

Her brother George, dressed in a crisp gray uniform, carrying an officer's cap under his arm, some
white starting to show in his otherwise raven-black
hair, his figure trim and athletic, his blue eyes full of
the quiet sadness of a man who had witnessed seven
years of war firsthand. She threw her arms around
him. He stumbled back, thrown off balance by her
enthusiastic hug. A Roman sentinel steadied him—he
was new to the moon, not used to its weaker gravity.

"You're *here!*" she exclaimed.

"I'm here," he said, and gave her a big-brotherly
squeeze.

She pulled back, breathless, and gazed at him with

shining eyes. "You're with . . . the Admiral's staff now?" she asked.

"I'm one of the Admiral's aides-de-camp," he informed her, and then gave her a good look. "They told me you were here. I had to come. And I'm glad to see you looking so well. I've never seen you looking so . . . so radiant." He arched a brow. "They tell me you're in love with the General."

She felt suddenly shy. Love had wrought its transformation. "Can you tell?" she asked.

He eyed her appraisingly. "I would say you're mad about the man," he said.

She let her arms slide from around his neck. "Oh, George . . . it's the most wonderful thing. He's so kind . . . and wise . . . and I know he's a lot older than I am, but I—I can't help feeling the way I do." She looked at him more closely. "But what of you?" she asked. "How are you?"

"The last seven years have been hard," he said. "I've fought like the Devil for Europe."

She grinned at his sly witticism.

"And what *of* Europe?" she asked.

He shook his head gravely. "She's a ruin," he said, "but we plan to rebuild her. And since we've brought this with us," he said, gesturing toward the crate, "we at least have a chance against Caesar's legions."

She gazed at the crate. "The superbomb?" she said.

"Come," he said. "I'll show you."

He took her by the hand and led her through the crowd. She was so overjoyed to have her brother George back, safe and sound, that her eyes misted over with tears.

Prussian soldiers in gray Wehrmacht uniforms guarded the *carrus* transporting the superbomb down the Via Scylla. When they saw George, they saluted and made way for him. Her grief for Henry would be easier to bear now that George was here. They could bear it together. George hopped up on the flatbed and gave June a hand up as the *carrus* moved slowly toward the Senate Hall.

"A testament to Prussian ingenuity," remarked George. "I can't believe Gallio doesn't have something similar."

"They might have mastered space colonization," said June, "but I've discovered their theoretical science is backward in a lot of respects. They're great builders, great copiers, but their culture has stagnated to a large degree. Roman innovation is practically nonexistent."

"Help me open the crate," said George.

They lifted the lid and leaned it against the side. Inside she saw what looked like a small metal whale, black and smooth, with fins at the back.

"The Prussians call it *Kleinknabe*," said George.

"*Kleinknabe*?" she said.

"Little Boy," he said. "We've got the payload, and Gallio has the missile. Between the two of us, we hope to stop Caesar's legions. Between the two of us, we hope at last to rid the world of tyranny once and for all."

Hesperus felt connected again—he was part of this army. Father Nordstrum's hand rested on his shoulder. The Hortulani crowded around Father Nordstrum like nieces and nephews around a favorite old uncle. They accepted Father Nordstrum. And because they accepted Father Nordstrum, they accepted him as well. Some clay-bred were here. So were some Indians from the Plains, and some local boys from Ste. Genevieve County. Even some Roman defectors from Lurio's army had joined their camp, feeling more allegiance to Gallio, great legend that he was, than they did to Rome.

The sun was just rising and shone through the mist to the east as a pale white disk. The moon, a razor-sharp fragment of silver, sank like a foundering ship into the dark sea of the retreating night. He stared at the moon. June was up there. With the General. With Gallio. That didn't matter anymore. Father Nordstrum looked at the moon with him.

"I'll make sure she knows about your sacrifice," he said.

Hesperus felt his eyes mist over. He would never get used to these unruly human emotions.

"Father . . . I'm sorry about Neil . . . it's just that I wanted to . . . to live."

Father Nordstrum stared at Hesperus for a long time, then nodded. "We all do, Hesperus," he said. He let his hand slide off Hesperus's shoulder. "We all do." He motioned to the Shrine, where Lurio's army was gathering in the thickening light of day. "I saw them come out here last night and check for weapons and booby traps in the rubble. As if I'd be dumb enough to try that trick again."

Hesperus surveyed the Roman troops in the Shrine. One held a black standard with the red Roman eagle on it. He saw a great tapering wingtip sticking out of the river, the downed larger vessel from the night of the air battle. The light of dawn spilled across the river in rich hues. For the first time in a long time he felt Woden inside him again. He knew he was ready to go through with this. He looked around at the Hortulani, the clay-bred, the dirt farmers, the townfolk, the Cheyenne, and the Roman defectors. He was part of them. And because of them, he felt he had finally found his human courage.

Hesperus looked at the moon one last time. He sensed everyone staring at him. They knew what he was now. They knew he was one of the last Benefactors on Earth, one of the last Benefactors anywhere. They knew what he could do. He would, he thought, become a small star, radiant enough to light up St. Lucius. He would assume the shape of his death. People would see the light from as far away as Ste. Genevieve County. They would see it from as far away as the most distant edges of the Territory. But would June see it from the moon?

He turned to Father Nordstrum. Father Nordstrum gripped both his arms and gave him an encouraging shake.

"God be with you, son," he said.

Hesperus nodded, screwed up his courage. "And with you, Father."

He turned around, climbed over the barricade, and walked down Bell Boulevard. He passed the rubble of St. Bernardine's Cathedral. He was a lone soldier amid all this destruction. The Romans watched him. He wondered what they must be thinking. That he was a messenger? An emissary seeking last-minute talks? He walked slowly. Overhead five mallard ducks flew south for the winter. He had a memory—one of Neil's memories—of June in the wetlands of St. Paul

watching the ducks fly south for the winter through a
sunset sky, the reeds and bulrushes bending in the
wind above the water, the clouds streaking the horizon
as with an artist's paintbrush. He was going to miss
this place—God's green Earth, as they called it. But
he was tired now. He knew it was time to go.

He reached the Romans.

The one they called Lurio stepped forward. Like
old times. He had never thought he would once more
have the opportunity, obligation, and duty to smite
Roman soldiers.

"You have a message, *servus*?" asked Lurio.

Lurio's Latin sounded like a death knell to his ears.
The man stood with his chin arrogantly thrust forward.

"Yes, Vice-regent, I do," he said, speaking Latin as
if he'd been born on the banks of the Tiber.

"And what message might that be?" asked Lurio.

Hesperus raised both hands toward the rising sun.
"We forgive you," he said.

For the last time he used the old parlor trick of
transformation, taking the suicide shape of a small
star. And in taking this final shape, he felt his old
power come back. He was truly one of the Heavenly
Host again. He sensed, saw, heard, smelled, and understood everything around him. He saw Father Nordstrum's troops take cover, dive down stairways and
manholes; he heard June's heartbeat on the moon; he
sensed his own people lurking beyond the edge of
death and extinction. Light radiated from his hands,
his face, his body—his soul. A fanlike blast of pure
energy surged toward the Romans, pulsating with the
ripe quantum radiation of home, vaporizing Lurio's
troops first into skeletons, then into ash. Here it was.

The end at last. And the end was much like the beginning . . . in its brightness, its glorious heat, its timelessness. His heavenly brilliance arched over the river toward Illinois. The *what is* became the *what was*, and, ending at last, became that much more precious. The godliness of Woden was so much more apprehendable in the infinity of death.

In death, there was no pain . . . no loneliness . . . just a blessed eternity of silence . . . and a connectedness that would never leave him again.

The *scriba* now showed not a blip but a fully digitized image of a spherical ship transmitted to the moon via reconnaissance satellite relay.

"It's big," said Admiral Doenitz. The translator translated for Gallio.

"Twenty-five miles across," responded Gallio.

The ship approached Orbis at twenty thousand miles per hour. Never had Gallio been so certain of victory, and never had victory tasted so bitter. The nuclear device the Prussians called *Kleinknabe* sped toward the troopship, camouflaged in a cloud of radar-deflecting debris. The sun brightened the debris, made it look like a flock of white birds flying through space.

"And this debris will hide our weapon from the enemy's radar?" asked the Admiral.

The Admiral was understandably concerned—a significant portion of Prussia's gross domestic product had gone into the development and manufacture of *Kleinknabe*. To see it blown out of the sky by Caesar's Imperial Guard would constitute a major loss for his already straitened nation.

"My *legio impello* has installed your payload on the

most advanced missile we have," he said. "This missile is programmed to evade up to one-hundred-and-fifty threats at a time. Much of the target-intelligent ordnance that Caesar fires at us will strike the debris in our diversionary cloud. *Kleinknabe* should get through. I'm only glad you have four more in production. Never negotiate with Caesar unless your gun is loaded."

A rain of blue fire erupted from the troopship, blasting many of Gallio's pretty white birds out of the sky. *Kleinknabe* swerved and dodged, easily evading missiles not duped by the diversionary cloud.

"Ten seconds till impact," said Gallio.

Kleinknabe pulled ahead of the debris. The distance between the ship and the bomb narrowed.

"Five seconds till impact," said Gallio.

A flash, a detonation, an Armageddon of crazed electrons and splitting atoms filled the *scriba* with a whiteness that was whiter than the whitest snow, sun-like in its intensity, expanding like Hades opening its jaws to devour the whole troopship in one voracious gulp. *Oh, save me, merciful Jupiter. Save me from what I have done.* He glanced at the Admiral. The Admiral watched without a flicker of emotion. They were kindred spirits. They recognized the exigencies of war. They understood the necessity of mass death—at Runnymede and out here in space.

The Admiral put his hand on Gallio's shoulder.

"What choice did Caesar leave us?" asked the Prussian leader.

Gallio gestured at the *scriba* as the nuclear fireball faded into the darkness of outer space. "We have made our noise," he told the Admiral. "Let's just hope Caesar hears it."

CHAPTER 41

Eric stood on the steps of St. Bernardine's Holy Cathedral once more, this time addressing not Lurio and his entourage but a gathering of his own people. The sky was slate-colored, and a few flurries drifted down. He had become their leader by acclamation.

"Publius Gallio has negotiated a peace with Caesar," he told the gathered representatives. "In return for this peace, Caesar is requesting limited and fair immigration of Roman citizens to Orbis. He has asked that he be allowed to die in Rome, and we have granted him this wish. Orbis will remain autonomous, and it will have its own laws and govern its own people. The Territory has officially seceded from the rest of the P.S.A. and is now a sovereign nation. I would ask all of you to aid, participate, and assist in the design and implementation of a charter of rights for our new nation. We are a diverse nation—Missourians, Hortulani, Romans, clay-bred, and Plains Indians—but we are all countrymen and we must decide for ourselves what our obligations and rights are to be."

He looked around at the band of fifty or sixty representatives. June was here, taking pictures with a Kodak box camera. Gallio and Mickey stood to his right, Moon, Filoda, and Whitefeather to his left. Cars and trucks moved along the access lanes hauling loads of rubble. Young people conscripted to dig ore had returned and were now removing rubble voluntarily from the Shrine.

"We will have many challenges to face," continued Eric. "The Indian Nations are worried about uncontrolled migration westward. I give them my word that any settlement will be fair and regulated. I propose that the white man and the Hortulani be allowed to settle only in selected reservations as designated by this Congress, mapped out only with the approval and consent of the Indian Nations. All the people of our new nation will have the same opportunities, just as they will have the same obligations. The Indian Nations will teach us the ways of the plains, just as the Romans will school us in the mysteries of space. The Hortulani will show us the miracles of the garden, and the clay-bred shall teach us patient labor. We shall learn from each other, and we shall help each other, and together we shall be strong. We shall turn the New West into a great and prosperous nation. We shall, all of us, have a fair and equal say in designing the constitution of the New West."

He paused, looked around, and saw, sticking out of the rubble, an old cross and orbis. He gestured at it and said, "Some may wish to practice the old faith of Catholicism. I say to you, worship Jesus. Worship the Benefactors, if that's what your heart tells you. Worship Jupiter. Worship Hortus. Worship the Great

Spirit. Find your way to the Holy Spirit any way you can. For in that spirit we will discover our strength. In that spirit, we will find the determination to rebuild. We'll march forward, with hope, integrity, and good-will. And we will pray, each after his own fashion, that our tomorrows will be better than our yesterdays. Two thousand years ago the Benefactors came to Earth and devised for us a flawed society. That society failed. Now it is our turn. In the spirit of mutual respect and freedom, let us build our own society. And let us build it better than the Benefactors did. Let us do it right this time."

In the spring, Gallio knelt in the bottomland along the Missouri River and stroked the first shoots of new wheat. The tiny but vigorous plants were the color of emerald, an unfathomable green such as he had never seen before, not even on Hortus.

"It's the quality of the sun, Imperator," said Filoda, through his *socius*. "The purity of the light gives these plants strength and sureness. And this soil is as rich as cake."

Gallio stood up, put his hands on his hips, and looked around his farm. They'd borrowed from the bank to buy the place. They weren't rich. And June was pregnant. But they had enough. He was a farmer at last, in the midst of the tranquility he had always desired, far from the battlefield, ten miles from town, close to nature, connected to the soil. They had a cow named Beulah. They had three goats. They had trout in the pond. In the back forty, raspberry bushes grew rampant—he sold them at the roadside for a quarter a pint. They had a car, a 1937 Pontiac with no back bumper, a cracked windshield, and a curious decal of an angry cartoon woodpecker clutching a cigar between its teeth. Eighty-five Hortulani lived in the orchard next door—neighbors. He had a wife. And soon he would have a child. Jupiter had at last smiled upon him.

"This land will do well," he told Filoda. "You must call me *agricola* now. I'm not the Imperator anymore."

Out on the road he heard a truck. He looked up and saw that it was Mickey Cunningham in his farm truck. He didn't know what he was going to do about Mickey. He shook his head. Mickey didn't seem to care that he and June were married now. Gallio thought he might talk to Mickey, gently advise him to attend more church socials or go to more Saturday night dances so he would have an opportunity to meet a greater variety of women. He was just about to wave Mickey down, intent on giving him some much-needed advice, when he heard a ruckus in the barn.

Two Hortulani ran out of the barn, being chased by Beulah. One thing about Beulah—she didn't like Hortulani in her barn. But the Hortulani, pesky as they could sometimes be, loved to tease her, and to tease him by letting her go and watching him chase her. He wasn't about to let his prize dairy cow wander too far, not after what he had paid for her.

He turned to Filoda.

"I'd better catch Beulah before your friends give her a heart attack," he said.

Filoda gestured at Mickey. "What about your guest?"

Gallio watched Mickey turn up the long drive.

"June will look after him. She's always been good to him. She'll be good to him again."

Mickey appeared at June's kitchen window. June looked up from her darning. For the first time in a long time he didn't have a bouquet of flowers for her. He looked pale and thin.

"Is it true, then?" he said. His voice sounded ragged with emotion.

"Is what true?" she asked. "Mickey, why don't you come in?"

"That you're havin' a baby?"

They looked at each other for a long time. Had there ever been a chance for Mickey, she wondered? Maybe in the few weeks following Neil's death. Maybe in the days surrounding Henry's execution when she would have turned to anyone. But not now.

"Yes, I'm having a baby," she confirmed.

His ears turned red and he looked ready to cry. "You never gave me a chance," he said. "You had to go with that spaceman."

She stared at Mickey. She was happy, and he was miserable, and that's the way the world was. What could she do about it?

"Mickey, I've been married eight months. And now I'm pregnant. You have to forget about me. You have to find someone else. You can never have me now. You should concentrate on finding a pretty girl in Ste. Genevieve County."

He squirmed miserably. "How can I do that?" he asked. "I've spent every minute of every day thinking about you for the last five years. It's hard to change course when the plow's dug the furrow so deep."

She continued darning. "I'm not anybody special, you know," she said. "I'm just a girl. There's plenty of girls in Ste. Genevieve County. I'm no one special at all."

"To me you're the most special girl in the world," he said.

"I know, Mickey . . . but now it's time to say good-bye. Now it's time for you to find someone else."

"What about the Odd Fellows?" he asked. "Won't we meet there anymore?"

"The Odd Fellows are over. We don't need the Odd Fellows now."

"Then how will I see you?"

"You won't," she said. "I think you should drive back to Ste. Genevieve County and stay there. It's the only way your heart's going to mend."

He looked at his hands. "I'll never forget you, June."

She swallowed. In the midst of her own great happiness, this man's heart was breaking. She didn't want to be cruel, but she saw it was the only way.

"Good-bye, Mickey."

He looked up. His lower lip stiffened as he got himself under control. "Don't say good-bye, June," he said. "It sounds so final."

"It is final," she said.

He didn't say anything after that. He simply hurried back to his truck and drove away, unable to give her even one last glance.

Moon had a miscarriage.

She was crying. Her face was pale. She looked like a clay-bred woman again, sickly, trembling, and weak.

"Clay-bred can't have babies," she told Eric. "Our plumbin's not built for it."

"Marciana turned you into a perfectly normal woman," he said. "Normal women have babies. They can also have miscarriages. This is just one of those things, Moon." He led her into the bedroom. "You lie here. I'm going to make you some tea."

"I'm sorry I lost the baby on you, Eric," she said. "I know how much you wanted it."

He stroked her forehead. "Don't worry about that now," he said. He helped her into bed. "You just rest."

He went to the kitchen. They lived in a new house in the Shrine, something called the Speaker's Manse—for that's what they were calling him now, the Speaker. He put the kettle on, got sassafras leaves from the cupboard, and waited for the water to boil. Ingrid always made sassafras tea whenever anybody got sick. He looked out the window. The Speaker's Manse was built on the site of the old Ecclesiarch's Manse. Now that the rubble had been cleared away, the grounds were much the same—minus the trees. The water boiled. He poured it into the teapot and waited for it to steep.

While he waited he looked out the window at the backyard. Only one of the original trees had been left standing, a crab apple near the back. He felt sad. They both wanted a child. For Moon, motherhood was a kind of litmus test, a validation of her new human state. The tree had tiny withered crab apples clinging to it, dots of red, like the blood Moon had left in the toilet. He wanted to give Moon the family she had never had. He put the teapot on the tray, along with biscuits and jam, and carried the whole works upstairs.

"Nineteen weeks," said Moon. "I wonder if it was a little girl or a little boy."

"Don't blame yourself," he said.

"I expect I'll be sore for a day or two," she said. "And maybe I'll be blue for a while too."

"You go ahead," he said. "It's to be expected."

"My leg keeps twitchin'," she said. "And I feel sick to my stomach."

"It'll pass," he said. "Paccia Marciana's on the way. She'll have a look at you." He poured tea. "In the meantime, take a sip of this," he said, holding the cup to her lips. "Nothing settles the stomach like sassafras tea."

She took a sip. "Are we going to try again?" she asked.

"As soon as you get better," he said.

"I think I'm going to shut my eyes for a bit."

"That sounds like a grand idea," he said.

As she closed her eyes, he walked to the bedroom window and looked out at the new town of St. Lucius. The new public buildings weren't like the old red brick ones from Catholic days. These were made from tan-colored stone barged all the way from Kiowa country—a peace treaty had been signed with the Kiowa three months ago. The new buildings were light and airy, set in wide-open spaces, and composed of wide, flat geometric shapes. Then there were the Roman buildings, with their traditional columns and arches, erected by the new Roman immigrants. Indian bands had erected lodges—wood structures with totems outside—by the river. Finally, the Hortulani had grown buildings: oversized gourds and melons catacombed with room-sized pockets—colorful, startling, alien.

He glanced over his shoulder at Moon. She was sleeping. They would try again. He gazed once more at the new St. Lucius. Across the Missouri River in West Shelby he saw the beginnings of a small Roman spaceport, approved by their own Congress last summer, a gateway for the trickle of expected Roman immigrants. This new world would be a different world. And in this new world, Moon would have her child. *His* child. They would try again. This world would be a better world for their child. A brighter, safer world, a more enlightened one. He pressed his hands against the windowsill as if to steady himself for the challenges ahead. They would try again, both with the child and with the world, and this time they would get it right.

For he was determined to do whatever it took to make this new world a true Garden.

And he knew he would succeed.

In the name of the Father, and of the Son—and especially in the name of the Holy Spirit—he would succeed.